WE ATE THE DARK

WE ATE THE DARK

A NOVEL

MALLORY PEARSON

47N RTH

Published by 47North, Seattle

www.apub.com

Amazon, the Amazon logo, and 47North are trademarks of Amazon.com, Inc., or its affiliates.

Excerpt from "Possession" from the collection *At the Gate* © 1995 by Martha Rhodes. Reprinted with permission of the author. All rights reserved.

ISBN-13: 9781662515408 (paperback)
ISBN-13: 9781662515392 (digital)

Cover design by Caroline Teagle Johnson

Cover image: © Victor Habbick / Arcangel

Printed in the United States of America

For my family, blood and found, chosen and bound.
We make magic together.

Show her you've discovered
all her holy spots

and watch her try to find another,
deeper forest. Everything she's kept from you
is yours now: these frilly private things,
this tiny book of screams.

Possession, Martha Rhodes

Prologue

The House Has a Mouth

Between two rolling mountains, split like a lip, a dirt road snakes its way through the trees to a leering house.

Something has knocked the windows from their panes, leaving behind black-eyed shells against rotten gray siding. The house's lovely peaks and spires crumble into suggestions. Black holes pock the roof and leave room for birds to nest. The fractured foundation bows, a slumped animal, a hunted thing caught with an arrow in its back. Wood peels away from the framework like curls of bark from a dead tree.

Once, someone swept the porch and its threshold, hung wreaths in doorways and star-colored lights from the eaves to banish the dark. Now the ceilings sag swollen with water. Floorboards buck like teeth in a freshly punched jaw. Whole rooms cave into rubble, green growth reclaiming the structure where it can cut its way through the remnants. Empty. Abandoned.

Down the black road comes a boyish call, tossed between the mouths of men like howling wolves. Shoes eat up gravel and trample grass thirsty for rain. A great crack echoes acres away when a stone lofts through a remaining pane of glass, the sound of a tree felled by lightning.

Miles from the house someone might hear the boom and think *thunder*, might watch murky clouds roll in behind their eyes. But the night remains clear of tapering spring rain. Wisps of condensation cling to the moon. A warm breeze overturns the leaves and promises coming summer, sage bellies cast upward toward the midnight glow.

Down the road an old church's bell tolls, shakes off its sleep. Its steeple is poised high and mighty; a crooked little cross atop it bends like an acrobat prepared to fly. Even the fireflies hold their breath and extinguish their lights, as if waiting to be found out. But at this time of night the town sleeps on with shutters buttoned up and doors latched shut.

Awake and alive, the group falls upon the house. If watched from that leaning cross, high above the world where the tops of trees shine dark and oily, they would scuttle and crawl, innumerable beetles upon a corpse.

"This place creeps me the fuck out," one of them says, neatly stepping into a rotten section of the porch and yelping when his ankle almost catches, the sound of his fear bird-shrill. Against intentional self-determination his mind recalls the last time the house bit someone, and the gnawed meat of the leg as flesh plunged through boards. He watches Tommy walk before him with a limp that hasn't faded, even after all this time.

Alex steps into a room full of sheet-ghost apparitions—and exhales when his brain makes sense of it, the specters just covered furniture jutting like white mountains. Some of the sheets have been tugged away or shredded into nests. Others are stained after years of rain dripping through the pocked roof. The ceiling bows close where it hasn't already collapsed, and every still-standing doorway is a gaping mouth.

The rest of the group piles in behind them. The house rocks with their disturbance. Their casual jeers make Alex feel self-conscious, overtly aware of the years the rest of the guys have on him—time they've spent engaging in familiar rowdiness, together, buoyed by Loring and its enduring nostalgia. But if his memory is correct, it's been nearly five years since this house's last visitor, when they boarded it up in the sheriff's final walk-through. Now it shudders with the weight of their life, overstimulated by their laughter, their spitting, their swallowing, the ravenous way they tear open boarded entryways.

"Watch it," Tommy calls, and Alex looks down at the place where the floor slopes away from them. Black splintered stars wait in the pockets where rot claims the old construction.

Alex was never afraid of the dark, not even as a kid, but anxiety strikes hard at the sight. A vision of being chewed up by the wooden teeth of the house races through him, a new pulse. His mind betrays him again—Tommy's calf torn to shreds that final innocent summer, blood coating his pant leg so thoroughly that Alex thought the denim might be red. He remembers the anguished gasp of Tommy's open mouth as it looked like the crumbling house itself cleanly snapped the bone. Up until that moment, Tommy and his best friend, Lucas Glasswell, had been invincible stars in Alex's sky, with the kind of golden popularity Alex always eagerly hoped they might pass down to a keen kid.

"Thanks," Alex says, when his voice finally crawls its way back into his mouth.

He hadn't wanted to come. The last time he saw the house was enough of a scar to convince him to turn down the invitation, repeatedly. But Tommy had asked him more than once, and Tommy never asks for anything.

"No one has been brave enough to go inside that house in years. If I can do it, you can grow the hell up and join," he had rallied, cuffing Alex on the shoulder and favoring his left leg with the swing. "Besides, what else are you going to do? Sit on your ass at home?"

Alex had planned on sitting on his ass at home. In two weeks, he'll graduate high school, and the late Loring spring is already warming in a way that makes Alex lazy with contentment. By June his time will be his again—long days spent swimming until he's so thirsty he considers drinking lake water, nights stretched out by getting drunk in Tommy's basement while the others pass controllers around to play something loud and violent, sleepy afternoons working at the gas station, where the only customers are truckers looking for something hot to eat and respite from the baking sun. The air-conditioning churning everything slow and dormant, katydids and cicadas a pale white noise even with the windows shut, sleep coming easier with the sound. Wasn't that what summer was for? Rotting away on a couch that molds itself to the shape of your body, watching reruns of reality TV until you can feel bits of your mind melting through your ears? He'd get his life together when the leaves fell again.

At home, things were safe and comfortable, and he could eat his shitty food and watch his shitty TV and avoid the copper tang that clung to Loring in the form of faded missing posters stapled to telephone poles. He could turn from the face of his childhood pinned to coffee shop notice boards, ignore abandoned cars left to die in overgrown fields, sleep without seeing things in crepuscular corners. He could leave the cornfields dry and brown, nodding under pale sun.

If he pretended the house no longer existed, there was peace. It lived on only through folklore—*Once, it held a family. No, once it held the sick and the dying. No, once it was home to a witch, and she was so hungry for a heart. She cooked the first person she saw. She split them down the middle and ate the splintered mess it made.*

Could a house hold that? It was all just energy—clinging, sticky, material. Could the shape of a structure remember the hurt administered within it?

Logic said no. But Alex had seen the place fester—watched it unfold in front of him at a bonfire, years ago, when the fight erupted and his sister looked at him across rising flames like it was his fault the night had gone to shit. How was he supposed to know that someone would get hurt? That the house would moan like a dying animal? That they'd go running through the trees, flying fast enough to steal the breath from their chests before whatever hunted them could catch up? That his sister's friend would disappear—just like that, never to be seen again?

It was all in the past, just like the memory. Just like Alex's chances of a lazy summer before he left Loring behind for good.

Outside, frogs croak rich, low sounds. The noise drifts in through the punched-out windows and settles over the dusty remains of the house. Down a hallway someone whoops again. Alex rolls his shoulders to pretend he didn't jump.

"Holy shit," Tommy calls. Alex sidesteps a crouching end table with a cracked leg and a painting of sunflowers that someone spray-painted over. Now it's a painting of sunflowers and the words *SSATANN WAS HHEREE* in furious, violent red. Alex wonders how long the words have been there—he can't recall them in the glassy memories of the house his younger mind clings to, all clouded by the posturing . . . Five years since he was thirteen and attempting to prove his bravery by standing in front of that bonfire, the last place he should have been. Five years since they taped the house off and stationed a patrol on the weekends to keep boys like him away from it. He inhales, smells distant smoke.

"C'mere and look at this," Tommy calls. "I *knew* there was something in here."

There's a dim doorway at the end of the hall. Jagged spears of wood, appearing to have once been the upstairs floor, now block the entrance. Alex picks his way through the mess and wishes his phone wasn't dead, wishes he didn't have to rely so much on the dim white beam coming from Tommy's. The gloom makes animals out of every penumbral corner, amplifies every crack and groan and pop. He thinks about the hole he nearly stepped into. Panic seizes his heart all over again.

Tommy turns. "Help me move this. I want to go in."

Alex fights the urge to make a rude gesture behind Tommy's back as he hoists moldy boards away. The ceiling is close enough that Alex has to duck as he follows. Beyond the black doorway, something moves—an animal maybe, or the cast shape of his body making shadow puppets on the wall. He focuses on the ground instead and obeys Tommy's grunts for help. They kick aside a pile of debris, centipedes scrambling away and the house wheezing with their effort.

Alex steps over detritus into what was once a kitchen. Beer cans make dioramas of Appalachia across the floor, gleaming blue and white under the pale glow of Tommy's phone. Tommy bends low to peer at something and Alex gingerly steps closer, nearly sliding out of his skin when he catches someone staring back at him in the dusk—but it's just a mirror, cracked and dirty, leaned up against the wall.

"It's like a museum for every pre-disaster party," Tommy says. "I'd bet anything that no one's been in here since I fucked up my leg." His beam jumps around the room, landing on countertops collapsing beneath settled dirt. The light stops on someone standing in the middle of the room.

Alex almost humiliates himself with a scream, but he's already embarrassed enough, so he kills the sound in his throat as his eyes adjust. Not someone. Not skin but bark, gnarled and textured, thick and old. A tree, growing in the middle of the house, warped like a hunching body.

"How?" Alex whispers.

"This is wild," Tommy says, laughing. He kicks a pile of cans and Alex flinches at the metallic sound, a shrapnel echo. He spins to look over his shoulder, suddenly feeling someone's eyes on his back, but finds only the empty doorway again.

"We should head home," he says, hating himself for his meekness. "Clearly this place is about to collapse."

But against his own will Alex keeps moving, too afraid to be left behind. Roots twist through the floor in jagged outlines where they splintered the boards. He wonders if Tommy heard him.

The light flickers again as Tommy circles the tree. Alex watches his grin fall away.

Down the hall someone screams, "Light it up, Briggs!" A resulting crash echoes around them, followed by swelling laughter. Alex flinches. Tommy's mouth drops open, then presses shut again, a marionette tugged alive by his brain.

Alex doesn't want to know, doesn't want to see it, but as Tommy calls his name, his voice shatters around the sound of it. Alex steps over roots. He tries not to think about the reverberation of footsteps behind him, like something else is trying to glimpse past the space he takes up.

There is a gouge in the tree where the bark hollows out and gives way to indistinct darkness. The cavern's edges are stained with a thick, sap-like liquid, black as blood. Deep slices in the trunk almost shimmer, coagulating, and the marks slide all the way down to the floor where there are—

Petals? Candle stubs? Black slashes like wounds in the bark, like someone had come at it with an axe and failed to fell it? Sickness rises in him. He swallows a few times and feels air lodge in his throat.

"Is that—" Alex starts, the words clipping their own wings.

In the shell of the tree, a skeleton stands. *Stands* is the wrong word, but Alex can't quite figure out what his brain is trying to tell him, a misalignment of neurons. There a skeleton stands. Cowers. Sleeps. Rots.

The tree snuggles up against the corpse with curling bark and new branches. It's just the natural progression of growth, really, but something about it is more than alive, cognizant of what the trunk holds. The bones are stark and white with snaking black patterns, like the sap just kept dripping, sickly and putrid. With horror, he recognizes the crumbling connections between delicate foot bones tucked underneath where the skeleton tried to curl up, fetal and afraid. Tattered remnants of a pocked shirt cling to the bones. Part of the skull is cracked like the thin veneer of an eggshell, and its dirty white sheen blends into the wood.

Alex sees spots at the corners of his vision. He blinks them into motes of gray.

"Jesus—we need to tell Lucas." Tommy's voice sounds a step behind his own thoughts. "Do you think it's her?"

Alex can still picture the missing posters around town, but now the girl's smiling face is replaced by that splintered skull, the collar of her shirt torn and bloody. He turns away, exhales hard through his nose.

When he looks again the skull is nearly smiling at him with straight and shattered teeth. Down the hall someone swears again and the chorus erupts in laughter, background music in the skipping track of Alex's mind.

The floor creaks beneath him and his heart doubles its speed. He steps back on trembling legs, reaching for anything to hold on to. He needs to get away. Away from Tommy, away from the tree, away from the skeleton.

His lungs swell, preparing to cry for help, and in the dun of the room something exhales against his cheek.

Across the moon-bleached fields of corn, the church bell thrums. The crooked cross tilts another inch toward its demise.

1

THE BIRD HAS A WAY WITH WORDS

Frances Jude Lyon swung her fist down and split the head in two.

The clay came apart easily, the bust she'd spent the last hour sculpting now nothing more than a caved-in face and drooping shoulders. The eyes veered in dissident directions. Its mouth mirrored a frown back at her. She dug her thumbs into the cheekbones, left tracks for tears to slide down.

There was a certain art to ruination. By rendering the piece unbearable, she could go back to the beginning and let muscle memory take over. That's what Frankie's mother told her, at least, and she had only been wrong a few times. The faults could be forgiven.

She dunked her sponge in the cup of reddened water set up beside her ceramic wheel and squeezed it over the skull. Terracotta sludge caught and slipped down to the jaw, exactly where she had hoped it might.

When Frankie pictured her home, she thought of water.

It wasn't necessarily a sensible thought. The mountains slept around her, ever swollen and cornflower blue. They were close enough to the studio to soak up any chance of evening light and prominent enough to be distorted by the warped glass of the front windows. Tourists came from all over the East to see them. In the fall they were a national treasure, alight in a million shades of sunrise, and in the summer they were passage for hikers seeking respite. Their outline was printed across the postcards Frankie had so carefully aligned beside the register, with a little gold star marking the valley that raised her.

But it was the water that mattered most to Frankie. The deep green of the stagnant lake behind Oph's farmhouse was the color of her heart after dark. The sound of lapping shoreline against loamy clay eased her every anxiety. Some nights when sleep wouldn't come, Sofia on her mind and her heart hurting like a paper cut, she'd imagine that sound like the coming rush of June bugs, picture the creamy echo of moon slivers against the surface of the water. It was the only type of magic she'd ever been willing to accept.

"Wow," Marya Sokolova said from her perch behind the register. Her eyes fixated on the mutilated skull, then flickered up to Frankie's. "I thought that one was kind of nice. You never let your face see the light of day."

Frankie shrugged, unwinding a wire and slicing it across the wet mess on her wheel. She re-formed the mass and slapped it down again, using her weight to center the shape into something that could be repurposed into a mug or a plate, dinnerware more likely to sell off the shelves of Lyon Ceramics. It made sense that Marya would assume they were self-portraits. After all, the busts did look like her.

But Frankie looked at the clay and found herself dangerously overwhelmed for a smarting moment. It didn't matter what anyone else saw. She could craft a face identical to hers every day for the rest of her futile, lonely life, but it would only ever be Sofia's.

Frankie could pretend, with that face held like water in her hands and the terracotta just as freckled with grit and earth as Sofia's skin had once been. She could imagine that Cass would pick her up after closing, Poppy in the passenger seat of the Ford, and they would drive around with the windows down. The vernal promise of late spring in North

Carolina would welcome them; they could coax a couple six-packs from the convenience store or the fridge in Cass's garage, get drunk down by the creek. Maybe, she imagined for a delicious moment, when she got home the crack under Sofia's door would be illuminated. She could stand in the hall and press her palm to the door. Listen to the distant hum of some muzzy song through the wood. Rest her forehead against it and relish the idea of her sister on the other side, breathing in her bed, taking up space. She'd leave her hand on the knob and wait for some invisible hope to welcome her inside.

In Frankie's traitorous memory, the empty space her sister took up blinked open and caught her watching.

Frankie had lived in several homes over the years, she and Sofia both. Home shaped like the place their parents bought when the twins came home from the hospital on an unusually hot spring day, a rambler with a leaky roof and rocky dirt too tough and unforgiving to make proper mud pies out of, though they'd tried their hardest. Home shaped like the townhouse where Fiona Lyon magicked them away after a divorce that was as abstract to them as the framed Cubist reproductions she hung crookedly over the fireplace. Home shaped like their aunt Ophelia's farmhouse in the middle of the woods. Everything Frankie and Sofia owned stuffed into two matching suitcases, blue for Frankie and yellow for Sofia because at that point the identical nature of their lives had started to chafe until it was nearly suffocating. Two closets in two bedrooms where twin black dresses hung, waiting to be worn for a funeral to come at the end of the week. Home shaped like Oph wearing their mother's face, standing in the doorway with her hands wrung out like rags against the curve of her stomach.

And finally—home shaped like the ceramics studio in Loring that their mother left to their aunt. Oph wasn't an artist and avoided the place at all costs, mostly preferring behind-the-scenes paperwork while she peddled overpriced candles online, the wax rolled in herbs and carved with sigils that represented things like "peace in the home" and "reversing a hex." So Frankie took over evening shifts, spinning clay on knee-high wheels throughout high school, first with Sofia at her side and then alone after her sister went missing and left Frankie behind to piece together the remaining fragments of her life.

Frankie opened her eyes. Past the glass, the mountains loosed a blue sigh.

There could be beauty here, too, even if it hurt to see, hurt to feel. The studio was at its most peaceful when the sun peaked overhead and filtered past the hills. The shelves of porcelain illuminated, dust particles momentarily transformed into vivid flakes of gold before they settled once again.

She studied the place on the floor where the stretched-out shadow of *Lyon Ceramics* staked its claim. In that still second, everything floated by on its usual track, without the sense of impending doom Frankie had grown accustomed to. While the gold light danced, the world was not ending, the world was not ending, the world was not ending.

Frankie spun the wheel in front of her again, running her sponge along the smooth surface to gather the extra water. The clay stained her white palms red and left them coated with earth. She thought, *I want to go home.* The summoned sound of the lapping lake roared in her ears.

Marya propped her shoes on the countertop. Her clothes, mono-chromatic and trendy in a ragged sort of way, somehow never managed to pick up the dust that layered everything else in the studio. Frankie resented her for that, and for the space she occupied. Over a year had passed since she'd finally been forced to hire someone to take Sofia's position, and Frankie still couldn't even properly pronounce the other girl's last name without feeling foolish. When it came to Marya, she usually felt foolish.

A year working with Marya. Five since Sofia disappeared. Hundreds of days strung together by the fragile wire of her waking alarm, long afternoons bent over a wheel, sleepless nights lying listless on stale sheets. Life had been on fast-forward since the moment her sister winked out of the world, each day a hurtling mess of minutes that left her scrambling for purchase.

And now Marya sat in the space that used to be Sofia's, distant and fickle as a new moon.

Frankie didn't think Marya was much help at all. She had a supreme lack of skill and a resting frown that could freeze over the lake of Frankie's heart. There were times when she reconsidered: maybe it really was better to be on her own, getting her work done as it was supposed to be done with no one left to get in her way. Frankie'd stuck it out all these years by herself, hadn't she, with only Oph balancing the books and stopping by to dust?

She had done it all alone. Why couldn't she do it again?

Because she was tired. Because Sofia's absence was still a monster that ate her up inside, no matter how starved and thin it became. And with Marya there—at least there was someone to witness her, a place to put the frustration.

"Would it kill you to put your feet down?" Frankie muttered as she tossed the used clay back into the bag at her side for recycling. She gave a pointed look at Marya as she walked past the register, weighed down with a bucket of opaque water and a dripping plaster tray with the imprint of the smashed skull. Marya didn't look up from her book. The apron she wore was as white as it had been in the package, her shirt untouched by the spray of a spinning wheel, hair free of red dust from its dark roots to its bleached ends.

The first few months after being hired, Marya had tried. That meant something, didn't it? But her only talent was inventory, and she ran Frankie's lone spreadsheet on the ancient shop laptop like a tyrant. The fact that she was still leagues better than everyone else Frankie had interviewed for the job said a lot.

"Yes," Marya grunted around the highlighter between her teeth. Fine strands of hair fell past her jaw, rendering her pale and wraithlike. "I have poor circulation."

Poor circulation! Frankie mouthed to the sloshing sink water as she scrubbed the plaster bat. She was tempted to wring herself out in front of Marya, congealing in crimson-tinged puddles around the drains in the floor. Her back ached and there was clay wedged under her fingernails. She'd kept her jaw clenched for days. Her shoulders pinched together, caught in the act of flinching away from an invisible blow. But the shop had to keep running. Marya, despite her lack of assistance, was an employee that had to be paid.

She wanted to go home. She wanted to go anywhere but home.

Sometimes it felt like Frankie had stepped out of her body and now watched the world from beyond. In the years since Sofia went missing, the trees had dropped their leaves and borne new ones. Posters printed with her face had disintegrated off telephone poles and melted in sidewalk gutters. Five birthdays had passed without acknowledgment. Now Frankie was nearly twenty-three and more alone than she ever thought possible.

Being a twin was a lot like déjà vu. There were days when she felt like she'd been left behind to feel all this pain because Sofia couldn't be here to bear it. *But I'm not a twin anymore,* she thought suddenly, mostly as a method of self-sabotage to break her own heart. Her chin trembled. It had worked.

Her pocket buzzed against her thigh, loud as a cicada clinging to a tree. She dried her hands by the sink and silently stewed at the clean tread of Marya's boots. Marya leaned casually back on her stool, knocking the highlighter against her lips. Frankie tugged hard on the knot of hair at the base of her neck with one hand and reached for her phone with the other.

The light coming through the windows was almost enough to obliterate the glow of her screen. She squinted at the text, tiny letters with enough density to anchor her back down on earth. The name attached to it made her heart thud with painful intensity.

where r u frank?

Her thumbs left wet little circles on the screen. It took a full minute to make her mind form words.

studio. are you home yet?

She tried not to get her hopes up. Focused instead on the air-conditioning ruffling Marya's hair, a group of women studying the listed hours past the glass of the door, the low stock of forest-green mugs on the front right shelf. As she attempted to even out her breaths with a seven-second inhale, exhale, count to four, a trooper's car blew down Main Street. The whirring siren made rainbows through the distorted glass of the windows. It was distracting enough to force Frankie to start counting from one all over again.

Her phone buzzed. Marya glanced up at the sound, and all thoughts of counting dissipated from Frankie's mind anyway.

sitting on ur porch FRANK. so yeah i guess im home!!!!!!!!!

"I think I'm going to close early today," Frankie said, the words spilling out in a rush. *Sitting on the porch. So close, so close.* "I'll clean up."

Marya sat before her, silent and quizzical. It was amazing that a person could be so completely still, Frankie thought as she took in Marya, statuesque form outlined by sun on the fair planes of her face.

"We still have an hour to go. Are you sure?" Marya asked. Frankie suspected Marya had killed most of her accent at some point—but a certain lilt clung to her words, a crispness that made her sound overly formal alongside Frankie's languid drawl. "I can stay, if you need me to."

Now she wanted to work? "I think I've got it all under control from here. But thanks," Frankie said. It was hard to feel sincere when Marya was an active reminder of her faltered failings. "I'll see you tomorrow, bright and early."

Marya seemed ready to protest, but she kept quiet. The silence toiled between them. Another buzz. Frankie didn't need to see the next text to know it was Cass, calling her home. She tucked her phone into her pocket and turned back to the sink, and she didn't look up from the water until the bell over the door sounded Marya's leaving.

With the sign flipped to *Closed* and the sun just starting to slip past the trees, Frankie locked up and clipped her keys to her hip. They made music there as she jogged around the building. She'd been waiting for this moment ever since Cass first called her and told her she was moving back home. She could already feel the waiting hug and see the hills framing Oph's sprawling house—no, her house too—with its familiar nooks and eaves and peeling paint, its slapdash siding, its sagging steps, its splintered lattice, its buckled overhangs, its weathered peaks. A house with her life in it, and a piece of her heart waiting on the porch.

With the chain coaxed away and a leg thrown over the seat, her bike ate up gravel. Taking Sofia's car would have been faster, but Frankie couldn't bear the thought of it, preferred to let it rot in the carport while the wind whipped through her hair. Low-hanging trees turned everything into a mosaic. The sky was the kind of blue so deep it was almost a reflection of water, the grass so green that summer *had* to be waiting just around the corner, with its haunches sore from crouching. The house split through the trees, yellowed by afternoon. Cass Sullivan stood with her brown arms propped on the porch railing. Beside her Oph was bright and rosy, russet hair curving where it hit the ruffled shoulders of her dress. The two of them were nesting dolls lined up one next to the other, perfect mirrors firm in their familiarity. Cass's dark hair was gold in the sun, her head cocked in hello but the smile on her face wavering and indistinctly mournful.

Home, Frankie thought, *finally home.*

She dropped her bike on the grass and let Cass crush her close.

It wasn't until Cass had thoroughly rocked her around that Frankie noticed the sheriff waiting in the doorway and the damp tracks of shed tears drying along Oph's chin. The sheriff held his hat and bowed his head. The shock of his intrusion was overwhelming. Every thought she'd had of home and safety was suddenly violated. It was almost as if, just by standing in her doorway, the sheriff was implicit in every aspect of the horror yet to come.

Cass's voice was rusty against her ear, her hands so warm against the small of Frankie's back. For a moment Frankie thought that if Cass let go of her she would blow away until nothing remained but her shoes in the grass, granules of dust catching in the easy breeze.

Someone was speaking. They were, weren't they? She stared through the slats of the porch, bored past wood grain. She could almost make out the ribs of the house with her eyes alone, peel back the siding and stain to dissect each insulated stud. When she looked up again, it was Cass's mouth moving soundlessly. Frankie couldn't make sense of what she was saying, words tripping over one another until they were just a mess of noise. Was she apologizing? What did she have to be sorry for?

"Frances, baby," Oph said into the lull, a hand outstretched with the intention of smoothing down Frankie's hair, and Frankie thought, *Maybe I will never cry again, not for as long as I live.*

In her mind, the edge of the lake lapped gritty red clay.

She was, of course, wrong.

2

To Have More than One Heart

Poppy Loveless could be cold, but she wasn't loveless at all.

If she were, she wouldn't have come back to Loring in the first place. Wouldn't have made the three-hour drive in her good-for-nothing car. Wouldn't have abandoned the life she'd built away from them after getting Cass's text, the scathing one that said:

jesus pops it's a funeral could u at least come home for that?

She was only a few days later than she'd intended. Years later, really, if the five she'd spent avoiding everything and everyone counted. At least she'd gotten in her car. At least she'd put her foot to the gas. At least she'd done the one thing everyone least expected of her. She would even stop at her childhood home first, to the shock and chagrin of the universe.

Growing up, they spent the least amount of time at Poppy's house.

There were several factors that played into those dynamics, from exploring in the woods as kids to sleepless high school nights passed under the stars. Most days were spent outside, swimming in the lake behind Oph's place when the weather was warm enough to allow it and piling onto Frankie's bed when evenings grew cold. There they'd form a tangled mess of limbs as they took turns adding lines to whatever grotesque drawing Frankie had started in her sketchbook, reading aloud to one another from a battered paperback. Poppy thought maybe she had spent more nights in the old farmhouse than she had in her own bed—snoring next to Frankie and Cass with the moon pouring through the window or pressed against Sofia in a sleepless wailing of the heart.

She was grateful for that fact—it meant she could keep her memories separate. She could look at her house and not be stung by it.

The years hadn't changed the place one bit. Her parents' house was a modest prefabricated box with recently redone siding and a flimsy foundation. The new paint was blue in a way that was probably supposed to be cheerful, but only gave it a mopey and shadowed hue. Its porch was a cement block that provided a pause before the door, with two pine chairs meant for sweet tea afternoons that her mother made at a woodworking class she took six years ago. They were clearly unused and had long since gone gray, like the window shades, like the morning.

Crows trespassed in the front yard, pecking furiously between blades of grass. Her dad must have just laid down the summer seed; he would be pissed when he saw the birds eating on his dime. An old tree behind the house blocked out the coming clouds and their threat of rain, but Poppy could smell it in the air, magnolias and azaleas and ozone. She took it all in from her place beside the run-down Jeep she'd bought with a season's worth of wages from the soft serve place in town, a graduation gift to herself before she'd left for college.

Now she had another graduation under her belt, and a year spent employed at an on-campus bookstore. Now she had unanswered job applications for archival departments. Now she had everything she'd thought she was supposed to work for, and nothing to show for it. What could she brag about? A degree? An empty space inside of her, carved and hollowed as an egg? Duke had given Poppy four seats for her stadium graduation, and humiliatingly, she'd only been able to fill two. The absence was a glaring hole—Sofia was gone. She'd never come to visit, never see the sublet apartment with its leaky faucet and wide bay window, couldn't comment on how adult the bedspread was, wouldn't prod Poppy's waist until they were both laughing, until they fell into one another, until they forgot what had been funny in the first place.

She was dead, and Poppy had returned to Loring to lay her to rest, just as Cass had begged her to, just as she'd promised herself she never would.

The idea was as soft and sick as overripe fruit—Poppy hadn't come back for more than three days at a time in the last five years, and now *home* was a funny word that she couldn't quite give power to. Loring and its inhabitants had never shown her much kindness.

Her hand ran over the velvet of her buzzed head. Her mom was sure to comment on it again, as she always did, every time they saw each other. She felt around for imperfections at the nape of her neck, for the spot in the back she tended to miss. She didn't trust a barber—it was her hand and no one else's. Except for that first time, when Sofia had done it. Sacredly and unafraid. A gentle hand against her scalp as tufts of hair fell to the floor. Slender fingers fluttering over her bare head. The way she had leaned close to Poppy's ear when she was done and spoke like cashmere: "You look beautiful, Pops," the sound enough to send a shiver down Poppy's spine, the brush of Sofia's mouth like a newly nested bird.

But that's what friends were for, right? And now Sofia was gone, and Poppy'd be damned if she didn't hang her head over her bathroom sink and buzz it down herself.

She could hear it already, her mother's first words like a slap, the same feeling every time even when the phrasing waxed and waned. *You look brutish. Severe. Unkempt.* Poppy didn't feel the sting anymore, just the initial faint pain. Her mother would always want a say in what made Poppy presentable, and in Loring, beauty depended on her capacity to blend in.

But maybe they could coexist, just like this: her sweet, distracted dad, her stoic mother, and Poppy. Whatever she might be. *Think of it like having temporary roommates,* she thought to herself. *Just until the funeral. It won't be very long at all. There's a lease to sign waiting for you back in Durham. A life that you built.*

She made her way to the house, the warm scent of honeysuckle swimming through the humidity. Scattered bushes still huddled close to the sides of the porch despite her mother's constant efforts to hack them away. It was the only comforting thing she'd experienced since parking her car.

She hesitated at the door, unsure if she should knock. Sweat beaded under her arms as her knuckles hung suspended in the air. There was only a beat of time to consider before it swung open to reveal her mom.

"Are you coming in?" she asked, in lieu of hello. Her gardening gloves seemed to have never touched dirt before, stark and yellow against her deep brown skin. Her hair was braided in neat rows and tied back at the nape of her neck. Maybe the coming storm had ended all hope for whatever yard endeavor her mother had planned to conquer that day. It must have already been a morning of disappointment.

Poppy said hello as she stepped inside, backpack slung over a hunched shoulder. She tried her best not to look like she was readying herself for the verbal blow to come.

"I wish you would stop shaving your head."

Poppy gave a teeth-baring grin as her only form of response.

"Was traffic bad or did you get a late start? Are you staying for dinner?"

Her mother used questions like bullets. These were aimed right for Poppy's temple.

"I'm just going to shower before I head over to Frankie's house," Poppy said, stepping into the living room where her father sat in a recliner by the TV. She bent down to give him a one-armed hug. It was always a quiet hello with him, and it made Poppy grateful each time. She said so with her cheek pressed to the top of his head. From the kitchen she could smell the aftermath of breakfast and chlorine from the neighbor's pool seeping past the screen door. Already overwhelmed, she left her parents downstairs and headed upstairs.

The size of her room always surprised her, no matter how long she'd been away. She felt as if she'd eaten the wrong pill—like her arms might jut out the windows and her legs pop through the floorboards until she wore it like a dress. It was done up for guests now, a dreary painting of an open window hanging above the bed. Solemn. Staged. Her mother didn't fuck around when it came to establishing an atmosphere.

She crashed onto the bed. Her feet dangled off the end. Just a minute to herself and she could face it all again. She could recharge and piece herself back together before the day demanded her presence, be in and out before Loring could remember it had once raised her. Besides, it was just a vigil. She was just going to Frankie's house, with Frankie inside of it. It was just Cass. Just Oph, with her awfully caring embrace, her horrifically motherly eyes.

She settled into the quilt, let her shoulders deflate. The fan hummed overhead, drying the sweat on her forehead. Her phone buzzed in her pocket and reflexively she flinched. Part of her considered checking the notification while the rest of her knew without looking that it would be a text from Cass.

She left it in her pocket and rolled over onto her stomach, considering the still knob of her bedroom door until her eyes drifted shut. Her phone chirped again, and her pulse thrummed with it through the delicate skin of her wrists. In the brown noise of her eyelids she saw Cass's and Frankie's faces, blurred ghosts. And there behind them, Sofia's, memorized until it hurt. She swallowed, begged her heart to loosen. She was afraid. She wanted to dig a hole deep enough to bury herself inside and refuse to crawl back out.

What if they never wanted to see her again?

She needed to get the feeling of the road off her back. With towel and clothes bundled in her arms, she headed down the hall to the shower and elbowed the door shut behind her. She left her glasses folded and fogged on the edge of the sink. When the bathroom had steamed to a level only hellfire could compare to, she plunged in, savoring the scalding water on her shoulders.

Just the thought of Oph's house sent her into a spiraling panic. The achingly familiar creak the porch floor made when they tried to sneak out late at night. The whinnying of the windows when they tried to sneak back *in*. Worst of all the scummy lakeshore out back, full of green tangled weeds so dense they were nearly black. The surface a rigid mirror, the kind of glass you could walk on until, as promised, it cracked beneath you.

Scrubbing shampoo over her scalp, she sighed, trying to empty herself of anxieties. Her eyes slit open and watched water stream down her arms.

Something moved behind the curtain.

Poppy froze with a hand pressed to her throat, watching the pale curtain move with the breeze that poured in from the tiny bathroom window. Just the wind. That was it. There was nothing—

The shadow dashed forward in a frenzy of movement, stalking back and forth behind the curtain. Poppy's breath was molasses thick in her throat. She struggled to inhale, the fear seizing her windpipe and squeezing.

"Mom?"

The word felt inane even as she said it. The last thing her mother would ever do was silently stand outside her shower. The strangeness of the image almost wrenched a laugh out of her.

The shape moved again, then stopped. She frantically mapped it out—hunched and humanoid. It seemed to pulsate behind the thin curtain, growing into something massive and imposing. It felt like the air in the room was being devoured. Poppy's ears roared. With a sound that came out like a frightened yelp, she ripped back the curtain.

There was nothing. Just her, alone, entirely too naked and vulnerable in the small bathroom, with only the toilet and sink for company.

Her glasses sat abandoned and she blinked water off her lashes. Of course. She was seeing shit.

In her room, she toweled off before the mirror behind her door, then carefully clasped a necklace back on. The vivid gold charm gleamed against the deep brown of her skin. Between her fingers it was alive, heavy with potential and brass, the shape of two snakes intertwining like the fearful clutch of her gut. She could hold it and almost feel the heat of Sofia's hands linking it around her neck. She could shut her eyes and remember Sofia's face like a rising sun.

"Oph helped me make it. She said that it's just like a ward my mother used to make."

Sofia, effervescent and eighteen. The memory of her hand stopped for a moment on Poppy's shoulder, cupping the place where it sloped down. She had just shaved her head for the first time, and she almost tried to lift her hair for Sofia before remembering the change.

"Ward?" Poppy had said around the beating of her heart in her throat.

"To keep you safe from anything big and bad in the world. My mom's journal said it dispels negativity," Sofia said, smiling. Her eyes sparkled as she passed over the little box she had put the necklace in, palm to palm, skin pale against the deep red velvet. Poppy could almost taste the color—decadent green of Sofia's gaze shining in the passenger side of Poppy's car, her hair the hue of the crimson box against the gray of the seat. "It draws in light, so you never feel lonely or scared."

In the mirror, Poppy watched herself bring it to her mouth, her shadow a jagged shape across the floor.

3

Yellow as an Ear of Corn

Cassandra Sullivan sat behind the wheel of her truck with her foot on the gas, unaware of the end to come. Through the windshield the mountains were achingly blue, that vein kind of color lying just beneath the skin. The sun stretched its fingers and made fat beams across the countryside.

Loring buzzed with energy. She looked at it and loved it with an affection so big it felt like falling. Afternoon light on the winding roads of the rural town remained a breathing thing, welcoming her back from her last abandonment with familiar arms.

The fact of the matter, the real meat of her hurt, was that she was always leaving something behind, even when she came home.

Memories made a keepsake out of her body. Cass had never hated her hometown, even when it wounded her—she could see the world and still love the little one that had raised her. And Loring was little, and it was sweet as a first sip of iced tea, and it was a myth made larger by missing it, verdant and sprawling and old as the mountains themselves. Animalistic in her muffled memory, all green and untouched. Even the vanishing spring air was muggy and gold, like she had a chance of seeing fireflies over the farmland despite the clinging chill.

Soon, she thought, lovingly. Just a little longer and the fields would be so full of after-evening haze that she wouldn't be able to find a spot of total darkness if she wanted to. The radio spoke a crooning sentence at her. Cass said it back, with affection.

The fields she passed were the same ones that had raised them. Before the Ford became hers, they took two-speed bikes down the crumbling roads, veering to avoid vultures defending roadkill prizes. They sped by endless lines of white-topped Queen Anne's lace, the black-eyed Susans a yellow sea. The creek cut a diagonal line between Poppy's house and Cass's, and there they spread blankets by the banks, eating browning apple slices speckled with lemon juice under the shade of ash trees. Cass remembered digging her thumbnail into the fruit, hearing the wet bite of it crushed between Poppy's teeth, Frankie and Sofia braiding wildflowers together after shaking off the ticks.

In the time since Cass left Loring, first for five semesters spent at NYU that she swiftly abandoned for three years spent in the city as a barista barely scraping up rent for her apartment, the town remained the same. She'd loved her time away, thrived in dank bars and sunny cafés and breezy parks until her money ran out alongside her luck. But she was a nostalgia hunter. There was nothing sweeter than returning to memory, and Loring had a magic of its own.

This time was a little different, in a way that still made her uneasy. Her parents had picked her up in a U-Haul, and Cass had fed her life into it. It was impossible to feel certain she was making the right choice, when she'd fought so hard to build something meaningful far, far away—but Loring could still be home, if she erased the clinging recollection of what she had built elsewhere. Frankie was here, after all. She was home on her own.

Frankie's house sat two miles past Cass's, down a gravel road populated by drowsy cows. She'd done the drive between them in her dirt-colored truck so many times that she felt she could shut her eyes and make it home with just the feeling of leather under her fingertips. Her mind rolled in time with the tires. Her phone sat on the passenger-side seat, open to the stream of texts letting Frankie know Cass was finally home. Anticipation made her palms sweat. She was scared that her excitement was really dread—that she would return to Loring after years of queasy emptiness and find it too changed to be hers once again.

The road dropped off where the farmhouse embedded itself in wisteria. It stood like it had just been given an uncomfortable hug, long and squeezed around the middle. Vines clung to clapboards that were once white but now boasted fifteen different species of moss. The sun shone on the massive lake until it glittered.

The lights in the house were off save for one that glowed through the living room window, Oph's shape a silhouette under the grim cast of the awning. Her mouth was a knot, a painful thing that lasted even when Cass met her on the porch and they hugged hard.

It stayed, even when the sheriff ambled down the drive, his tires crackling against the rock, headlights shining two brilliant pupils against the shadowed house. It stayed even as he hauled out of the car and walked slowly up the porch steps.

If he recognized Cass from that bonfire so many years ago, his face didn't betray it, though something awful in her stomach dropped at the sight of him. He cleared his throat twice before he spoke, the lilting cadence of his Loring twang all at once comforting and terrible. "I'm afraid I need to share some bad news."

Then: Frankie arriving, falling into her arms, smelling like Sofia, her cheek damp on Cass's shoulder. Frankie's collapse at the sudden understanding passing between them—that their precipice had dropped into a craggy descent. *Missing* was a word sharpened and honed until it pointed directly to the end, and Cass's fear was a claw cutting its way up her throat. She had been so right to be afraid.

The days to come flickered by like blinking fireflies. Even when it felt impossible, the light in the living room burned on. They grieved. Then came the shift.

With the windows open, the air in Oph's house was lively with the scent of new wildflowers pushing past the fly-speckled screens. Peonies nodded beyond the glass, bending to the will of the wind. They sat together at the kitchen table, she and Oph, knocking back burning sips of whiskey as they slapped down cards. Her eyes were heavy with salt, her tongue furred in her mouth. She could feel Frankie hovering in the kitchen, irritation leaving footprints around the room.

"You should sit down," Cass called over her shoulder, grimacing as Oph swiped a stack of dimes and flashed a winning hand back at her.

"You should focus on winning a round for once," Frankie retorted distractedly, with no real heat. "My sister is dead, and Poppy has the audacity to be *late*."

Dead was a heavy hand on Cass's shoulder. She avoided looking at the other seats at the table, like acknowledging them might summon something too painful—Sofia's leg banging against hers, head tossed back in one of those wicked laughs that always shook the room. Sofia's hands in her hair, coaxing braids out of the unwieldy curls. Sofia's head in her lap, heavy as a purring cat.

Cass slid a card forward. Frankie had lent her one of the oversized T-shirts she usually slept in but on Cass it might as well have been a gown. Every time the hem brushed her knees, she swiped at it like a mosquito.

"Have you tried calling again?" Oph suggested, sniffling hard. All the crying had left her with a stuffy nose.

"Only a million times," Frankie said, barbed as wire.

"You know Poppy," Cass answered. A sleeve drooped off her shoulder. She tugged it back up and glanced at the back door, where leaden clouds waited past the pollen-fuzzed panes. "She'll show up when she's good and ready."

Cass knew Frankie well enough to predict that the answer wouldn't satisfy; Frankie didn't like good and ready. She liked punctuality. Dependability. Frankie hovered over them, a hand on the back of Cass's chair. Cass wanted to lean into her side, feel her warmth against her cheek, but sometimes Frankie spooked like an animal, needed to be warned.

"Take some of the dogwood tincture if you're antsy," Oph said to Frankie, following up Cass's card with one of her own. Her red-rimmed lids betrayed the two weeks of their collective late nights, their grief, their anger.

"Not in the mood," Frankie said, "but thanks."

Oph liked material cures. Tinctures that consisted of tiny vials of extracts, herbal teas, foul potions, well-meaning spells. A candle burned down until nothing remained. Plates of coins and folded paper and a freshly cut fingernail. Names scrawled on paper and frozen behind a bag of peas for the next seven years. Hair clipped and woven in a fingerling braid, pinned between the wicks of two tapers, flames racing to the finish. The years that Cass had been a part of the Lyon family's orbit lent themselves closer to apprenticeship than observation. She was a curious student in the heart of an interior practice. But her understanding of witchcraft was still starved—Oph gave them evidence in predicted test grades, tea leaves still hot in the bottom of a cup, tarot cards called by name before they were flipped and revealed with a satisfied *shwick* of the hand. But even Oph brushed her practice off as ordinary, claiming that her sister had always been the better witch. Cass had only met Frankie's mom a few times. She'd always been a little scared of her.

Asking for more was out of the question. These days, if the conversation veered toward witchery, Frankie left the room.

"Queen of Spades, thirteen points," Cass said with a grin, pushing a stack of cards toward Oph. To Frankie she called, "What were you saying about winning rounds, bitch?"

It was Oph's turn to curse. She incanted a hundred hangnails upon Cass's hands and made it extra nasty. Frankie laughed for the first time.

"Completely unnecessary," Cass said. "Quit being a sore loser and deal me in again."

She enjoyed the magic of it all, even if she wasn't entirely convinced of its effectiveness beyond parlor tricks. But she liked the way Oph seemed to look at the world and see its roots. She liked tucking the rose petal beneath her tongue and wishing for love, hoping with some fraction of her heart that it might come true.

Frankie liked things that made physical sense. Given the chance, she would spit the petal out.

Fat bees bumped against the back door's dirty glass. Cass bent the edge of a card and shook her leg, craving some kind of movement to keep her from bouncing out of her body. Frankie scanned relentlessly out the window.

"A watched pot never boils," Oph called.

"Good thing I'm not making pasta," Frankie said.

"If you're angry when she gets here, she's going to be angry too," Cass warned. The new round began and Oph slapped down another set of hearts. They both drank at once.

"Well, she has no right to be."

Frankie tended to simmer, searing inside herself until her mouth opened and smoke poured out. It was part of what tore her and Sofia apart in those final months, and what fractured the rest of them in the end. The rift bit into Cass and left the impression of teeth.

It was hard to remember what things had been like before Sofia disappeared, before everything started to disintegrate. Frankie's easy laugh had slipped from her memory. Cass's grasp on Poppy was thin as a fistful of water. Whatever the four of them had once been was a childish invention, a prayer for a lasting link left unanswered.

Cass had expected them to grow up together, to attend each other's weddings, to hold each other's hair as they puked into toilets and to raise their kids like some kind of queer commune. They had been that way all her life—closer than sisters. Soul-bonded. No one knew her like her women. No one would ever see into her like them, past the walls of her heart.

But then, that summer after their senior year. The bonfire where everything fell apart. The night Sofia didn't come home and Poppy drove them all over town until her car gave out for the hundredth time. Weeks of search parties, of Frankie split as a binary star, Poppy like a burning pyre, Sofia's car a mausoleum on the side of the road. Poppy's bruised knuckles and suitcases packed for college, Cass off to New York, Poppy to Durham, Frankie left in Loring with a Sofia-shaped hole in the ragged place where her heart had lived.

Sofia was declared a runaway. Their collective grief hardened in different places.

Cass called and visited when she could, even when it ate her up— feeling too big to be a child and too small to be anything else, the sun radiant on the surface of the dining table that she bought with a job that she applied for in an apartment where she paid rent, barely holding herself together because she had a hometown that everyone told her to leave, so she left it. *Were you seeking something more? Did you ever find it?* There was no correct answer.

Cass still loved them, despite all the years she had longed to turn off her hurt. Poppy stopped answering their texts, avoided Loring like it was a plague sent to eradicate her, while Frankie grew thorns and retreated within herself. What could Cass possibly ask from them now? From Loring itself?

Well—to see her first firefly of the season. To lay her head on Frankie's shoulder, to press against Poppy's back, to feel the rise and fall of their breaths through the bone. To laugh. To feel pretty and loved, in a feral sort of way. To hold a cool glass to her cheek, sweating, to suck the rind of a lemon, for summer to emerge and stay forever, to come home, to never feel the need to leave again.

And what did she have in the end? Just the ache of anticipation.

Tomorrow was the memorial. Already, neighbors had left casseroles on the porch along with their condolences, green beans steeped in processed soups. The night before, Oph had taken to deep cleaning the refrigerator to give herself something to do. Frankie had kept the curtains drawn and the lights down low. Cass had stayed the night like she always did before she left Loring, lying in the bedroom beside Sofia's, absentmindedly stroking Frankie's hair. Even if things were different now, they could still have this—the casual touch that had always grounded them to one another.

"I don't know how you can just sit there," Frankie said. "I feel like I'm going to buzz out of my body, and we still need someone to cater the memorial."

Cass slapped down another winning hand. Oph left the table with a huff and headed toward the mantel-altar hybrid in the living room, overflowing with candles, dried flowers, and framed family photos, most of them consisting of overedited photos of Sofia that Cass was certain she would have hated to see on display. Their collective black box-dyed hair phases deserved to die in quiet.

"What do you want us to do? I'm fresh out of tears," Oph said, fumbling with a box of matches. She sparked candles across the mantel, one after the other after the other, and flashed a hurtful look at Cass. "This is getting ridiculous, I never lose to you."

"Maybe I hexed you," Cass said, wriggling her fingers.

"Please, my wards are strong," Oph scoffed, then aimed the rest of her words at Frankie. "Just feed them whatever slop the neighbors brought us. Goddess knows we won't be able to eat it all." She lit a pink taper candle, then a white. Cass could hear her already, the same spiel she'd rattled off for years. *Pink for the bond we share, everlasting. White for a blank and purifying slate. Out with the old, in with the new.* It felt a little silly, now that she was twenty-two and magic seemed as flimsy as who she'd been when she was seventeen. But wasn't it nice, to see a physical representation of your hope in front of you?

"I agree. Sofia wouldn't care," Cass added. She swirled her drink in one hand while the other clutched the ornate back of a yard-sale dining chair. Frankie kept her arms tightly crossed, body rigid. Her shirt hung loosely around her torso. She looked peaky.

"You should eat something," Cass added after a beat.

"You should mind your business," Frankie said, but she lifted the foil off one of the plates that littered the countertops and bit down into an apple pastry.

"Come on now," Oph scolded. She tied her hair back with a scrap of fabric that looked suspiciously like it used to be a satin baby doll dress and held her hair with just as much effectiveness as one might expect. "Let's all just be glad to be together, no matter the occasion."

Occasion. Cass ducked her head. This wasn't a damn bachelorette party. She drained the rest of her drink and scrubbed at an eye, fighting the sting. "What's the Russian up to today?" she asked, desperate to talk about anything besides murder and grief and Poppy Goddamn Loveless.

Their weekly phone calls over the past year had consisted mostly of Frankie venting to Cass about her employee's lack of comprehension of what a job entailed.

"Probably burning down the shop or something," Frankie answered through a full mouth. An avalanche of crumbs decorated her shirt. In the dining room, Oph was back at the table flipping through an ancient binder of CDs.

Cass rolled her eyes and pushed away from the table, playing cards drifting to the floor in the rush of movement. "I need to pee. If Poppy gets here while I'm gone, try not to get into a fistfight, please?"

She tugged on a strand of Frankie's hair as she disappeared through the kitchen doorway. Frankie swatted at her and missed by an inch, and Cass laughed at the attempt. "Already?" Oph called after her. Cass couldn't tell whether she was responding to the need to pee or the idea of a physical altercation. The sound of a chair pushing in warred for recognition over the suddenly blaring radio and Oph's declaration of "I love this song!"

Cass headed down the hallway to the bathroom, eyes catching on movement at the top of the staircase. She did a double take, searching for the shadow she'd just seen, but there was nothing, only gray light making shapes against doorways. The floor creaked down the hall, the kind of sound her mom would have told her was *settling*. Cass found it to have the opposite effect.

With the door shut, the bathroom was eerily quiet. The music was muffled, Oph's and Frankie's voices gone. She peed at record speed and washed her hands with a bar of soap that was mostly lumpy flower petals. She stared at the streaming faucet, suddenly unwilling to meet her gaze in the mirror. In the smallest glimpse she caught how the light yellowed her under the eyes and her dark curls frizzed with humidity or an unseen current. Anxiety curdled in her stomach and the nerves ran all the way up her chest, hair prickling across her arms and her scalp.

When she turned to the old door and tugged, the knob wouldn't yank free. She twisted again. It stuck fast, like someone was holding the knob on the other side, pinning her in place. It was the kind of prank they would have pulled in another life, before it stopped being funny, before there'd been nothing left to laugh about.

"Hey," she said, tasting fear. She pulled harder. Distantly she heard a succession of hard knocks, then footsteps. "Frankie," she called, "let me out."

There was the sudden, cold sensation of someone's eyes on her back. All at once she felt that turning to the mirror would show someone else standing beside her, body pressed up against the door. The room dimmed, overhead bulb going murky—her breath went down hard as a swallowed stone.

The lights blinked once. The world woke around her. The knob creaked and twisted and left Cass stumbling into the edge of the sink. She rushed out to find Frankie standing at the end of the hall by the entryway, face open in surprise.

"You have a terrible sense of humor," Cass tried to snap, but it came out like desperation.

Frankie blinked back at her. "What the hell are you talking about?"

Cass's lungs were a pincushion. Every inhale pained and pricked. She pressed her hands, dewy and shaking, to her thighs. "Why would you—" she started, but three hard knocks sounded again, demanding their attention.

Frankie glanced at her for a stolen moment, restrained emotion written in her face and mirroring Cass's own unraveling—a fraught cocktail of anxiety, confusion, and defeat. Then she shook her head and tore open the door.

Poppy stood on the porch. The afternoon was so ominous and gray behind her that it almost made the moment funny. Poppy's head was freshly shorn, her eyes bleak and narrowed, chin tilted back on the defensive and lips parted in question. Her shirt had a hole in the shoulder that revealed a patch of dark skin, but she wore it intentionally, like finery. She was beautiful and brand new, soft and just the same, and for a moment Cass almost forgot that Poppy had left the rest of them behind.

Until Frankie reminded her and said, "Would it kill you to pick up your *fucking* phone?"

4

Mountains with Deep Pockets

Wordless and wide-eyed, seer and seen, Marya Sokolova spent her life listening to other busy mouths tell her who she was meant to be.

Marya was good at keeping quiet. Her mother ground lessons into her with a hard pinch of her cheek. Her friends poked the truth from her in scraps and made up what happened in the gaps of her admissions. The rest of the world leered over her, begging for a performance.

Loring breathed lazily past the promise of rain. Marya perched by her apartment window and sucked impatiently on a cigarette, rolling her ankle against the wide sill. Across the scattered shops that made up Loring's Main Street, the sky painted huge swoops of grayed-out blue. She could just make out the studio, closed for the day. Beyond it all the mountains rose. They were beautiful cerulean things, with an outline like a woman sleeping on her side.

She exhaled smoke with a pang in her chest, a feeling of falling that reminded her of how much she craved a goddamn Coke. She tilted her head back against the framed sill and tried to shut out the sound of running water.

The man in her kitchen wouldn't stop fucking with the faucet.

He stood under the fickle ceiling light, both bulbs long since burned out. One hand he kept jammed down in his pocket and the other he used to start the water again, hot then cold then hot again, trickling stream then roaring rush.

"Do you have to do that?" she asked.

He looked at her with the wounded eyes of a scolded dog and turned the water off again. He liked it best if she left the sink filled to a dangerous level, where he could drag his hands through scummy and sour water. Some days she'd come home from work and find that the basin had overflowed onto the linoleum, and he'd endure her chastising with a shaking head.

Strands of hair stuck to her cheek. Almost dusk and the humidity still sweltered. She wasn't quite used to it yet, the swampy, suffocating heat of the South. If she'd admitted that out loud, Nina would have laughed at her. But she hadn't spoken, just exhaled long and painfully through her nose, and Nina wasn't there. It was just Marya and the man in the kitchen, hangdog and dour.

A fly crawled across the sill. She stubbed her cigarette out beside it, sending it into a frenzy, and immediately she lit another, feeling guilty for it and terribly pleased.

"This is the last one," she promised. She smoked for several minutes of quiet, snatches of conversation floating up from beneath her window, the hum of bugs already building in the bushes below.

A final huff of air slipped from her mouth. She ashed her cigarette beside the first and fished for the pack in her pocket, extending her legs to loosen the hold her jeans had on it. When it was free, she unceremoniously tossed it out the open window.

"Last one," she said again, getting to her feet and kicking around crumpled pants on the floor in search of her wallet. She wouldn't smoke another, but she'd buy a soda. It was hot and she was thirsty and she could only kick one habit at a time because today wasn't the day she was going to die, no, not yet. She wished there was someone there to hold her to it, to tell her not to buy another pack for as long as she lived, to split the Coke with her so she wouldn't knock the whole thing back and feel her teeth fuzzing in her skull. She looked at the man, but he pointedly ignored her and went into the bathroom instead, likely to toy with the toilet handle until Marya threatened to kick him out. It was an empty claim—she'd never have the guts to ask for space. But he didn't have to know that.

Regardless—she found the wallet in a dirty pair of jeans. Tossed a bag over her shoulder. Toed on her shoes and hefted her bike down the apartment stairs into the coming storm.

Loring bloomed on.

"Downtown" was a speck of life growing relentlessly out of the country. Really it was nothing more than some mom-and-pop shops and Frances Lyon's ceramics place where Marya barely covered the cost of her rent, a deli where the guy who stocked shelves liked to knock knuckles with Marya because he saw how supremely uncomfortable it made her, benches built into uprooted sidewalks and dedicated to people named Tammy or Steve who grew up over yonder, never left, until they were tucked beneath the great green earth. The town was smaller than anywhere else Marya had ever lived, with its own insular conversations and gossipy tensions, its delegated ways of life. At times, Loring made her hyperaware of her own isolation. Mostly she was satisfied to have an excuse to hide.

She sailed her bike past languid afternoon traffic. Faded missing posters remained, stapled to the splintery posts with a face just like Frankie's smiling back at her. Marya kept her eyes on the road, already itching for a smoke.

It took focus to keep her grip tight on the handlebars. She banked right and swiftly picked up speed as the road declined. Potholes demanded that she swerve every few seconds. Straitlaced poplar trees framed the asphalt, leaves flipping casually as the storm rumbled closer. She could already see the soda and a salty bag of chips in her mind, illuminated by a halo of light like the finest reliquary a cathedral could ask for.

Marya chained up her bike in the supermarket parking lot. In and out, just the essentials. In a matter of minutes, she'd be home again, where she could stretch out on the couch and watch television until the sky slipped into night without her realization.

She strode down aisles with a basket balanced on her hip, scanning for something satisfying, noting a mental checklist as she headed into the baking aisle. The oven back at her apartment was temperamental, but a cake could be finagled out of it.

Gradual thrumming filled the store. She peered out of the front windows, shoulders falling when she saw the sheets of rain. The man would be pleased. Marya returned to her shopping a little slower this time and caught the flicker of matter just as the world shifted.

It would be impossible to say that she was surprised to see Sofia Lyon standing just feet away from her, bleached bone fingertips clutched around a plastic container of icing. That was the complicated thing about ghosts; she couldn't look right at them and expect to see the truth. Without the missing posters to supplement her, she might not have immediately understood who she was looking at, might have thought that her mind was inventing images of Frankie to haunt her past work hours. But Marya had learned to watch from corners and catch the right angle. With a sideways glance, she took Sofia in: the close crop of her deep red hair, the slope of her shoulders where a ragged shirt clung to bruised skin. The awful green of her eyes, like grass after rain and new garden growth—that brightness made Marya desperately sad, as if Sofia still had the potential to turn to Marya and suck a living breath into the open chasm of her chest.

Experience had taught her that wherever Sofia was, Frankie would likely follow, as she had for the past year. Marya was a little more surprised at the prospect of running into Frankie than the corpse of her twin sister.

It was like the universe wanted her to suffer, she thought, as her boss rounded the corner with two others trailing after her. The specter of Sofia's hand flickered away, and the canister of vanilla icing, in its impervious plastic casing, thudded to the floor with an echoing slap. It rolled to a stop at the toe of Marya's sneaker. She shifted the weight of her basket to the other hip in an awkward shrug and raised a hand in greeting to the surprised faces of Frankie and her friends.

Sofia dappled like bits of scattered light, and Marya watched the vague pockets of her crushed skull deepen and warp, the periwinkle edges of her skin blurring where the world bent around them.

Yes, she liked Loring. She liked it because it wasn't her mom's apartment in Queens. Because Nina wasn't there to stir up guilt in her for leaving Raleigh, because some days it was so beautiful that it made her want to cry. Because she might be a body with no homeland but maybe this could be hers, the hazy pink skies, the tender blue mountains, the huge ash trees. She liked how impossibly lush it was in the summer, and how viciously dense it became in the winter. She thought the way the mountains held the valley town made the whole place feel a little more heavenly and loved. Maybe she liked to feel heavenly and loved.

Or, maybe, perhaps, Marya liked it because she had never seen a haunting like Sofia's.

Since the first day at the studio, Sofia's incorporeal form had clung to her sister, buzzing in and out of sight, sometimes stronger, sometimes weaker. Marya understood that kind of apparition to some extent—a body needed energy to be seen, and Sofia could only leech off those around her for so long without a flicker.

But there was a fine line separating Sofia from the familiar, and Marya was a curious animal. Sofia was not the old woman Marya used to see in her mother's bathroom mirror, not the little girl who lived under the front step of her apartment building, not the man who turned the faucets and stood over Marya on nights when she forgot to salt the floor before her bedroom door.

Sofia had a shadow with a mind of its own, that defied all the laws of a haunt that Marya thought she knew. It was an inky and menacing shape, opaque enough to block out the light, shimmering and gray where its size and matter staked a claim. It followed. It stole from Sofia, left her silent and sullen and faint. Sometimes it attempted to sink its way into Sofia's skin, sometimes it tried to peel itself away, always pulling at her, ever prodding. It filled every room with a malignant presence—too physical, too imposing, too present. Now it pressed itself up against boxes of brownie mix and bags of chocolate chips, fuzzy at the edges in a way that encouraged a headache at the base of Marya's skull.

If her mom could see her like this, she'd warn Marya away from it. That was how she had raised her, after all, with a healthy fear of black corners and apparitions in the hazy pockets of dawn, a shared and familial understanding that had kept them safe for years to come and go. There was nothing to be salvaged from the unknown. It was smarter to step back—to remove herself from the equation, turn from the begging haunt and give it the space required to move on, with a prayer said in the night to a whole and watching moon.

Marya had never been afraid of the dark before. But she looked at Frankie, wearing the face of a dead girl unseen beside her, and thought her fear had the potential to grow.

5

THE HEN HOUSE AND ITS UNSTEADY LEGS

There was no discernible point in time when the night became unsafe.

It was like this: Once, the shadow cast by the house was just that—a shadow. Mass blocking light. A space that the pomegranate sun tried and failed to paint crimson with its glow. Trees that showed their bellies for oily rain. Birds that shied away from rusty sunlight to steal tomatoes from the garden.

Finder fed the geese beyond the porch. There the grass grew tall and wispy as an old woman's hair, peppered with ants, white flowers dotting the field like spilled flour. She'd take the stairs two at a time, grain in her basket and one of Mother Mab's patterned kerchiefs holding the hair out of her face, and step into cast shapes made purple by the absence of illumination. It was special: an opportunity for Mab to trust that Finder would get the job done without needing visual proof.

When Finder thought back to those moments, it was always with an ache. Maybe it would have been better if she'd never known the difference between day and night. If the sun had gone on, a brilliant, red, shaking mirage overhead, so glazed and warm that it never failed to remind Finder of the shift into evenings when her nose bled into the sink without sign of stopping and each drop dyed the water copper. If the moonless night had never come so all-encompassing that seeing her hand before her face was impossible without a candle held in the other.

Maybe it wouldn't be so awful if the Ossifier agreed when she talked about the sun. If now, when she returned from feedings within the fence prickled with fear, Mother Mab didn't snatch the grain basket from her hands and the kerchief from her hair, spitting somewhere on the floor to punctuate her scolding.

"All this night and day again and again, Finder chick," Mother Mab would say, her gnarled fingers tight around the stolen kerchief as Finder rubbed her sore scalp. "I'm tired of your prattling on about imagined light and invented fantasies. Keep it up and I'll toss your skin-quilt out in the woods and let something eat you for a change."

The Ossifier would stand quietly in the corner by the stove where the room was warmest, hands clacking as he rubbed them together. His breath would rattle and shake. His sniffles would suck the air from the room like the bellows of an accordion perched against a thin, trembling knee.

"Don't you remember it?" she would ask the Ossifier on the rare occasions that he'd meet her gaze with milky eyes, desperate for someone else to say *yes Finder, the sun was red and rotten like the inside of your cheek and the underside of your tongue, and the light made everything a blushing pink just after dawn, and the Hen House cast a jagged outline on the dry grass every day after two and a quarter.*

Instead, the Ossifier would flinch away when Mother Mab snapped at him, her hair wild in every direction gravity could tug it, wrinkled face screwed up with a mixture of irritation and impatience. Finder's question would go unanswered as tasks were doled out. She'd spend the rest of her everlasting night scattering grain for the chickens in their hut with a candle perched on the porch railing. The fence delineated the breadth of her world. In the distance, she'd watch the trees stand upright in the pitch, listen to something hunt beyond the dark.

Now, in mornings distinguished only by the faint gray that tinged the horizon, Finder would watch as Mother Mab counted seeds for their breakfast. Five in the left hand, six in the right, and then with gusto! Tossed down into a bowl of cream, thick and sour. Eleven was such a wonderful number when paired with lovingly pared fruit.

She hadn't always been called Finder. First, she was just Creature, barely a girl at all but a thing with two legs and ten fingers, skin mulled like wine beneath the red sun's glow. On one of her worst nights in those early years of living with Mother Mab, the Ossifier had prodded at her elbows to feel the bones beneath that skin, rubbed his white thumbs along her knees until she could almost see the tracks his dusty finger-prints left behind. It'd taken Mab's broom thudding into his chest to get him to back off. Finder caught him rubbing his fingers together for nearly an hour afterward, her skin staining them a burnt rouge.

She had arrived in a basket on the porch back before the world went dark, smelling of the starched crispness of freshly hung sheets. The house had nearly bucked her off. She couldn't blame it—it was used to creatures coming out of the woods in search of something to feed on, half-dead wraiths with no right mind of their own. But when Mother Mab opened the door, she'd found not the dead but Finder squalling and a great brown bear pressing its nose against hers, tugging at the basket handle with its teeth.

Superstitious to a fault, Mab brought the bear inside first and fed her a plate of fish. Then, after they finished their respective breakfasts, she went outside to retrieve Finder.

"You'll be called Creature until you can earn a name," Mother Mab said to Finder once she was old enough to know what the words meant, drying her palms on an apron so dirty it barely managed to bend around the wrinkles of her skin.

"Yes, Mother Mab," Finder had answered.

The thing was, she hadn't been sure what was worthy. Before the thick night came, she spent her days working, washing clothes and stirring pots on the stove. Afternoons passed picking berries in the woods, lying on her back in the grass as the blood-red sun crawled across the sky.

Her answer came in the form of a seedling.

She'd been the first to spot the crack in the floor. While the Ossifier sat in the next room, settled in Mother Mab's second-favorite armchair and whittling a bleached bone, and Mab bundled bouquets of river reeds by the woodstove, Finder read from a thin volume of stories on the kitchen floor. Finder was a little over seven years old then, signaled by the cauterized lines burned into her thigh, rising taut, a tally for each passing collage of days. She was just tall enough now to reach the fourth shelf, the one with familiar titles like *Transmutation in the Form of a Bone* and *Assisting a Spirit in Passage* and *Shapeshifters: The Goat Man Walks after Three*.

That day, years before the sun winked out of the sky, a page splayed open about a demon that grew from spilled blood like seeds planted in earth. It was a rooted thing that latched itself into whatever could feed it, whether that be body or loam or liquid, and it was said to obey the ones that learned its name and called it from their reflections. She was a little too scared to look directly at the illustrations and had to cover them with a hand while she read—the demon's gnarled head and the shadowed shapes it tore into with its teeth left her sick with near hallucinations of her own outline stepping into the light.

Mother Mab stalked past and gave Finder's book a kick, shutting it with the pointed toe of her boot. "Don't read things like that," Mab said. "I won't be the one to ease the nightmares that will come with it."

Finder looked up from the closed book, annoyed, and her eyes landed on the seedling.

Somehow, underfoot and fickle, it had crawled its way through the floor. The fresh green of its leaves left spots at the corners of her vision. She brushed a tentative finger against it and felt something sing deep in her blood. It was a warning sensation, like the hum of insects right before a storm.

"Mother Mab," she called from her place on the floor. "There's a plant."

The Ossifier let out a wounded noise and sucked at his thumb where his knife had nicked it. Sparse pale hair fell across the lines of his forehead. The house keened as Mother Mab stopped beside her. "What are you talking about, chickling?"

She pointed at the sprout. "It's growing through the floor."

Mab's kneeling was a messy ordeal. Her skirts were mud caked at the hems and her ample hips didn't take well to bending low. But she got down beside Finder and peered at the seedling. A deep-set wrinkle bisected her narrowed eyes. The Ossifier watched them, thumb held between his lips.

"Oh, Creature," Mother Mab breathed. "Do you know what this means? It's a tree, come to bear us fruit and join our house." She reached out, quick as the crack of a whip, and caught Finder's chin. Her fingers pressed dimples into Finder's cheeks. "This is a wonderful thing you've seen."

Mab released her, worked her way back up to standing. She smiled down at the girl on the floor—an eerie sight. "I think it's time we gave you a name, Finder."

So she became indispensable to Mother Mab, always spotting something just before it was needed. Until the night. Until she watched the sun drain from the world.

Before bed, she'd blow her candle out and paint the room a million shades of black. Stare at the slanted ceiling of her attic bedroom, knotted eyes peering at her from the wood. "It happened," she'd whisper back at them. Maybe Mother Mab and the Ossifier sleeping beneath her would hear it, feel the words seep behind their shut eyelids.

Maybe it bothered her most because she knew it had to be her fault.

One moment, the window beside the door to the porch was awash in red, scarlet pouring through the panes of glass like wine. In the distance, it melted with the smoke of village chimneys and cast a wide berth over the mountains, dirt so fiercely tanned that the whole world might as well have been leather. One moment and she'd been memorizing the shape of those hills, the dips and arcs, the landscape she had known her entire life. Then the next second—fast and painful as a breaking bone—a black curtain dropped over the land and her vision had no chance of adjusting.

And what Finder saw was different, wasn't it? Wasn't that what Mother Mab had always said? So why wouldn't they believe her, when they had lived in the red world, too, before the woods became too dangerous to step into and the grass grew too high to wade through?

Sofia would believe her, Finder knew. If she would only come back—if she would only answer Finder's whispers into the tepid surface of the bath, if she would only feel the way Finder shook when she sat by her window and begged the glass to show her the other girl's face.

Sofia had loved the tree. When Finder brought her to it in the sleeping house, pressed Sofia's hand up against the bark, showed her how it twisted its way through the floorboards, Sofia's eyes had welled with tears.

"Oh, it's beautiful, Finder, it's lovely," she had said, her voice shaking harder than her white hand against the purpled bark.

Finder had thought it would make her happy, to see the magic of it all unfolding before her. After all, there was nothing Sofia loved more than magic.

But Finder knew what it felt like when something was so beautiful that it hurt to see. It was how she used to feel when she looked at the sun.

Sofia had always understood her better than anyone else.

6

ROTTEN LIKE FALLEN FRUIT

The dress didn't fit. Frankie pinched the waist, felt the black fabric give, watched it pillow away from the plane of her stomach in her reflection.

The house was loud as a body, with all the same digestive hums and groans. Downstairs she could hear the music of them—Cass and Oph arranging flowers in the collection of vases Frankie had ferried home from the studio, Poppy distinguishable by the third set of footsteps pacing in the kitchen.

Frankie felt lucky to have slipped away—it ached to picture the heavy hanging heads of Oph's peonies, cut and clustered.

In an hour the house would fill with everyone she had spent the last five years attempting to avoid, well-meaning mothers and overcurious classmates and fraudulent lurkers preparing to drink in the grief. Frankie turned from the mirror and dragged a harsh breath in through her nose. It was too much—her mind a mess, her body ugly in the dress, her heart a fractured thing slamming against her rib cage.

A creak sounded in the hall. She snapped her head up and watched the empty doorway. Some traitorous part of her hoped that she would find her sister standing there, waiting to be invited inside.

Sofia had always been a size smaller than Frankie, something that reminded her that they had been different beings after all. That Frankie hadn't lost herself inside of the myth of her sister. But now they were almost the same—Frankie shrinking and changing while Sofia remained stagnant.

She slipped out of her bedroom and down the hall to Sofia's door. The hesitation lasted only a moment, her breath a brutal stone in her throat and her hand hovering over the knob, before she pushed her way in.

The air inside was stale, duvet mussed like it had never been made after the last person to sleep on it. Frankie avoided looking at the photos on the wall or the scattered papers and pens on Sofia's desk—instead she went right for the closet and began to flick through hangers.

The floor gave another whisper and she glanced over her shoulder. Downstairs, Cass laughed. Here the shadows were deeper, faint buzzing clinging to the quiet corners. The hair on her arms stood on end, electric.

"Hello?" she mumbled, testing. But silence answered.

She faced the task with new determination. The closet was exactly how it had been since they first moved into Oph's. Messy, unorganized, packed as a finch's nest. The dusty scent of jasmine. Heady woodsmoke clinging to a sweatshirt, so faint it could have been conjured by memory alone. Frankie brought the sleeve to her cheek and inhaled, her eyes shut, her chin trembling.

Hinges creaked somewhere down the hall and she dropped it immediately. She snatched a dress off the hanger instead and laid it out on the bed. There it made a corpse of its own—a sister-shaped space against all the quilted thread.

She made quick work of the too-big dress over her head before stepping into Sofia's. It was still a little small—the zipper caught halfway when she tugged it up—but at least it didn't make her feel like she was drowning.

"Do you need some help?"

"Jesus Christ," Frankie gasped, hand pressed to her throat as she spun and found Poppy in the doorway.

"Sorry," Poppy said, uncomfortable. "Didn't mean to scare you."

"What are you doing up here?" Frankie asked.

Poppy glanced around the room before her eyes rushed back to Frankie, who stood with her hands pressed to the collar of the dress, zipper hanging open and exposing the flayed fabric of her bare back. She felt entirely too exposed. Something in Poppy's face sharpened, burned by the sight of Sofia's preservation.

"You were taking a while," Poppy said finally. One hand toyed with the pocket of her slacks and the other pressed against the buttons of her shirt, as if checking that they were still in place. "I wanted to make sure you were all right."

There were a thousand answers she could volley back, but Frankie settled on: "I'm fine."

"I kind of doubt that," Poppy said. She stepped further into the room and made a twisted motion with her hand, urging Frankie to turn around. When Frankie stared back, dumbfounded, she sighed. "Let me zip you up."

Frankie obeyed after a beat of hesitation and faced Sofia's bed. Poppy braced one hand at the small of Frankie's back, and the other dragged the zipper up. Frankie fought the urge to shiver at the proximity.

"You look nice," Poppy said to the nape of Frankie's neck. "Sofia would have thought so too."

It would be easier to be agreeable, but Frankie had never been easy, not even when Poppy had known her. She laughed instead. "Thank god my dead sister would have liked my outfit, that makes this whole thing a thousand times better."

"That's not what I meant."

It was awful, to understand someone so well and still think of them as a stranger. There had been a time where Frankie shattered moments like this by swinging an arm around Poppy's neck and pulling her into a hug, that easy closeness, that reassurance in a matching pulse. She remembered casual affection. She remembered comfortable silence. Her palm resting on the bone of Poppy's shoulder, warmth under her hands, their heads tipping to meet in the middle, temple to temple.

The silence was sharper now, had teeth of its own. Frankie smoothed down the front of the dress. The clock on Sofia's nightstand blinked back, twelve o'clock forever and ever, from some ancient time when the power had gone out and no one had come in to correct it. A floorboard creaked in the doorway and the two of them turned to look at it. She could taste her anxiety—tinny, heavy, tongue dry in her mouth.

"I know it's not what you meant," she said, trying not to be poisonous. A headache built behind her ears. "Sorry."

"All good," Poppy said, avoiding her eyes. "Do you mind if we get out of here? Being in this room makes me want to crawl out of my skin."

They stepped into the hallway and Frankie turned the doorknob as it shut behind her, unwilling to make a sound and alert the world to where they'd been. At the top of the stairs Poppy looked at her askance, otherworldly and aphotic.

"I'm actually fine," Frankie promised halfheartedly. She paused—and then, against all odds, tried to smile. It was probably a disturbing sight. "Go ahead."

Poppy stared back, disbelieving, but turned and led the way down the stairs, where they found Oph sprucing up the last bouquet on the coffee table. Cass stood by the mantel-altar above the fireplace, littered with framed photos of Sofia.

They spanned decades. The pictures of the two of them as children were nearly indistinguishable: unruly red-headed babies half-drenched in mud. Most were of Sofia alone, after they'd started to hate taking photos together. Then it was Sofia after an unfortunate middle school haircut when she'd teased the top layers and tried to dye it black. Sofia with her eye makeup smudged into dark clouds. Sofia just a few months before disappearing, hair cropped short against her head, lashes full and lovely, mouth twisted with satisfaction in a way that reminded Frankie too much of their mother.

"There you are," Cass said, suspiciously cheery, as if anticipating an argument or preparing to ease the aftermath of one. "Frank, I wanted to ask—is Marya coming?"

"It's not in her job description," Frankie answered, paling. Seeing Marya stare at her in the supermarket like she was some kind of end-time omen had been enough to make her blood hum.

"T minus forty-five minutes," Oph said.

Frankie pressed a fingertip to her ear to dull the shrill buzzing that kept needling at her, worsening her headache as the kettle started to shriek from the kitchen. A thump reverberated through the room and Frankie shivered—something had followed them out of Sofia's room. She felt the air pulse, swelling heat of space and matter.

But it was only Cass, catching a picture frame before it could tumble to the floor, Sofia, Frankie, and their mother all smiling behind the glass. Grotesquely unaware of what was to come.

The week before her mother's death, a coyote had slipped out of the woods framing the lake's shore. Its feet left prints in the season's first and only fine dustings of snow. Standing on the porch and listening to the birds' titters as it crept around the edge of the trees, Frankie watched with her family.

Fiona Lyon pointed. "Look, it's hungry, it wants to eat the birds."

Sofia had buried her head against their mother's side but kept one eye free of her cowering hands, afraid to look at it directly. Frankie leaned on the railing separating them from the sloping grass and the lake, lips parted in wonder. The coyote inched closer.

Fiona's voice dropped to a whisper. "See it creeping in? It's stalking them."

Frankie nodded. "I see it," Sofia said, small.

Then Fiona whooped, loud and crackling, and the birds took to the sky in a mad rush. The coyote flinched. It darted back into the trees and Fiona put a warm hand on Frankie's shoulder, pulling her back against her hip. When her mother called again across the waving grass, Frankie's heartbeat formed wings.

"No more birds, coyote!"

How had she ever doubted her mother's power? Her bravery? Frankie looked at Fiona's laughing mouth, slack in wonder and shouted joy, and felt awed by the sight of her.

Fiona had been so kind that last week, sweeter than stars, as if she'd known the horror would come. As if she had looked into the future, like she did all those nights when she thought Frankie was asleep, her empty eyes gazing into a shallow dish of black water, palms pressed against the bathroom mirror and mouth drooping into a vacancy, leaving Frankie behind for somewhere distant and more promising. She kissed the top of Frankie's head each time she saw her. She left dog-eared books on Sofia's nightstand. She stood in their doorways right before bed, *good nights* and *I love yous* falling from her mouth like snow, looking like a Pre-Raphaelite angel. Her hair a great auburn cloud, her necklaces tangled across her white collarbones, her eyes gleaming like coals in the dark.

The coyote came back the day after her funeral. Frankie found dead birds among the flower beds in the yard for weeks, until they were nothing, until they were pockets of bone and sinew and whatever plastic had lived in their stomachs.

But the bouquet beside her mother's urn had been lovely, even when it began to wilt.

7

CELLAR, PIT, GRAVE FOR A WITCH

The people came in droves. Neighbors parked in the yard and left ruts in the rain-softened earth, balancing gift baskets and farm stand flowers on their arms, all interspersed with people they'd gone to school with who didn't care about Sofia until she was nothing but bones.

They needed napkins. Poppy promptly disappeared, and Oph and Frankie were absorbed by the crowd until she could barely spot their heads among the corral of shoulders, so here Cass was, searching for paper towels in the cryptically terrifying dirt cellar of the Lyon house.

It was a descent into hell. The stairs were derelict and steep. There was barely enough room for her to fit a foot on each one; she had to turn her ankle to take diagonal steps the whole way down. The only light depended on reaching a pull-chain in the middle of the black room, and Cass had to trail a hand along splintery shelves to reach it. She cursed under her breath, stumbling over boxes and soft items that she prayed were bundles of curtain and quilt and not the burrowed corpses of nocturnal animals.

It had been years since her last time in this basement, but the image of it held fast in her memory. The walls were lined with shelves of jars and a rickety sliding ladder, the floor littered with storage bins. But without a bulb the jars were plunged in darkness and the whole room grew dank and clammy.

Overhead, the floor creaked as people milled between the kitchen and living room. Cass told herself it was comforting to hear them up there, close to her, separated only by old beams and boards and insulation. It was supposed to be an intimate event, but the number of footsteps seemed to multiply. Below, she sank into the cool dirt, like the earth had been freshly tilled and now here she was, stirring up the mud.

She swung one hand back and forth in front of her as she struggled to find the chain. That burning bulb would be her solace. The dark was so relentless that it almost hurt to breathe. Her eyes stubbornly refused to adjust.

The hair on the back of her neck prickled. She was reminded, suddenly, unwittingly, of that claustrophobic moment in the bathroom. Frankie had brushed her off when Cass brought it up, insisting that she hadn't even been near the door. But someone had held that knob in place.

Another wide, desperate arc of her hand. Maybe the chain was missing. She prepared to give up. This was a lost cause, and she was no longer interested in being the kind of friend that ran errands for people in mourning when all she wanted to do was sleep for a few days and grieve for herself.

Cass took a step forward into deeper black, leaving the rows of jars behind. The cellar had never seemed so cavernous before. She cursed herself and her sensible funeral dress, patting around her pocketless thighs for a phone that wasn't there. *You are very brave,* she told herself. *You're not afraid of shit. You're killing it right now.*

Something moved in front of her.

"Absolutely not," she said. The words sounded foreign to her, like they had been sucked away from that vacuum of a room. She squinted and froze, her vision taking on a reddish tinge, a faint hum rising in the back of her head like a generator left to run through the night.

The ground was uneven. Maybe whoever built the house had carved it into the mountain and left it raw, letting the ground curve and slide. Maybe the forest had grown its way inside with its roots spiderwebbing her path. Her pulse made a metronome out of her blood. She swung her hands out again, wishing for the chain, holding the image of it in her head like Oph had taught them when they were kids and wanted something terribly.

"Think of it with intention," she'd said.

Cass intended, hard.

She stepped forward into a pocket of unnervingly frigid air. There was a distant click, like the igniting of a gas range. Another step and the cold abandoned her as she bumped into something firm and warm and person-shaped. Her gasp met the sound of labored breathing in the pitch dark.

Panic surged past her lips in a silent scream. The air she sucked in couldn't make it to her lungs fast enough. Each blink echoed flashes of red. She backpedaled, her mouth forming a yell for help that came out as a weak gasp as she stumbled over boxes, again. There was a person standing in the room. She had bumped into a *person*. In the *fucking cellar*.

Her throat found her lungs, and the sound cracked as she shakily called Poppy's name. When no one answered, she tried again, louder and terrified and desperate. A set of footsteps panicked over her and called back down the stairs.

"Cass? What the hell?" Poppy's voice rang out as a pale rectangle of light filtered in from the top of the steps. It was just enough to give Cass a moment of calm as she reached for the chain again and grabbed it at last, yanking with enough force to nearly rip the bulb itself from the beams of the ceiling.

The cellar illuminated a sick yellow. She whipped her head around, searching for the person that had been beside her only moments before.

Her throat was raw. She thought she could smell smoke, somewhere far off, someone burning leaves in the woods.

Poppy stepped carefully down the stairs. When she spotted Cass in the middle of the room, her face fell from concerned to confused. "What are you *doing*? Why did you scream?"

Cass clutched her throat. Shivers racked her shoulders. She knew she must look wild, but she couldn't catch her breath, couldn't stop looking over her shoulder at the rows and rows of herbs. No one else in sight.

"I know this sounds ridiculous," she whispered, "but there was someone in here."

Poppy clutched the railing. "What do you mean? You're the only one who went down the stairs."

Cass sputtered. "I hit someone when I was trying to find the light. I *felt* them." She was unsteady, rewired. The dirt floor beneath her seemed to swell with life, like the house had a heartbeat of its own.

Poppy looked around the room again before stepping the rest of the way down. Light broke her face into abstract planes. The chain from the bulb swung back and forth, back and forth. There were no jutting stones, no warping roots—just packed earth.

Poppy gently squeezed Cass's shoulder, as if afraid she might send Cass further into her spiraling panic. When Cass let out a shaky breath and leaned into her hand, Poppy gave her a weak smile. "Let's get out of here. Whatever you touched or saw is long gone, I guess."

Cass immediately turned to the stairs, before Poppy had the chance to move. "Can you cut the light?" Her voice tremored. "Please."

Poppy shook her head softly but pulled the chain before hurrying up after her. At the top of the stairs, Cass soaked in the dusk-lit kitchen. All that mess and she hadn't even found what she went down to the cellar for. She could still feel the pressure of the chest she'd bumped into. She knew the sensation of being in the room with someone else, how two sets of breath could fill a silent space, how the darkness tensed when someone else was beside her. She knew it sounded unhinged, illogical. But it had happened. *Something* had happened. Just as she had felt with her hands on that doorknob, turning, pleading, wishing.

She slipped out of the kitchen, Poppy trailing close behind as they blended into the crowded living room. The curtains were drawn back and ultramarine evening pooled outside, the mountains just curves of countryside in the distance. Cass had to force her eyes away from the glass and focus on the faces that flitted by instead, murmuring their condolences to Frankie and Oph.

Then she saw him, and a sickly feeling pooled in her stomach.

8

PEACH, PEAR, PLUM

In the aftermath of her death, in that room full of people drawn by Sofia's memory, Poppy's line of sight caught on the stillness of Cass's body. Cass never paused for anything and now she was so frozen that even her breath had stopped. Poppy followed her gaze and watched him come slowly down the stairs, his head bowed like preparation for a prayer, lips parted and eyes tinged red.

Murderer, Poppy thought, *murderermurderermurderer.*

Aloud, she said, "What the fuck is *he* doing here?"

Lucas Glasswell paused by the table of strange food they'd scrounged up. His suit was tailored, his colorless hair overgrown and hanging in cloudy eyes. The fine bones of his face pushed against hoary skin. His parents hovered beside him, the sheriff's hat clashing with his suit and his mother's hair immaculately cropped to her chin in a severe bob. Poppy watched her put a hand on her son's shoulder, steering him away from Oph, eyes flat behind her hair.

Who had let him upstairs? Poppy imagined him standing in Sofia's stagnant room. His hands on her things, his shoes on her rug, his breath in her space. She thought she might be sick.

"Cass," she said, eerily calm. "What is he doing here?"

Cass finally moved. The ghost of something clung to the corners of her downturned mouth and a sweaty curl stuck to her forehead. *What did you see down there?* Poppy wondered, before Cass interrupted her thoughts.

"Everything is fine. We just can't let him talk to Frankie," Cass said, already scanning the room.

Candlelight danced along wallpaper. Through the doorway, Poppy could see Oph standing in the kitchen, pouring tea for a woman who looked suspiciously like their seventh-grade math teacher. Frankie wasn't there, wasn't in the living room, wasn't standing among the mismatched dining chairs.

"Where is she?" Poppy whispered, mostly to herself.

"Who are you looking for?"

Her voice was unmistakable. The sound of it brought her back to the supermarket, to fizzling overheads and an unmistakable sense of dread. Poppy schooled her expression into something neutral. Marya's hair, black roots and pale strands nearly translucent, was swept behind her ears with two conspicuous pins. She had a neat beauty mark above her lips, catty-corner to her Cupid's bow. Poppy couldn't tell if she had put on some makeup since they last saw her or if the Loring heat had provided the pink blush across her cheeks. Her clothes were dark and elegant. From her arms, the scent of lilies carried itself through the air, wrapped in crinkling brown paper.

"Marya! We were looking for *you*, actually," Cass answered immediately, delight replacing the cold fear in her face. Not much had changed over the years—if a girl had functioning lungs and a tendency to look like she wore mood rings, Cass would flirt with her.

"Oh?" Marya answered, scanning the crowd with a stare so intense it seemed to suck light from the air. "You must have had a premonition."

"Ha," Cass said. "Ha ha, yeah, totally. Truthfully, I'm looking for a girl that goes by Frankie. Frank. Frances. Happen to spot a moody redhead on your way in?"

"I was planning to ask you the same thing," Marya answered. Her eyes grazed the top of Cass's head and landed on Poppy. "Is there an urn that I put these by? I don't really know what the protocol is."

Cass laughed a little, shaking her head. "Oh, no, it's funny really, see, they're still doing an autopsy on her body, so we don't get to bury her for a while. Oph's the only one that's seen her. I mean, luckily." She corrected herself instantly, face falling for a moment.

"Yes," Marya said softly. "I know. I'm very sorry."

The last thing to make Poppy cry had been Cass's voicemail about the sheriff's arrival and Sofia's body in the tree. She had thought herself beyond grief, hardened, impenetrable. Her eyes prickled again. She dug her nails into her palms.

"Thanks, but we really need to find Frankie," Poppy cut in.

Cass nodded hard enough to make her hair bounce. "Totally. Totally, totally, totally. Listen, Marya, a lot of weird shit is happening, and I'm not sure that now would be the best time for—"

"Marya?" Frankie materialized from the dark hall, dabbing her hands dry on Sofia's dress. "I said you could take the day off."

Poppy remembered the feeling of the zipper. Frankie's cheeks were splotched with pink. Poppy could picture her standing in front of the bathroom mirror, splashing water on her face and practicing how to breathe. Frankie's eyes cut to Cass, suspicious.

"I am off. Just stopping by to pay my respects," Marya answered as Cass held up her hands in innocence. She extended the package of lilies. "My condolences, Frances."

Frances, Cass mouthed to Poppy, gleeful. Poppy smiled back a beat too late.

Frankie started to retort, but Cass interrupted in a rush of words. "Welcome to our rejected grievers club," she said, slinging an arm around her shoulders. "I've been looking for you all over the damn place. Membership is exclusive around these parts."

Poppy averted her eyes from the casual affection of Cass's arm around Frankie's shoulders, wishing she could touch them without feeling like an alien, wishing suddenly that she could be anywhere but this room.

"I've been in high demand," Frankie answered, eyes searching for the nearest exit. It took her a beat before they landed on the bouquet Marya kept extended. Marya nudged it forward again.

Cass gasped, wickedly delighted. "Frank, you love calla lilies!"

Frankie was suspicious as she took the flowers from Marya and held them to her chest. "Calla lilies were Sofia's favorite."

Poppy couldn't look at them. Even the scent was too much, cloying.

Marya's gaze softened. "Lucky guess." They watched each other, tense and taut, as if sizing one another up for the very first time.

"Well, anyways," Cass said pointedly. "How about we go check on the refreshments?"

Frankie shook her off gently. "Sure." She looked back to Marya, guarded. "You'll be at the shop tomorrow, right?"

"Wouldn't miss it," Marya agreed. She gave Cass and Poppy a little wave before melting back into the growing crowd. The light slid off her hair, absorbed into her clothes. She flickered like an apparition.

"She's kind of creepy," Poppy murmured. "Her eyes look right through you."

"Yeah, it's severely hot," Cass answered solemnly. Frankie pushed at her shoulder.

"I guess I need to put these in some water," Frankie said, glancing around the room. She stopped as someone angled toward them. Her face went blank and dead, eyes shuttering.

Poppy looked up. When Lucas saw her, he smiled, vacant as a mountain motel.

She almost instinctively put her body between Frankie and his advance. The thud of his dress shoes on the floor was the sound of a timer counting down the last remaining seconds of Poppy's resolve. He walked with power to his name—it was built into his genetic matter, as if his father's position as sheriff coursed through their blood. He'd always been that way. Buoyant and unshakable, leering and familiar as a church on a street corner. And for three insufferable years, which none of them had had the complete capacity to understand, he'd been Sofia's boyfriend. Now her body waited in a morgue, and he stood here smiling.

The problem was that Sofia was so easy to love. Poppy had adored her the moment she saw her, just kids, coltish and unkempt and rowdy. There was a certain brightness to her, like holding a hand up to the sun and watching the thin edges of the skin go molten. She was beautiful in a startling way, with the boyish jut of her shoulders, her wide hands, neat knuckles, teasing bite of her mouth. She was a witch's daughter and spoke like she was telling a fortune. She was quick to laughter and prone to teasing. Years down the line—after they'd learned each other, after the barriers fell away—Sofia liked to trail her fingers down the deep curve of Poppy's neck, and Poppy would hold her breath, just hoping to let it last a second longer. There was a thrill in being the subject of a magical girl's devotion. Poppy couldn't blame the rest of Loring for loving her. After all, the whole world would have worshipped her if it had only had the chance to try.

But Sofia had loved *him* too, and it had killed her in the end, hadn't it?

She'd insisted that he was kind and patient, interesting and smart. Affectionate. Well spoken. That was all fine if you wanted to believe that. But Poppy thought he was an absolute fucking prick. She wondered if he had wiped all memory of Poppy Loveless the moment she left Loring, just as she had tried to do with everyone else, drawing a boundary between the place that had only ever made her feel scrutinized for all the ways she couldn't fit and the future she believed herself capable of living.

"Frankie," he said, extending a hand. He had a way of speaking that had stuck over the years—like he was reciting particularly boring bits of information from a pamphlet. "It's good to be with family at a time like this."

Frankie made no move to respond to the handshake. Lucas's faint smile remained as he dropped his hand to his side. He was broad shouldered, strong, shaped by years of physicality. Sofia had been strangled, the coroner said, and after she was dead, she had been beaten until she cracked like an eggshell. Poppy looked at Lucas's hands again.

"She's got all the family she needs," Cass answered. She straightened her spine and puffed out her chest. To Poppy, she looked a little like a pigeon pecking underfoot, but the effort was appreciated.

He looked past Poppy, like she was part of the wallpaper. "I just wanted to extend my support. We're all grieving right now."

"There's plenty of suffering to go around here," Poppy said. The words came out hoarse, and Cass's gaze burned against Poppy's cheek. Poppy couldn't meet her eyes.

"Plenty," Frankie echoed.

Poppy flushed with warm pride. How long had it been since she'd felt like they were on the same side?

The shadow across Lucas's face was the stretched-out angle of a sundial. If Poppy were to close her eyes, maybe she'd be able to picture the black bruise that had bloomed across his cheek courtesy of her fist. "Of course. Anything you need, just let my family know."

"Sure thing, thanks for the heads-up," Cass answered. "Grab a plate on your way out."

He fixed her with a chilled look as he was swept into a conversation with an old woman concerned about the state of missing chickens in the county. Frankie immediately ran a hand through her hair, completely drained, shoulders drooping. She looked exhausted.

"What if we just sat on the porch for a little while?" she asked, her voice almost a whisper. Cass reached for Frankie's hand, looking to Poppy for confirmation. When she gave a nod back, Cass blessed her with a soft smile. Something in Poppy's chest thrilled at even being included in the question.

They snagged a bottle of wine and slipped out the back door. The moon waited beyond an awning where decades of bees had bored nests into forgiving wood.

But their spot had already been claimed. Marya stood at the railing of the porch, jacket drooping off her shoulders and elbows pressed into fading white wood. The moon made her cheek skeletal when she turned. A cigarette stubbed out in an ashtray beside her left the smell of smoke clinging to the air.

Poppy looked to Frankie for a reaction, but she was already halfway to a rocking chair. She flopped down and pulled her knees to her chest, abandoning her shoes to the slats of the porch. They hung in the quiet, drinking in the night.

"I didn't mean to steal your spot," Marya said. "I was on my way out. I just . . ." Something far away settled into her eyes. "I thought I saw something. I mean, someone. Go out that door." She pointed behind her vaguely toward the back door.

Marya angled back to the milky surface of the massive lake and Poppy followed her line of sight. Foliage ate up the edge of the water until there was nothing but blackness at the horizon line. Poppy squinted, trying to make out a shape among the trees. Cicadas crooned and bullfrogs croaked and red crepe myrtles bloomed like brush fires. But the breeze just rustled the branches, no one in sight.

Poppy settled into another rocking chair beside Frankie, long legs stretched out in front of her. Cass held out the wine until she could knock it against Poppy's shoulder. Poppy looked down at it, inhaled, and took it by the neck to swig directly from the bottle. Frankie's chair bobbed soundlessly. Marya leaned over the railing until it creaked.

"I want to kill them," Frankie said. "I want to find whoever did this to her, and I want to kill them."

Poppy looked at her. Frankie stared at the lake, her rocking chair slowly swaying.

Frankie, for all her containment and impulsiveness, felt so deeply, gave everything she had to the people she loved. Once you were hers, it was impossible to break that hold. Poppy knew. She had tried, and now here she was all over again.

"Then let's kill them," Poppy said firmly.

Cass nodded. "Okay, fine. We'll make them pay. Just lead the way, Frank."

Marya looked at the lake like a witness, and Poppy settled back into her chair.

It was good to be with them, like this. Almost like she had never left, like she never would again.

Almost.

But there was a new thrill to the familiar—a building crescendo inside of her—the idea that things were changing, and the chase was beginning, and if she didn't start running now, she'd never be able to keep up.

9

AND I BEG FOR SLEEP

Late that night, after the moon turned a creamy yellow, after the house cleared out and Marya left and Frankie stood in the hall listening for the last footstep, after she sank into a steaming bath with her clothes still on because the thought of the dress falling to the floor hurt too much and she shivered so hard that she bit her tongue, after they knocked on the cracked door and Poppy knelt beside the tub as Cass washed Frankie's hair, after Poppy wrapped her arms around her in a hug she thought might never come and she hid her face in the jut of her shoulder, after they took her to bed and curled around her in the mess of sheets, after the house went quiet, Frankie, at last, slept.

It had been easier once, to love them, to be loved by them. It was an unavoidable thought. But the rules could be suspended for a moment, each touch just a passage of time conveying something left unsaid. Nothing was okay, but things were changing, and some things were staying the same, and the least she could do was try to keep up with them all.

Night crawled past the rising moon. She kept the lilies beside her bed in a new coffee can, a wet ring on the nightstand where metal met wood. Behind their lids, her eyes fluttered back and forth, undisturbed by the sounds a shifting house makes and the changing early morning light.

All through the night, something watched her from the doorway.

10

But Receive Only Life

Late that night, after they finished the wine, after she said nothing but a quiet goodbye to Frankie, after she watched the line of trees until the leaves blurred into writhing bugs beneath her unfocused gaze, Marya biked home.

Her apartment was a cave. She tiptoed inside as if afraid to wake something sleeping in a black corner. Pale moon came through the broken blinds of her window and she shivered hard at the sight. The cool evening clung to her skin, sank down to her bones.

Her body was a machine, a puppet tugged by its strings from room to room until she stumbled to the bath. Dazedly, she ran the tub faucet until it was nearly hot enough to boil. Strands of hair from the last impromptu haircut she'd given herself floated on top of the water, delicate and strange.

"Move over," she said to the corpse of Sofia Lyon. The girl stared up at her from the bathwater. She was whole, in her time-of-death apparition, still muscle and meat. What remained of her hair was matted with blood, the white of her skull showing through rotted skin where something blunt had neatly shattered the bone. There was a forward angle to her neck where the hyoid had cracked under someone's grasp.

It made Marya think of anatomy textbooks, and failed classes, and new ways to disappoint her mother. Sofia's shirt, shredded and stained, floated where it touched the water.

Sofia scooted back. The water sloshed. Her shadow crawled up the wall like a hungry animal and fell into the doorway, hunching to watch them. Marya flinched away as she kicked off her funeral attire and stepped in, heat scalding her down to her skeleton.

"Leave us alone," Marya said to Sofia's shadow, but it only rocked back on its heels until it was half-obscured in the hallway, the faceless shape peering around the doorjamb. From a certain angle it was too humanoid—smooth ridges marked the eye sockets and the maw of its mouth, fingers clung to the doorknob and darkened the brass. The man stood behind it, his face falling like a star. He flinched back from the shadow too. She tried not to look, tried not to think about the specters waiting for her next move, but felt it watching her all the while.

Marya leaned forward, the ends of her hair dripping. The dead girl's eyes were trained on her shadow. She took Sofia's face gently in her hands and tilted it back and forth, examining the bruises across her remaining blue neck, the slide of her waxy skin beneath Marya's fingertips.

"They love you so much," she whispered.

If she were in Sofia's place right now, dead as a drowned animal, would anyone want to kill for her? Would they swear to destroy anyone who hurt her, like Frankie had for her sister?

"They want to kill who did this to you," Marya insisted, watching Sofia's eyes go misty and cumulonimbus. "Can't you just tell me? Can't you let me help them?"

The overhead light flickered as Sofia dragged her fingers across the surface of the water. Her lips parted like she might speak, but Marya knew no words would follow. Sofia was a silent corpse, terrified of a threat that Marya didn't understand.

Marya pressed her fists to her eyes until she could see nothing but blackness and pinpricks of stars.

11

FAMILIAR AS HER OWN FACE

The first time, they met by the lake.

Finder had been as young as spring. She'd only just received her name the year before—the tree had grown thicker, with branches that cowered against the ceiling.

It was the best kind of day, one where she finished her chores early enough that she could volunteer to find the pokeberries Mother Mab needed for dye. That meant the lake. That meant Finder's shoes left by the shore, dress shed like a skin, head held under water until her lungs threatened to burst. Just the idea left her with the sweet swollen-fruit feeling of it, a reminder of her life as sharp as a year burned into the thigh.

There was a path that led to the water. Finder could see slivers of the lake through the trees as she followed it. Sun made red rings on the surface, reeds bobbing in the breeze. She held her boots by their laces and listened to them bump together with each step. The ground beneath her feet was warm with the aftermath of light—the sun had only just slid behind the trees, still alive enough in those days to participate in the memory.

The sound of the shore was a familiar heartbeat. Water crept up the rocks and smooth stones cracked against one another like bones tumbling down a hill. But as she broke past the tree line and watched the world span open, red sun on purple waves dotted by black trees across acres of nothingness, she noticed a flaw in the image.

A girl stood in the water.

Finder stopped, as if her stillness might camouflage her among the foliage. But the girl's eyes found her at once. The tide tugged at her calves as she pushed forward, her shirt stuck to the skin beneath it, hair curling against her forehead and dripping around her ears.

"Hi," she called, voice warm and rough as a star-studded stone, and Finder watched her smile as she said it.

Finder knew there had to be others her age—she had seen traces of them around the homes where she and Mother Mab delivered laundry in the daylight years, flashes of fabric and hair and flesh as they darted across porches, down creaking stairs, into the dirt roads. But they were as foreign to her as her own origins.

"Hi," Finder said to her first girl.

The girl's smile grew. She waved with the hand that wasn't clutching the damp hem of her shirt. Finder felt like she was looking in a mirror, like this person was an echo of who she could have been in another life with another face.

The girl was determined but the water was murky. She fought to lift her shoes through algae and clay. Finder went barefoot down the coast and pebbles shifted under each step. They met where the water lapped, the girl's shoes reddened with muck. They were strange things, laced up and colorful under all the earth, with thick soles.

"I guess I ruined my sneakers, huh?" the girl said, looking down. She held out a hand. Her nails were a deep crimson, and this close Finder could see, from the drying tendrils pressed to her forehead, that her hair was too.

"Sofia," the girl said. "What's your name?"

71

Finder took the offered hand. Sofia had a gap in her teeth, nearly wide enough to prod the tip of her tongue through it. Finder had to look up at the other girl—the sun framed her skull like a comet.

"Finder," she said after a beat, thankful that she had a name to give after all.

Sofia's eyebrows rose. "Finder," she repeated. "Good name." She hauled herself out of the water, a wet sleeve sagging around her shoulder, freckles dotting her all the way from her nose down to the loose dark cling of her collar. There was a sureness to the way she walked, a certain impossible gravity.

Finder started to open her mouth, but then she wasn't sure what question she even wanted to ask. Her thoughts soured on her tongue as Sofia looked over her shoulder, lips curled up in question.

"Where did you come from?" Finder said at last.

Sofia gave the water a respectful nod. Her voice was commanding, and it hung in the air between them. "Through the door, just like my mother taught me," she said. "Isn't that the polite thing to do?"

"I wouldn't know," Finder said, face heating with embarrassment.

Sofia scrubbed a shoulder against her cheek, smearing running rivulets of water. "Where am I?" she asked, sounding pleased by the question.

"Well, you're—you're in the Fissure," Finder said.

"Good." Sofia's grin was wicked and bright. Her eyes crinkled at the corners. "It worked. It worked!" She clapped once and Finder jumped.

"What worked?" she asked.

Sofia leaned closer, like she was sharing something conspiratorial between them. This felt like a precipice. *How beautiful,* Finder thought. Her first girl and her first adventure.

"My mother once showed me how to walk between lives," Sofia said, with delight. "Would you like to know about the world I came from?"

It was simple, after that moment, when the hard and fast lines of Finder's life blurred until her world bloomed, opening itself up for her like a night flower.

The first meeting came and went, with Sofia hurrying into the woods and asking Finder to show her everything, everything, everything. They ate berries that stained her skin and Sofia touched it all with those reddened fingers, Fissure bleeding onto her alabaster body. As they walked, she slid her arm through Finder's and didn't shy away when Finder flinched. When they lay on the gritty shore and watched the red glow filter through trees, she grabbed Finder's hand and used it to point out things she wanted to learn about. And when she had to go, she took Finder's face in her hands and spoke to her with barely an inch between them.

"I won't be able to come back for a while," Sofia said. "It's the rules."

Finder swallowed. Her cheeks shrugged under Sofia's palms. "I don't understand."

"Once a year, that's all I get." Sofia furrowed her brow when she spoke. It was a very adult expression for her childish face. "Just once. This place isn't meant for a body like mine. But I'll come back if you'll look for me. Promise you'll look?"

"I'll look," Finder answered earnestly. Sofia squeezed her hand once, then again. Then she turned and walked into the water until the top of her head disappeared beneath the surface. She was a ripple, then nothing.

Finder stared at the shore for a long time.

She knew what would happen if Mother Mab or the Ossifier saw Sofia—it was an unspoken understanding that came with the realization that her universe existed along a strung-out line of many. She had been punished for much smaller inconveniences than the sudden appearance of a girl born out of a different world.

But she wanted—God, she wanted—Sofia to come home with her, to see the house with its crooked foundation and tendency to sigh like a sleeping dog. She wanted someone to wash the windows with, to read books with, to drip candles with. Finder had never been so aware of her loneliness before.

When did the knowing start to hurt? It was difficult to pinpoint the exact moment—maybe it was the second she'd seen Sofia standing in the water—of the understanding that life before the first girl would be rendered a shimmering daydream never to be seen again. Maybe it was the time they were caught. Maybe it was the year Sofia stopped coming, and Finder's first girl became her last. Maybe it was the fact that with Sofia's disappearance came the theft of the sun—and Finder was starting to think that maybe the light had followed Sofia into the dark.

She was older now. The lines in her thighs were burned in sets of tallied fives, one and two and three and four, twenty years gone by, twelve passing since that first meeting. She had known Sofia for over half her life and spent five years mourning her absence.

Now there were remnants of the other girl everywhere, seen only by Finder's eyes. A scorch mark on Finder's wall beside the window where Sofia knocked over a lamp that last night and Finder burned her fingertips trying to catch it. A necklace that had once been Sofia's until she took it off and latched it around Finder's neck, a twisted gold symbol like sleeping snakes now kept under the wedged lip of a loose floorboard. The board's splintered edge catching on her socks and tearing holes in the heels that ached to be mended.

They had been friends. Finder thought the word too sweet to eat so she kept it out of her mouth.

It was simpler now that the landscape beyond the house was impossible to traverse. Mab had warned her of the creatures that toiled in the dark and prevented her from stepping past the boundaries of the fenced-in home, far from the lake and its residual hauntings of girls rising out of the water. And while Finder tried to forget Sofia, she learned of the monsters—great phantasmic things that lurked in the deep woods, once human and now only the madness left behind when a life was snuffed out—kept at bay by wards woven by Mother Mab.

Until she saw the shadow on the porch, years later, when they read by candlelight day and night and day and night and the tree had long since split the floor nearly in two and pushed past the ceiling overhead.

Finder prepared for the coming monster just as she always had—by calling forth the witch.

"Mother Mab," Finder said from her place in the second-favorite armchair, book balanced on her knee. "There's something at the door."

A fire burned blue in the hearth, sparks crackling off disintegrating wood. Two heads bobbed up at her words. The Ossifier's from his dinner plate, and Mother Mab's from the herb bundle she'd been wrapping with thread. She left it beside her chair and went to the door to peer out its little glass eye. A grunt of acknowledgment slipped free.

Mother Mab swung the door open. The figure behind it stood about Mab's height, stocky, cropped brown hair atop the head.

"Excuse me, miss," came the voice, pitched low. "I've been walking the dark for some time now, and yours is the first home I've come across. I wondered if you might let me come in for a glass of water, and maybe a place to sleep for the night?"

As the candles caught the figure's face, Finder's stomach dropped. She had read about creatures like this. Geese that took the form of people, snakes that grew two legs and knocked on the door with scaled knuckles.

The face before them looked normal enough, with reddened cheeks and an aquiline nose, wide-set eyes rippling with reflected wicks. Their skin was so pale that even the black air couldn't disguise them, tinged with pink like the memory of day. Maybe they were a normal person, if appearances could be trusted. Maybe they were a walking snake.

"I don't let strangers in," Mother Mab said, though Finder knew that wasn't true. She and the Ossifier had been strangers once.

Mother Mab watched the person for a long moment, wrinkled hand still clutching the door. "But my Finder girl is the one that's seen you, and what she sees never brought me ill will before, only luck and fortune and trees through the floor." She glanced at Finder, as if confirming. Finder blinked back. "But you'll have to earn your keep, kidling."

The stranger laughed. "It's sir, actually. I'm no kid. My name is—"

"When you're in my house," Mother Mab said, the porch giving a delighted little shrug beneath the boy's feet at her words, "you'll be referred to as Creature, till you earn a name like Finder over there."

The boy looked at Finder. She felt the bitter zing of lightning far off down the tarry road. He nodded with a wry smile. Then his focus glided into the kitchen where the Ossifier still sat with his dinner, eyes set deep in his white skull like stones in a bezel.

"Is that a tree?" the boy asked, his brow furrowing.

"I told you it was so," Mother Mab answered.

And so Finder's dark world expanded, and her heart warred against her. Some small fraction of her mind had hoped that the figure would be Sofia, even knowing the pain that would unfurl in the aftermath.

The next day, the tree sprouted three new leaves.

12

A Cavern Shaped like a Head

In the days between Frankie's declaration of action and the desire to push ahead, she moved on autopilot, staying in bed too long, lying awake too late. She needed for things to be different, for a moment to catch her breath, for some evidence that she wasn't a lost cause.

It was morning, and it was a Wednesday, and it was a brand-new devastation.

"I don't think I can go to the studio today," Frankie said to Oph from the kitchen doorway, her feet bare and cold on the linoleum.

Oph looked up in surprise. Her hair was pinned high on her head, suds clinging to her pink dish gloves. The radio made everything syrupy. "What's that, doll?"

"Everything feels wrong." The words came out in a rushed mess. "Things were different when we had a goal—when finding her was still a possibility. Now, I—" Frankie's voice caught painfully.

Oph stripped the gloves off and faced her fully, a hip pressed to the edge of the sink. "You don't have to do anything you don't want to do," she said, soft, as if Frankie might spook. "Hell, we can sell the studio if that's what you want."

When Frankie's mother died, Oph spent weeks in the studio with the sign on the door flipped to *Closed*. Frankie and Sofia couldn't bring themselves to follow. Their grief grew mold in different dark spaces.

When Frankie finally approached Oph there after school one day, she'd held her aunt in her arms and let her sob, kneeling in the mess of mugs and plates and bowls Oph had smashed around them. "It's all I have left of her," Oph had wept, distorted with pain. "She's my sister, and this is all I have left."

Frankie had never told Sofia about it. Maybe she might have, eventually, when the telling wouldn't have hurt Sofia so much, when they were old enough to understand the wake of Oph's implosive disintegration. But that option no longer existed.

Something in Frankie's chest undid itself. She wouldn't do that to Oph—not now, not yet. "It's okay. We'll figure it out. I think I just need a break." Oph squeezed Frankie's hand, and Frankie had to look away from the edge of pity in her eyes. She cleared her throat noisily. "I'm just, um, going to call Marya and tell her I'm not coming in."

She stepped onto the porch, screen door banging behind her. Morning mist tangled in the mountains as the beginning of summer shouldered its way through the new green growth. Frankie sat down at the top of the steps, anticipation pulsing like a bitten tongue. She pinned her phone between her shoulder and her ear and picked at a loose thread along the hem of her shorts. The call rang once.

"Frankie?"

"You don't have to work today," she answered, abrupt.

"Are you sure?" She thought that might be a twinge of disappointment in Marya's voice, but she pointedly ignored it. Why did everyone want to know how sure she was about everything she did? Why did she always have to be *sure*?

"I'm positive." She waited for a snarky answer. Instead, there was a moment of quiet, and then—

"Are you hunting?"

Frankie tried to mask her surprise. "What do you mean? Hunting what?"

"The murderer," Marya answered. "You know, like you said after the funeral. If the answer is yes, then I would like to help."

Who said I needed your help? Frankie thought, pushing at a bug with a leaf as it struggled to climb through the cracks of a warping stair. Awareness pounded in her temples. Maybe she *was* hunting, now that it seemed it was the one thing left she could do. Her sister was dead, her mother was dead, the world was dying and breathing over and over again. But there was a killer walking the earth—she could ruin them.

Marya spoke like she could feel Frankie thinking. "I'm good at that kind of thing."

Frankie couldn't see her face, but she knew when Marya was smug. It made her prickle with something she wished was resentment. She lifted the bug out of its cavern and eased it onto the next stair with a nudge of her finger and felt a pang in her chest, like the sharp sound ceramic pieces would make when she took them out of the kiln, stoneware settling into their new bodies. She could handle Marya assisting at the studio, even if her help was lackluster. But bringing Marya into her life, into everyone else's lives, it felt a little like—

She let her heart ache at the idea. It felt like Marya was stepping into the vacant space Sofia had left behind. And Frankie wanted that space to hurt. She wanted to look at it, empty and glowing around the edges, and feel burned by it.

It took some restrained effort to even out her voice. "Prove it then. We'll be there in fifteen."

Frankie was positive she could hear the smile in Marya's goodbye when she hung up.

She propped her elbows on her knees and avoided looking at the spot where Sofia's car sat under the carport. There had been questions when her sister first disappeared. She was the more personable twin, the one everyone spoke to first, the one capable of change, ever exciting, strange, joyful. If one of them was the type to run—if they wanted to go, never look back, if there was one that might leave Loring behind for something bigger—it was always going to be Sofia.

But Frankie knew from that first day when they found the car abandoned by a ditch, where the trees grew close and the sun tapered out. Not a runaway but stolen. Not dead but murdered.

Sofia would never leave Frankie behind.

Past her eyelids she saw that rising fire. The snarl on Lucas's face, the blood on his shirt, the hot red of his cheek where Poppy's fist had connected. The chaos, her feet hitting mud, branches cutting her cheeks, a scream twining with the close wail of sirens. Sofia wouldn't leave Frankie, but Frankie had left her, had tried to leave her so many times before.

Now her brain had convinced her that she was not allowed to look at the carport, or the world might end. Instead, her eyes bored into the trees where a million different greens lived and danced. She stayed like this until the crunch of gravel under Cass's Ford loudly announced itself.

"Helloooooo!" Cass called past the passenger window, the sound bright enough to power the engine alone.

Frankie hurled herself into the seat. Leather clung to her legs immediately. The cab had always smelled a little like cigarettes, though she had only ever seen Cass take a drag from one once, and the face she'd made in the aftermath was enough to know there wouldn't be an encore anytime soon. Still, she inhaled deeply—it smelled like coming home, like falling asleep on the couch and being carried upstairs in someone else's arms.

She was grateful when her house disappeared behind them, free from her game where she had no option left but to lose.

"Where are we going?" Frankie finally thought to ask. The road was the washed gray of old pavement, dappled with light. Impressions of color flickered past the windshield. At the end of the tree-formed tunnel the mountains stood blue, everything lush and oversaturated as May died and gave way to June.

"We're picking up Poppy." Cass shifted gears, her small fists a funny sight against the large steering wheel.

"You really think she wants to help?" Frankie asked. Her stomach flipped.

Cass gave her a disbelieving glance. "Can't you at least feel a little excited that we're all together again?"

She couldn't. She was a different person now, heart buried in the floorboards. They'd left her alone with it—the fear, the anger, the mistrust, the apprehension. All those years in Loring, waiting for someone to come home. To tell her it was going to be okay. Frankie was only ever missing them, only ever wishing they would notice.

When they pulled up to Poppy's house, she was already halfway out the door. Frankie could see the shape of someone in the doorway as she scooted over to the middle of the bench seat and made room.

Poppy slid in beside Frankie. Morning lit up the sharp angles of her and made them softer, her legs nearly too long to fit in Cass's narrow footwell. Their thighs pressed together—Cass connected to Frankie and Frankie connected to Poppy.

She tensed for a moment, preparing to pull away. But the version of her that had existed before Poppy and Cass was too distant for contact. They knew everything about her. And now that Sofia was gone and Frankie wasn't who she thought she might have been, they were the only people who ever would.

"Your mom pissed already?" Cass asked, deftly maneuvering the truck back onto the road.

"You know how she is," Poppy mumbled. She propped her elbow against the passenger door's handle and watched scattered houses pass by. Her hand pressed where the shadow of her hair was shorn close to the scalp. This close, Frankie could smell perfume and deodorant, the linen scent she'd always associated with Poppy. "Where are we going, anyway?"

"We're off to—"

"Marya's apartment," Frankie cut in.

"Seriously," Poppy said, flatly.

"I love when Frankie tells a joke," Cass said, grinning. "It's like watching a robot mimic human behavior."

Poppy snorted, and Frankie simmered. "I'm not joking."

"You're hilarious. Give me her address, then."

"What makes you think I know her address off the top of my head? I'm her employer, not her stalker."

Cass raised her eyebrows. They disappeared beneath her hat.

Frankie glared back. "It's on Peabody, off Main Street."

"Fuck yeah," Cass said. "This is perfect. I can totally see you standing in the street, trying to figure out where to get a boombox so you can hold it up to her window."

"I'm going to throw myself in front of that tractor."

Cass glanced up at the rearview mirror, where a farmer puttered slowly behind them, massive tractor nearly occupying both lanes. She shrugged. "It's not going fast enough to do any real damage."

Poppy interrupted before Frankie could say something spiteful. "Can I ask what we're actually doing, and why Marya is involved?"

"We're going to follow Lucas," Cass answered brightly. "Trail him and see where he goes. Then we're going to search for evidence."

"And Marya asked to join," Frankie said, feeling her face go hot, like the words were an admission of weakness.

She waited for an argument. But Poppy just pressed her mouth into a line.

Cass pulled onto Marya's street and made Frankie, reluctantly, point out the apartment. From inside the truck, she could see a figure sitting by the window with the glass pulled up a few inches to let some air in.

Cass waved up. Marya waved back. A few seconds later her door opened and she hauled herself into the bed of Cass's truck, leaning up against the rear windshield. Cass unlatched the little window behind Frankie's head that connected the bed of the truck and the cab.

Marya peered back at them through the opening, flushed with excitement. "Ready to hunt?" she asked. Her voice was gravelly, like it'd gone unused for centuries and now she'd awakened from some eternal sleep.

Beside her, Poppy let out a sound like a wound, and Frankie reflexively pressed their legs tighter together. She'd forgotten how comforting a touch could be. Now that she'd started, she didn't know if she could stop again, couldn't reel herself in and fence the emotion within its boundaries.

Poppy had kissed her once, at a birthday party in Tommy Kowalski's basement in the eighth grade. It was one of those almost-sour memories—embarrassment so sharp that she had to picture something else to cloud the image out every time. Why was it that her most vivid recollections were moments of devastating self-doubt?

It wasn't that she was ashamed of the kiss. The press of their lips had been brief as a butterfly's life, her very first, too quick to mean more than flushed cheeks. Frankie was just fourteen, her mother dead three years before. She hadn't thought herself capable of attraction to begin with—not like the other girls her age, at least. And she hadn't quite understood what the word *lesbian* meant.

It was the fact that the kiss had been coaxed out of her. It was a bottle spun in a group of kids thinking they were bigger than their bodies. Lucas Glasswell leaning back on his hands, chin pointed forward in a dare. Sofia demure with her hair pulled into a high ponytail. Cass standing in the corner with a cup of the sickly sweet sorbet-Sprite punch Tommy's mom had made, insisting that she didn't want to play. Poppy sitting with her knees drawn to her chest, box braids long and twisted with color, Frankie perched on her heels like an animal prepared to run.

Green glass went clockwise. She watched it turn, and when the bottle's slender neck stopped on Poppy's knees, Frankie willed her heart to stop its mindless thumping.

Tommy whistled, long and low. Sofia looked at Frankie with wide eyes, then at Lucas, then at the floor.

"You don't have to," Cass said from her place outside of the circle. But the boys ignored her in favor of laughter, and Frankie could hear only the thunderous crash of her blood in her ears.

"Shut up," Lucas said.

Frankie looked at Sofia for a split second, her mouth hanging open in conflicted silence, and Tommy added, "Aren't they lesbos anyway?"

Then Poppy pushed forward and caught Frankie's cheek. She pulled her in with one perfunctory tug around the nape of her neck and pressed their lips together. Poppy tasted of vanilla lip balm, heady. Just that quick peck was enough to make Frankie's pulse explode like a splitting atom.

It wasn't that it was Poppy, necessarily—they loved each other in a way that romance would never satisfy—but that kiss answered every questioning bee boring into the soft wirings of her brain, a hive in a dead tree. One kiss and Frankie went quiet, her anxious train of thought replaced by *of course, there it is, the feeling I've been looking for.*

"I knew they were dykes," Tommy said, clapping Lucas on the back. Cass stood with her arms crossed over her chest. Sofia's eyes dug into her twin's face in an unreadable expression. Frankie didn't pay them any mind, didn't even feel the sting.

In the years between then and eighteen they were binary, unkissed by anyone else. At least, that's what Frankie believed. It was almost impossible to tell what Poppy was thinking unless she decided to reveal it to you, and all Frankie wanted was to be the person she came to. To feel that tug again—Poppy's hand on the back of her head, pulling her into a secret that only the two of them would ever understand no matter who sat back and saw it unfurl. Frankie was a closed door, but she liked to think that was something they had in common—that they could be together in their isolation.

Now in the Ford—Cass's grip loose around the wheel, Marya leaning against the rear glass, Poppy's thigh against hers—Frankie felt that complete sensation of seeing someone and being seen by them too.

Cass spurred the truck forward. Poppy looked at Frankie. She didn't pull her thigh away.

13

THE RATTLED LINES OF ROTTED WOOD

"This is starting to feel like a waste of time," Frankie said. Marya watched as she slumped and ran her fingers through the length of her hair, knuckles snagging on a tangle.

Marya turned back to the community center that they'd followed Lucas to. The truck's bed seared her thighs and she ached miserably for a cigarette. Instead of begging someone to drive her to the nearest convenience store, she uncapped a lukewarm bottle of water and swallowed a few times.

"What do you suggest we do instead?" Marya asked.

The idea was this: Follow Lucas. See where he spent his time. Cass said that she'd once heard that killers return to the scene of the crime— the decrepit house where Sofia's body was found was quarantined by the police and wrapped in caution tape, had been off limits since Lucas's best friend Tommy plunged through the porch. But maybe Lucas would lead them somewhere else, somewhere that mattered. Maybe he'd killed her in one place and taken her to that house after. Maybe he'd killed her in the house and stashed the weapon in the high school's lacrosse field. Maybe he hadn't killed her at all, and this *was* a waste of time.

Marya asked about it because she had to, even if it meant a crest-fallen look crossing Frankie's face. The police had investigated Lucas the first day that Sofia was reported missing. But the next morning his father spoke to local news declaring his son's innocence, a hard hand on Lucas's shoulder, assuring that they would do everything in their power to find Sofia. She wondered if anything might change now that they had a body, or if the community would take one glimpse at what the Glasswell family represented and look the other way.

Now Sofia was dead as roadkill and sitting across from Marya in the rear of the truck. Her hair glowed a burnished copper under all that afternoon light. Where her ashen skin remained, it shone blue-tinged.

Sofia held a finger to her lips, smiling faintly, and Marya, unsettled by the sight, didn't say a word.

"He's so fucking boring," Poppy said, one foot pressed up against the truck's passenger airbag in a manner that made Marya incredibly anxious. "He's been working out for two hours. That's masochistic."

Marya felt strands of her hair cling to her sweaty forehead. The sky above them was mockingly clear, a brightness so pure it hurt to look at. She trained her eyes on it to keep them from settling on Sofia's beetle-eaten jaw.

"There's no point in following him," said Frankie the Optimist. "We should go to the house instead. The police have to have missed something important there. If we drive over to the station, we can demand that they do a more thorough search."

"Oh, true. Let's walk right into the police station and start giving orders. Frankie, you're telling me you trust the Loring Sheriff's Department to do their job properly after all their 'help' with the original search?" Poppy asked. She glanced at Cass, whose forehead was pressed to the steering wheel. "No offense," she added after a beat.

"You really think I'd take offense on behalf of my dad?" Cass said.

Marya didn't ask for an explanation, afraid of making her confusion more evident. She was embarrassed to be out of the loop.

"Well, you can get arrested," Poppy continued to Frankie. "I'm not going somewhere if police might be lurking around. With my luck, they were probably the ones who did it and are just trying to cover up their tracks, and we'll be next in line."

Marya nudged her boot against Sofia's foot. She typically tried her best not to touch a ghost, but the impermanent nature of Sofia drew her in. The contact immediately sent a chill through her body. There was a slight sensation of resistance, and then the shoe passed through the bony remains of Sofia's toes. Her shadow bent like someone had cracked a bat over its head. Marya grimaced.

"Great point," Cass said to Poppy, pointing an affirmative finger in her direction. "Frankie, if you want to go ahead and see what the inside of a jail cell looks like, I support you, but I'm not stepping foot into that house."

Frankie sputtered. Marya cut in before the conversation could spiral away. "If she was found in the house, then where was she last seen alive?"

The cab went quiet. Sofia leaned against the truck, a cat seeking warmth. Her shadow arched away from her. The exposed bone of her skull was so gruesome, the crooked angles of her knees so awkward, the hunched bend of her spine so inhuman. It was always worse once Marya started to know a ghost. She thought of the man in her kitchen, his hands shaking against the tap. Hadn't she learned anything by now?

"He was the last one to see her," Frankie said thickly. "There was this bonfire party Tommy threw, a 'last hurrah' thing before everyone left for college. It got messy." She cleared her throat, and when she spoke again, she'd clipped the frayed edges off her voice. "The police showed up, and everyone ran. Tommy got hurt, and Lucas claimed that he stuck around to help, but he also said—" She paused. "That he lost her, that she went running through the trees. That was it."

"They found her car the next day," Cass added. "On the side of the road about a mile from Lucas's house."

"We searched the woods for weeks," Frankie said miserably.

"That was five years ago?" Marya asked, though she already knew the answer. Frankie just nodded, staring past the windshield.

"Do you think that was where it happened?" Marya pressed. Sofia let her temple rest in her gory palm. "Near his home?"

"Clearly," Poppy said, "since he's the one who did it."

"We don't know that for sure," Cass interjected. "I hate the son of a bitch, but everyone is innocent until proven guilty here."

The community center's doors swung open and Lucas strolled out, sweaty and red in the face. Marya ducked down in the bed of the truck. Sofia's head followed as he walked, eyes glassy.

Marya stared at Sofia's corpse. She should just tell them. Who cared if they didn't believe her? Who cared if they thought she was crazy?

It was deceptively difficult to reveal her thoughts, ridiculously easy to be afraid. Apparitions she knew and could make sense of. But that other jagged entity leering at her from the corner of the truck bed? Its body as opaque as clay, limbs bending, midtransformation? The distant smell of smoke, like the shadow itself had been charred? How to explain it in a way that would make them see. That wouldn't push them away.

The urge died in her throat. She had a history of giving too much away and regretting it immediately after.

Sofia turned back to her as Lucas climbed behind the wheel of his truck and pulled out of the lot. Cass shifted gears, the truck roaring to life underneath Marya, dragging her mind from its sticky thoughts.

The most painful part of it—she had to admit it, couldn't avoid it—was that she liked being around them so much more than she thought she would. Enjoyed their easy banter and affection, appreciated the years of history they traded between glances and touches. When was the last time someone had treated her like that? Like she mattered?

It must have been Nina on one of their last days in Raleigh, sharing a cigarette on the back steps of the bar and pressed together from shoulder to wrist. Smoke mingling past their lips still red from a kiss, Nina's black eyes warm on her cheek, her ringed fingers squeezing a knee. Back before Marya packed up everything she owned and left without a word.

She met Sofia's eyes and pinned her mouth shut. This would be her burden to bear. She'd watch after Sofia, find out what tethered her to this world, and make it right.

Above her the clouds were bulbous and bright. Leaves leaned over the road to blot out the sun. The others talked beyond the glass, voices dancing on top of one another. Marya sat against the uneven ridges of the truck's bed, feeling like an outsider and refusing to let it bother her. How lucky she was to even be along for the ride.

The truck slowed. Sofia had flickered and warped, and now there were patches of her body that seemed more solid than others. Marya looked through the translucent pockets of Sofia's cheek into the closely gathered trees as Lucas's truck rolled past a narrow road. "I think he's turning," Cass said. "I can't drive any further without him noticing. Let's stop and look around here."

She pulled over where a patch of dirt led into the trees, and they left the Ford behind on the shoulder. New growth poked through the underfoot rot as they walked into the woods. Past the skinny trunks and overgrown brush, Marya could make out a farmhouse and a red barn, so vivid that she saw a green mirror image of it every time she blinked.

Marya realized that this was the spot they had been talking about, where Sofia's car was found. The smell of woodsmoke was strong—strange for the early heat. Frankie led the way and ducked as her hair snagged on a branch. Marya had the inane urge to tug it free, but before she could act Frankie plunged forward with the rest of them hurrying behind her.

"It's been years," Poppy said as she caught up with Cass. "What could possibly be left?"

She had a point. The whole idea seemed futile, but they scanned the area as the sun dripped lower in the sky. Marya watched shadows become yellow, more pronounced. The crunch of animals in the foliage sounded deceptively like footsteps.

She tripped and caught herself against the skinny trunk of a tree. The bark was ragged under her palm.

"Marya?" Cass called back.

"I'm fine," she answered immediately. She took another step forward and her vision distorted. Sound deepened, gained weight. Marya heard her blood in her ears and saw the leaves around her begin to tremble, as if this pocket of forest was one great snow globe shaken by an unseen hand.

A force slammed through her. She flinched and grasped at her stomach, fear cooling in her belly. Horror seized her like a rope around the throat as a dark mass seeped through her frantic grip and slipped past her skin. It spilled into the grass, shimmering, limbs re-forming before it stumbled onto solidifying feet and darted off through the trees. Sofia's shadow had never split so far from her. It had never been so scared. It had never made contact with Marya like this, physical and pliable enough to move through her body.

"Are you alright?" Frankie asked, eyes narrowing with concern as they passed over Marya.

When Marya was a kid, she woke one night to the sound of someone crying for help. Past her shut window, Marya watched a girl struggle to jump the tall fence that bordered their little green patch of Queens. She had moved through the air like syrup, the edges of her blurring with the foliage. When Marya called for her mother, she expected reassurance—instead she was yanked from her bed and away from the black glass.

"Don't let it see how weak you are," her mother had hissed. "That's the kind of creature that wants to lure you out of bed and eat you whole."

This shadowy apparition stumbled through the trees like that blur of a girl had, panting so loud and hot in Marya's ears that she nearly brought her hands up to cover them. The shrill carry of a scream bulleted through her mind, like a shrike like a gunned-down elk like the crack of a felled tree. The shadow collapsed and caught on the thorns of a bush, foggy matter tearing as it tried to stagger to its feet. It let out an awful, dying sound.

She took a step. Her body moved like it was ripping from reality. The shadow keened and plunged its limbs through the meat of its empty head. It had no face, no eyes to see—but she could swear that it turned and looked at her. Instinct told her to get the fuck out of there, just like her mom had demanded of her all those years ago. Instead, she pushed forward, crashing through brush, trying to get closer.

"Marya?" Cass called again, somewhere distant, a past life.

The shadow wept, unintelligible desperation falling from its body. Marya watched it run ahead where the growth petered out to expose the barn. The ground rose to meet it, falling again to the dry grass. Sofia was afraid of it, and the man in her apartment was afraid of it, and Marya herself could barely look at it directly—so what could have frightened Sofia's shadow enough to send it running from its host?

The dark shape began to dissipate, fragments of gray splitting away from the central body. Tendrils of smoke rose like black snakes and slid up the side of the barn. It seeped through the cracks in the wood and leeched life from the red. When Marya stopped just past the line of trees, the shape was gone, the memory of it a cast vacancy in the grass.

The structure leered before them. Brittle silos crumbled under the weight of overgrown vines, the air heavy with the scent of rot and juniper. Marya tilted her head back to take it in, swallowed hard around the rising emotion lodged in her throat.

"What's wrong?" Cass asked, out of breath. "Why did you run?"

Marya looked back. They were panting, apparently having chased after her, confused and more than a little irritated at being left behind. "Sorry," she said when she could command her breath to do her bidding. "I thought I saw—what is this barn? Is it abandoned?"

"It's part of the Glasswell property," Frankie answered. "Why?"

Marya's breath kept catching in her chest, stinging with pain. She could feel how afraid the shadow had been, all over her, down to the bone. It had taken something from her when it passed through her body—too much energy, enough to make her heart pound. It was so corporeal. It had stood up on its own and taken off, leaving Sofia behind. Marya had assumed it was a residual haunt, some memory of Sofia's that replayed where distant trauma had occurred. Maybe this was its imprint. The manifestation of Sofia's agony, her end, domineered by something more sinister than the bridge between life and death. But was the shadow reacting to a past hurt or a present monster, unseen? She inhaled hard through her nose. Her breath still wouldn't come. Marya, beyond all other hope, wanted to understand.

Her fingertips were still too cold for sensation. Slowly, at the risk of sounding delirious, she said: "I think we need to go inside."

Across the field speckled with wildflowers, the Glasswells' sprawling house rose like a pristine preserved relic—filaments and teeth, pale painted brick shining under the sun, the massive estate eating up mowed fields and landscaped gardens. Neatly trimmed hedges lined the boundary of the lawn, forsythia making yellow clusters along the driveway. In the distance, she could hear the familiar crunch of tires on gravel. Someone coming home.

Marya lurched. She pressed a hand to her abdomen again, almost expecting something to burst through the skin. But it was just Frankie yanking her back into the trees and out of sight, fingers tight around her wrist.

The shrike call echoed, stinging in her ears.

14

FLAME WITH FLAME, PIOUS WITH PROFANE

Passing sun made the late afternoon a sleepy gold, the sky crow-dotted, air heavy with cut grass and gasoline. They gathered around Oph's dining table. Frankie placed her hands on the wooden slab like she was preparing to perform a magic trick, dragging over layers upon layers of interlocking rings left behind from unattended mugs of the past. It was a myriad of Venn diagrams of those who had sat there over the years, chronicling the spaces where they overlapped.

The screen door banged and a cool breeze followed the thud. Frankie sat at the head of the table. She looked at Marya in the seat across from her—the high bridge of her nose, the mess of her hair beneath lamplight, the steady knot of her fingers. Marya, with the slightest tilt of her head, looked back.

"We need a plan," Frankie said, as if establishing a universal form of control might make it real. She could smell coffee, earthy and rich, as Oph made magic out of a French press. The table already held a bowl of fruit, a basket of rolls, and a stack of mismatched dishes. Yeast and sweetness cloyed around the table.

"We can't just break into someone's barn," Cass insisted, stabbing a strawberry with a tiny fork and popping it into her mouth. She always snatched that one out of the drawer before Frankie could slam it shut, insistent that it fit in her hand better. "Especially not one belonging to the damn sheriff."

"Do I want to be here for this conversation?" Oph asked.

"Cass is right," Poppy said. Cass beamed. "It would be a terrible move. We have no legitimate reason to be there, and we'll be fucked if someone catches us."

Marya pressed a thumb to the corner of her mouth as if tucking a word away, and Frankie pointedly didn't look this time.

"What happened to 'he's the one that did it'?" she asked, inclining her head toward Poppy. She traced rings on the table, an anxious tick. "Isn't that evidence enough? You said it yourself. If we believe that Lucas killed her, the only way we're going to prove it is by finding something ourselves. The sheriff would never prosecute his son without enough external pressure."

"Well, I'm not going to get arrested just because Marya got a vibe," Cass said. She glanced at Marya, sheepish. "Sorry."

Marya's eyes drifted, mouth thoughtfully pursed.

"You saw something," Frankie said, and Marya looked up at her, surprised. "Didn't you?"

Marya—always contained, always reserved, always a step ahead of Frankie—had stood before that barn with fear written all over her. Frankie knew what that kind of fear felt like. All-encompassing doubt, stomach-devouring discomfort.

To Frankie, it made sense. Salting the earth behind her was never going to be a simple task—they were talking about Lucas Glasswell, after all. He had killed her sister. He had ruined her life. What mattered here, truly, besides his downfall? Besides the memory of a sister, that sanguinary tang, slick as a swallowed heart?

Nothing. She wanted an answer.

Marya faltered. "I don't know. It was just an idea."

Poppy reached for a roll and held it delicately, not taking a bite, just pinching it into sections. A neat divot of frustration marked her forehead. To Marya, she said: "I don't get why you want to be here."

"She's helping us," Frankie said immediately.

She thought about the night of the memorial, how Poppy had held her soaked body close like nothing terrible had ever happened between them, how suddenly everything was strange and she couldn't sort out where they stood at all. She wanted Poppy to look at her. She wanted to feel like something was okay, for once. But Poppy just started to rip the roll into furred little pieces, her words measured. "Helping with what, exactly?"

"You know—what we talked about."

"What did we talk about again?" Cass asked, squinting in confusion.

"Finding Sofia's murderer and killing them."

"Oh my God," Oph huffed. "Someone please tell me if I need to leave."

Frankie didn't want to feel this way—overstimulated, out of control. "We're going to bring her justice. If that means asking for outside help, then we should at least try it."

"Exactly, she's an outsider. She never even met Sofia," Poppy said.

Oph couldn't take her eyes off the crumbs that littered the table.

Marya attempted to interrupt. "Listen, I'm not trying to—"

But Frankie crossed her arms over her chest. "If you don't want to be here, then go. It's not like anyone else is offering up a better idea than Marya's."

Poppy sighed. "Frankie, you can't be angry when we're just—"

"I can't be angry?" Frankie's heart pulsed red. "Do you know how long I've been here by myself, just trying to hold things together? It's not like you stayed! You didn't join search parties or put up posters! You never even picked up the phone, let alone stopped by." She tried to cool her temper. It cooked her anyway. "You *left*, Poppy."

"Frances," Oph warned from the doorway.

Cass touched Frankie's wrist, something that was probably supposed to be comforting but only made Frankie want to disappear.

"I don't have to explain myself to you," Poppy said quietly. "I don't owe you anything."

"So, what, you're better off without us? You'd rather let go of our entire lives?" The words were so hot in Frankie's mouth. "She was *ours*. Plural. The things that we went through together—"

Was it possible to just forget the ways they'd injured each other? The year of silence after Frankie went under the lake water and bobbed breathless to the surface, Poppy seizing her by the shoulders. Smoke. Darkness falling over the woods, Sofia pleading for everyone to stop, Poppy's fist reared back a second before it collided with Lucas's jaw—

Frankie dug her fingertips into her biceps and twisted until her eyes were focused past the warped windows instead of on Poppy. "Jesus. Listen. I'm not trying to be a bitch. But you left, and we needed you. She would have been so—"

Frankie stopped herself before she could wound with the words. Her stomach bottomed out. What did she know about what Sofia would have wanted? The two of them hadn't even been on speaking terms when her sister disappeared. They never would be again. "It sucked without you here," she said at last, miserably.

Poppy tossed the remnants of her bread down onto her plate. Cass's face showed a very visible wince.

"I didn't know you felt that way," Poppy said roughly.

Frankie's words were small in her mouth. "How was I supposed to tell you? You wouldn't answer our calls."

Poppy used to pick up every time, even when she probably shouldn't have, Frankie ringing her number with her phone pinned between her shoulder and her ear and walking her bike along a breadcrumb trail of yellowed streetlights down the main road. The coaxing was as simple as smiling into the receiver at the sound of Poppy's sleepy voice. Begging her to sneak out and get shitty food at Sunset despite Poppy's insistence that she had a test the next day, that her mom would kill her if she found out, that Frankie was an enabler who wanted to ruin Poppy's life.

Only a little, Frankie would say, grinning. *I'll pay for your cheeseburger.*

And Poppy would show up with a hoodie over her pajamas and her glasses magnifying the indigo circles under her eyes, leaning over the passenger seat and pushing the door open for Frankie, bike finagled into the back. They'd drive down dark streets to the twenty-four-hour spot where they'd carved out a booth of their own from the start of freshman year.

Then it was the promised cheeseburger and Coke, fries painted with ketchup and drenched in vinegar. Poppy fiddling with the strings of her hoodie like she was resisting the urge to tug the hood up over her freshly shorn head, looking so different and somehow entirely herself, cheekbones more angular, piercing gaze less likely to drift. Frankie settling her chin into her palm and smiling—catching Poppy's eye and saying *you look so right like this, you're so you, everyone has already said how good you look.* Frankie had wanted to say *every girl at school,* but they weren't quite ready for that yet. It was hard enough for Frankie to learn her own identity, let alone assign a life to someone else. Besides—in a few weeks, Poppy, Cass, and Sofia would leave for college and Frankie would stay behind, growing smaller in their rearview mirrors until she winked out of existence completely. She wouldn't know the people they would grow to become.

Then it was Frankie prodding the tip of Poppy's sneaker with her own under the table and saying *you'd tell me if there was something on your mind, right? You wouldn't just keep it to yourself?*

And in the hollow of her heart, thinking: *When she goes, she will meet others who will take care of her, and she will never need me again. They will love her because it is easy to love her. They will listen to her because she has so much to say, and she will have no words left for me.*

Frankie's phone buzzing on the table. The text preview from Cass that said: u know I have ur locations u bitches, how dare u go to sunset without us???????? Poppy's eyes flickering from the glowing screen back up to Frankie, her face a boarded-up house, condemned and quiet. Her winched smile pulled from whatever recess she had sunk down into.

Yes, I'd tell you.

The memory summoned pain like a rotten tooth, roots left in the arteries. Could you hate yourself enough to make up for someone else's indifference, an anticipatory hurt? Frankie wasn't sure. But she could try.

Cass finally broke the pause in the dining room and shattered Frankie's reverie. "Are we going to finish talking burglary plans or what?"

Oph disappeared into the kitchen with a huff. Dishes clinked distantly.

"No? We're just going to sit here like it's a book club?" Cass knocked her knuckles against the table. "Well, in that case, Marya, why don't you start by telling us a little bit about yourself? Starting with are you in a relationship, and if so, how serious is it *really*?"

"Jesus, Cass," Poppy snapped. "That's exactly what I'm talking about. This," she said, gesturing to the women around the table until her index finger stopped on Marya, "is nothing more than an entertaining paycheck to you. Why bother getting yourself involved?"

The intensity in Poppy's focus was all-consuming. Frankie, despite herself, couldn't tear her eyes away. There was a part of her, some hungry thing, that needed the answer too.

Marya's voice hitched. "I know it's strange for me to be here. I just wanted—"

Poppy scoffed. "Wanted what? To play murder podcast?"

"Come on," Cass warned.

Marya laughed. "No, that's fair. I want to help you in whatever way I can." She met Poppy's eyes across the table. "I'm not trying to be another enemy."

Frankie found herself suddenly eviscerated by it all. She wanted Marya to stay. She wanted her to go. She wanted Poppy to fight back. She wanted to fall asleep sandwiched between her and Cass, with one of their favorite movies playing in the background. She wanted her sister to be alive and she wanted to forget that she'd ever once had a family at all.

"I don't know why I'm even still here," Poppy said, standing. The overhead light painted her face in shadow when she met Frankie's eyes. "Do you understand what we've given up for her? For you?"

Frankie's chest felt too tight. She closed her eyes.

Poppy continued, her voice breaking. "I have a life outside of this. I have interviews for jobs that I need to keep my apartment. I have *an apartment*. Cass might have moved back and you might have never left, but this is not my home. I'm not sticking around to watch you throw your life away just because hers is over."

Frankie's fingernails dug into her thighs, hard enough to break skin. She was too afraid of what might come out of her mouth if she tried to speak.

Poppy shook her head. "I think it's better if I go now. You clearly have all the help that you need." She left for the front door, barely pausing to shove her feet into her shoes. Frankie started to rise but Cass stopped her, already halfway to the porch.

"Give her some space. The past few days have been really shitty," Cass said. "We're all trying to figure it out." Frankie thought she meant the words for Marya, but she found Cass looking at her, mouth a heart-wrenching line. She started to answer, but Cass was already out the door and bounding down the porch stairs.

"I should go instead," Marya said, hip pressing against the edge of the table as she rose.

"No!"

Marya blinked back at her, surprised. Even Frankie wasn't sure why she had said it—agreeing would have been sensible, but she was tired of putting up walls. She needed one thing to be easy.

"Wait." She stood, too, watching the coffee tremble in her mug with the movement. Marya pushed her hands into the pockets of her jeans and shifted, head tilting between the abandoned table and the doorway. "We need to get a few things straight if you're going to help us."

Marya's mouth fell open. She shut it after a beat and nodded.

"I should fire you," Frankie said.

Marya winced. "Please don't. You're the only spot in town that offers dental insurance, and I'm a cavity away from bankruptcy."

Frankie scoffed. "Well—you stress me out. You kind of suck at your job."

"Subjective," Marya answered with a shrug.

"It's a fact. I'm stressed right now." Frankie grimaced when she caught Oph in the doorway, definitely eavesdropping. "No! I don't want a tincture for that." Her aunt disappeared back into the kitchen, hands raised in defense. Oph's notorious droppers full of plant extracts were famous only for making her queasy.

The corners of Marya's eyes crinkled with contained delight.

"I don't want you to get any ideas," Frankie continued. "Don't start thinking that you're irreplaceable just because you're with us."

Marya tapped her temple. Her watch slid down her wrist. "Got it. Expendable."

Frankie sucked her teeth. "And it's just that—you'll have to give us all some time to get used to it." She avoided Marya's eyes, the words coming out sharper than she intended—why did she always have to barb herself? Why did she always have to make it sting? "I need you to give me a real reason why you should get involved."

"I can't just offer to help you?"

Frankie sighed through her nose. "Poppy's not going to open up if she doesn't trust you. And right now, you're at the bottom of her list, with me right above you. I need you to give me a reason that won't make her balk." She paused, swallowed hard. "Because we don't even know where to start, and this shit is hard, and it would mean a lot if you helped make it a little easier. And if you don't, I really will fire you."

Marya laughed, head tipped back. Frankie had to turn her face away so she wouldn't show the smile that stretched there.

"You don't hold any punches, do you?" Marya said. "You can tell Poppy, you can tell Cass, you can tell God, I don't care. I've lived here for a year and I've watched the posters around town fade and get replaced twice already, and I know by now that you couldn't take a break even if it meant the whole world being changed for the better. I want to help because if she were my sister, I would die before I gave up searching, and if I had to go through that alone I don't think I could make it." She paused, dark gaze burning into Frankie's cheek like a stubbed cigarette. "Because I'm kind of fucking nice. And you hired me to help you in whatever capacity I could. So here I am, helping you."

Frankie's heart seized in her chest. "I'm not alone," she said hotly.

"I know you're not," Marya said, her voice gentler.

"I can't pay you for helping us," Frankie added, just to sour the flutter in her chest.

Marya laughed again. "I needed a new hobby anyway."

There was a terrible sinking in Frankie's stomach, a kind of private self-hate that made her wish she was alone where the threat of tears wouldn't be so humiliating. Her voice cracked open like a confession. "We should look in the barn, right?"

Frankie wanted to believe in instinct. She wanted proof and evidence. What else was there, other than her aimless hope? She tried not to look down the hallway where the stairs rose to their bedrooms, as if Sofia were watching them from the top step.

"There's no harm in trying," Marya murmured.

It was exactly what she had hoped to hear. "Then stay," Frankie said.

Marya held up her hands in surrender. "If that's what you want."

Frankie rolled her eyes and pointed at the dining table. Marya went obediently, settling back into her chair.

"Okay," Frankie said, mostly to herself. "Good. Fine. I'll be right back." She turned to the kitchen and startled. Oph stood in the doorway again, silhouetted, and Frankie's breath halted. "Shit," she exhaled, trying to erase any specters from her imagination. "You scared me."

Oph stretched out a hand and Frankie crossed the room to accept it, the grasp warm on her own. At least she would always have this constant—Oph, wearing her mother's face.

"I need you to be careful," Oph whispered. "Your mother would haunt me until the day I died if something were to happen to you." Her face crumpled, just a fraction, and she squeezed Frankie's fingers hard enough to break her heart in the process. "I already have enough to answer for."

"I won't do anything dangerous," Frankie said, embarrassment creeping into the words. "I'm just trying to do the right thing."

"Promise that you won't get yourself in trouble." Oph squeezed again when Frankie hesitated. "Hey. I said promise me."

"I promise," Frankie said.

Oph's smile was full of relief. "That's settled then. How about another pot of coffee for the table?"

15

Halted by Coming Wind

Poppy's piece-of-shit car wouldn't start, insistent on embarrassing her further, so she hit the steering wheel a few times for good measure. She called it a thousand different names before getting out to lift the hood, standing shamefully in Frankie's gravel driveway.

"Need a ride, drama queen? Your steed looks like it's in corpse mode." Cass poked her head under beside Poppy, shaking her keys in her face.

"Release me, witch," Poppy answered, measuring her oil, mouth flattened in concentration. "What part of 'I'm leaving' wasn't clear to you?"

"You never actually mean it." Cass's eyes followed as Poppy wiped oil from her hands with an old fast-food napkin filched from the glove compartment, wrinkling her nose in distaste. "You love to be all, 'Oh, just let me go, Cass, don't follow me or you'll regret it, Cass, let me rot and die alone, Cass,' but imagine how lonely you'd be if I actually listened to you."

Poppy laughed, the joy in her chest warring with comfort and fury all at once. Cass's face flashed with delight at the sound. Poppy tried to school her expression back to annoyance.

"I wouldn't put it that way," she said at last.

Cass scoffed. "You're a terrible liar," she said, slamming the hood of Poppy's Jeep back down and giving it a familiar pat. "Come back inside."

"Oh, absolutely not. That was a shitshow."

"And whose fault is that?"

"All of ours," Poppy ground out, "for even allowing it to happen. She knows nothing about us and it doesn't seem like Frankie even likes her, so I don't understand the point of bringing a stranger into this and making it more complicated than it has to be."

"Ha, Frankie doesn't like her, that's rich. I think Frankie is just deeply sexually repressed—"

"I really don't want to think about that!" Poppy grimaced.

"—and would benefit from us helping her pull the stick out of her ass."

Poppy returned to the driver's seat, twisted the key. The engine let out a nasty snarl and refused to catch. Cass put her hand on Poppy's and held the steering wheel in place.

"Give it up, Loveless. Come in and I'll make you tea. With lemon, how you like it."

"She's not okay, Cass. Frankie—she's—we shouldn't even be here. You remember what happened before, the last time she was upset like this. She almost *died*. And that was just because she found out Sofia was going to follow Lucas to college."

"Don't say that," Cass answered immediately.

Poppy shook her head. "You know I'm right. If we encourage this and she hurts herself, then what? That's on us."

"You haven't been here, and you haven't talked to her. You don't know." Cass's eyes were stern behind the shadow of her curls. Guilt like fungi sprouted in the dark pit of Poppy's belly. "She's not—I swear to you, this isn't like before. She's fine. She just needs our help."

Poppy had been the one to find Frankie face down in the lake. To pull her from the water and watch Oph nearly crack her ribs doing CPR. Her best friend blue and broken, a mouth she had kissed choking on lake water. It had never been the same after that, no matter how hard they tried, no matter how well they pretended it wasn't real.

Cass leaned down to her window, face suddenly inches away. "What was the point in coming home if you're just going to leave again?"

That was the question Poppy had been asking herself, wasn't it? Why didn't she just drive away right now, spend her summer working in Durham for some shitty chain restaurant with terrible tippers? Her meager savings wouldn't last more than a couple weeks, and she'd hoped to put it toward something she didn't have to sublet. Her mom would laugh in her face if she asked for money. Her dad could potentially be convinced if she could set aside her pride. But pulling out of Frankie's driveway and leaving for Durham would be the smartest thing Poppy ever did.

She wanted to be angry. She wanted to hate them all for making her feel this way, like she was tethered to them, like she couldn't get away no matter how hard she tried. She made fists in her lap until her knuckles strained. She felt, inexplicably, the burn of coming tears high in her nose.

It had been this way with her for years, a sadness so profound that it hollowed into preemptive hurt, her mind inventing new ways to strike at the soft animal of her heart. She had forgotten what it was like to stop armoring herself. How was she supposed to live like the rest of them, in a place that only ate away at her, without demanding something more?

Loring was insular and unforgiving. It made her ungainly, vexed with her body, incapable of and uninterested in carving out a space in a sea of white faces. In fighting for a place that didn't depend on the familiar comfort of her friends. Leaving it all behind and letting the ache fester in the cavern of her isolation seemed the only solution. She'd spent so many years imagining all the ways Frankie would finally leave her—would lie sleepless in the dark and picture Cass's silence on the other end of a phone call, wounding herself with the fear and permitting it to eat her alive. But that was the problem with pain—she hoped it would make her harder, ready her for inevitable collapse. She was still waiting to feel like it had worked.

Cass, out of everyone, understood the most. But her love for Loring couldn't be disparaged. She was too willing for romance. Too blessed by beauty.

"I'm just tired," Poppy said.

Cass smiled and tapped Poppy's cheek with a finger. "Me too, baby."

The sound of tires on gravel startled them both. Cass turned to face a fancy little car with a silent and functioning engine. She shared a knowing glance with Poppy. They both recognized the face behind the wheel, and the sight of it warmed Poppy with a fraction of relief. Years spent at Frankie's house had introduced them to a menagerie of unusual people, and Sissa wasn't easy to forget.

She slid from the car before it even seemed to roll to a stop, effortless and elegant as a peacock. A long coat trailed behind her despite the warm breeze, her hair huge and full of life. Lines marked her face where she'd spent years smiling.

"What's everyone doing out here?" she said, grinning. "Party's inside."

Poppy pulled the key from the ignition, admonished. They followed her in.

Sissa left the door open, and by the time Poppy made it up the porch steps again she was spinning Oph around in her arms, the two of them laughing. Frankie stood in the doorway, eyes wide in surprise.

"Did you know about this?" Cass said to her, glancing back every few seconds as if checking to see if Poppy would run in the opposite direction. The thought was tempting.

"She was supposed to be here for the memorial, but Oph said there were some travel delays," Frankie answered. "I thought that meant she wasn't coming."

"You know I wouldn't leave you like that! Blame it on three canceled flights and a twelve-hour drive." Sissa released Oph, who teetered on her sock feet, smiling so wide it looked painful.

"And the others?" Oph asked, quiet and hopeful.

Sofia had mentioned other witches in her family to Poppy once, the two of them stretched out on a blanket down by the creek bed. She had talked as she dragged her fingers up and down Poppy's forearm in a way that was sickeningly distracting—stories about being a kid with her mother and Oph and Sissa and their coven, women crowding rooms, something always boiling on the stove and filling the house with spice, the laundry always running and shampoo-scented bathrooms laden with damp towels and candles burning day and night, regardless of a fear of fire. Alma, Eve, and Ishanvi used to come around every year with Sissa, until they suddenly didn't. The silence that followed left an eerie triad behind, and the twins' mother pretended as if they had never existed. Sofia liked to come up with fantastical stories about what could have caused a rift between the women, like failed hexes or blood rituals or deals with demons in the afterlife. Poppy just found the idea of a family like that fascinating and felt a little sad at the idea of it imploding. But most of her attention kept landing on Sofia's mouth. She had probably missed crucial details along the way.

"It's just me," Sissa said softly. "Sorry, honey."

Oph made a dismissive sound. But she looked pleased to see Sissa, her mouth curling up as she discreetly wiped at an eye.

Sissa entered the kitchen with authority and started rummaging in the cabinets. The skinny heels of her boots clicked on linoleum. The house filled with sound, the warm clinking of porcelain, the distant bang of the open screen door, the gentle tinny echo of Sissa's rings on the handle of a mug.

"I need tea!" Sissa cried. "And whiskey! If you're willing, my love."

Oph dutifully followed Sissa into the kitchen with a half-empty bottle, and a beat later Marya emerged from where she'd been abandoned in the dining room. "There's a beautiful woman making a lot of noise in there," she said.

Poppy focused on the wallpaper, discomfited in the face of Marya's easy tone. It had been hard enough to come back to Frankie and Cass, to be known so completely. She was still fighting to reclaim a past comfort, still tearing it down with damaging words. Now she had to start over again and reveal herself to someone new.

"You'll get used to it," Frankie answered. She touched Poppy's arm, the warmth of her fingertips enough to make Poppy jump. Frankie pulled back and asked in the most pleading tone Poppy had ever heard her use, "Sit down?"

She relented.

16

TRAMPLED UNDERGROUND LIKE SWEET SILK

In the hours they spent in the Lyon house eating, drinking, laughing, crying, Cass's heart swelled with the pleasant lulling warmth. The tense morning was shattered by the space Sissa took up—somehow, in a matter of hours, she had softened every corner and filled every room. There was noise everywhere: innumerable shoes by the door, bags in every bedroom and mugs on every table, the oven baking something sweet and buttery to life.

Oph and Sissa fell into familiarity. They talked and teased like sisters, though Oph was a whole head shorter with all the warm hues of afternoon while Sissa towered long, lean, and brilliantly jewel-toned. Cass watched the two of them with wonder as they fixed espresso and a pot of steeping chamomile on the stove. Oph, auburn hair tied in a knot at the nape of her white neck and a summer dress hugging her full body, and Sissa's buoyant curls coiling to her shoulders where the straps of her top pressed deep lines into dark brown skin. They moved like they knew the other's next step before it happened—they spoke like they had plucked the words from one another's mouth. Still, they left a space in every room as if anticipating a third person in their orbit.

Sometimes Cass felt she could imagine the outline of Frankie's mom, standing in that solid cutout between Oph and Sissa.

When Frankie wasn't around to argue, Sofia used to claim that their family performed magic—*real* magic, metaphysical manifestations, herbs packed into bundles and mirrors covered with black cloths, glass mutated to portal and incantations to reality. When their mother died, it splintered everything—the illusion of an intertwined three and their capability in creation. But even without Fiona, they were a family, women crafting alchemy out of the mundane. They were scattered across states, but distant threads kept them tethered. Sissa had been a part of Frankie's and Sofia's lives for so long that Cass sometimes forgot they weren't all tied by blood.

It made Cass impossibly jealous, desperately longing, painfully adoring. She loved the easy way they fell into each other. In her most private of desires, she had always thought the four of them would be the same way—linked by mutual histories, so beyond friendship that they might as well share DNA.

Now Sofia was gone. Marya stood beside the memory of her. Poppy was staggeringly different, hardened by fear, and Frankie was miserably the same, just waiting to explode. Cass stretched like a thinning game of cat's cradle between them all. They were standing on a precipice. Cass was so afraid of what waited at the bottom.

But she sat in Frankie's living room and let herself be lulled by the easy intimacy. *I will have this moment,* she thought, *and it will hurt tomorrow—but at least it will be mine now.*

Oph settled into the couch beside Cass with her elbow propped on the arm and her cheek pillowed in her hand. The joy on Oph's face was genuine, but her eyes kept flitting over to Frankie, the slightest furrow of concern marking her brow.

Music picked up on the stereo, Oph's CD case splayed open. Sissa swayed into the room. She carried a cake alight with a cluster of candles, as if every day that passed between them had been a birthday. The flames painted Oph in shades of overjoyed pink, and Sissa laughed, raucous and booming and high. The sound was so like Sofia's that Cass felt the hard sting of tears. Pieces of a story jumped from mouth to mouth: *remember when Fiona slipped in the mud holding my birthday cake—she ate it anyway, even covered in mulch—she told me not to throw it away, that it would be a waste—what a bitch—I would kill to hug her again—*

Frankie sat on a stool they had dragged from the dining room. Poppy hovered beside her with a hand shoved deep in her pocket, like it had reached for Frankie and settled there instead out of insecurity. It should have been different—they were together, the room bright with laughter and lamplight, cake on the table. But the dissonance ached in Cass's chest; an old, fevered wound that wouldn't heal over.

Marya said her goodbyes when Sissa started to snore in the armchair. Cass shouldn't have stayed the night but by the time they all drifted off to find a place to sleep, the sky was pale with dawn. She crept out when the sun had just finished rising, sleepless and humming with energy, Frankie and Poppy still curled together unknowingly on the couch.

A stream ran through the mountains and ended somewhere in the middle of the valley. It wrapped like a snake. It had seven forked tongues. At a point along that Loring rut in the earth, on the banks of rich dirt that pushed cattails to surface, sat Cass Sullivan's house.

She was affectionate about it. The house was a tall, thin man in a neighborhood of homes shaped like luxuriously plump ladies. Its very long and very broken nose jutted out in the shape of an awning over very steep and very splintered stairs. She had played on those stairs. She'd tried to do pull-ups on the awning. She had failed, and probably cracked the wood in a few places.

The yard was well kept, well watered, well mown. Her dad saw to that.

In the bruise of their kitchen, her mom was a vision in blue. Cass closed the front door quietly and watched her cook. Camilla Gutiérrez-Sullivan's robe was Cass's gift from last Christmas, meticulously hand-embroidered with her name. The stitched letters flowed like ivy in their deep green thread across the blue satin: *Camilla,* they crooned. She flipped something on the stove, the air around her heady with hot butter. The bracelets adorning her wrist jingled with each toss. *Camilla,* they sang. Her sleek dark hair was tied back, loose strands cradling her face like sweet flowers. *Camilla,* they whispered.

"Cassandra," said her dad from the hallway. It was not a croon, a song, or a whisper. It fell like an axe, cutting the room down the middle.

He stepped into the kitchen in his uniform. It always made Cass uncomfortable; she didn't like thinking about the gun on his hip, heavy and hot in his belt. The badge on his chest caught the yellow kitchen light and sent it scattering like a split atom.

He sat at the kitchen table with a grunt. Cass let her bag drop to the floor and hovered in the doorway, wishing she hadn't left Frankie's in the first place. Why had she thought she could come home, like it would be different? Her dad had always made her anxious. There was a gulf between them she couldn't cross. It left her with questions instead, unanswerable needles prickling along the back of her neck—why he was so cold, why she was incapable of pleasing him, why her every action and word were compared to her brother's.

But she'd put herself in this position. She was broke. The city apartment was gone, its remnants scattered around her childhood bedroom, half-unpacked. Sofia was dead. Cass was exactly where she was meant to be at exactly the right time, the universe guiding her home. The minor inconveniences could be dealt with if she could just keep that hope at the forefront of her mind.

So she flattened her voice and asked, "Ready for another hard day at the station?"

"Cass," her mom admonished.

Something sizzled and hissed on the stove. The smell suggested eggs. She watched yolks dance in the pan and reached for a bag of granola on the counter instead.

"How's your friend doing?" her dad asked, in a tone that suggested he would rather feed off the scattered bones of all roadkill within a five-mile radius than hear the answer. The deputy had always been suspicious of her ties to Sofia and Frankie—mostly because he resented Cass's time spent away from home, her incessant haircuts, the time she'd dyed her bangs crimson and they'd ended up a muddy maroon, the picture she'd posted online kissing her first girlfriend a week after dorm move-ins, the gap year that had lasted for three, the money she threw away on rent and an unfinished education.

"She's killing it," Cass replied, chewing noisily with her mouth open and hoping he would look her way to see the mess she made of the oats in her teeth. He refused, too used to her tricks, eyes trained on his phone instead. "We spent the evening contacting the dead and making corn-husk dolls to hex our enemies."

Her mom clucked, then leaned past the open doorway that led down the hall. "Alex!" Camilla called. "Breakfast!"

Cass slid off the countertop and retrieved her bag, swallowing with a dry tongue. "You're leaving?" Camilla asked, glancing over at Cass. "You just got here, honey, you should eat something real."

"I'm not hungry," Cass said. "We're going to work on the case later at Frankie's house and I need to get some work done beforehand."

Her mom turned fully this time, but the deputy cut her off. "You need to leave the detective work to us, Cassandra. You're only going to make things harder for that girl."

Cass smiled. "Thanks for the expert opinion. Maybe I will when you actually do something productive."

Camilla prepared to scold her as the deputy scoffed, but Cass took the stairs that led up to her bedroom two at a time, bag thumping against her thigh, nearly colliding with her brother at the top. Alex stumbled a bit, eyes moving anywhere but where Cass stood, deep purple curves beneath them.

"Hey," Cass said. "You good?"

"Fine." He tried to shoulder past her, but she caught his arm.

"Wait, do you want to hang out after you eat? I really wanted to ask you about—"

"No," he said sharply. His face fell, but Cass had already stumbled away. "Sorry, I'm meeting up with Tommy today. Maybe some other time."

Cass stepped out of his way. "Sure," she said to his back as he thudded down the stairs. He disappeared into the kitchen as a conversation between her parents lulled, voices churning among the spitting pop of frying food and television.

Cass paused before Alex's room, where the darkness was stale and complete.

She'd always been the messier Sullivan. Clothes mapped out every spot she'd stood in her room, kicked off her pants, toed off her socks. Notebooks remained splayed and waiting with an uncapped pen down the center. Cups of water stood on her bedside table in varying states of fullness, like she was preparing to play a song along their rims.

"I know you're the oldest," Camilla would repeat, standing in Cass's doorway and wrinkling her nose. "But I wish you'd take a hint from your brother and clean this place up."

He had changed in the five years she'd been gone, slipping past her somehow unseen. Had she peeked in his room over breaks since then? Seen the piles of clothes toppling from his desk chair? Noticed the drawn curtains?

She had let herself be distracted by the promise of a new life, while Alex continued to go to school, spend his free time under the disconcerting influence of Tommy Kowalski's crowd, and eat dinner at a set table with their mother at one end and their father at the other, Cass's seat left empty. And just over two weeks ago—though time felt untrust-worthy now—he'd found Sofia's body in the belly of a tree.

Past his doorway, she thought she saw something move, staring back at her in the absence of light. Heart pounding, she rocked back on her heels, but the shadow moved with her, just a shape her own body cast into the room. She forced herself to her room and shut the door behind her, enveloped in quiet solitude.

More than anything, she wanted to know what he'd seen.

17

DROOPING, ALL THE BIRCHES

"You're a magician," Sofia said, looking at Finder's hands with a smile big enough to suggest that she would eat them if she could.

"It's just work," Finder answered. "We do it every day."

The sun was high as a hawk's nest. It made everything a pleasant crimson, igniting the top of Sofia's head and shadowing the pockets of her eyes.

Sofia dragged a finger through the loam, sketching out a symbol between her and Finder's folded knees. Sofia had just turned fifteen. Finder noticed that she always came to the Fissure a few weeks after her birthday, when spring was in full bloom. Finder was ornery with youth, grated by Sofia's insistence on being right. She could never be taught. She always thought she had come to the conclusion herself.

"No, it's not. It's magic."

Finder looked down at the bundle of dry grass and twigs. There were flower petals tucked under the string that knotted them together, roses from Mab's garden. She shrugged and tossed it to Sofia, who caught it like a jewel and held it close for study.

"What makes it any different than what your mother does?"

Sofia's pleased expression slipped, and Finder regretted asking. It didn't seem fair—Finder told Sofia everything. She told her of Mother Mab, the Ossifier, the house. She told her about the things that walked in the woods at night, pocked like scars. How Mother Mab said they were people once and now they were the aftermath of death, seeking a place to go, looking for somewhere to put that energy down.

In the hundreds of days between each one that Sofia got to spend in the Fissure, Finder read every hour she wasn't working, wrote detailed notes on the things Sofia asked her about—wards and walls, charms and hexes, creatures and herbs. She kept diaries that she bundled in thread torn from the bottom of her skirt. Then she'd hand them over—a birthday gift.

Sofia looked at the book beside her shoe now, dragged her thumb along the rough edges of the pages. The cover was dark as the dirt and nearly disappeared among it. "I don't want to talk about my mother right now," she said, with finality.

It was so hard to get information out of her. For someone as talkative as Sofia was, she remained extremely private, and Finder felt she had to flay herself open to catch a hint of what Sofia was thinking. When she was alone, Finder would tally what she knew like melting candies in her mouth: Sofia had a mother. She lived in a world separate from Finder's. Her mother made magic like Mab did, and taught Sofia about it. The rest Sofia had deemed inconsequential.

But there was something heavy on Sofia's mind. It caught in the corners of her mouth, dragged it down.

"You're upset," Finder said, because she had two hours before Mother Mab would come looking for her and she wasn't about to waste them.

Sofia rolled her eyes. She reached out and cuffed Finder's chin, a familiar gesture that made her nearly keen forward in pleasure.

"I'm not upset," Sofia said. "I'm thinking." She rolled the bundle in her hands. "You said there's rose petal in this?"

"Rose, cinnamon, clove, shatavari, damiana. And vanilla, whole, not extracted." Finder counted off the ingredients on her fingers. Sofia examined it until the cloudy look slipped from her face and she finally smiled again, a sight so bright it might as well have been dawn.

"You're amazing, Finder. You really are. You don't realize—this is going to change everything." Sofia set the bundle down, carefully, on top of the diary that Finder had given her.

Finder's face flamed under all the praise. She pressed her own smile into the place where her skirt stretched over her knee. "I could be more helpful if you would tell me what you need it for."

It hadn't been easy to get the materials for Sofia. Finder had risen that morning with the hope that her girl would be back—the one day of the year that she woke without dread. She left an excuse with Mother Mab, expertly crafted after a year of isolation, and slipped into the woods to find Sofia waiting by the shore. As soon as their eyes met, Finder felt that rush of happiness. Until Sofia shattered it with the request. *A love spell.* Finder had nearly lost a finger beneath Mab's butcher knife for filching things from the cupboard.

"You're nosy," Sofia said lightly, but she fixed Finder with a hard look that chilled her down to the soles of her boots. "Why should I tell you?"

Finder shook her head, trying to dismiss the fact that the question had existed in the first place. "I didn't mean to—"

But Sofia started to laugh. Finder's frown stayed until Sofia tapped her cheek with a fingertip, still smiling. "I'm kidding, Finder. God. You take everything so seriously. It's not a big deal, it's just kind of . . . embarrassing."

Sofia looked down at the symbol she had drawn, two twisting forms, like snakes. Her eyes were thoughtful, like she was having a silent conversation with it. Finally, she said, "I think I could be safe with him."

"With him?" Finder asked. She sat on her hands to keep herself from reaching out and snatching the bundle back.

"My mom always said not to perform a love spell unless I was sure," Sofia said. Finder stayed quiet—she was afraid if she interrupted, she might never get the answer she wanted. "She said that she regretted the one she had done as a teenager, that she was never sure if my dad actually liked her in the first place. But I want—" She tilted her head back and took in the trees above them, leaves shaking, afraid of the wind. "I want a family, Finder. I want something like what Poppy has, two parents, a regular home. I want to feel safe, and I want to have a future. I don't want to be like my mother. I don't want to depend on my friends to hold me together in place of the real thing and still manage to lose it all in the end."

Poppy? Finder wondered, the flower unfurling in her mind. She felt chastened. "A love spell is not the answer."

Mother Mab had told her as much, when the women who came to their front door with offerings in baskets begged for something that might make their husbands stay. "It's never what they really want, Finder chick," Mab said. "It just makes them both hurt more."

"You told me it works," Sofia said coolly.

"It does," Finder insisted. She wrapped her arms around her knees. "It's just—it's not going to solve all your problems. It's infatuation. It doesn't replace genuine care."

Sofia fixed her with a glazed-over stare. "You just want to keep me all to yourself," she said loftily, like it could be a joke if looked at from a certain angle. But Finder knew her better than that. She had only ever known her. "I'll still be yours, Finder. I just want him to see me and think that I'm the one thing he's always been missing."

And do you want him? Finder wanted to ask, but she was already afraid of Sofia's hungry look. *Or do you just want him to want you?*

"Whatever," she said instead.

"Hey," Sofia murmured, her eyes searching Finder's until they pinned her in place. "Thank you. Seriously. You've brought me so much comfort with this. You're incredible, Finder."

Later, Finder watched her walk into the water, the myth of a friend that belonged solely to her. They would see each other only three more times before Sofia stopped coming.

If there had been a spell to bring people back, Finder would have done it. She would have jabbed the end of a finger with a blade until it bled. She would have pulled a tooth from its socket in her jaw. She would have plucked her eyelashes, one by one, and kept them in a jar, crushed into nothing among salt and rosemary.

She'd read all the books. There was no spell, and she was alone.

Until—him.

Despite all her longing, it took some time for Finder to get used to the space taken up by a fourth person. The boy (she couldn't call him a creature, not after she'd been one herself, and it had made her feel smaller and smaller each waking day) was a quiet one, ghostlike in the narrow house.

In the week that he'd lived with them, Finder spoke four words to him: *here*, *no*, *okay*, and *please*. There'd almost been a fifth, when he pointed to the thin-legged chair at the table that stood a foot taller than the others and gleamed ivory white and asked what it was made of, but the Ossifier answered before she could summon the word to her lips, the word rolling from his mouth like it'd been greased and oiled. *Bone.*

The boy was strange. Which wasn't saying much considering he was only the second man she'd ever met. He was stout and broad shouldered. He cleaned up after himself, unlike the Ossifier. He liked to fry an egg for lunch, drizzle honey on slices of toasted bread, sprinkle sugar on the egg before slicing into the oozing yolk. Sweet and wrong all at once.

Mother Mab was delighted to provide him with tasks. The Ossifier was overjoyed to watch. Finder was embarrassed to be sharing simple jobs she'd done her whole life; it was easier to just do something her way than to wait for the boy to catch up. But admittedly, it was nice to have someone else to hold the lantern in the dark.

The path that led to the coop was overgrown with dry grass. As it rustled in the wind, Finder tuned her ears, watched for oddities along the fence's line. The field was a lightless jungle. Finder waded through it, basket bumping against her hip and the boy hurrying behind her with a lantern held high. The glow cast a wide red circle around them.

Early in the cycle between deepest and faded black, the air held a certain thickness. It coated Finder like syrup, like sugar boiled down until only paste remained. She felt as though she could reach out and gather strands of atmosphere to tuck away in the basket. Taffy that would cling to teeth.

The lantern could only just barely illuminate the beginning of the path. She prickled with discomfort. It took everything in her not to glance over her shoulder and keep a steady eye on the boy behind her. In the distance, a dull sound echoed, like the stretching of an animal as it released a breath. There was a discordant slam—the gate that once broke the low line of the fence banging in the breeze. Finder kept her eyes trained to the ground. It was nothing.

Brush crashed in the distance, a riotous, bestial pacing. She imagined the ward to be physical—some impenetrable wall surrounding them, creatures dragging nails down stone.

"You do this every morning?" the boy asked. His words bumped up and down with each step they took. He let out a little *oof* as he stumbled and righted himself once again. This part of the yard tended to slope down, and it was difficult to traverse when the sun no longer existed and you hadn't known it your whole life like Finder had.

"Yes. Where did you think all your eggs came from?"

It was the longest sentence she'd ever said to him, and his breath huffed in response. The lantern bobbed. "I heard there was a village up ahead," he said, only half an answer.

"There is."

"I was headed that way," he admitted. "But my torch went out just before your house. I saw the lights through your windows and thought it might be worth stopping in."

Mother Mab once told her that she'd enchanted the windows to keep unwanted visitors away. That she had constructed a ward the crooked master of the trees could never penetrate. It might have been a lie, something said to comfort Finder in the newfound dark, but Mab had never been the type to console. No one knew magic like the old woman. Finder had seen her gnarled hands warp river reeds until they were husks of dolls. Had watched steam curl from pots into shapes like dogs and trees and women with swollen bellies. Who was she to say the ward wasn't real? And who was this boy to see right through it?

Finder's grasp curled tighter around the basket handle. She wanted him to walk in front of her, where she could study his movements.

She comforted herself with this: she had been the one to see him. If what Mother Mab said was true, then what Finder saw would bring them only good fortune. But she'd watched the sun wink out, hadn't she? And that had brought only the lurking dark beyond the faltering fence.

The boy placed the lantern at the base of the coop's ladder. He reached for a rung to haul himself up, but Finder held out a hand in the dim glow to stop him. The faster they got this done, the better. And Finder always did things faster.

She crawled up the ladder with the basket tucked into the crook of her arm. With one palm braced against the wall, she worked the door open. When it popped free, the smell of warmth washed over her, musty feed and feathers. But inside, the coop was silent. And there was something else that stood out to her. A metallic tang, clinging to the edge of her nostrils.

"Light," she called to the boy with a gesture at the lantern. Then she grimaced to herself. "Please." He passed it to her without a word. She fought down a sense of satisfaction at his immediate action.

Finder lifted the flame to peer inside the tarry coop. Red glow caught in the corners of the box, danced across strewn feathers and something wet splattered across the walls. Her breath caught. She forced herself further inside the small door as the basket slipped from her arm and thudded to the ground. Her hand splayed against the wood and stickiness clung to her fingers. When she pulled away, disgusted, she saw that it coated her skin.

The chickens were torn apart. The coop was crimson where the blood and the lantern light combined to paint it. Every one of them was dead, the nests overturned, eggs smashed to broken bits. Whatever it was had not eaten them. Why didn't it eat them?

"Finder?" the boy called from below. "Do you need some help?"

She couldn't look at him. The breeze ruffled the scattered feathers. All that flesh. Mounds of carnage left behind to rot.

"I saw it first," she said.

"What's wrong?" the boy pushed, wavering.

She reached to tuck her hair back on instinct and felt wetness brush against her cheek. Her stomach tossed at the thought of blood smeared over her skin. When she faced him again, the boy sucked in a sharp breath.

"They're all dead," she said calmly, backing down the ladder. That same distorted animal groan whistled past them again, the thunderous snapping of dead wood underfoot. She didn't dare look to where the field ended and the woods began. She thought of the lake. Of Sofia's head, disappearing beneath the water.

"Well," she said, "hurry up. Let's go tell Mother Mab."

18

LET THEM ARM AND LET THEM TUMBLE

Marya woke to the sound of trickling and the sensation of being watched.

"Shit fuck," she said, pushing out of bed and stepping directly into a puddle. Her mouth was tacky—she didn't remember falling asleep. Her phone rang on her bedside table, but instead of answering it she went for the baseball bat she'd propped against the table's edge, anxiously anticipating an intruder. The man stood in the doorway wringing his hands. His head rolled so far forward she was afraid it might tumble off his shoulders.

"If you wanted me to wake up, you could have just touched me," she muttered, peering down at the water and prodding at it with the bat. It was scummy with soap along the surface, bubbles making refracted coins of light. "Where's it coming from? The bathroom?"

The man shook all over. He let out a desperately scared groan. Her irritation dissipated immediately, and she reached for him. She stopped just an inch from him.

"Show me," she said, and he grabbed her.

Cold dove into her, severe and all-knowing. She could feel the way his echo cowered, the wicking strength of his haunt pulling from her to remain visible. He was afraid of something. That made her terrified.

Marya watched the man waver, caverns opening in the absences of his body and bits of wall and hardwood showing through where he wisped away. She pushed past him and felt the shift—the chill left her empty and weakened.

The hallway was too dark. The air was sour and green, the muzzy aftermath of her spilled shampoo rising like crushed leaves. She crept toward the bathroom, listened to the faucet spitting distantly. Water collected around the doorjamb. The man's following footsteps creaked behind her.

Sofia floated face down in the tub, bare back and shredded fabric bobbing above the water as more roared from the faucet. An imposing shape clung to the corner where the showerhead dribbled—made the ceiling a smoky black, sapped all the color from the room—with its spine hunched and too humanoid under the flickering overhead light. Sofia's frenetic shadow slipped down the shower wall and crashed into the bath. Water torrented over the sides and drenched Marya's feet. She lurched away in surprise as the shadow reached out a manifested hand and yanked Sofia up by the hair.

Marya's hesitation lasted only a moment before she darted forward. The shadow turned as the slicked-over formation of its lidded eyes and gaping mouth registered her attack. She didn't consider consequences, just swung the bat at the creature as Sofia's head lifted, dripping from the water, the specter's long, pointed fingers raking against her scalp. Sofia's mouth fell open in an imitated scream, chest heaving.

Wood hit the mottled shape of its head, and the mass let out a pained wail. Marya's bat passed through it until it smashed into tile and left a splintered crack running up the wall. The showerhead coughed out a spray. The creature flinched away, screaming like an animal in a trap, water sloshing in every direction. She readied the bat for another swing. But the shadow—its dimensional body, that unreal presence—hissed as it disintegrated into the water. The faucet spat black until it ran clear at last.

Marya crouched and yanked Sofia up by the armpits. She pressed past skin and down into frozen bone in a manner that made her stomach turn. Sofia looked at Marya, mouth slack and stuttering, water streaming down her cheeks. She began to fade, the weight of her lightening in Marya's arms—she watched the droplets on Sofia's skin fall through the disappearing pockets of her body, landing in the overflowing tub.

"Fuck," Marya said again once she found her voice, Sofia's outline now just the red imprint of looking away from an unshaded bulb. The man reached beside her and turned off the faucet. She raised her head and shivered in the cold room, surprised that he'd summoned enough energy to move something physical. Now he coalesced without Sofia's desperate pull. His mournful face became more pronounced, body resaturating, shoes rippling in pooled water. He tipped his head at her and pressed his mouth into a regretful line. She was glad she hadn't attempted to exorcise him.

"Thank you," Marya whispered, "for telling me."

Her phone rang again from the other room. This time she rushed to it, newly aware of her body, bat rolling with a clatter across the wet floor.

"We're downstairs, bitch!" Cass said happily, crackling over the connection. "It's time to commit a crime!"

Marya stared at the puddles, at the man's indistinct shape in the hall, at the foot of her door where the bat had rolled to a stop. Her landlord was going to crucify her.

"Cool," Marya said, as if she were confessing to murder. "Be right down."

"You're ready, right? Do you need us to come up?"

"No!" Marya answered harshly, and then she corrected herself. "I mean, yes. No. I'm ready and you don't need to come up. Give me five minutes."

It took her ten to push the water around with the few towels she had, and three more to yank on clean clothes that weren't drenched by the bath. When she finally made it downstairs, Cass's headlights were bright and atomic. Cass leaned over Poppy to wave out the rolled-down window, while Poppy fixed Marya with a hard stare. Frankie sat in the bed of the truck with her arms crossed over her knees.

"You alright?" Frankie asked, when Marya had hauled herself into the back beside her.

"Never better," Marya answered. Her shirt stuck to her spine, still damp with anxious sweat.

The night was sweltry with the scent of onion grass and honey-suckle, of burning wood and beauty. It was dark enough that she could barely make out the distant mountains. Cass drove fast, too fast, and Marya was grateful for it—anything she could have said to Frankie would have been snatched away by the wind. She closed her eyes. Against the lids she could still see the gruesome aftermath of Sofia face down in the water. She tried to slow her pounding heart with a hard breath sucked through the nose, but it caught in her throat, too painful to swallow. Frankie's arm bumped Marya's thigh and imme-diately pulled away. Marya slitted her eyes open and focused on that instead—the stinging point of contact anchoring her back to the hard metal beneath her.

This time, they parked further from where Sofia's car had been abandoned. Cass tucked her truck just beneath the cover of a low-hang-ing ash tree. "No one will suspect a thing," she said with a loving pat against the hood as they poured out of the truck. "Hunters stop around here all the time."

Marya didn't like the idea of others sharing the forest with them as they wove through the trees, her feet unsteady in the foliage, sneakers sticking in muggy dirt. Everything was different at night. Her world was reduced to what she could see a foot or two ahead of her, Cass's flashlight, the relentless cricket hum.

"This is ridiculous," Poppy said as she stumbled, barely righting herself in time. "We're all going to end up in jail."

"No we won't," Cass answered quickly. "I checked. Town hall potluck tonight—my dad said the sheriff goes every week and brings his whole family." She gave them all a thumbs-up. "I forgot how cute Loring could be. I'm kind of sad we're missing out."

"I told you that you could've stayed home if you wanted to," Frankie said to Poppy. Cass scoffed at that, and her beam of light bounced. Poppy shrugged, needled. Her eyes landed on Marya, and immediately flitted away again when she caught Marya looking back.

Marya didn't blame Poppy's suspicion—to them, she was a stranger with no stake in Sofia's life, and she could imagine what that looked like to a family in mourning. But she was laden with their grief, and Sofia was trying to tell her something, and she was going to do everything in her power to understand.

The barn made a black cutout against the sky. The Glasswell house stayed dark. Overhead, the moon was a sliver so thin that it felt like a mirage.

Frankie led the way. The barn's entryway was composed of two massive doors barred across the middle, and a Dutch door cut out in its side. The top half of the Dutch door hung open just an inch—the bottom was padlocked shut.

"I'm obsessed with the sheriff's idea of security," Cass said, pushing on the top half of the door with a casual hand. It swung open to reveal the black guts of the barn. She hauled herself up and over the bottom half of the door, turning to wave the others in. Frankie followed. Marya went last, after Poppy's shoes hit the ground. She took one more look at the sleeping house waiting in the distance. Then she swung herself inside.

The belly of the barn was damp with life, full of muffled exhales and animal noises, flecks of dust shining beneath the beams of their flashlights. Marya's chest was tight. She liked to think that she'd seen the worst, that there could be nothing as devastating as the terrors she'd already witnessed. But the barn was so dark. She waited for something to lunge at her, to tear her heart from her ribs and devour her whole. Spirits had only ever left her cold and empty, without inflicted hurts. But after the shadow in her bathroom, she doubted her grasp on the capabilities of a haunt.

The only sound was the soft whinny of an anxious horse. She watched Frankie peer in stalls, heard her murmur something absurdly gentle. Cass stuck close to Poppy's side, their shoulders brushing with each step.

"What exactly are we looking for?" Poppy asked, and it was a reasonable question. Marya didn't quite know. All she could think about was that terrifying mass slipping through the cracks in the walls, its limbs twining in Sofia's hair. All she had was a gut feeling and the memory of an apparition.

She let feeling pull her. Mosquitoes buzzed beside her ear. With her eyes closed everything was magnified—the smell of mud and feed, the call of a distant bird, a bead of sweat running from her shoulders to her hips.

Then—there it was, a frigid exhale, the cool promise of sapped energy. A spot in the center of the room drew her in, right in front of an empty stall. Hay bales were stacked beside it. The stall door was closed, terminating just below her shoulders. Marya waved a flashlight across it once and almost left it behind.

But the beam landed on a shape on the door and held her in place. It was a strange thing, twisted and scrawled, carved deep into the wood. Marya bent and trained the light on it, tracing her thumb along the outline of two intertwined snakes.

There, with her knees bent and one palm pressed to the earth, the ground nearly pulsed with heat. There was a distant repetitive thud like a blood-slowed heartbeat, thick and lively. A shape flickered in the corner of her eye. She blinked, hard. Something had happened in that spot—she could feel it like the memory of another life, a reoccurring dream.

A touch landed on her shoulder. She turned, expecting to see one of the others, and found Sofia crouched beside her.

It was a shock to see her, as if the near drowning had been her true death. Marya imagined she could feel Sofia's breath on her cheek. She was clearer now than she had been in the bath, more defined with Frankie so near. Sofia held up a hand, bruised and rotted as a trampled peach, fingers crossed in a tight twist. They rippled, her twined index and middle mimicking the shape carved into the stall door.

She rocked forward and Marya almost stumbled back onto her heels. But Sofia just pushed down into the dirt. Marya kneeled forward to copy the action and watched Sofia line her hand up against Marya's, thumbs pressed knuckle to knuckle like a promise. Together they pushed against the ground, and Marya felt a rushed *thumpthumpthump*, that rabbit-kick, that body breath.

Sofia let out a little hiss, something inhuman and strained. Her grip curled as if trying to tear down into the earth. But instead of digging into the dirt floor, Marya watched the outline of Sofia's hand tremble, the shadow splitting away and sliding up the door, clawing desperately at the wood. It tried to rip the symbol away. But the snakes remained, rippling under her flashlight. The shadow's fingers flickered until they slipped past the door and fell away under the beam of light, Sofia prone and still beside Marya.

"What are you doing?" someone asked beside her ear, and this time when she glanced back it was Frankie crowding her, wide-eyed and wondering, her beam landing on Marya's dirty hands.

Marya considered a lie. But a partial truth seemed simpler—she pressed a finger to the symbol on the stall door. Poppy paused behind them, Cass peering over her shoulder. Four beams trained on the spot where her fingertip met wood, snakes twisting up and away, away, away.

"What is it?" Cass asked.

"Sofia's," Poppy said.

Frankie frowned. "You're sure?"

"She gave me this," Poppy whispered, doubtful, wounded. "She said it was supposed to protect me." Cass's flashlight followed Poppy's gesture to her neck. A charm hung from a thin chain—two matching snakes knotted around a slender line. Her hand glowed bronze against the bright gold pendant.

Marya dragged her eyes down the wood, back to the dirt and its pulsing heartbeat. And there, in the crack between the stall door and the packed earth, Marya saw the distinct shape of two solid feet.

She fell back, scrambling away, a sound torn from her throat. The others scattered like spooked birds taking flight. "Go!" she whispered, harsh and fast. "Someone else is in here!"

They ran for the halved door. Cass was over it in a second flat, vaulting herself past the hatch, Poppy and Frankie following just as fast. Marya stumbled after them with one last glance over her shoulder, waiting to find the sheriff there with a shotgun trained on their backs.

Instead, she watched the feet step forward. Gray filtered through the wood like a body fragmenting into mist until it formed a shape more solid than the natural haze of night. It wasn't Sofia's harrowing shadow—or at least, not the iteration Marya had spent the day battling. This shape grew taller and more distinct until it was a body of its own. It held the same shimmering quality as the shadow, mass blocking light. But its masked features sprouted roots curling up toward the barn's sloped ceiling. Its mouth was a black and endless cavern, unhinged and hanging, like it had gorged itself once and hunted now for something more satiating. Its fingers were longer, its angles more pronounced. Sofia's slumped form bowed before it. Her crushed forehead pressed into packed dirt.

The body walked through the stall door and stepped over Sofia. It tipped a gnarled and rooted head in Marya's direction. It began to stalk after them.

For once, she was a good woman's daughter. She ran like hell.

19

SILVER MOON SLIVERS

The ride home was tense, with Poppy perched in the center of it all—Cass's knuckles squeezed to the bone around the wheel, Frankie rigid in the passenger seat, Marya coiled in the back like a waiting animal. No one could summon the strength to speak. Poppy's nails pressed into her thigh, where she channeled all her focus.

Sofia, Sofia, Sofia, Poppy's mind incanted, a desperate plea to raise the other girl from the dead. At some point before Sofia was murdered—or maybe even in the exact moment—she'd been in Lucas Glasswell's barn.

Poppy wished he had been the one to fall through the porch the night of the bonfire. She wanted to hit him again, wanted to watch the socket of his eye go purple beneath her fist. She wanted to pull his heart from his chest and eat it before him, dripping red.

Okay, maybe she didn't want that exactly—but the desperate need for action buzzed like drunkenness. She had to shut her eyes, the sight of the black road too endless to consider.

Cass dropped her off, and Poppy crept into her parents' house. Somehow it still remembered her enough to remain silent, the stairs muffled under her feet, front door clicking shut with a little chirp.

She shed her dirty clothes and jewelry and collapsed into the too-small bed, ankles hanging off the end and a knuckle shoved between her teeth. She tried to cry. Her chest strained with the effort. But nothing ever came, her pain a knot bound up in her throat, and Poppy fell into the dream like a body from a balcony.

She floated on the tepid surface of the lake behind Frankie and Sofia's house. She knew it instantly, that familiar brush of algae, the cold that soaked through her clothes. Above her, the earth had been robbed of its stars.

As she drifted, she watched the center of the sky slit open. From it, colorless dust poured out, snaking tendrils of shadow. They curled down from the starless black to where she floated and prodded at her stomach, her cheeks, her throat. They coaxed her mouth agape. They crawled inside—

And rushed through her, ice water now vascular, claiming her blood for its own. The current began to drag her down, so slowly that she almost didn't notice until the lake clouded past her parted lips. Thrashing was an instinct but her body seized up, a skipped stone. She opened her eyes in the murk and found Frankie before her. The skin of her face had peeled back and the veins beneath gave way to gore, the water rushing red red red around them as she snarled—*all your fault.*

When Poppy woke, she couldn't move.

Something stood in the corner of the room.

Frantically, eyes trained up at the ceiling, she tried to work her mouth, her fingers, any appendage that might make it possible for her to claw her way out of this. The only sound was the tidal rush of her blood in her ears.

From the corner of her eye, she saw it move. A turn of its body revealed the black shape of a shoulder shadow-puppeted against the wall. But its outline was darker than night, hazy around the edges. Through the spot where an elbow should be, the doorknob showed, brassy and solid. Her eyes dragged up the hulking body to a head—long, curling lines sprouted from the skull, rippling and roiling, tendrils prodding the air. Some delirious part of her wanted to reach for her glasses, as if putting them on might dispel the sight. But her body wouldn't obey when summoned.

It took a step forward. She could see that it had a reflection, from a glimpse of the mirror above her dresser. Somehow that made it so much worse, and so much closer to her. *Stop,* she thought, *stop it, let me out, please.*

A shrill noise pierced her thoughts and took over her frozen mouth. It buzzed distantly, a television left on through the night. A voice boomed into her skull, gritty and charred, like someone had sucked in a lungful of smoke and held it inside, like the vocal cords had been shredded and destroyed.

I WILL TAKE THE ONE I DESIRE TO THE TREE, it said with Poppy's mouth, and who was that? Who the fuck was that? Why was it speaking what did it want what did it mean—*WHERE MY ROOTS WILL DRINK THEIR FILL.*

The sound slipped from her mind, leaving her empty. She blinked once, twice. Someone spoke again, this time beside her ear, faint and wispy. They shook her hard, hands so cold on her fever-body. Her tongue was lead in her mouth. It lay heavily against her teeth, a slick creature now foreign to her.

"What?" she finally worked out.

Poppy twisted her head against her pillow and looked at Sofia.

"WAKE UP!" Sofia screamed, her face locked up in agony, the words a breeze carried through the air, a gift in the form of a nightmare.

Half of her face had been crushed. Bone poked through the skin, mottled and gory. Her mouth hung open, a tooth missing from the front, one of her canines. Her bottom lip was split. The one eye that wasn't bruised and bloody shone a pure green, earthy and alive and all hers, and the sight of it made Poppy gasp. That intake of breath shook her back into her body.

Poppy reached for Sofia and grabbed empty air, alone in the room once again. She heard someone sob, an awful, heart-wrenching sound, before her brain caught up with her mouth and she realized the tears were her own. The shadow shape and Sofia were gone.

When she crawled from the bed, she hit the floor knees first. Staggered up. Kicked the sheets from around her ankles. Ran.

Down the hall, Poppy heard someone call her name. But sound held no honesty anymore. She was in her car before she could make sense of it, turning the key and begging it to be good to her for once. The engine caught like an answered prayer and she sped into the coming dawn, the sky barely blue.

Trees whipped by. She was going too fast. Panic pounded like a second heart. *Sofia,* she thought or said aloud or wept, and then had to force herself to shake the image from her head. She couldn't think about it. Couldn't. Couldn't. Couldn't.

She'd go to Frankie's. She'd be safe there. Oph would help her, hold her close like a mother might, run her soft palms along Poppy's cheek until she fell back asleep.

But when the car rolled to a stop, she was back where they'd started the night, parked in the dirt-covered embankment. Her headlights lit up the trees. The road was still, katydids hushed. She slid from the car on shaky legs and walked to the edge of the forest. The air was saturated, muddled.

Through the trees she could see the outline of that red barn, stark against pale trunks. Every black shape was a new figure looking back at her. Rocks jutted past the dirt and cut into her bare feet.

Poppy could still feel that gravelly voice. Her throat was raw, as if she'd been screaming. Maybe she had. She raked a glance along the white bellies of the new leaves and thought about Marya standing beneath them, her head tipped in anticipation. Thought about running. About the sight of that symbol carved in the wood, about Sofia wielding something sharp enough to cut.

Poppy tried to quell her trembling, afraid to close her eyes and see Sofia in her bed. The idea was nothing unusual—they'd been there a hundred times before. She had reached for Sofia's hands, guided them to her body, the soft planes of her stomach and thighs, let her wrists be pushed into the mattress as Sofia settled over her and bit down on Poppy's lip, let the tender sound slip from her mouth. And when the pain bloomed, she had arched into the touch and pulled Sofia closer.

Now the memory soured—Poppy kept seeing Sofia's crushed skull, blood running down her cheek as she gasped against Poppy's throat.

"Come back," she said, shattered and pathetic. "Show yourself to me."

But who was she asking? Sofia? The gore of her, cracked and spilled open? The entity reflected in her mirror, populated in the vacancies between trees?

Poppy could feel it watching, that remembered voice slicing down her spine. If it was going to come for her, then she would choose her demise. She would grab the blade of her grief and feel it slice her open. She would choose it even now, waiting for morning to destroy her last fragile grasp of the universe. She would choose it even after losing her again.

The sound of someone's tires on the road awakened her. She turned and found a figure behind the wheel watching her through their window. Something about the person's profile was familiar in a way that prickled. Their eyes met for a suspended moment, Poppy's face twisted into a grimace, and the woman—it was a woman, wasn't it, with the hanging line of her hair?—narrowed her gaze before she was gone.

Poppy ran her fingers over her snarl-split lip. Just a swallow was enough to set her throat on fire. She trailed down until she settled at her collarbones, reaching for her necklace. But it was gone. In memory, she could see it—waiting on her nightstand, beside the bed where Sofia's broken body had called for her to wake.

20

SPLIT-STRING PUPPET

When Cass pulled up to Frankie's house, morning sunning itself across the hills like a cat, she found Poppy asleep in a rocking chair.

"Hey," Cass said. "*Hey.* Poppy. What the fuck, dude."

Poppy sat up, blinking. There were circles carved under her eyes, her clothes rumpled; she was still in her pajamas, just a T-shirt from their high school basketball team and a pair of shorts that used to be Sofia's a lifetime ago. Her feet were bare, one tucked beneath her thigh. She looked wrecked.

The slats of the porch creaked loudly beneath Cass's sneakers and the sudden movement of Poppy's rocking chair. She watched Poppy run a hand down her face. "What time is it?"

"It's like, ten, probably. Did you sleep out here? All night?"

The front door interrupted them with a rusty click, revealing a bleary-eyed Frankie with her hair poking out in a million different directions. "Y'all can just knock, you know?"

"I was busy asking Poppy why she slept on the porch," Cass said.

"You slept on my porch?"

"I had a nightmare, okay?" Poppy said sharply. "I just didn't want to be at home."

Frankie's face softened. "You could have come inside," she said. "You know where the spare key is."

"I didn't want to wake anyone," Poppy said. "Sorry for sleeping on your porch." She got up and straightened her shorts, eyes trained absently downward. Cass touched Poppy's arm and jumped when Poppy flinched. She let her hand fall away.

They followed Frankie inside. Sissa knelt by the fireplace striking match after match, tossing them into a pile of smoldering wood when they didn't catch. "Finally," Sissa sighed when she saw them. A scarf knotted her hair on top of her head and another wrapped around her shoulders, patterned and sleek, dragging dangerously close to the hearth. Cass stared at the cup of coffee beside Sissa's feet, and the edge of the fabric that kept nearly dipping inside of it.

"We need a few more players for hearts," Oph said, leaning into the doorway and speaking around a mouthful of something. "Are y'all staying? I just took a sourdough loaf out of the oven."

"I wish we could. You know I'm ready to beat you again," Cass answered with a wink.

Oph's lips curled down. "Where are you going?"

"You're leaving already?" Sissa asked at the same time. The fire began to catch.

"You know it's basically summer, right?" Frankie said, eyebrows raised at the growing flames. "I have to open the studio, and then we're, um, hanging out after."

"Right, 'hanging out.' I thought I told you to quit messing around with that stalking," Oph said, her eyes flattening into something stern enough to make Cass sweat along her hairline. "It will never end well."

"Is that a premonition?" Poppy asked. Cass watched the firm set of her mouth. How bad could that dream have been?

Sissa snorted and caught Oph's eye. "Not a chance, that's just common sense." Her gaze dragged back over Poppy, who appeared uneasy in her pajamas and bare feet, and she sucked her teeth in displeasure. "Go grab something out of my suitcase, darling. You can't hunt like that."

Poppy silently obeyed, and Sissa turned back to the fire and tossed a handful of something green into it, face lighting up as it sparked and burned away. A faint herb-tinged scent filled the air.

"Just—be careful, please," Oph finished, exasperated. "And come home for dinner."

Frankie flashed a thumbs-up to her aunt, but Cass watched the way Frankie's eyes clung to the hearth's fire—like she could raze the logs to ash with her stare alone.

They piled into Cass's truck. It might be a clunker, but the engine was less likely to break down than Poppy's piece of junk, even if it did only properly seat two and a half of them. Frankie's sneakers squeaked against the floor as she slid into the middle, but Poppy jumped up into the bed of the truck, leaving the passenger-side seat open. Cass glanced back at where Poppy leaned against the rear windshield, shoulders pulled up close to her ears. Worry flickered through her, lined with hesitance—she couldn't remember how to bridge the gap between them.

They met Marya at the studio with a crisp apron already tied around her waist and the sign on the door flipped to *Open*. She smiled when they came in and the shape of it lit up her face. Cass found herself pleasantly surprised by the familiarity of it, of Marya, of realizing the moment when you were happy to see someone.

While Frankie and Marya worked, Cass sat with Poppy behind the counter, the four of them finally gathering into a huddled circle when the shop was empty enough to craft a new plan.

Sofia was last seen the night of the bonfire. The police raided the clearing and sent everyone scattering—Sofia, separated in the madness, never came home. By the next morning, they'd started to search, the police scouting with what little force they had, Frankie and Cass and Poppy stuffed into Poppy's car with its hiccupping near-death engine. Lucas appealed to the town on their only local news station, asking for anyone who had seen Sofia to report it. Weeks of silence passed, and Sheriff Glasswell finally filed her as a runaway and boarded up the abandoned house.

Then her body was discovered, five years later, by a group of guys—one of which was Cass's brother, Alex—tucked away inside the abandoned house that had torn Tommy Kowalski's leg into a bloody wreck. Sofia had been left beaten and fractured in the center of some kind of ritualistic circle: white petals, melted candles, spilled wax. And Lucas now spent all his time at the gym, continuously building up a threatening amount of muscle.

Even if he had been awful to them over the years, Lucas had always been soft for Sofia in a way Cass found inconceivable. He would carry her things, open doors for her, buy her little gifts that brought barely concealed satisfaction to Sofia's face. She liked the attention, and being one of the few couples at their high school that people *talked* about. But the few times Cass had met his eyes over the years, the vacancy behind them left her sick to her stomach.

They had all seen the symbol in the barn.

"We know she wasn't killed in the house, because it was still empty when the police searched. Someone did it elsewhere and got past the barricade to hide her inside. But maybe the barn could have been where Lucas hurt her. It's only a two-mile drive between it and the abandoned house, and he's likely the only one who would know how to avoid the cops staked outside." Frankie was distant, her tone clinical. She tapped clay-covered fingers against the register. "Do you think the sheriff knows and is covering for him?"

Cass scooted around on her stool, trying to get comfortable. "If so, then we've already lost. But Lucas is a self-obsessed freak, and he'll slip up at some point. You remember the time we asked Sofia to go with us to prom as a group and he told her if she did, he wouldn't go at all?"

Marya wrinkled her nose. "I think we need to go straight to the source and confront him with what we found."

"Oh yeah, right," Frankie said. "He'll probably just tell his dad that we broke into their barn, and we'll be arrested for trespassing in the first place."

"We need to go to the house," Poppy said.

They were silent for a moment, the truth of it sinking in. It seemed obvious—if they'd found a sign of Sofia's distress, there had to be something else out there, waiting for them to make sense of the fragments. That didn't make the idea any easier to swallow. Cass had been perfectly happy living without a reminder of the place where Sofia's body had rotted, alone in a crumbling house. She needed no new ways to torture herself.

"Then it's decided," Frankie said. "I'll close up and we'll leave." She pushed away from the countertop, sneakers squeaking against the damp floor.

"Wait, wait, wait. Are you sure we should be trespassing again after nearly getting caught the last time?" Cass asked as Frankie's footsteps receded, somewhere on the other side of the studio.

"We're practiced now," Frankie called. "And that house is abandoned, unlike the barn." The sink started running and she raised her voice over it. "We'll be in and out—no one needs to know. Unless you're planning to narc and get some good points with the deputy?"

Cass rolled her eyes. "Chill, it was a good point. I just don't think this is something we should rush into, and I already promised my mom I'd be home for dinner."

"Oh man, can't miss meatloaf."

"Okay, bitch, my mom's meatloaf is good," Cass said to Frankie. "At least let me show up so she doesn't freak out on me. They've been treating my move back home like I'm sixteen and annoying all over again, and I don't feel like getting in an argument."

"Oh, you're not annoying anymore?" Poppy asked, the teasing tone in her voice faint but present.

Cass pointed at her. "That's a good one. I walked into that."

"Later then," Frankie said, undoing the knot of her apron. "Can you sneak out when they go to bed?"

She'd done so plenty of times before. But this time felt different, loaded with potential.

"Fine," Cass said, swallowing around the stone in her throat. "I'll drop y'all off at home and swing back around by midnight. But someone is going to have to sit in the back again, so just lie down if the cops pass us. They're probably printing wanted posters with our faces on them already."

She left them behind to close up, with orders to meet her and the Ford out front in five minutes. As she headed for the gravel lot behind the studio to bring the truck around, rocks crunching under her high-tops and keys jingling on her belt loop, something caught her eye.

There was a dark figure standing beside the tree that blanketed her truck. Low-hanging, blackening branches obscured its shape. She froze, heart immediately slamming against her rib cage.

Then the figure stepped forward to shed its shadow skin and became a cop. Specifically, it became Sheriff Glasswell, Lucas's equally haunting father. Cass was not comforted by the fact that he was not actually a demon. In the growing umbrage, his skin appeared mottled and wrong. She gripped her keys until they made indents on her palm.

"You the chief deputy's kid?"

"I guess," she answered.

There was a poised pen in his hand. "I was about to write a ticket for this truck. Is it yours?"

She nodded. She didn't trust herself to speak. He stepped closer. "Thought it was poised to park here overnight, but if you're here to move it, I'll let you off with a warning."

How kind, she thought miserably. What she said was, "Thank you, sir."

He slapped his pad of tickets against a thigh and looked her over. She fought the overwhelming urge to shiver. "Be safe out there, young lady," he said, before his boots crunched past her and he slipped into the patrol car parked on the street.

Jackass, she thought. With the door slammed hard behind her, she felt safe for a moment.

Then she looked up through the windshield and found a figure looming in the same place she had seen Glasswell standing. It had to be at least seven feet tall. Its smoky form nearly reached the branches of the willow tree overhead. In the deep shadow, she could just make out its wide hands curled against the bark, inhuman, horrifying. Frozen, she watched it stagger forward, a clot of shadow, one of those hands slamming down hard on the hood of the truck.

She let out a shriek and flipped on the headlights in a rush. They illuminated nothing but bushes. With a gasping breath Cass let her head fall against the steering wheel, pulse pounding in her ears.

"It was nothing," she said aloud, like the words were a spell that could banish the slamming of her heart against her rib cage. The sound of the hand hitting her hood played on a loop. "It wasn't there."

She thought of the basement—of something's echoing inhale beside her head, the hard press of its body in the dark. She knew it had been there. It was as real as her own breath.

"It was nothing," she said again. The threat of tears made her mouth swollen and dry, each swallow raking across her throat.

She shifted into drive and turned onto Main, leaving the shadows to die in denial, her tires rolling ruts in the gravel and brush.

21

THE REEDY PROMISE OF A BROKEN JAW

In the warped glass above the bathroom sink, Finder prodded at her nose. Blood dripped patiently into the basin and its slow-draining water. Even the slightest movement would open the interior gash again, as it had off and on all day, Finder's handkerchief now stained a wet and heavy black. Candlelight illuminated the roundness of her face and made the shadows of her skin more purple.

So the chickens were dead. So her nose was flowing crimson and wild into the sink. So Mother Mab had lashed out at her when she'd told her the news, delivering a curt slap to Finder's cheek and gripping her chin to shout more firmly into Finder's face, her jaw working furiously as she spouted off a list of disciplinary tasks to complete. Finder spent the day hauling fowl corpses into the house for Mab to clean and scrubbing thin sprays of gore from the coop's walls. But this was easy this was normal this was Finder's life and Finder's house and she'd seen the chickens first, hadn't she? She'd seen them and brought the darkness down and maybe all those years ago she'd been the one to send the sun to its grave, stealing the red from the sky, left with all that plummy black.

Still—this punishment was bearable. It couldn't be compared to the devastation after she was caught with Sofia.

It was all Finder's fault. She took too much from Mab's stores, gave too much of herself away. But Sofia had been so desperate for her help. Her face such a wound. Finder had just wanted to show her the tree—just wanted to share that little fraction of something beautiful, real magic, the kind of awe-striking thing she knew Sofia would adore. Sofia had been so sad that last time, regretful and pleading for help. Finder wanted to make her smile.

"Oh, Finder," Sofia had whispered that night, perched there on her knees pressing her hands to the bark, her eyes falling open like clones of the empty moon. Turning that milky gaze on Finder, miles away, like she was already gone. "I didn't mean for it to happen like this."

Then the creak of the stairs under Mother Mab's heavy footsteps, and the slap raised and ready. That hit had rattled her brain in her skull, Mab's palm still smarting with the shape of Finder's jaw. There had been shouting, words that rang like distant bells in the back of Finder's head, the room still spinning as she fell to her knees and cried out for Sofia to run. Mother Mab sending the Ossifier after her. Finder's arm nearly yanked from its socket as she was dragged to her room, the door barred for the following week and only cracked open for a meal a day. Mab had been almost remorseful on the final morning, when she stood in Finder's doorway, a harbinger of hurt. "That girl was dead the moment she stepped foot in this plane, chick. It's a bargain, crossing so close to death—she made a deal with something that would have happily devoured you both in its fulfillment."

Finder had stared at the wall, curled in on herself in the stale sheets.

"I hope you understand," Mab finished. "I am only trying to keep you safe."

Is this safe? Finder looked at the glass before her, at the jagged edges of her face like fault lines. Her nose ran darkly down her chin.

She wiped the trickle of blood with her knuckles and hooked a finger around her candle's base, slipping back into the hallway, socks catching on splits in the wood floor. Her body ached for rest. When she turned into her room, she let out a gasp that crawled halfway to a scream before she willed it silent.

"What are you doing here?" she whispered to the boy perched on her bed, looking supremely uncomfortable.

"I thought I heard something," he said. In his lap his hands wove together and unraveled. His shirt was buttoned up to his throat. Unruly hair fell beneath his ears.

"It was just me in the bathroom," she answered. "You can go to bed now."

"No." His voice was firm, sure of itself in a manner that surprised both him and Finder. They blinked back at each other. "No, I mean—I heard it outside my window. It was this sloshing noise, like something walking through water."

She thought of Sofia pushing past the lapping waves, her clothes clinging to her skin. Finder looked at her bedroom window as if expecting a different face in the reflection but found only the orange candle glow of her own.

"Well," Finder said, a little annoyed that he seemed to expect *her* of all people to have an explanation for every frightening thing. "You'll get used to that." She blew out her candle with a puff of air. Complete darkness stole across the room.

She sat down on the bed and pulled her knees up close to her chin. The boy remained statuesque.

"Are you alright?" he asked.

"Fine," she answered. Outside, a night bird called, low and throaty.

"I'm sorry she hit you. It wasn't your fault."

"I know that," Finder spat, not trying to be curt but finding it impossible to keep the edge out. "You'll get used to that too."

"Okay. Well, good night," he said, hovering, before finally getting up and making his way to the door.

Finder rolled over in bed, pushing her cheek against the downy pillow, sighing open mouthed into the fabric. She heard him pad quietly down the stairs to the sitting room, with the crackling fireplace and rows of books and battered armchairs, where he'd slept every night for the last week or so, maybe two, maybe three. What was time when you lived in the dark?

She remained sleepless, her mind replaying her every mistake.

When morning came, signaled only by Mother Mab looming over her with a lit candle, Finder gathered the grain basket. The chickens were dead, but the geese still circled the porch, honking loudly beyond the warped wood. Just looking at the black doorway made her heart pound in defiant fear. But she pulled her hair back and rolled the sleeves of her dress to her elbows, looping the basket against the crook of one arm.

"Wait," the boy said as she stepped over the threshold. He lifted a lantern from the dining table and held it up, illuminating their faces. "Let me join you."

Finder stepped over the threshold into the night with the basket bumping against her hip. He hesitated. "Are you coming?" she called over her shoulder, and he hurried after her.

She stayed close to the house, eyeing the fence's border as she tossed handfuls of grain out into the yard. Over the years she had adjusted to the dun world; the faint glow of the lantern was enough for her to make out the tangled grass, insects skittering away from the light. Beyond the clearing where the house nested, her eyes met the pockets between trees where the darkness stood tall and black.

The boy's voice was unsteady. "Did you hear that?"

In the distance, she listened to the locust hum, the gentle twittering of birds made more haunting by the lightless world.

"No," she said. The geese squawked low in their throats and pecked at the ground, pushing aside the grass. The smell of earth and feed rose peaty from the ground. "I didn't think you were the type to be afraid of the dark."

"I'm afraid of the thing that killed your fowl." He glanced around again, uneasily. "Is there a body of water near here?"

"There's a lake about a mile out," Finder answered. "A decent walk. But I haven't been there since—"

She cut herself off. Water, rippling gory and spectral, drooping cattails bending to the current. The pomegranate color of the evening coming over the sky. Sofia's head rising like a submerged animal. There was a moment where she wondered if the boy remembered the sun, or if maybe it was a dream she'd had, a delusion that had trailed her for years and years, some piece of her broken and unable to make sense of the things she saw and heard and tasted and touched.

"Since the light?" he asked, obliterating her last sense of rightness in the world.

"You remember the sun?"

He laughed, but the sound was sharp. "Everyone remembers it."

Not Mother Mab, she thought, not the Ossifier. Only Finder. Only ever Finder.

"Where did you come from?" Finder asked, thinking *where was your home before this and why did you leave?*—but also *what kind of creature are you and were you sent here to haunt me and make me see things I'd thought were gone after all? Were you sent to take her place, to punish me for wanting her back?*

The boy grinned. "Secret."

Finder stomped back to the porch.

"Hey," he called after her, "I'm just kidding." She kept stomping. "I'm from the Basin."

She cut her eyes over to him, keeping her pace until her feet met the porch stairs. "That's nearly a three-day walk from here."

"I told you I'd been walking for a while."

She thought back to the endless night when he'd appeared as a shadow waiting beyond the house's threshold. Her traitorous brain replaced the image with a past hurt, the tree tearing apart the floorboards and Sofia leaning against it, tears nearly silver on her cheeks. There was a split second where Finder imagined telling him all about Sofia.

"Why did you leave?" she said instead.

"You won't believe me."

"I'm gullible."

That made him laugh. "No, you're incorrigible."

She scoffed. But then she caught the serious cast of his eyes.

"They banished me."

"Why?" she insisted again.

"I had a nightmare," he said, with a wry twist of his mouth, "and I saw the end of the world."

He had an earnest face. It seemed impossible for him to force his lips not to turn up. It was so expressive—everything about him was, really, always talking with his hands, furrowing his brows. That was what convinced her he was telling the truth. He was still smiling, like he was sorry.

"What if I don't believe you?"

"What happened to being gullible?"

"I'm a skeptic," Finder said, drily.

"Now she's honest," he said to no one, arms thrown wide and head tipped back to the black sky.

"So what, we all die now? You saw our violent ends?"

The boy fixed her with a heavy look. "I saw a body eat the sun, and when the sun couldn't satisfy it, I saw it rise from the water and spread throughout the valley and the holler and the Basin, and I saw it root down into the earth, and I saw it poison everything in its path. I saw it devour living people and empty souls."

"Oh," Finder said.

"I think we're nearing the end, Finder," he said, softly, like he didn't want to scare her, "and I want to kill this beast before it has a chance to finish us off. That's why the Basin banished me. Because they didn't want to deal with the truth I'd given them."

"I thought it might have been because . . . ," Finder started, and then stopped, blushing, feeling like a fool.

"What, you thought they kicked me out for wearing boy clothes?" He laughed and gestured loosely to his body. She blushed harder. "Yeah, they weren't happy about me being a man, either. But it went over a little easier than telling them I had visions of their violent deaths every night since the sun disappeared."

"So you walked all night, knowing there was something out there?" Finder asked, waving her basket at the woods.

"With my lantern I was able to make it across the mountain." His expression fell, haunted. "But I could hear it following. It made this wet drag, Finder. It was like—like slaughtering an animal, or lifting a drowning thing from the water."

When he looked at Finder, his vivid determination fell across her face. "It was real. I can't stop seeing it, and I won't stand here and let whatever predetermined devastation happen. I think it followed me here, and I want to find it and destroy it, if you'll join me."

It was almost like she could feel the woods breathe behind them, a long and measured exhale, the pleasure of a shared awareness. Her body nearly froze with the settling fear. But she went up the stairs, geese honking in the distance, still alive despite it all.

The last person she'd helped suffered because of her foolish impulses. Finder had been so desperate to keep Sofia that she had destroyed what little thread remained between them. Now she had been abandoned in the dark.

But the Ossifier had followed Sofia into the woods. Finder had watched it happen, before she was dragged from the doorway. And though he denied catching her, claimed that he lost her somewhere out in those unforgiving woods, Finder had always been convinced of the possibility. The Ossifier was a liar. It was entirely reasonable that Sofia hadn't returned because of something he did to her. Or maybe whatever creature the boy saw found her first.

The thought was hot enough to scorch, and Finder wanted to shove it back to the recesses of her mind. A selfish, terrible part of her preferred the monstrous answer. A creature was beyond her capability and comprehension—from behind her bedroom door, Finder never could have kept Sofia safe from what lived beyond the fence. The Ossifier was a different horror, one that belonged to Finder alone, one that she had brought Sofia directly to. That blood was on Finder's hands.

If the Ossifier hurt Sofia, she decided then and there on the porch steps, she would kill him herself. She would kill anything. She would become a hunter.

The fear took root in her. But she could find proof. She could go into the woods, face death, look the black water in its face.

Finder turned back to the boy. He hadn't moved, just watched her reach for the doorknob.

"Well?" he said.

"Fine. We'll seek it out, since you crave death so badly." She shouldered the door open. "But let's have breakfast first."

22

SONECHKA AND HER LIKABLE BIRDS

Something carried her to the tree.

It's a thought that continues in her mind without a beginning or an end, a trailing sentence that waxes and wanes. She'd been too far gone to walk then. Her skull all wet and cracked. Something scooped her up, held the limp hang of her neck against their shoulder, strong grasp around her waist.

Now she's no longer herself, just a shape that's been standing for some time, cold from the wind, mouth heavy and dry, so unbearably, irreparably tired.

She's becoming a repeater. A doll with a string in its back, learning the absent world—death not a final animal but the sensation of seeing a million unrecognizable colors. Just as brutal and sensitive as the plane she was a part of before, when her blood pumped her to life.

Moments between consciousness: There she is, blue in the back of Cass's truck, bruised in Marya's bathtub, prone in Poppy's bed, standing over Frankie's as she sleeps, reaching for Finder across heart-colored light. She presses her rotten hand to her rib cage, trying to hold herself together. It hurts to even think the names.

Repeater girl. Say it again because it's better than losing it completely.

But she is forgetting. Her own name escapes her now, and her fingers are just cellophane things without prints. She can't remember the sensation of solid ground. Her toes drag the earth.

It is so hard to haunt, so much harder than slipping away. She wants to drink it all up. To go where she once stood, danced, slept, kissed. She wants some taste of the life she had, back before her shadow's reflection became an entity of its own. Before it began to swell with life, heavy with feeding, its rooted head hanging over an arched and imposing back.

It follows her, impatient. It wants to bring her somewhere it believes she could belong. It's hard to be mad at it, her changing shadow, when it operates under some other creature's thumb. Hadn't she felt that way once? Trapped by something larger than herself, out of control, clinging for any possible hold on power? Hadn't she tried to conjure a future that felt like hers? She remembers slicing herself open, red dripping into flame, remembers tilting her head to look the dark figure in its face.

A LIFE FOR A LIFE, the creature says, bending to meet her eyes over the fire, and she's afraid. A deal is only ever an imprisonment if she can't uphold her end of the bargain.

At times she straddles worlds. Everything is sharper in that darkened plane, past the fence's boundary, chickens clucking in a black yard. Sometimes she blinks and the abandoned house stands atop its hill under the cruel white of the sun. Blink and there it is again in the plummy night, warping with a heat wave ripple. Something begs to be summoned. It demands completion. It tears her shadow from her spine and pits it against her. It can see all the hollow spaces where she failed to devote herself. The doors of the house strain against their hinges. The floorboards splinter, and something spills out through the cracks, roaring like the winds of a hurricane.

Blink, and evening softens all the broken boards. The house stands under the deep blue mirror of the sky, all peaks and siding and lattice, porch like a skirt slipping from its hips. The old tree, emptied of her body, pokes gaping holes through the house's roof—branches crawl toward the clouds as if they might one day take flight.

She fights for solidity. The dirt road taunts her dragging feet. She stood here once, before she gave herself over to the red world and her offering ripped her in neat halves. That awful night. Burning wood and spilled beer and dewy grass and hot breeze. That boy's mouth on the back of her neck, whispering a wish there, trying to tether her to him. She had worked so hard to make him want her. Why did she resent him when her efforts finally paid off?

The fire building tall, flames reflected in Poppy's eyes and the smarting flesh of her split knuckles. The choice in that gaze, coaxing her forward, asking her to decide.

Poppy—the name summons something long buried. She touches her mouth. Thinks of water beneath her hands, of falling through time. Has she made her mother proud?

Sofia. Right, that's her name.

She flickers and changes.

23

Names and Their Mysterious Origins

Poppy waited for them in the dark. Fear was a stone in her belly—she folded her arms and cupped her elbows to hush her shivering. She was too cold for summer and the moon was a white fingernail clipping and her head ached with the reminder of a voice booming through it.

Tonight she'd see where they'd left Sofia's body behind. She would no longer be able to deny it.

The first time they went to the house, all those years ago, Poppy could smell magic in the air. A fire burned somewhere. She felt timeless, at once ancient and young, learning and learned, her head tipped to the sky and her jacket draped over her shoulders to let the breeze hold her body.

They'd left Cass's truck on a dirt road and walked the rest of the way through the woods. No one had an address. It was a sensation more than a destination, a knowing of the land, an unspoken recognition of seedy corners and the promise of danger.

"If they don't want to get caught, they're doing an awful job," Cass had said, rubbing her hands over her bare arms. "You can smell that fire from a mile away."

Poppy could smell something tinny, too, like roadkill and kerosene and hulled metal. The path twisted intestinal through the woods. She kept her eyes trained forward, unwilling to look directly into the darkness. Overhead, the moon was orange and harvest heavy. She could just make out the glow of flame intercepted by flickering opaque shapes, like the trees had split away from their trunks and stood up to face her. Distant music carried toward them, a spell—*come closer come closer come closer*. The fire waited like a lamp down the hall.

"Is Sof already here?" she asked, trying not to sound as exposed as she felt.

"I texted her," Frankie said, which wasn't really an answer.

"She said they would be here around eleven," Cass amended. Her fingers were tucked beneath her armpits now.

They broke into a clearing where the fire climbed higher than their heads. Poppy could see fragments of wood pallets among the flames, some furniture broken down. There was an old house near the gathering where someone must have pilfered the tinder. Some had driven all the way down the muddy road and parked around the building flames, where they could perch in the back of their car or truck among nests of quilts. Poppy desperately searched for Sofia among them, against the stubborn urge to remain casual.

"You good?" Cass asked, looping an arm around her waist. Poppy almost flinched, almost pulled herself away, but she fought the instinct and remained rigid under Cass's touch, steeling herself to ignore the glances everyone else would throw their way. Shame settled heavy in her—she shouldn't have to worry about what other people might think when they saw Cass with her like that. Straight girls got to be affectionate with one another all the time. Why did every minute have to be a coming out? Why did she have to flay herself open for these people who cared nothing about her?

"Hey. I'm talking to you."

Cass rested her hold at the hem of Poppy's shirt. A tender brush of a thumb against her abdomen was all it took to yank her back to the present moment.

"I'm okay," Poppy said. She leaned into Cass and willed herself not to spiral into missing it before it was gone.

They sidestepped places where the ground was uneven, the sky spilling with star-glow. Firelight made every figure around it into a wriggling creature. But then she saw—the familiar shape of her, the outline of a body she knew as well as her own.

"There she is," Poppy said, humiliated when the words came out like a sigh of relief.

Lucas had his arm around Sofia as they perched on the tailgate of his truck, and Poppy watched his skin illuminate red as if she could ignite it with her gaze alone.

Music crooned, exactly the kind of twangy tune that always made her feel like she was watching her body from the outside, marveling at how out of place it could be in the land where it had been raised. Poppy picked up the pace. Her long legs covered the sloping side of the hill faster than Cass's or Frankie's could, and they had to hurry to keep up with her. Sofia turned, eyes flashing with delight when they found Poppy's.

Lucas didn't acknowledge them at all, just tightened his hold around Sofia's shoulders.

"Remember," Frankie said, in a quiet tone that suggested she hadn't meant for Poppy to hear it at all. "You said midnight."

"I know, Frank, midnight, no later. Have I ever lied to you?"

"Finally," Sofia said once they were in earshot. Her smile was a notched arrow. "I was starting to think you wouldn't come at all." Lucas reached across her and placed a lit joint between her lips. Sofia inhaled as her eyelids fell. Poppy wanted to look away, but her gaze landed on Sofia's mouth.

"Chill," Sofia said when Frankie sighed in her direction, smoke following the sound of her voice like one of Oph's extinguished candles. She leaned back on an arm and fixed her sister with a challenging stare. Poppy followed it and found Frankie frowning back in disapproval. "It's mostly mugwort anyway."

That made Frankie's frown deepen. Poppy didn't claim to be an expert on what Sofia sometimes wrote out as *magick*, but she'd been on the other end of one of those mugwort cigarettes before—lying on her back among Sofia's sheets, tipping her chin up for the joint to be pressed to her lips, inhaling and watching the green of Sofia's eyes go hungry. "For prophetic dreams," her girl had said, before kissing the corner of Poppy's mouth. "To see our future."

"Ours?" Poppy had asked, wanting it so badly that she thought she might cry. But Sofia just touched her cheek like she was already saying goodbye.

"Does he know that?" Frankie asked. Lucas scoffed. Sofia plucked the joint from his hands and held it out for Poppy, cocking her head in question. Poppy bent and took a drag from between Sofia's fingers, where her mouth had just been moments before, lips nearly brushing the skin there. She could hear her blood in her ears. Her eyes flickered low beneath the lids and caught on Sofia's palm, where a ragged cut split her heart line in two. Poppy fought the urge to reach for it.

"Me next," Cass said, earning another smile from Sofia—a real one, where her eyes crinkled like fine tissue paper at the corners.

Sofia tugged at the hem of her skirt as Cass smoked, and Lucas looked back at the sound of his name. She'd always been fidgety when she was nervous. But what did she have to be nervous about when Poppy was the one shaking?

Up close the house was a leaning animal in the night, illuminated by thrown embers. Poppy could see people standing on the porch and tipping back beers as the breeze rustled foliage all around them, the whole forest coming to life.

Footsteps sounded behind her. "Dude," Tommy said as he clapped hands with Lucas. He gave the rest of them a cursory glance, ending with a half nod in Sofia's direction and a self-satisfied smirk. Something twisted in Poppy's stomach, displeasure at remembering that others saw Sofia just as she did—beautiful, magnetic, coy. But when she turned Sofia was looking at her, gaze warmer than the fire.

The music shifted. Something a little heavier ground out of someone's speakers. Chills rose on the nape of Poppy's neck. Cass laughed when Frankie muttered indistinctly and Poppy tuned back into Tommy's slow voice, the same drawl he'd had since they were kids, deeper now.

"I told Alex to bring his own shit," Tommy was saying, thumping the back of a fist against Lucas's chest. "He's in the house."

"Please don't tell me you're doing drugs with my little brother," Cass said sharply, all laughter draining away. Lucas glanced to Sofia like she might interject, but Sofia reached out a hand and let it rest against the pendant of Poppy's necklace, leisurely running the pad of her thumb over it. This close, she could feel the heat of Sofia's skin before it pressed against her collarbone. Poppy leaned in like a devotee. If she could have pulled away, she might have seen Lucas's face shutter. But it took everything in her to even stay still.

Tommy scowled. "Oh shit, my bad, I forgot I was talking to narcs. You gonna write us up, hall monitor?"

Poppy turned just in time to watch Cass scowl back. "No, but I'll be the one forced to take care of him tonight, and I'm not in the mood. He's thirteen, Tommy."

"Do you know what I was doing when I was thirteen, Sullivan?" He scoffed. Then his eyes gleamed with pleasure. "Probably the same things you were doing," he added, holding two fingers up to his mouth and wiggling his tongue between them suggestively.

"Fuck off," Sofia snapped, suddenly cold. Lucas and Tommy both glanced at her. She kept her shoulders tipped back with the joint pinned between her fingers, still absently fiddling with Poppy's necklace. The smoke made a halo around the tufts of her hair and the space between the two of them. Poppy knew that look, saw the challenge in it, remembered loving her senselessly. "If you ever speak to her like that again, I'll peel your fucking skin off your bones."

There was anger in the flat line of Tommy's jaw, but he just pushed away from the tailgate. "Whatever." To Lucas, he said: "Your girlfriend is a cunt."

Lucas followed and shoved Tommy hard, but his face remained neutral. "I'll be back later," he said to Sofia.

"Excuse me?"

Even Poppy was surprised by the sound of her own voice, flat as obsidian. Her heart was a caged bird. It slammed against her ribs, begging to be set free. She hadn't meant to speak, didn't intend on getting mixed up in whatever Tommy was trying to start—but she saw crimson at the corners of her vision. Sofia kept her frozen in place with her thumb on the gold.

"Jesus H. Christ, it's like a family of wardens," Tommy said.

Poppy leveled Lucas with a stare and spoke before her bravado could abandon her. "You're gonna let him talk about her like that?"

"He's not worth it," Sofia muttered, giving the necklace a tug. Poppy wanted to ask who exactly she meant—that if Lucas wasn't worth it, after all this time, why did she keep choosing him? Why, when Poppy knew that she would have given Sofia anything she could have ever asked for? That she loved her. That it ached.

"She's right," Frankie interrupted, tipping her chin in Tommy's direction. "Apologize to her."

"I'm over this," Tommy snapped. He backed up and Lucas trailed close behind him, shaking his head.

But Poppy rocked forward, possessed, ignited. She felt the necklace slip out of Sofia's grasp as she stepped into Lucas's space. "Tell him to apologize."

"For what?" Lucas drawled. It was clear that he wanted to be intimidating, but Poppy was taller than the rest of them, her eyes resting just at Lucas's nose. She liked how close she came to meeting him face-to-face, so she bit her words extra hard.

"For calling her a cunt."

"It's really not a big deal," Sofia said, but she was watching Poppy like she was a star cupped in her open palm.

Lucas stared down at her for a long moment before the façade of his face finally shattered. "Apologize, Kowalski."

"Oh my god," Tommy groaned. "Who fucking cares. I'm sorry. You're not a cunt, but the rest of your friends are." He took off toward the house without another glance in their direction.

"Happy?" Lucas asked Poppy, sneering.

Poppy's mouth stretched wide, more grimace than anything else, her heart rising like an orchestra. "No," she said, and she punched him.

Lucas staggered back, clutching his jaw, but Poppy was there again, shoving him hard in the chest. Her knuckles sang. She was elastic, her body ready to react. Everyone was watching them now, the crowd a collection of open-mouthed gasps that quickly dissolved into whoops and flash videos.

"Stop!" Sofia called, hopping down from the tailgate. "Please, Poppy, don't."

Poppy, her broad shoulders, her victorious smile, her glasses slipping down her nose. Her face growing warm as sun on the mountainside as they stepped closer to the fire. She was an entirely different person, unhinged and untethered, hungry for more. Lucas's nose bled down his chin, splattered against the pale blue of his T-shirt. He lunged forward as if to swing at Poppy but Sofia was suddenly there between them and pushing them apart. Poppy couldn't even hear her. Lucas's finger was in her face but she was still smiling, and no matter how close he came, she didn't flinch.

Among the rising jeers, she could pick out Cass's desperate babble: "Oh fuck, fucking hell, Frank, this is bad."

But Frankie was laughing and laughing and laughing, the sound high as a newborn bird, hard enough to promise a stomachache. Everyone stared. Poppy looked at Frankie and her face was a picture of joy, a laugh mirrored there when their eyes met.

And then someone yelled, "Cops!"

Poppy saw trees go red and blue before she heard the distant whoop of the sirens. Suddenly she stumbled into a run, and when her brain caught up with her legs she realized it was Cass pulling her along, Frankie already a length ahead of them.

Wait, where is she, we left her behind, I need to—

Her thoughts died just as fast as they came, Cass's hold so tight, the ground pocked where past rain had collected, Poppy's feet catching on roots and rocks and the skinny arches of felled trees. Branches scratched fine lines across her cheek that stung in the wind, running and running and running and—

Sprawling, Frankie first as the ground suddenly sloped down, then Cass quickly following, the hand laced with Poppy's yanking them both to the ground. Poppy hit it hard, somersaulting once, twice, before she landed on her back.

"Oh," she said when her breath returned to her chest.

"Shh," Frankie said beside her ear.

The three of them pressed low to the ground, Cass whimpering about her wrist until Frankie hushed her again and examined it with tender fingers. The woods were bathed in color. They heard distant voices, the sound of a megaphone. Something crawled behind Poppy's ear. The forest teemed with life, watching the disaster unfold and feeding off the chaos it created.

"Where's Sofia?" Cass whispered, an echo of Poppy's earlier thoughts now gone sour.

They had left her behind. Poppy had left her.

Then the beam of light landing on them, burning her up—Cass's fed-up dad saying, "Goddamn it, Cassandra."

A ride home in a cop car. Poppy's mother waiting silently in the dead door frame. Poppy storming away to her room after a fight that would render them strangers—then slipping right back out the window, her feet thudding on the grass.

They wouldn't learn until hours later, dawn annihilating the dark as they gathered in Frankie's bedroom. Cass tended to the scrapes on Poppy's elbow as Poppy wrapped Cass's wrist and Frankie dialed Sofia repeatedly, the line falling flat with each call.

"Holy shit," Cass whispered at last, her phone in her hands and her chin resting on her knees. The glow illuminated her face.

They watched it unfold on someone's grainy video—running and yelling, people darting for the abandoned house to hide, Tommy leaping onto the porch and the rotting wood snapping beneath him. The roar he let out as his leg plunged through, the eruption of screams. Lucas nowhere in sight, though he would later claim that he had been right behind Tommy, just out of frame and ready to help.

And Sofia, gone. Her car waiting like an open casket.

All my fault.

She would think of that night for years to come. Would dream of it in hot, white bursts—the anticipation in her chest, Sofia's hold around her necklace, Poppy's fist and her thumb safe outside of it. How it had all been a catalyst. How she had understood in that moment that everything she wanted was just so slightly out of her reach. That it would never be hers to love, only hers to lose, and it would always be her burden to bear.

24

WORSHIPPED ONE DAY ON ETERNAL ALTARS

Frankie eased the front door shut behind her and clicked the latch into place with a careful hand. The house was dark and silent, save for the living room lamp. She'd showered and eaten something cold out of the fridge, scrunched her fingers through the damp wave of her hair. The breeze made her shiver as it dried against her neck.

Cass was late. Anticipation and anxiety built inside of Frankie until they were one melded rhythm that sounded like *tonight, tonight, tonight.*

"Where are you off to?" Sissa asked.

Frankie jumped. "I'm starting to think y'all try to scare me on purpose," she said, meeting Sissa's gaze in the dark where she perched on the porch swing. Something half-knitted had been abandoned to her lap. A candle lit up the left side of her face, bisecting the curious expression there.

"You sound like your mother when you talk like that," she said, wistfully.

People loved to say things like this to her, always had—*you look like your mother, you sound like your sister, you remind us of the dead, you're here and they're not.*

"I wouldn't know," Frankie answered finally, smarting.

Her mother had taken her to lunch once when she was a kid. Frankie had cried a little bit in the car's back seat where no one could see her—private, happy tears, the overwhelming joy of being chosen. She'd always compared herself to Sofia. She'd always wanted to be better.

Across from her in the diner booth, Fiona swiped a thumb over Frankie's cheek, though the damp tracks had long since dried. "You're such a sad little kid," Fiona said, leaning down until they met at eye level. "I wish I could tell you it won't be that way someday. But I think I'm still trying to grow out of it, too."

Frankie remembered her heart breaking. But she also remembered looking at her mother and thinking, *if I can be like her by the time all those years pass, I can handle the sadness too.*

Except now there would come a day when Frankie grew older than her mother. And she was still fucking sad.

Sissa went to her as if she could see the feeling written in her face, smoothing back Frankie's hair. "How about we have a cup of tea before you go? You look stressed."

Frankie looked at the empty driveway, her phone silent against her thigh. "I'm running late."

Sissa's gaze darkened. "You know, your aunt is too proud to say so, but she's been making herself sick with worry. I hope you're not getting yourself wrapped up in any trouble, for her sake."

What was trouble, really? What could be any worse than the way Frankie felt in this moment? Her grief had become so enormously a part of her that it was nearly something she wanted to live for. There would always be a compulsive need to prove that she was good for something after all.

"I can't trust anyone else to help her. I need to do it myself. If I don't, then no one will, and I can't let that—" Frankie's throat constricted. Sissa had known her since before she was born. Frankie's family mythology was Sissa's too—she knew all about the rosebush and when Oph pulled thorns from her mom's thighs after a drunken fall, about

Sofia's shitty haircuts and the time Frankie went under the water until they had to pump it from her lungs. But somehow the thought of another person seeing her cry—familiar or foreign—made her want to die.

"I'm trying to do what's right," she repeated, as if she knew what that meant. "I just want to know what I'm missing."

"Come inside," Sissa said. She squeezed Frankie's elbow. "Just for a moment."

She went right for the kitchen. Frankie reluctantly followed. Sissa deftly turned on the finicky stove burner and filled the room with a low glow. Cabinets shut with a bang as she searched through tins of tea and a stock of handmade candles, cursing Oph under her breath for rearranging. The kettle squealed on the stove as Sissa struck a match and held it to a cone of incense. With her empty hand she waved myrrh into the air.

Floorboards creaked in the hall as the kitchen filled with haze. The scent drew Oph to the doorway like a fly to honey, sticky and sweet. She was already in her pajamas, softly tucking a yellow robe tighter around her middle. Behind hanks of hair her eyes were sleepy, her mouth slack with comfort. Something about Sissa's presence reduced Oph's authority. It softened her, brought her down to Frankie's level. There was someone else there to take care of them both.

"Tea?" Sissa asked over her shoulder, and the nod Oph gave her was heavy and aware in a way that almost made Frankie feel like they'd forgotten she still stood in the room.

When Oph finally turned, her expression had hardened back into something masked. She led Frankie to the dining table with a gentle hold around her wrist. "Sit," Oph ordered as she took the seat at the head, face cleared of emotion except for the little tug of her chin that Frankie recognized as fear.

It was all just a party trick, smoke and mirrors. But something twisted in Frankie's stomach. She hesitated, ears rushing with the heavy sound of her own heartbeat, and pulled out the chair to Oph's right.

Sissa joined them with a delicate teacup. The rim was chipped where Sofia once dropped it, and fine leaves swirled along the surface of the steaming water. She stopped beside Oph's seat, resting a gentle hand on the back of her neck. They bent together.

Oph knocked back the cup. Sissa sighed like she could feel the warmth of the liquid, the sound of her breath gold and dreamy. Frankie could just barely make out the clinging bits of green stuck to the sides of the ceramic. She wanted to bend closer, even as the logical part of her brain resented whatever the leaves might spell.

"Here," Oph said. They peered into the cup together. "A line leads away."

"Oh, don't say that," Sissa whispered, but her face was slack with wonder.

"It's a long journey, just beginning." Oph's pupils were blown wide. Frankie couldn't look away. "A snake marks tension in her path. Or maybe roots?"

"Roots," Sissa said excitedly. "Definitely roots."

"Tangled and overgrown and in need of being hacked away," Oph answered.

"It will be dark as night?" Sissa asked.

Oph splayed her fingers against the table. "Darker."

"Come on," Frankie interrupted. "This is pointless."

They looked at her. There was a half smile on Oph's face, a vague thing that made the shape of her unfamiliar and eerie. All her clucking joy had drained away—in its place was an absent summoned self that reminded Frankie too much of being a kid in her mother's presence, wildly out of control of her future.

"You are playing with something you don't understand," Oph said finally.

How could they know what Frankie did and didn't comprehend? They hadn't seen what she had over those early years, those fractured pieces of memory—her mother slumped in front of a mirror, a spilled glass of water on the floor. Forehead pressed to the floor with her palms up in offering. Blurred figures circling her, flickers of shadow that Frankie caught in unreliable glances. Her mother's voice blending into something else, portentous: *I have a daughter and I pray she may outlive me. Keep her safe so that I might continue in her memory.* A daughter—only ever one, Frankie desperately wanting to know which one of them her mother's words were meant to represent but too afraid to learn the answer.

Books left open and pages dog-eared, passages that told of offerings and séances, of unearthly power, of planes and worlds beyond. Text in her mother's hand, pen pressed hard enough to tear through the page, instructions that spoke of slipping under the water and emerging in a spirit-walking world. Images that left Frankie terrified and sent her scrambling for Sofia's room—their secret knock spelled out against the wood—and Sofia lifting the blankets to let Frankie crawl in beside her. *Sleep, bird:* her sister's voice from the other side of the bed, groggy and distant. Only then would Frankie shut her eyes.

There was no point in lying. If they could claim to see her future, then maybe they knew her steps before she could take them, her path a glowing line across the world punctuated with the abandoned structure where her sister's body had waited alone.

"It's just a house." Frankie faltered, like she didn't quite believe the words herself. But it was the truth. It was just a house. Sofia was just a girl, flesh and blood like Frankie was, just as fickle and capable of death.

"Frances," Oph said, like a eulogy.

Sissa stared into the cup. "It's more than that. You know that just as well as we do."

But it wasn't an omen, an albatross in the dark. It was just a gravesite.

"I'm doing what I can to fix this," Frankie said, "I feel like I'm the only one who's even trying. She was my *sister*." She looked at them, her family who had raised her in some shape or form. "Doesn't that mean anything to you?"

She meant, *wasn't my mother something like a sister to you? Didn't it tear you apart when she was gone, too?*

"I wish I could see more clearly," Oph said, so softly. "But Fiona was the best of us. She was so good at what she did."

It always came back to her mother. Prophet, priestess, glass-walker. Her mother blowing mugwort smoke out a cracked window, beckoning Frankie to come and sit with her on the couch, pressing her cheek to the top of Frankie's head. Humming so low in her throat that the sound took on the quality of ritual.

They watched her. She looked back, feeling petulant, like her feet were planted at the edge of a jutting cliff.

"You shouldn't go," Sissa said at last. Frankie started to retort. "Oh, honey, we already know you will."

"You can see that?" she asked.

"Not exactly," Oph said. "We just know how you are."

How you are. Frankie's spine itched, like her skeleton was trying to climb its way out of her skin. How unsettling it was to be known. Who she was now was an entirely different creature than who she'd been before her life fell apart; venomously uncharted territory.

Oph circled the table. She stopped behind Frankie's chair and touched her shoulder, gently pinning her in place. "You have your mother's wildness in you. You have her magic. I can't tell you what to do, or force you to believe me, but I wish you would stay."

Frankie's chest tightened. She could smell myrrh, the cling of incense, charcoal and antiseptic tinctures. *Hers,* she thought, *never mine.*

"Please, leave it alone and go to bed."

Frankie looked at her aunt in the reflection of a framed painting, the glass dusty and speckled with candlelight. Behind her Oph was ghoulish and all-knowing.

"I promised to keep you safe," her aunt insisted, her mouth a dark cavern in the ghostly mirror image, "and you're making me a liar."

The crunch of gravel under tires announced the Ford's arrival. Frankie shut her eyes and let herself be grounded by that hand on her shoulder.

"Cass is waiting on me," she said finally.

They let her go, screen door banging.

Cass and Poppy waited in the cab. Frankie and Marya stretched out in the back. Wheels rolled over asphalt beneath the starry and cloudless black. With her skull pressed to the rear windshield of the truck, Frankie dragged her gaze upward and buried her fear somewhere abyssal.

Heart in her throat, pulse in her wrists, she grieved for Sofia's body decaying in a room meant for examination, never to see the stars again. She grieved for herself, because here she was looking at the big sky and watching the mountains make slumped shapes beneath it and feeling so small in this massive and discombobulated world that she wanted to cry.

The night was alive. The night had teeth in rows and rows.

Her thigh kept brushing against Marya's, the quiet warmth of it too nice to pull away from. It was that delicious sensation of summer, when the air was so heavy with honeysuckle that each breath came wet and leaden under all the pollen. Still—Frankie felt fire-light, bird-nimble.

The road gave way to dirt. There were more churches in Loring than there were grocery stores, but the old one they passed with its rotting steeple always felt like something impenetrable and ancient, a portal to a different plane. A cross clung crookedly to the spire, tilted in a balancing act.

The house came too quick. Goose bumps curdled along Frankie's arms as the early summer heat gave way to a breezier altitude. Her shoulder knocked Marya's when they bumped over roots and she prayed that her chills weren't visible, embarrassment peeking past the collar of her T-shirt.

Once, it'd been a beautiful Victorian. She could see it in the gingerbread trim dripping from the roof, the sharp juts of the gables. Scalloped wood siding previously hammered carefully into place now hung like baby teeth ready to be pulled. The windows blinked back at them, gaping wounds in the sides of the house. The truck rolled to a stop at the base of the hill sloping up toward the house's porch. Frankie forced herself to drink it in. *You are my sister's coffin,* she thought to herself, letting it hurt as much as it needed to.

A brush of fingertips against her knee deepened her chills. "Okay?" Marya asked.

Her gaze was so intense, murky eyes shimmering with stars caught up in the brown. Frankie blinked back, and sucked her bottom lip between her teeth to force herself to think before she spoke.

"Fine," she said, after a beat.

"Let's get this over with," Cass said as she slammed the truck door behind her.

Frankie hauled her way out of the bed, full-on shivering now, teeth chattering. She always forgot it would be like this—that the mountains would carry them high above the heat until there was nothing left but biting air. She wanted to ask the others if they felt as awful as she did in that moment—if they looked at this house and remembered that night, Sofia's chin raised in challenge, Lucas's sneering face. Poppy's fist swinging before Frankie could make sense of it. Running and running, losing Sofia once, losing her forever, leaving her behind—and the groaning of the house splintering and Tommy's distant scream.

Why had she left? Why hadn't she waited? Why hadn't she reached for her sister instead, snatched her wrist, pulled her to safety?

The porch was in an even sorrier state now. Years of disuse had allowed it to sink further, and Frankie was hesitant to test its integrity. She swiped her clammy hands on her shorts. Now she saw the death trap for what it was, smelled distant smoke on the air.

I want to go home, Frankie thought, her mouth dry as she imagined water rushing to the shore, but she didn't know if it was true, didn't know if home meant what it was supposed to mean. She allowed herself a split-second thought, even as it seared her—*I want to go home with Sofia.*

Poppy shouldered the door open with one hard shove. Caution tape still clung to the windows. They took careful steps across the sagging porch and the floor went soft beneath Frankie's shoes.

"This place is a dump," Cass said. Her voice bounced around the sunken room.

"It's always been a dump." Poppy stepped gingerly over a pile of what seemed to be some of the ceiling and peered down a dark hallway.

Frankie swept a flashlight across the doorways, the night making creatures out of every shape and sound. Anxiety jogged in time with her blood. Is this what Sofia had felt, the night that she died? Watched by every corner? Had she been dead already, by the time they stuffed her into that tree? Had she called out for Frankie? For any of them? For their mother, long dead?

If the universe were fair, this place would be impenetrable. They would have razed it to the ground after the wood ripped the meat of Tommy's calf right open. There would be police in here right now marking down every minuscule detail with the intention of bringing justice for Sofia.

But the house still stood, and it was empty save for their breath, and the thought made Frankie want to be sick. Because the police either didn't care who killed Sofia, or they knew already. And either idea was enough to make her want to stop moving altogether.

Collapsed ceiling blocked off some entryways. A jagged path remained where the boys who found Sofia had carved their way through. It led to a sunken doorway, wide and watching like an eye. Over Marya's shoulder, Frankie could make out the shape of the tree. Deep silhouettes left inky impressions and the flicker of her own shadow made her jump, imagining for a second that her sister was following her room to room, a cast shape against the peeling wallpaper.

"In here," Marya called, ducking into the doorway.

Frankie pressed a hand to her collarbone to ease the pinch of her grief. She addressed the trunk with a straightforward stare, flashlight a stark accuser against the bark. Marya stepped forward. The house gave a dull creak. Frankie felt Cass behind her, huffing quietly under her breath, and Poppy cleared her throat in the doorway. Something skittered overhead, and suddenly Frankie was thinking of rats and beetles and her sister's skin and she really was going to be sick, to collapse, to fade until nothing remained.

Cass touched her back. "Go outside if you need to," she murmured, thickly.

Frankie nodded. Words were impossible. She kept moving, one foot in front of the other, circling the tree. The trouble with being a twin was the sharing of a face. Sometimes when she pictured Sofia, all she could see was her own reddened cheeks, the wild vines of her hair climbing toward the sun. It was hard to separate the two of them and still feel alive. She looked at the tree and imagined herself looking back.

It stood before her, gouged and shredded. Caution tape hung in limp tendrils. Her light reflected against the yellow, sharp enough to make her squint. A sound slipped from her lips; an involuntary gasp, loud and too low. Marya's shoes crunched glass to her left. They stood together in the dark.

"I thought—" Poppy started, but the words fell away. Frankie mentally finished the sentence for her. *I thought I'd see her.*

Because she had. She'd thought, for one awful and endless moment, that she would step into this house and stand before this tree and see her sister curled inside its trunk, body bruised and blue, grin eaten away into bared teeth. Marya looked into the gouge like she saw that very thing. Her eyes went soft, her mouth an uncertain line. Cass looked away.

Instead of a body, there were tiny flowers growing in the trunk. The first sprouts of unfurling chrysanthemums bloomed. They were bright against the bark, pale shades of white and yellow, spilling onto the floor in bunches. Poppy brushed a knuckle against one of the flowers, the sodden tracks her tears had left down her cheeks glistening under the illumination of their flashlights.

"How are they growing here?" Cass whispered.

"This place is wrong," Marya said finally, her voice rough with disuse. "There's something—" She cocked her head, tracking. "Can you smell the smoke?"

Frankie had thought it was just her memory, the bonfire high and wide. But it was weighted like winter, warm as cedar. She stepped closer to the tree and tried to memorize the sight of the flowers growing there, feeling like she was looking at a crack in the universe, something she was never supposed to witness. She didn't know what to say, so she sucked a deep breath through her nose.

A broken mirror leaned up against the wall behind the tree. Frankie's reflection moved beyond the trunk, her flashlight refracting back at her, and for some reason the sight was awful enough to send her reeling back. Her eyes trailed further down the bark, following drips of sap along the rigid edges. At the foot of the tree the floor began to split. Roots tore between planks of wood and snaked around their feet, dead flowers floating among them. Circles on the ground surrounded the trunk—places where wax had melted down and stained the boards. Candles. Her mind said *ritual* then immediately leapt back from the thought like it had been burned. She knew, of course, had read the police reports. But the visual was chilling. Something in her flared, solar-hot.

She thought of her mother, blank stare in the looking glass. Of her head held underwater, water choking in her lungs.

It didn't mean anything. They were stains. Not proof. But she knelt and ran her fingers over the little rings anyway. Then Frankie tipped her head back and looked into the black belly of the trunk. In her mind she saw herself stuffed inside of it, the girl with her face and her life, repeated.

Everything was oversaturated. When Frankie spoke, the sound came out wrong. "I don't think I can be in this room any longer."

Marya crouched beside her. The dark made her gaunt and terrifying, but Frankie found comfort in the sight, in looking at a face and not knowing it well enough yet to fill out the missing pieces. She held out a hand. Frankie took it. Together, they got to their feet.

They were headed for the doorway when Frankie caught something new in the mirror's reflection. There was a shape behind her, featureless and trembling, with exaggerated limbs and a hunched stance. But when she spun to face it, she saw only Poppy in front of the tree, reaching for it.

"What are you doing?" Frankie asked. The shadows wriggled around them. Her heart thundered in her ears and the dank smell of rotting earth mixing with dead fire overtook her. Had she really seen something, or was it her mind's nightmarish invention?

"Poppy," Cass said. "Come on. Let's get out of here, there's nothing left."

Poppy didn't move. In the dusk she made a haunting shape, flashlights illuminating the deep pockets of her cheeks and the long lines of her lashes. Marya stepped toward the tree with a hand outstretched, like she was ready to pull Poppy away.

"Is everything okay?" Marya asked.

"Poppy," Frankie repeated. She wanted to leave. Now. If she stayed in here one moment longer she'd fall apart, she'd lash out, she'd—

"This isn't funny." Cass's voice held a tinge of fear. She moved toward Poppy now, too, stumbling over something and righting herself in a rush.

Marya held up slow, splayed fingers. Poppy's mouth hung open. Her eyes, usually heavy-lidded and intense behind her glasses, were glazed over.

MY ROOTS WILL DRINK THEIR FILL, Poppy said, in a voice that belonged to no living thing. Her lips didn't move. Her mouth was a frozen gasp.

Frankie's heart stuttered in its rhythm, stopped and kick-started all at once. Cass rocked back on her heels. "What the fuck, Pops?"

AND MY LEAVES WILL SWELL WITH BLOOD, HEAVY LIKE RAINWATER, RED LIKE FRUIT AND TONGUES AND WOUNDS. I WILL TAKE THE ONE I DESIRE TO THE TREE AND THEY WILL BECOME ENERGY, AND ENERGY WILL BECOME ME.

Marya's hand hung in the air, suspended.

"That's not her voice," Cass said, but it came out like a plea. "It's not."

Poppy's jaw twitched, her palm flat against the bark. The whites of her eyes appeared like pupal insects. *I LIKE THE SHAPE OF THIS ONE,* the voice said. *SHE WILL BE A MEAL FIT FOR A GOD, A GIRL MADE FOR MY TABLE.*

"Stop it," Frankie said, blood rushing everywhere, everywhere, everywhere. "Whatever you are."

ONCE I ATE A GIRL WHO CRUSHED SOURLY BETWEEN MY TEETH.

The flowers started to rot and die before their eyes, sweet pastels turning a sickly gray. They melted around where Poppy touched the trunk, slid over her knuckles, underneath her nails. Frankie felt the world warp as spidery fingers pushed through the melt.

Something began to crawl out of the tree.

The manifested hand locked around Poppy's other forearm. She let out a ragged scream as it yanked her toward the tree.

"Grab her!" Marya yelled.

Darkness ran up Poppy's skin, staining her wrist. Frankie rushed at the tree, grabbed Poppy, and yanked as hard as she could. Fire laced across her wrists. She tried to beat at the fizzling thing that held Poppy and let out a piercing yelp when a tendril of shadow lashed out at her, whipping her across the forearms and leaving a scorching red mark.

But she pushed harder, plunging her hands into the dust as it crawled across Poppy. A spinning cord seeped out of the trunk, rippling, parasitic and apocalyptic. It was like looking into the burning embers of a dying fire—like seeing night come to life—like watching the ground split open and reveal the core of the world. It snaked around Poppy, whirling between them, wisping into the air.

Frankie held tight to the nightmare of Poppy's arm, her cheek pressed against a trembling shoulder, and planted her feet as firmly as she could. The shadow constricted around Poppy and dove into her open mouth.

The pain roared through her until Frankie thought she'd look at her skin and find flames. Then, just as suddenly as it began, the hold released her and she blinked away spots of white as she fell with Poppy. They crashed to the gnarled floor. There was a moment when none of her senses came when she called them, her ears dull and ringing, her nose scathed by the scent of cooked ash.

"What the fuck, oh my god, holy shit," Cass blubbered, rushing to lift Poppy's limp shoulders, cradling her head. Poppy blinked back at her in surprise. "Can you hear me? What the hell was that?" Then she let out a pained gasp. "Frankie, your *hands*."

Marya flashed her light across Frankie's palms. Against Poppy's arm they were crimson, blistered, destroyed. Her fingertips almost seemed to smolder. Marya sucked in a painful breath between her teeth.

Frankie felt Marya cradle her hands, and she jerked away as pain rocketed up her arms. "Let me see," Marya murmured, and Frankie relented, even as her nerves burned. Something impossible had seared her skin. Something had taken over Poppy and enveloped Frankie in turn.

The house creaked, foundation rattling and groaning, and Poppy blinked up at the ceiling. "What happened?" she asked hoarsely.

Cass held her close, rocking her back and forth. "I don't know. I really don't know."

"We need to leave," Marya commanded. "Now."

No one argued.

25

MASHENKA, MASTER MASK MAKER

Her mother called the seeing *volshebstvo*—sorcery. A trick of the eye. Thin places, where feeling could tear past one world into another. Some people were closer. Some toed the line. Marya had no choice—she'd been born halfway across the edge already, until there seemed no delineation between monster and mind, spirit and safety.

But she'd never seen anything like that house.

They sat in the farmhouse kitchen, the only sound the warbled ticking of the cuckoo clock. Marya was overtly aware of a shift. Whatever had lashed out at them in the house was bigger than Sofia's frenetic black outline. The tree had served as a conduit, some kind of incubation of the dark, and the creature that crawled from it and plunged down Poppy's throat was an entirely new monster with a deeper capacity for devouring.

Now there was a fractured understanding: The shadow trailing Sofia had grown, subverting Marya's assumed familiarity. Something larger had to be giving it power, or orders—something terrifying enough that it could scare her shadow into a vicious transformation. Now whatever fed Sofia's shadow was expanding, and it was coming for them, and it was going to eat them from the inside out, and Marya felt powerless in every other sense than sight.

The kitchen smelled of cloves, a lingering spice that made Marya want to smoke. Cass stood by the kettle, ready to kill the burner's flame as soon as the water started to boil. Poppy slumped low in her seat, eyelids heavy, and Frankie leaned next to Marya at the table with her hands extended. Marya lifted them gently and eyed the red tint of her skin.

"It looks worse than it feels," Frankie said.

"You don't have to lie for my sake," Poppy muttered, her first words since they'd left that awful house, where that thing had used her mouth to speak.

They should have never gone. They should have never started messing with things they didn't understand. Marya shouldn't have encouraged them, should have known that Sofia's violent shadow meant something was wrong, that they needed to abandon this and her and move on and pretend none of it had ever happened. She should have told them how afraid she was. How utterly out of control she felt.

Cass rummaged in a cabinet. She produced an old jam jar labeled *BURN STUFF* on a faded note, setting it down gently in front of Marya with a pointed look before returning to watch the kettle.

Marya cracked it open. It smelled like honey. She gingerly cleaned the blistered skin with pads of alcohol, then dipped into the jar and touched the substance to Frankie's burns, following the lines where the skin cracked like razed earth. Frankie flinched before she exhaled and forcibly relaxed her hand.

Marya tried to be as gentle as she possibly could, pressing open Frankie's fingers and spreading the salve along the red marks that stretched to her wrist. She sifted through a first aid kit they'd found beneath the kitchen sink, mostly full of cartoon-themed bandages. When she found an old roll of gauze, she began to wrap Frankie's palms.

The wounds were almost made worse by the lack of understanding of how they were possible. Marya ran a thumb across her handiwork, the watch on her wrist catching lamp glow and glinting it back and forth across the room. "Does it hurt?" she asked.

"Not much," Frankie answered. Her tone wasn't very convincing, but her gaze was fierce. It took effort for Marya to tug her eyes away.

It was her fault this had happened in the first place. She had gone and done the one thing she'd always been lectured not to do. She had followed the spirit into the dark.

"I don't understand," Cass said, too loud in the hushed room.

"Join the club," Poppy said. "How do you think I feel?"

Cass glanced at her before turning back to the kettle. Her voice cracked, emotion seeping through. "You're—you're sure you didn't say those things?"

Poppy's face lit up with discomfort, her jaw working. "That wasn't me. You know that."

There was a long beat of quiet. "I know," Cass said at last.

"We can make it make sense," Frankie said, watching Marya wrap the gauze around her second upturned hand. "We have to go back."

"No," Marya said immediately, and every woman looked at her. She scrambled for the right words—this was her chance to make it right. She had known that there was something off before they even stepped into the house. She should have turned them all around. "That was— that was evil, and it attacked Poppy."

"I didn't realize you were such a believer," Frankie said, starting to tug herself out of Marya's grasp but faltering halfway through.

"If you're not, then explain to me what we just saw."

Marya had received Frankie's hard stare more times than she could count in the past year—but this one faltered and went flat, as if she had summoned something painful to the surface and bricked it up behind a wall.

"We were stressed," Frankie said.

Cass scoffed. "Who are you trying to kid right now? You out of all people should know that—"

"I should know what, Cass?"

The uncertain line of Cass's mouth wavered. "You should understand," she said finally.

"It wasn't *stress*. It was physical. We all saw what it did to you and Poppy," Marya said, earning a scoff. To Poppy, she added: "Why did you touch it?"

Quiet hung around the room.

"It was—in my head, taking over. I wanted to feel the flowers and know they were real, and as soon as the thought came to me, I had to do it. But holding them felt like the opposite of proving that they existed. Like I was losing part of myself in the process." She looked around the room, expression complicated. "I just want to know why this keeps happening to me."

"What are you talking about?" Frankie asked.

"I've—seen things—like whatever was in the tree," Poppy admitted. "Before today."

They all looked at her.

"Like what?" Cass asked. "I mean, I have too, but I'm not making myself sound crazy until you guys do."

"Shadows?" Marya asked, barely above a whisper. She stared into the vacant doorway of the kitchen, watching for movement, for the house to creak and give itself away. She could hear Frankie swallow.

"Yes," Poppy confirmed.

"Whatever," Frankie said. "Shadows, then. What are we supposed to do about that?"

That opened a floodgate. Poppy in the shower, Poppy in her dreams, Poppy alone in her bedroom. Cass behind the wheel of her truck and in Frankie's bathroom. Frankie in the house staring into a shattered mirror. Each of them had seen *something* inexplicable.

In the past, Marya had been instructed to keep those mystifying moments to herself, to harden the knowledge into something compacted and stabilized. Her mother would have killed her if she could see her now, if she hadn't already tried that time she listened at the door and heard the hot rush of what a seventeen-year-old Marya was describing to Nina in her childhood bedroom—the terrified imprint of the girl who tried to jump the fence, the shadowy woman who wept by the bus station, the dog that followed Marya back and forth every day to school for a month until she watched a car drive through the empty outline of its hind legs.

But to keep this to herself was to put the rest of them in danger. Somewhere along the line, her hope for understanding had transformed into a need to keep the rest of them out of harm's way. Still—she kept failing, no matter how hard she tried.

"I've—" she started, trembling, thinking about Sofia's body translucent in the trunk of a car, face down in rushing water, "I've seen—"

But the kettle whistled and Cass scrambled to stop it and Marya's heart dashed like a scared animal in her chest, and maybe that was her sign that she should just keep her mouth shut, now, forever, until she was worm food in the dirt.

"Seen what?" Frankie prodded, tapping on her wrist.

"I've seen the shadows too," Marya said finally. "Everywhere I go."

"So, what do we do? Do we ask—you know?" Cass said, waving in the general direction of the house, at the shoes left by the door and the unwashed mugs littering the sink. She rinsed one and peered at it before filling it with a tea bag and hot water. Poppy accepted it from her, downcast and shaded.

"Let's try to figure this out before we get them involved," Frankie muttered. "Whatever happened in that house, we can handle it."

As if summoned by their hesitation, the stairs creaked beneath soft footsteps, and Sissa floated into the kitchen trailed by the tail of her robe, glinting a deep green. "It's past three in the morning, in case y'all weren't aware," she said breezily. "Some of us were trying to sleep."

With a gentle hip she bumped Cass aside and filled a different mug from the kettle.

"We're aware," Frankie answered quietly, flexing her hands, stiff in their gauze. Marya watched her move and winced as the skin stretched.

Sissa looked between the four of them, her eyes bouncing beneath sleep-heavy lashes and widening when they landed on Frankie and her bandages. One hand tugged her robe tighter while the other clutched her mug. "What's going on here? Are you okay?"

"Do you believe in ghosts?" Poppy asked.

Sissa let out a little bark of a laugh. "Ghosts, demons, the whole shebang. Of course I do." Her stare landed somewhere in the hazy distance. "Don't tell me you don't?"

The four of them remained silent, each of them afraid to speak it aloud. Marya heard the echo of her heart in her ears.

"What's this really about?" Sissa said, her smile faltering.

"Nothing," Frankie said.

"We went to the house," Cass blurted. Frankie glared at her, wounded.

Sissa's face shuttered. "Your aunt told you to leave that be. A couple hours ago, in fact, if my memory is correct."

"And *you* said that I'd do whatever I was going to do regardless," Frankie said sharply. Marya, her hand still resting beneath Frankie's, gave the tip of a finger a little pinch. Frankie looked back down in surprise, cheeks flushing.

Marya tipped her head to Sissa. "What do you see when you look at us?"

Cass leaned into the steam from her tea. Poppy kept her arms crossed tight around her ribs.

"I know you've felt it," Sissa whispered, then cleared her throat again to make room for volume. "It's like all this time, you've been standing in the dark, and now you've stepped into the light. It's disorienting. We've all been there before, seen power like that." She glanced toward the living room, as if hoping Oph might come in and save her from the interrogation.

"So just tell us," Frankie urged.

"You wouldn't believe me," Sissa said, so sadly. "You never do, kiddo."

"How am I supposed to believe? What should I say, that magic is real? I don't *care* if it's real, Sissa, because it doesn't change anything. Either way, they're dead and they're not coming back."

"Your mother could make something out of nothing," Sissa said dreamily, like Frankie hadn't even spoken. "She was our magician—give her water and she'd spit up wine. She brought me flowers from a red world once, and they didn't wilt until she was gone."

Frankie's face was a wound. She looked so young like that, small in her chair under the flickering overhead light, the bags under her eyes heavy and purple. "Quit talking in riddles," she said.

"You've looked magic in its face," Sissa started. Her eyes were wide and star-blown. "You've conjured and crossed a boundary, and you need to accept the magic for what it is now that you've called it to spaces where it did not previously sleep. I can see it on you. It clings to your shadows."

A deep, mournful line formed between Frankie's eyebrows. Marya wanted to press a fingertip to it.

"You shouldn't have gone," Sissa finished when they remained silent, tugging mindlessly at the strings of her robe. "But you would have in this world or the next, and there's nothing we could have done about it."

The corners of the room seemed to deepen at that. Marya's eyes eclipsed, snagging on the slightest movement, waiting for Sofia to fade into frame, for the spidery outline of her to reach for them. But stillness prevailed.

"I don't know what you expect me to do now," Frankie said, thick with emotion.

"I expect that when you go looking for trouble, you'll be careful about where you prod. I expect that when you find her it won't make a single thing better, but I hope it'll help, despite it all."

"Teach us how," Frankie said roughly. "I'll learn, if that's what you want."

Sissa shook her head, coils of hair slipping from behind her ears and falling around her face. "You're not ready."

Some of the despair replaced itself with anger. "Like hell I'm not."

"You have to be willing to give something up," Sissa said softly, "and you have nothing I want."

Frankie's lips moved soundlessly, flickering through the emotion, until she pressed them shut and turned away.

Sissa placed a hand on Poppy's back. "Go to bed. Misery loves a sleepless mind."

Marya hesitated. When their eyes met, Frankie's were vacant and defeated.

They filed out of the room as Sissa led them toward the stairs. Poppy and Cass followed Frankie with the clear intention of spending the night, and Marya didn't know where to go, who to be, what kind of body to encompass.

"You can stay if you want to, you know," Frankie said, and it was reassuring to hear even if her tone was standoffish.

She was almost ready to say yes, almost ready to accept the olive branch, but Marya caught a glimpse of the four of them in the mirror over the fireplace and had to hide her flinch. Her first thought was *Sofia?* when she caught sight of the figure. But it was only Frankie, stepping forward and leaving Poppy exposed in the glass. Standing beside Marya, Poppy moved anxiously, looking upstairs into the dim hallway and tapping her foot in some staccato rhythm. But for a too-long second, the Poppy in the reflection remained still and shadowed. A ghost imprinted on the glass.

Marya's heart refused to slow. "I can't tonight," she amended. The lies calcified in her chest.

"Fine," Frankie said sharply, already turning away.

Fear hung in the air between all four of them, heavy and sour, a specter of death.

"See you tomorrow?" Marya called after them, her question echoing up the stairs. Cass called a mumbled greeting back to her but it fell into silence, indecipherable.

She biked home in the dark.

26

A Heart for a Heart, Entrails for Entrails

She wished that someone could have told her it would feel like this; that when you began to lose your mind, you lost the rest of you, too, until you were barely an impression in the air, mass that required space to move through.

Poppy moved through space. But then space moved, too, ominous and wriggling around her.

Poppy was a dweller. That's what her dad called it, at least, a cleverly pitiful way of saying that she felt everything *more*. All night she saw that endless moment in a string of forevers—reaching for the tree before her mind could make sense of the action, shadows winding up her skin and pushing their way down her throat.

It had been three weeks since Cass's first call. They were days she'd meant to spend back home in Durham where her sublet waited and job applications sat unfinished. She had a small stipend from her last semester as a teacher's assistant, but her savings were dwindling, and she'd done laundry three times already, trying to keep the meager wardrobe she'd packed clean and sufficient in the heat. But all of that felt like an anecdote from another girl's life. She was a whisper of who she'd been when her mother opened the door on that first day back in Loring.

Three weeks since the call and three days since she'd touched the tree. Now sensation held a different meaning—there was a disconnect, a fog over understanding, where her senses didn't quite match up with her expectations. Sometimes she reached for the soft cotton sleeve of a shirt, the rippled surface of the quilt on her bed, water thin and cooling in the bathtub, each moment unrealized. Her fingertips would find only a vacancy where no connection was made, a breakage in her perception of the world. What had that apparition taken? Why her? Why was she losing her mind, watching it slip away from her in radiant tendrils of color?

She woke smelling smoke one night and ran down to the kitchen, thinking someone had left a burner on. There was no way to tell how long she stood in front of the stove staring listlessly at the gas range. All she remembered was her father flicking the kitchen light on as dawn spread beyond the windows. All she could hear was that quiet concern as he asked her what she was doing.

She didn't know. Didn't know. Didn't know.

She slept fitfully. Woke with a start each day like someone had flicked on a blinding switch, flipping the world from dark to bright.

Time kept walking past her. Three days turned into another week— though she woke every morning unsure of what day it was, always thinking she'd overslept for something important. Now the four of them spent most afternoons at the studio taking inventory or gathered around Oph's kitchen table, coffee clutched in hands already overwarm and dewy from the settling heat. They scrawled plans for not-stalking out on the table with torn bits of paper and dull pencils. They would watch Lucas every day for the next week to come, cataloging the places he went. They would not go back to the house.

Poppy felt Oph's and Sissa's eyes like a focused ray of sun on the nape of her neck.

June swept past them, swampy and bleached. It itched down Poppy's spine. In the spare moments where thoughts made sense, she considered the days flicking by and wondered if she should leave it all behind, try to let go until this terror was barely an impression on her world. But it was an impossible dream. She was stuck here until she could understand what had gone wrong, wax cooling over her, a statue in the mystery of her memories.

Slips of time were lost to her, whole hours when she remembered nothing but great swaths of black. Her mind played tricks on her, a stereoscope flicking through images in her head. Blink and there was Sofia beside her on the bed, mouth open in that gory gasp. Blink and something darted beyond the shower curtain. Blink and Sofia sat in the car, dazzling and rosy with her fair hand on Poppy's thigh, an electric thing, a current of dreams. Blink and there was the trunk of the tree and her shaking fingers pressed against it.

They followed Lucas a few more times, each time uneventful. She let herself be tugged across Loring, between the mountains. More than once Frankie caught Poppy floating away in her head and confronted her about it.

"You look rough," Frankie said one day as they hunkered down in Cass's truck. Lucas loaded groceries into the back of his truck. "Are you sure you don't want to take a few days to rest?"

"I'm fine," Poppy insisted.

And she was. There was nothing else she could be other than fine; she'd lost the words for scared, for anxious, for uncontrolled.

Sissa caught her another day as Poppy walked out to her car, leaving Cass and Marya and Frankie behind to plot. She was spent, her head pounding. The other woman's arms were weighed down with shopping bags, various thrift stores advertised on the sides, the wide legs of her pants dragging in the grass.

"Help me with these before you go?" she asked. Poppy relented and took a few bags from her, heading back up the stairs to drop them in the entryway of the farmhouse. She could still hear the others, conversation melding into something intense. She turned to go and Sissa caught her arm before she could disappear. "What's on your mind, doll?"

Poppy shook her head, then hesitated. "I haven't been sleeping well."

"Wait here," Sissa answered. She disappeared down the hall, her boots clicking. When she returned, she clutched a little satchel close to her chest. Poppy accepted it and wrinkled her nose when she peered inside at a collection of green herbs.

"Is this legal?" she asked.

Sissa nudged her shoulder. "It's mugwort. Steep it and drink it as a tea for some sweeter dreams." Her face softened. "You look like you need something other than a nightmare."

Poppy thanked her and went home, where she dozed on the couch while her dad watched TV in his recliner and her mother clinked dishes in the kitchen, a house-made lullaby that eased her into fitful rest. She woke to someone snapping in her face.

"What's up with you?" her mother asked, forehead furrowed. "Are you getting sick?"

"A cold, I think," Poppy answered roughly, her throat strained. "I think I just need some tea."

She methodically ate pasta cold from the fridge and brewed the mugwort on the stove. The scent of it rose like splitting earth and all she could think about for a dazzling moment was putting her lips on a cigarette that Sofia had just taken a drag of. She downed everything in the mug, despite the steam and the sharp memory. Her fingers went to her throat when the swallow caught—the skin was bare and too hot. She couldn't remember where Sofia's necklace had gone. She racked her brain, trying to picture the last place she had taken it off, but her eyes kept fuzzing over.

Within an hour she was drowsy again, this time prone on her bed with the moon already high in the sky and her limbs slack among the blankets.

She'd heard once that if you held a picture in your mind while falling asleep, you'd dream only of that thing. Behind her eyes she traced an image of Sofia, vivid and shining like every bullet of light in the wide-open sky had been created with the green of her irises in mind. Went back through memories savored like hard candies under the tongue, slow-moving things that she rolled around in her mouth for times like this when she desperately needed comfort.

A fevered kiss shared in Poppy's bedroom, open mouthed and warm. Her hand knotted in Sofia's hair. Sofia's palm smooth against Poppy's scalp. Their knees connected beneath a blanket while a movie played unwatched on the television, their skin sticky where it'd been pressed together for hours.

When she slept it was dead and hollow, and she dreamt of nothing at all.

Still, it was something. A moment of peace. Maybe she couldn't see Sofia again, alive or dead, but god it was a respite to think of her, a pause from these slips in time these blank-eyed stares these underwater sounds that wouldn't give her a damn break wouldn't leave her alone wouldn't let her breathe.

Poppy moved through space. Girl become ghost.

Then, catastrophe.

It happened in Oph's kitchen, sun filtering past the curtains. Marya cut apples beside the sink at Frankie's instruction. It was a stunningly regular sight—Poppy couldn't remember a time they'd all gathered without Marya included, her presence more familiar than not. Frankie fiddled with the coffee maker, trying to coax one last cup out of it, even though it was nearly dusk by now and coffee would keep Poppy up all night if she even had a sip. It likely didn't matter—she'd spend the night sleepless anyway.

Poppy hovered by the sink and held the edge for stability. Her feet were ungainly against the linoleum, the permeating scent of wood-smoke and faint rotting flowers making her head light and leaden all at once.

"He doesn't do jack shit," Cass called from the dining table where she doodled on an old menu, yellowed at the corners. "It's not worth following him. I think we should confront him about the symbol in the barn."

"We could always go back to the house." Frankie looked over her shoulder at the empty doorway. The television puttered in the living room, where Oph and Sissa sat.

"We agreed already," Marya murmured. "It's not smart."

Poppy looked at the reflective side of the toaster, where her warped face stared unblinkingly back.

Frankie thumped the heel of her hand against the coffee maker. "We're running out of options. I swear this thing was made to piss me off. Cass, can you look at it?"

The rake of a chair pushing away from the table grated against Poppy and she cringed. Cass leaned in to look at the coffee maker. Marya popped a slice of apple into her mouth and nodded along to a faint jingle coming from the other room as she chopped.

"Finally," Frankie said as the machine sputtered. The sound was too much. Poppy blinked and blinked and blinked, black spots fizzing like flies at the corners of her vision. The room was suddenly too warm, constricting. She blinked again and the moment dragged longer than a year, a decade where her eyes mechanically shut and opened.

Marya glanced at her, a slice of apple pinched between her fingers. "Want one?" she asked. When Poppy stayed silent, Marya asked, "Are you alright?"

Poppy clutched the edge of the countertop harder. She caught a glimpse of herself in the mirrored glass of the microwave and felt her heart skip and stop and start all over again. Her reflection stuttered.

"Pops?" Cass asked.

Fine, she wanted to say, *oh I'm fine, just let me sit down, just let me—* Frankie peered at her with concern. Poppy looked at her and saw Sofia. Her chest went cold, her breath painful to even inhale. "Maybe you should—" Frankie started.

The sharp sound of a ceramic shatter cut her words off as Poppy felt her arm swing out and sweep a mug off the counter, tugged by some invisible string, her body propelled with it. Blink and the pieces lay in a sodden mess at her feet. Blink and watch Cass stumble back, Marya lean with her, Frankie's mouth drop open in a gasp.

"What was that?" Sissa called from the other room.

They froze. "Nothing!" Frankie called. She held up a cautious hand to the rest of them. To Poppy she said, "What's wrong?"

Something tore through her chest, rippled through her veins. Poppy tried to make a fist and found that she couldn't. A burning feeling rose in her throat, and for a moment she thought that opening her mouth might release a great plume of smoke. Her body just a chimney. Bonfire crux.

"Aren't you tired?" Poppy's lips said, the words fried. Her tongue lay heavy against her teeth. Her body slumped against the counter. Her voice was still her own but rougher now, flint-sharp. The shadow she cast gave a violent quiver.

"What are you talking about?" Marya asked.

Poppy moved like a marionette, fingertips crackling. A thrumming sound filled her ears as her body began to tremble. One outstretched hand pointed to Frankie. She stared down in amazement at it.

"Aren't you tired of acting like a hero?" her voice said, burning up through her throat. *Stop,* she thought, *please, stop.*

Marya rocked forward and tensed as if ready to strike. Poppy snarled back at her, sensing the movement. "You follow her blindly. You let her order you around when she's the one who let her sister die. She failed, and still you follow."

Her voice altered itself. It hurt her own ears to hear it. The twisted remnants of her words mixing with the clangor of the thing inside of her was an entirely new monster.

"No one follows me," Frankie answered. "Cass asked you to come home. We wanted you here, with us."

Poppy's lips parted to bare her teeth. "What are you now, Frances, without her? You're a twin with no proper master and no knowledge of where to go next."

The words hung in the kitchen. Down the hall, where all sound had faded to an insect buzz, three soft knocks sounded.

Frankie's face fell like debris from a burning building, like Poppy had just cracked her ribs open and yanked out her still-beating heart, meat swelling past her fingers with a desperate plea. *I could eat a heart,* something thought with her mind, she could bite down into it, feel the hot pulse. It would be so simple.

"Whatever you are, you're making a mistake," Marya said through her teeth. Something flashed under the hot yellow light of the kitchen, and Poppy grinned wider when she realized it was a knife, a thin slice of apple skin still clinging to the blade. To Poppy, she said: "Don't let it stake its claim," calm and slow.

Poppy's head rolled back, momentarily blinded by the white sun of the overhead light. She let it fall forward against her chest. Someone laughed. Maybe it was her.

"Poppy," Cass started, choked with the threat of tears. "Please—"

Her leg swung out, her foot connected with an intact chunk of the mug she'd broken. It caught air and smashed against the wall, the delicious crunch of a car crash. The sound filled the kitchen with an echoing haunt, and she almost expected to find several versions of this contorted body she wore waiting outside each doorway.

Her eyes slid down the knife in Marya's hand. She tasted blood behind her teeth. "Stick me once and you'll come home to the wretched earth with me, won't you Masha Sokolova? But you know this. You always have."

She watched Marya's collected façade melt into something sharper, head cocked in question. Wisps of pale hair covered the delicacy of her cheek, and at that moment, everything about her was dangerous and severe. The paring knife remained firm.

"We warned you before," Marya said. "She's not yours to keep and you've borrowed beyond what you were permitted."

Poppy released her grip on the counter to trace lazy lines across her own face, shadows pooling in the richness of her skin. When she spoke, it was a saccharine baritone.

"Doesn't she make a lovely vessel, Masha?" Her fingers, feather light, brushed over long lashes and full lips, guided by some unknown force. "Isn't she worth keeping?"

Poppy let out one huge rattling exhale. She clenched her teeth around the sound, struggling to gain control over herself. Her body sidestepped the shattered remains of her mug. She was still grinning as she moved toward Frankie, head rolling. Marya stepped between them. In a moment that seemed longer than time would allow, Poppy reached past her and gripped Frankie's chin; and Marya held the little knife to her throat.

"That's the thing about twins," Poppy murmured roughly. chin upturned to relieve the pressure of Marya's knife, teeth clenched hard enough to hurt. "They really do have the same face." She tilted Frankie's head back and forth, examining it, and Marya pressed the threat of the knife a little harder. "But you would have been a much more suitable candidate."

Her skin itched. Her grip pressed harder into Frankie's jaw. She could feel a trickle of blood as it ran past her collarbone, down her shirt, the point of Marya's knife stinging against her throat.

"Leave her body," Marya said firmly.

"Oh, fine," her mouth declared wickedly. "You're no fun at all!"

Just as easily as it had overcome her, she was emptied. Poppy struggled to click back into her own head. The room fizzled and hummed with the atmosphere of dim fluorescence, and three loud knocks sounded again, this time on the countertop next to where they stood. Her knees gave out. She fell to the floor, bare skin pressing into bits of the shattered mug, and cried out as sensation returned to her.

In seconds there was Frankie, her face up in Poppy's, hands hovering around her cheeks. "It's okay," she whispered. "It's okay, it wasn't you, I know that, I know, it wasn't you, you're okay." When they touched, Frankie's bandages pressed to the fevered skin of Poppy's cheeks, she felt herself start to cry, her chest shaking with the effort.

Frankie held her up. Cass's arm was warm around her shoulders. Marya, somewhere distant, asked, "Why would it do that to her?"

Why? That's what Poppy needed to know too. Why her, out of everyone in the world?

When she looked up from Frankie's damp shirt, she saw Oph standing in the doorway, her hands tangled anxiously in the front of her skirt as she took in the scene before her.

Shakily, Oph said, "What have y'all done?"

27

DRIVE FROM MY HEART THIS TENDER TERROR

"I told you it was a bad idea," Oph said as she led them to the water. "I told you not to go to that house. You are making it impossible for me to keep you from doing something reckless."

"I thought you knew me better than that," Frankie said. Her face shimmered, dewy where heat overtook her. The lake stretched out under the hot sphere of the evening sun: a red dot blinking back at them like an unexpected camera flash lighting up an iris.

"That doesn't mean I think you should go ahead and do it," Oph ground out. She stooped to scoop water from the lake into a glass bowl, the liquid swirling green as a dead girl's eye with algae. "She's possessed, Frances. I was trying to prevent this from happening."

She resented *Frances*. "That's not fair," she said, with too much vitriol. "If you knew this would go so wrong, why wouldn't you say so?"

"You have to be joking. What do you think the tea-leaf reading was, a game? When have you ever listened to me?"

Frankie's pulse rushed in her ears. Control was a myth. There was no way to stabilize herself in this moment, everyone sliding away from her, away, away, away. She glanced back at the house, where the others waited inside. Waited for her next grand idea, her perfect solution, her reassuring direction. The idea made her want to crumble into nothing, to turn and walk into the lake and let it wash her clean or claim her entirely.

"I'm trying to—"

"Make it right, I know," Oph snapped. Then she softened. "I'm sorry. You know I am. You have to know how all of this is destroying me, too. But what if there is no right answer? What if this is what we get? Can you live with that?"

"I just want to help her," Frankie insisted hotly, "and it feels impossible."

Oph looked at her with so much intensity that Frankie had to avert her gaze. "Then trust me to take care of you."

Her aunt led the way back up the sloping yard, water sloshing down the front of her skirt. Sunset filtered over the whitewashed eaves of the house. Once, Frankie would have seen that kind of evening and thought *home*. Instead, she was overcome with the sense that night would come and never leave again. She looked down at her hands, at the ugly red skin, the angry lines peeking past white bandages. There was something kind of reassuring about them. Something that looked a little like she felt on the inside.

Inside, Oph heated the lake water on the stove. Sissa peered into the pot with her chin perched on the other woman's shoulder and her eyes trained on the clock, mouthing silent seconds. Oph deftly sprinkled herbs into the pot, stirred carefully clockwise in sequence with Sissa's counting. Each time she asked for a new ingredient, Sissa pressed it into her palm before she could finish speaking.

Frankie watched them sway and move as one, muttering under their breath, passing energy where their skin brushed. The two of them were her family, like Cass and Poppy—and now maybe even Marya— had become, blood or not, just the same. The realization made her ache. They were her family, and so they hurt her. It had always been that way, hadn't it? Her mother had started it, slack jawed and buried. Then Sofia. Even if she hadn't really meant to, not at first.

Poppy sat at the dining table, head in her hands. Marya clung to the back of Poppy's chair like she was trying to comfort through the wood. Frankie paused beside Cass and leaned into her, seeking stability. Cass looped a finger around Frankie's wrist and the tender skin prickled.

"Please don't tell me I have to drink that," Poppy said. She cleared her throat. Frankie could feel the ache of it in the sound alone.

"No, doll," Oph soothed. "It's for bathing."

Poppy raised her head and flushed. Frankie watched her eyes hop around the room, likely counting the amount of people who'd be involved in Poppy sitting naked in a tub of dirty lake water. "Here?"

"We're just washing you with it," Sissa said, wriggling her eyebrows. "Like a baptism, if that's the kinda thing that turns you on."

"Don't be vulgar," Oph said with a harsh poke to Sissa's side.

Poppy grimaced. Oph clicked off the burner. She brought the pot over to the table and placed it beneath Poppy's chin. The steam curled around her throat and Frankie wanted to wave it away, wanted to give Poppy some room to breathe.

"Inhale," Oph said.

Poppy's chest steadily rose and fell as she obeyed, arms crossed in defense and fingers digging into the flesh of her biceps. In her mind Frankie saw those hands lashing out again, felt them snatch her chin in a perfunctory grasp.

It wasn't her.

"Something in that house latched on to you," Oph said.

"Awesome," Poppy answered thickly. "Why me?"

Oph's expression was complicated, and she chewed on her bottom lip as if she didn't want to speak the answer aloud. "You know—in situations like these, it's hard to tell."

"Be honest."

"It's possible that you're in a weaker state," Oph murmured. "You're grieving, and you've been . . . disconnected for some time, left vulnerable. You lost someone that you care about and you're feeling out of control. Someone like that is irresistible—there's so much energy to feed on."

Frankie watched Poppy's expression darken.

In the years they'd been apart, it had been simple for Frankie to resent Poppy's absence, to despise Lucas's existence. Anger meant blame, and blame meant accountability, and accountability meant she had somewhere to place the empty ache of being the one left behind. It was the unknown that truly scared her—the void where feeling should live. But dignifying that void with her attention meant acknowledging that Poppy had been alone too; isolated and afraid, without anyone there to ease the fear. At least Frankie could have picked up the phone and dialed Cass's number, knowing there would always be someone waiting no matter how poisonous she made herself. But who had Poppy turned to? When had she lost her capacity for belief in the bonded thread that they'd once been?

Frankie had watched the tree come to life under Poppy's hand, felt the sting of shadow cooking her fingertips. She had been a witness. Did that make her a believer too?

"May I touch you?" Oph asked gently.

Poppy nodded, body slackening. Oph unbent one arm, laying it flat. Sissa did the other. They dipped bits of cloth in the water and wiped them across Poppy's skin. Setting sun made the room glow red and the water simmer auroral. Poppy's face distorted and changed. There was a moment when the surface of the water rippled and Frankie thought she caught Poppy's reflection shifting into something new, but the image was shattered by Oph dunking the cloth again.

"What will this do?" Marya asked. The light illuminated her hair until the strands were pink all the way up to the black roots.

"It's a cleansing spell," Sissa said, like the settling creaks of an old house, distant and unnerving. She circled the table, lit a tall black candle. "It will exorcise the negative energy that clings to her and hopefully prevent it from coming back."

"And what about the candle?" Cass asked, clearly trying not to sound like her resolve had crumbled into ash.

"It will absorb the energy as it leaves her," Oph explained.

Frankie shifted uneasily. Time moved agonizingly slowly as they covered every exposed inch of Poppy's skin with the warm mixture, wiping at her fluttering eyelashes, her sharp cheeks, her long throat. Every time Oph wet the cloth the water grew murkier. The sun went down and color seeped from the room with it, purple to blue to gray to black.

Cass announced herself with the gentle prodding of her fingers as they folded between the bandages on Frankie's. The room was so dark, illuminated in firefly spotlights by the dripping candles. Frankie shut her eyes. The glow of the flames pressed against the thin skin of her eyelids. Strands of her hair stuck to the nape of her neck. She was thirsty, uncomfortably so.

"Let go," Sissa murmured. Her voice hung like fog in the air. It clung to Frankie's skin, damp and dewy.

Who is she talking to? she wondered, her tongue awkward in her mouth, gravity pressing down her shoulders. Her eyes parted again. Poppy's head hung over the water. Frankie watched her mirror image expand and warp, re-forming itself into something larger, deeper, an endless pool, a distant glow, a tunnel growing and pushing and carving its way through the mountain until it cut through one world into the next and she had to—

Close the thought out, try to hold herself together.

"Don't let her wander," Sissa hissed. "Keep Poppy's image in your mind."

But there was only one face Frankie could see, in satellites of black starlight. It looked like her own.

Not her. I'm not ready. I can't.

She could feel her pulse against Cass's. It swelled like her heart was on the verge of bursting.

"Can you feel it?" Oph asked.

"*Yes*," Poppy and Marya said together, in a rush of emotion. Poppy's voice broken and wounded, Marya's thrilled and alive. Somewhere in the room came the quiet sound of weeping, and Frankie couldn't tell if it was Cass or Sissa or a memory, something summoned to life by Frankie's pounding heart.

She's my sister, Frankie thought, *she's mine. Why isn't she here with me?*

Her hands burned, itching beneath the bandages. She wanted to crack the water's surface like a falling cross, steeple left naked in the sky.

She tried to scrub her mind of the hurt. Tried to erase the images of Sofia that had haunted her over the past few weeks, the idea of her battered body wheeled from that old house, the sketches she'd seen pinned in the sheriff's station. The edges of a photo of her twin where she caught sight of dirty bone.

Instead, she summoned a memory that burned like hellfire. In her mind there was a live wire, a current of energy that powered a sister-shaped hole. A socket, a place to plug her body into. She let it envelop her, tingling down her forearms. Once, she'd had a sister. Now she had only the promise of continuation. The days had come and gone, the house empty save for her and Oph. It had been a loud sort of quiet, and Frankie an aching sort of alone, and most nights—almost every night—she curled numb and sleepless, telling herself that *tomorrow it will be a better day, a different day, one that matters.* That she'd figure it out along the way. But it had been her life, the whole time.

She sucked in a ragged, killing breath.

Sofia emerged in the expanse of her shut eyes, distorted and reflected. Her sister's hair, a little darker than Frankie's and sheared off boyishly short and charming, wisping against pierced lobes. Her broad shoulders, freckled arms, that scar below her knuckles where she'd burned them on the radiator in her room. Frankie could hear her painful shriek and then her laugh, that full-bodied joy circling the two of them until she dissolved into giggles too.

It was so impossibly vivid. She felt as if she could lay her head in Sofia's lap and revel in the brush of her fingers curling into Frankie's hair, thumb soothing the sore spot above her ear where a headache would sometimes form. A touch that lingered, burrowed into her body and nested.

Frankie thought, *let it be real.*

There was a humming sound in the air, persistent. When she exhaled, she felt someone sitting before her, taking her breath into their own chest, swelling like the bellows of an accordion.

It was this: Staggered silence at first. Even the humming in her ears faded. It was Frankie aware of her body in a way that was physically unnerving: electrified to the tips of her scorched fingers, conscious of her teeth in her mouth and the minuscule hairs along her arms.

She opened her eyes and stood in the basement.

"What the fuck?" she said. She said it again, just to savor the words, and then thought it a few more times as punctuation.

It was a black pit and still she knew it instantly—she'd walked that basement a million times, felt the churned earth of its floor that she'd stumbled over to reach jars of preserves. This was her world. She'd know it in light or dark, life or death.

Light. She needed to find the bulb, its hanging chain. Sight would make sense of it.

The cellar smelled like a grave, fleshy and earthen and unsettling. Her feet, bare as they had been when she sat at the dining table, were cold against the packed dirt.

Frankie wondered, distantly, if her body still waited upstairs with their interlinked circle and some wounded part of her had ruptured and split. She wondered at the dim silence. She wondered, painfully, if she was alone.

She swung her arm for the chain. When she exhaled, the air seemed to swell around the room and fill every crevice of space until something across from her breathed it back in. It was a gentle gasp, the filling of an empty chest.

"It's okay," she whispered, wishing, hurting. "It's just me."

Another step forward. Chills rose along the exposed flesh of her thighs.

"If you're here, please say something," she whispered. "I miss—I miss you so bad, Sof, you have no idea, you don't realize. I'm so sorry, for everything. Please, say something."

Another swing. She found the chain. There was a strange sense of déjà vu, like she was standing in someone else's life, a different mind and body. She felt the inhale-exhale exchange again. Someone stood in front of her. She could sense the shaking heat of their body.

She pulled the chain. Nothing happened. Panic, burning her up, searing her like a fresh wound.

She pulled again. And again. And again, harder, until the chain snapped free and she let out a staggered cry.

The darkness deepened. She smoothed her hands down her shirt, trying to reassure herself with the physical presence of her body. But these clothes were different—she was wearing a dress, an old one that Sofia had let her borrow once, on a night when they'd snuck out and met Cass and Poppy in the woods and Sofia had burned photos of her and Lucas (their first breakup, with others to follow), drunk on wine and the heady scent of smoke. The dress had been too thin to stand up against the breeze that night, a flimsy green fabric without much body but deep pockets to make up for it. It was too thin now too. She was cold and afraid. But she patted her way down her thighs and plunged her hands into the pockets, wondering if—

There was a box of matches tucked away there, just as there had been that night. She saw herself striking them and tucking them into piles of dry brush. Coaxing the fire to grow.

Shivering, she pulled the matchbox from her pocket. The body before her sighed, so soft she almost couldn't hear it.

Blindly she struck. The match exploded on the first try. In the glow of the flame, a face lit up before her: blue and wounded, like a sister.

"Oh, Sof," Frankie said, shaking so hard she was afraid the match would go out. "Sofia. Oh god. Tell me how to help you."

There was a cool touch on her cheek. She leaned into it and the match trembled. The flame nearly reached her fingertips now. She didn't care. Let it cook her hands all over again.

Sofia burned in the dark, bottom lip split, teeth crooked and sweet. She flickered in the flamelight—one moment grotesque and shattered, the next whole as life.

"I'm so sorry," Frankie said again. *Who killed you?* she thought, far away, but her mouth said *I love you, I miss you, I love you, I miss you, come back.*

The room appeared alive around her, like each jar along the walls had a pair of eyes looking back at her. Sofia seemed to feel it too, pupils expanding until the whites rolled back into her head. A buzzing sound echoed distantly and Frankie cringed away from it.

"Wait," she said.

Sofia's hand slipped away from her cheek. It rose between them, beside the burning match. Frankie watched her sister's fingers twist together—they twined and rippled and wriggled, two snakes melding into one.

"I don't understand," Frankie said, her voice shattering. "What are you trying to show me?"

Sofia blew out the match.

"No!" Frankie cried, scrambling to strike another, but the dark moved fluid-fast and stone-heavy, and when she blinked her eyes open again she was in the candlelit dining room. Cass's palm sweated against hers. Poppy bent over the water, mouth parted in a dreamlike breath.

Frankie whipped her head around, as if Sofia might be standing somewhere among them. She stopped on Marya. The other girl was looking right back at her, eyes blown wide, mouth messy, hair stirred by an unseen breeze. Frankie felt suddenly and inexplicably seen. Like her face said it all—like Sofia had stolen her skin and worn it as her own.

"Something was here with us," Oph said, tears in her mouth. "Couldn't you feel it?"

Couldn't you feel me? Frankie thought, her heart a desperate animal, her blood a humming insect.

Marya's eyes flicked to the pot of water. Now it was inky and nebulous, color sucked from the air and desaturated. Poppy's head lolled forward and Oph caught her by the shoulders just in time. One by one they followed Poppy's limp shape, focused on the graying water, the tremble of its surface—one by one they watched it spill over the edges, sloshing and foul, Poppy's reflection coagulated into something sinister. Frankie couldn't tear herself away from the form reflected within it—rooted and gnarled and imposing. She wondered at the shape of its body and tried to parse the image out: Sister, demon, or both at once, curled into one desperate monster? Where was the line that separated them? How could she know the boundaries?

Dread was a cold stone in the pit of her. She could still feel Sofia's fingers on her jaw. Whatever lived inside of Poppy and reflected in that water, horned and waiting and massive, was not her sister. That shape in the basement—the blue ache of her—that hallucination was Sofia. Frankie didn't want to admit how real it had felt, to see her there, the bend of her mouth and the crush of her skull. But for the first time in this whole faltering mess, maybe she had found something physical to hunt, in the dark circle of that scrying bowl.

When she blinked, the creature was gone. Their intertwined circle pulled apart.

28

ANYTHING CRACKED WILL SHATTER AT A TOUCH

"It's mirror magic," Sissa said, definitively.

Marya watched the pot shimmer as Poppy's head tipped limply forward. It had seemed like only a few passing seconds, Oph's mouth moving soundlessly, Marya's ears popping in the quiet. But she felt the *shift*.

Poppy sucked in a sharp gasp, her eyes blinking open in a rush. Oph soothed her with an arm around her shoulders, surrounding her with a murmur of *you're okay, you're okay now, everything's alright*. Cass was at her side in a second, inspecting Poppy all over and pushing the bowl of water out of her face.

Frankie met Marya's gaze—and took on the apparition of her sister.

It was just a flicker, a shifting of atoms, a trick of the mind. Her jaw hardened into a satisfied smile. Her brows rose and filled. Her ruddy cheeks went pale, blue-tinged, her shoulders broadened, her hair cropped close to her cracked skull. The image trembled and righted itself and there was Frankie again, shivering, biting down hard enough to make her lip bleed.

Marya's assumed answers dissipated with the shadow in the water. The narrative shifted—all this time she had watched Sofia move through space, her shadow following close behind, and now it had turned its head and augmented into something nastier. What she had thought to be a residual haunting was an entirely new poltergeist.

"Whoa, whoa, whoa," Cass said, looking up from her inspection of Poppy. "Someone needs to explain what exactly that means."

"Fiona used to communicate like this—"

"Sissa," Oph said, laced with warning.

"Frankie knows what her mother's work included," Sissa answered, testily.

"Do I?" Frankie challenged, but the mirth was gone and glazed over with fear.

Cass sighed. "Frankie might know what you're talking about, but the rest of us are in the dark, okay?"

Oph dipped a fingertip into the liquid, face falling. Sissa held Oph's arm and leaned into her side, like the touch alone might provide one of them with support. It'd been a long time since Marya had felt close enough to someone to let down her guard and seek that comfort.

"Fiona was skilled in mirror magic," Sissa explained. She squeezed Oph's wrist and the other woman closed her eyes. "She'd scry for us, at times. Lose herself in reflection and enter a purgatory."

"Purgatory?" Poppy asked, hoarse in the quiet.

Sissa contemplated. "It's not exactly what you're thinking. Think of it more like a destination, not a sentence. It's a spirit realm that powers the immortalization of a soul and allows a person's essence to continue existing beyond the planes of our reality."

"Those are nonsense words," Frankie said.

"Energy," Sissa continued. "It sticks around. It's like the sensation you get when a light's left on, or the TV is muted. You can feel that *buzzing*."

"Sure," Frankie continued, eerily still, "but what does that have to do with my mother and my sister?"

"The thing about magic is that it is an exchange of disbelief and power." Oph pressed a finger to her temple. "You have to suspend your doubts and let your thoughts follow a bisect—death, and the rift before it. A fissure between us and the other side. We have tried to peer into that realm," she said, sharing a private look with Sissa. "But your mother is the only one of us who's ever entered the Fissure."

"It's a risk of mirror magic," Sissa added. "The goal is to build a communication link when you play with mirrors, because they're such simple doorways. They'll let anything through. But if you do it incorrectly, you'll wind up in the Fissure, and it's nearly impossible to come back without losing part of yourself. Fiona is the only one of us who ever entered it, and she did so to learn and share it with us, because she was the most unhinged person I've ever had the pleasure of knowing." She patted Oph's arm lovingly. "No offense."

"You think some part of Sofia is trapped there," Marya said. "And that whatever trapped her is affecting Poppy, too."

Sissa nodded again. Marya's mind whirred. Was Sofia's shadow the piece of her immured by the Fissure? What had come for them that night? Who had summoned it? Was Sofia's death really part of a ritual, her skin so bruised her bones so pliant her blood so—

"But how?" Poppy asked. "Sofia didn't mess with that kind of thing."

"Either you're wrong about that," Sissa said, "or whoever killed her did 'mess with that kind of thing,' and trapped her in the Fissure before her soul could rest."

"So we're being haunted by some creature from that place?" Cass asked.

Oph frowned, eyes narrowed. "It's likely that the spell took place in that house where she was found," she said, "and your visit there stirred something up. It's also possible that you've interacted with this magic before, and the disruption of Sofia's body set something free that was previously caged. Mirror magic is a complicated science. We can't hear her—we should be able to pull more, to understand what kind of . . . trauma she might have faced. But there's something standing between us."

"This is bullshit," Frankie said, damply.

"What else do I need to do to prove it to you, Frances?" Oph sighed. "You watched your mother work all her life. If I were capable of looking for Sofia in the mirror, I'd do it, believe me. I'd do anything to keep you safe."

Marya watched Frankie run a hand down her face, shoulders slumping with exhaustion.

"Each of you has seen things that you don't understand," Oph continued when Frankie remained stubbornly silent. "You said that the tree came to life and something in it reached for Poppy. And now we're telling you what we know, and you want to deny that?"

Frankie's face crumpled. Her eyes trailed to Poppy in defeat. "If this is magic, then there's nothing I can do to find who did this to Sofia. And that's not an option."

Sissa shook her head softly. "We'll help you. Maybe Sofia is just lost—and we'll do whatever we can to change that."

"Then we go into the Fissure, and we find her," Frankie said.

"Nope!" Oph answered with a clap. "No way, certainly not. You are not skilled enough to enter a mirror without your soul being literally torn apart. I'm sorry, but I won't allow that to happen."

"So what, we sit around and let *her* soul be torn apart? Why can't you try to help her?" Frankie cried.

"*We* are not skilled enough to do that successfully. We'd likely end up summoning something that could follow us back into our world. I loved her just as much as you did, Frankie, but this is not a game." Oph folded her hands together, pleading. "You need to stop. You're lucky what happened in that house wasn't worse."

"You're going to let her suffer just because you're afraid."

The room fell silent. Oph's face was grave. "Of course I'm afraid," she said, chillingly calm. "And you should be too."

Marya, all at once, feared Oph and the implications of her hushed anger. She was out of her element. She wanted to tell Frankie it was all going to be okay, even if she felt like a liar. She wanted to call her mother and ask for help. Wanted to rest her head against Nina's shoulder and feel her cup the back of her skull. To know that someone would come when asked.

Marya's mother used to say that the women in her family were susceptible to a haunt. They were always too trusting, too desperate for something to understand. As if Marya's life were some predestined thing beyond her grasp.

Seer. That's what her mother had called her when Marya confided in her about the spirits, a proud joy arriving in the revelation of their shared awareness. Her mother had also called her a shame to the family. Regardless, it was a good word. *Seeing.* The right word, maybe, and yet still untrustworthy.

Marya watched Frankie give her aunt a challenging stare. Oph met it with just as much venom.

Finally, Frankie twisted away and said, "Just tell me what I need to do, and I'll do it. Any ritual. Any séance. Any tarot reading or tea-leaf study or candle burning. I don't care. Just tell me how to find her and I'll make it happen."

Pity made lines around Oph's mouth. "That's just the thing, isn't it? You don't see how deep this goes, how you're in over your head. You don't even realize when you're already standing in something else's hand."

Frankie wouldn't meet her eyes.

Oph softened her voice. "Please. Leave that house and this whole mess alone. I know how badly you're hurting, more than anyone else in this world, but you don't understand the power it has over you. There are worse things out there than killers, believe it or not." She paused, her words falling into a plea. "Promise me? You'll leave it alone?"

Frankie's face shuttered, some heavier thing shoved down and contained. Her eyes avoided Oph's as she said, "I need some air." She turned and pushed past the back door, screen slamming shut behind her.

"That went well," Poppy muttered.

"I'll—" Marya started, suddenly uncomfortable. She felt their eyes on her and paused, expecting someone to stop her.

"Go ahead," Cass said, nodding permission. "We'll catch up."

Marya didn't wait for her to change her mind. She found Frankie at the lake's edge, feet in the water, arms hanging at her sides. Marya got close enough that she could press her fingertips against Frankie's wrist. She bit down on the thought with her teeth tearing the tender skin of her cheek. Desire made her feel reckless. She had only ever been impulsive at her worst.

"Leave me alone," Frankie said, as soon as she heard the footsteps. But when she caught Marya's eye, her face softened just a fraction. "Oh, I thought you were Oph. I don't want to talk about it."

"Good thing I'm not here to talk about it," Marya said, stopping beside her. Outside, the world was balmy, but still a chill sank deep into her bones.

She could say it. She could say: *Frankie, since I met you, I've seen your sister. Since I met you, I've known she was dead without being able to prove it. Since they found her body, I've seen her in everything, untethered and raw and aching.* Or she could lie in some roundabout way: *I saw the shadow of who Sofia once was, and it was like waking from a nightmare.*

"I have something to tell you," Frankie blurted. Her arms came up to hold herself, and her fingertips dug into her biceps. "I saw Sofia in the basement."

Marya blinked at her. "When?"

"Inside, just now. I—I was like, transported or something. I opened my eyes and then Sofia was there, but she couldn't speak or answer me and she looked so awful—" Frankie scrubbed at her face with the heels of her hands. "I don't know what it meant. I just had to tell someone."

Marya looked at Frankie's cheek and felt control slip away.

"Sometimes," Frankie continued, breath stuttering, "I think I can feel her everywhere, like she's standing right beside me. And I feel so crazy." Frankie eyed her. "Do you think I'm losing my mind?"

This was her chance. Let it hurt. Say it and allow it to implode. "Of course not," Marya said softly. "If you're crazy, then I am too."

"That's really comforting," Frankie said drily. She kicked at the shore. Muddy earth splashed into the water with a gentle *hiss*. Marya watched the ripples in the water, echoes spreading and changing and growing.

Say it, she thought.

Every word was a secret. There was a hard pit in her stomach, an hourglass standing on its end. Each time she dared to picture Nina's face, the dingy tint of the bar, the street in Raleigh where her old apartment had been, the hourglass flipped. She'd left Nina behind. She'd disappointed her mother past the limits of love. Just the thought sent her back to the past, where magic wore a different skin. It was the burnt-out crispness of a fallen star, a harder beauty. The clinging ache after a burn.

"I should go inside," Frankie said. "It was wrong to leave them behind like that."

Marya shook her head. "Poppy has Cass. You needed space."

Frankie shrugged. There was a suspended tension in the way she held herself, and Marya decided all at once that she couldn't bear to be shut out a second longer.

"Wanna get out of here?" she asked, committing to disaster and dragging a finger over Frankie's wrist, right where the bandage stopped. Frankie turned to her and smiled.

Frankie led the way, bikes weaving, the coming solstice so alive that the world hadn't quite gone completely dark. Marya felt endless, young in a way she'd never been before. Frankie's hair blew behind her and streetlights lit her up like camera flashes. She stopped where the road dipped into a pinched valley and abandoned her bike against a guardrail. The embankment sloped down into the trees, and she started forward without looking to see if Marya would follow. There had never been any question of yes or no, only when, only how fast.

They stopped at a creek twisting under a heavy-headed willow. Frankie dropped to her haunches, let her fingertips drag in the water. The current rose to meet her. Everything was blue and dire.

"We used to come here all the time," Frankie said as Marya knelt beside her, watching ripples claim moss. "I haven't been here in five years."

She spoke around Sofia's name. It was clearly a way to ignore everything that had just happened, like Frankie was trying to reconstruct the fragments of the life she had once had. Marya allowed it. If there'd been a chance to escape her own haunts, she would have tried too.

"I used to have a place like this," she said, surprising herself. Frankie pressed her chin to a bare and freckled shoulder. "I'd walk to the park from my mom's place in Astoria. My favorite spot was where all the fishermen would sit with their poles leaned against the fence. They listened to great music."

It was nothing, and it was still too much, and it was a thorn in her heart.

"I didn't know that," Frankie said. "I don't think I even knew where you lived before Loring."

Marya's voice went wry. "Well, you don't know much about me, do you?" She'd meant it teasingly, trying to prod, but there was a beat of embarrassed silence.

"You never tell me anything," Frankie said to the water.

Marya laughed. "You hate me. Why would I offer information that you don't want?"

"I don't hate you," Frankie said quickly.

"Frankie. You threaten to fire me, like, once a week. You told me you would have been better off hiring a dog to do my job."

"I was kidding," Frankie said, blushing in the dark.

Marya rubbed her cheek against the sleeve of her shirt and laughed again. "Sure, hilarious."

"I can be funny."

"Oh? Tell me a joke, then."

Frankie bumped her shoulder against Marya's, something so casual that it sent nerves tingling across Marya's entire body. "You're really cool, Marya."

Marya laughed until her eyes crinkled shut at the corners, head tipped back. "You're a dick," she said. "It's amazing that you have such great friends."

"I have a stellar personality."

Marya turned and found Frankie looking back at her. She'd swept her hair behind her ears, stare gone stormy, a loose wave curling against her dewy forehead. A thrill crept down Marya's spine, dangerous, too fast. Something about this felt like a precipice. She wanted a road map. A boundary drawn, so she wouldn't cross a line.

Frankie's shoe was almost touching Marya's. It was startlingly inti-mate. She fought across the rift between leaning closer and pulling away.

"Can I tell you something?"

"Didn't we go over this already?" Marya answered lightly.

She expected an eye roll, a laugh if she was lucky. But Frankie said: "I'm scared," like she meant to say anything else. Everything smelled like earth, like first fallen rain, like a rising plume of fire, smoky and rich. In a moment that rang like the chiming of a bell, Marya reached over and squeezed Frankie's knee, letting her fingers rest around the bone for a beat before she pulled them back.

Dangerous. Finally safe. Too much. Not enough.

"Of what?" she murmured.

"Forgetting her," Frankie answered, the words rising between them like a wave, just as fast and hungry.

"Oh," Marya said, the syllable drawn out. She'd meant to follow the word with Frankie's name but doubted herself in the last second—everything faltered. "You couldn't even if you tried."

"You don't get it," Frankie said. She was talking with her hands now, making big shapes in the air. "She used to sit where you're sitting now. We would drive to school and walk through the library together, and when I had nightmares, she let me sleep in her room even though it kept her awake. She had this way of putting things off—homework, chores, it didn't matter, but it pissed me off every time, and now I just want to feel angry again over something so meaningless. I wore her clothes all the time and they always smelled like her, and I used to tell her I hated it but I'd do anything to get that back, and I never will.

"How am I supposed to come to terms with that? We weren't even speaking in the last few months before she was gone—we had a ridiculous fight, and I did something even more ridiculous in the aftermath, and Oph kept telling me to apologize but I couldn't. I wanted Sofia to choose me for once. I wanted her to come to me and tell me she was wrong. And now I—I think it should have been me instead, and I would have taken her place if she had just—god, I don't know. Shouldn't I just want to forget?"

Frankie pressed her fingertips to her eyes. "I wasn't allowed to miss her. I had to hold everyone else together when she was gone. I had to keep looking, every single day, and I had to keep hoping for her, and I'm stuck here trying to figure out why she's slipping away and that hurts more than remembering."

Marya wasn't sure where to put her hands. She felt an ache rise in her throat, but it had been years since she'd cried. She couldn't remember how to start. Her fingers twisted in the grass between them.

"I wasn't good enough for her," Frankie whispered into her palm. "But she wasn't good enough for me either. What am I supposed to do with that?"

Marya froze, anticipating, afraid. Her hand waited limp and upturned in the grass. She imagined Frankie's sliding into it. Squeezing. It was an annihilating thought, one that razed her heart to ash.

But Frankie just leaned forward and pressed her forehead against Marya's shoulder. This close, her hair smelled exactly as Marya had imagined it would—grassy, clean, smoke-tinged. A fire smoldered down to coals.

"You were made for each other," Marya murmured, and her mouth brushed against Frankie's hair as she said it. "You are her mirror image, and no one can take that from you. You'll remember her and spill that memory into everything."

Frankie inhaled, deep and strained. "Too late. I've made myself unbearable to be around."

"I can bear it."

Frankie scoffed. It was a broken sound, disbelieving, wounded. "Don't say things like that."

"I mean it. You have so many people here to fill in the gaps," Marya said, fervently. "You can give parts of her to me and I'll keep them safe. I don't hate you at all, Frankie. I mean that, even if you don't believe it."

She nodded against Marya's shoulder.

"I guess I should fire you now that you've seen me like this," Frankie mumbled into the cotton. "Or kill you, so you can't give away my deepest darkest secrets."

Marya laughed. "Just give me a raise for emotional damages."

When she lifted her head, Frankie was smiling, and if her eyes were a little glassy, Marya didn't say a word. The grass rustled as Frankie stood and extended a hand. Marya hesitated, her heart crawling its way up to her mouth, and took it.

That smile did everything to her. What did Marya's fear matter, really? What did a secret mean? Was she better for being more contained, for her isolation, for her failure? She had let down her mother a million times with her openness and her fallibilities. Who could she disappoint now? She had already scorned all the ways Nina had taken care of her, and her mother pretended she was dead. Marya might as well live like it.

If it was mirror magic they needed, she would figure out how to give it to them, even if it meant her own inevitable end.

"Come on, they're waiting for us. Let's go home," Frankie said.

They went home.

29

UNSPOILED BY THE AXE

The evening of their deception was a fervent one. Finder and the boy crouched around a washtub in the kitchen, scrubbing at a mountain of soiled clothes. The day had passed quickly, and soon Mother Mab would call them to the table.

"Tonight should be the night," the boy said in what was surely supposed to be a whisper but came out closer to a shout. Finder frantically sloshed the laundry tub, looking over her shoulder for Mab's or the Ossifier's watchful eyes.

"You'd be smarter if you learned how to be quiet," Finder hissed. Then, just to be annoying, she said, "What makes you think you have the authority to decide what we do?"

The boy scoffed. "It's not authority, it's sensibility. There's no benefit to waiting. Whatever killed the animals is out there, and it's likely coming for us next." He looked around the room, watching for eavesdroppers, and leaned in closer. "I think we should go to the lake."

Finder plunged her hands into the soapy water. She watched it ripple away from her wrists and thought about a girl rising from the reeds, shirt wrung out and dripping, delight on her face.

"Why?" she asked.

"I dreamt it came from the water," he said. "You said that's where the path in the woods goes, right? Where else would we hunt?"

Remembering was a painful thing. Behind her eyes she saw Sofia running through the curling snake of trees, the Ossifier stalking behind her.

"I need you to make it stop," Sofia had said that last night. "I need you to take it back. Break the spell. End it all. I don't want him to want me anymore."

"It doesn't work like that," Finder whispered. Sofia had come too late in the day. The sun was falling behind the trees, turning everything scarlet and haunted.

"You don't understand." Sofia tore her hands through her hair like she might be able to rip her thoughts out with it. "I don't—I don't love him, Finder. I thought I did. I thought I wanted him to want me. But now it's all falling apart. I leave soon and I can't bear the thought—" She stopped herself. "I chose him because I thought it was expected of me. And now I can't leave her behind, Finder. She'll think I don't care and I—I love her. I do."

"Who?" Finder asked. She'd never seen Sofia like this—open awe in her eyes, like she'd surprised herself with her own words.

"Poppy," Sofia whispered. Her voice was reverent. "Fuck. And she probably hates me now, after all this. I messed up, Finder. I've hurt people."

I warned you, Finder wanted to snap, wanted to teach Sofia something for once. But she faltered and said, "You could never hurt anyone."

Sofia's smile fought its way forward. "Oh, you're sweet. I always forget how sweet you can be."

Finder smarted. "I am not."

But Sofia cuffed her chin, eyes all rimmed in silver. "It's a good thing, silly. You're kind to me even when I don't deserve it." She watched Finder, waiting for her to crack.

"I can't break the spell," she said, mostly because she felt out of control, because she could gain something in the way Sofia's expression fell.

"Please," Sofia whispered. "I'll never ask anything of you again if you give me this one thing. You were right, okay? You can say it as often as you want. You were right. I need your help just one more time."

Finder avoided Sofia and focused on the ground instead, toed a stone with her boot. "I'll have to collect things from the house."

"Oh, thank you, you're amazing." Sofia cupped Finder's face. "You're so smart, Finder. Everything you say is like learning how the world works all over again."

Finder's cheeks went hot under Sofia's hold, influenced by the joy of being seen as something more.

That reflected moment felt like a warning for inevitable disaster. But in the present, all Finder could think to say to the boy was *hmm*. So she said "Hmm," under her breath. "I can't promise you'll find anything worthwhile, but I'll take you there if you really want it."

The boy cut his eyes at her, but she caught the satisfaction in them. "Well. Good. When do we go?"

"When everyone else has gone to bed. And no one hears a word about it," Finder whispered, "unless you like the feeling of a birch branch against your back and three days without dinner."

The boy scrubbed hard at a linen skirt, teeth flashing with a grin. "I mean, it depends on who's swinging the switch, am I right?"

It was exactly the kind of joke Sofia would have made, and it forced a lump of emotion to harden in her throat. "Puke," Finder answered as she rose to her feet. Her fingers were pruned and raw, her head hollow with exhaustion. Mother Mab called for them again, a piercing sound that made Finder suddenly and achingly nostalgic for being a child.

Dinner was a hen plucked clean, an after-murder corpse. With each bite salted against her tongue, Finder saw arcs of blood sprayed across the porous wood walls of the coop. She had to squeeze her eyes shut against the sensation, will it away.

"Something wrong?" the Ossifier asked, the words the sound of tearing paper, scissors snipping through burlap. He tapped once beside her plate. Finder didn't meet his gaze, couldn't, but she held the image of him in her head: thin eyes slitted like a snake's, the curt termination of his nose, the ends of his pale hair curling around the edge of his jaw.

"Not a thing," Finder answered at last. She pushed aside yellow circles of potato from where thinned blood soaked into them. Swallowed around her dry tongue.

Mother Mab grunted past a chicken bone. "You know better than to waste food," she scolded. The Ossifier shoved away from the table, bone screeching against the floor, and brushed his hands against his chest.

Finder watched grease pool on one side of her plate, where the table leaned a little to the right. There was a moment where she thought *this has already happened to me.* But maybe it was just the memory of breakfast and every meal before it. A music box world, one tune, a repeating sound that would last until the mechanics gave up. In a past life, Sofia would have been the one to appear with the tree's new unfurling leaves, not the boy. They would have had their day together in a timeline where no one else existed.

She asked to be excused, avoiding the boy's questioning expression. Mother Mab watched her scrape her plate into the garbage and hissed between her teeth, swearing that Finder would never eat another meal as long as she lived if she left food behind again.

When the house fell quiet, the only light blooming from a candle beside her bed and dancing against the glass of her window, Finder dressed in her most sensible clothing. Pants cinched hard around her waist with looping threads of leather to keep them up (they'd been the Ossifier's once, and he was a waif of a thing, but Finder hadn't kept her food down in days, felt her bones thinning and changing). A loose linen shirt tucked and cuffed up around her elbows. Tall boots resoled a hundred times with ivory bone. Sometimes, when she walked, she could just feel the minuscule tacks the Ossifier had hammered back into the soles pinching against her feet.

Her reflection moved with her in the window's glass. She blew out the candle with a wisp of a breath. They met at the bottom of the stairs, in the dark.

Finder had walked this house all her life. She knew the creaks and groans its floorboards gave, how wide she could open a door before it crooned, where to jimmy the latch until it relented. She knew how to sneak a girl inside, how to bring her to the trunk of an ancient tree. So she led the way and the boy followed close behind, his steps quick and his breath hard.

On the porch they lit a lantern. Her hand glowed pale orange and the brown grass went gold. The air was clammy and close. Crickets chirped away from their shoes. She ignored the coop at the edge of the fence, focusing on steady steps and sure footing.

"How long did you say the walk was again?" the boy asked, already huffing as they made their way toward the line of trees. It'd been years since Finder had walked in the woods. She was safe in the house. What reason had there been to leave, after her last? It was only a reminder. A vigil. The breeze rustled the leaves on the trees, a scattering sound that had her heartbeat quickening.

"Just under an hour, if we're quick." The boy did not seem like he would be quick. His breathing was labored, his steps irregular. She picked up the pace, hoping to lead by example.

The lantern cast a circle of protection around them. For a moment Finder found herself believing in that glow of gold, that perhaps anything the light touched would not be able to hurt them. In the distance, dry leaves crunched beneath unseen weight.

"What is *that*?" the boy asked, as the lantern glinted against something on a tree, shining white among all the darkness.

It was a person. No, it was a doll. No, it was bone, whittled and carved and nailed to the trunk of the tree.

It was about the size of Finder's torso and had the head of some small animal, holes carved where eyes would have once sat, teeth laid out in jagged rows. The limbs were loosely knotted pieces clattering in the wind. It swayed and jerked.

"The Ossifier," Finder whispered. They were still close to the house; it was feasible for the haunting figurine to be his. But in the past few years, he'd rarely left the boundary of the fence. And why would he string it up at the path's beginning, like a warning blaze? Unless he knew about the creature they sought. Unless he believed the bone doll to be some kind of ward against whatever lurked in the woods.

"Why would he make this?" the boy asked, creeping closer to it. "It's horrifying."

"Your guess is as good as mine," Finder answered. When she turned back to the path, the lantern swung with her and lit up the trees. More bone dolls hung from their trunks, mismatched arms above their heads, lolling necks rolling in the breeze. "Though it seems they're leading to the same place we're going to."

"You have to know something," the boy said, following her again as she pushed deeper into the woods. "You've spent almost your whole life with him, haven't you?"

"How do you know that?" Finder stepped over a fallen tree. Her skin crawled, like she'd walked into a spiderweb.

A huff and then the boy was over the tree too. "Would it kill you to slow down a bit? Mother Mab told me, when I asked if you were her daughter."

Finder narrowed her eyes. The peaty smell of rotting earth warmed the air. They must be getting closer to the banks now. "And what else did she have to say on the subject?"

"She said that you'd been left on her porch just after you were born, but she considered you her child."

Finder had to fight the warmth in her chest. Mab didn't deserve much credit in the motherly department, despite her title, but some awful part of Finder's heart awakened at the idea of being claimed. A *daughter*. She'd never really considered herself to be one of those before.

After what felt like another silent mile of stumbling steps, the boy spoke again. "Does that make the Ossifier your father, then?"

Finder scoffed. "Don't be insulting. The Ossifier belongs to Mab just as I do."

"Your brother?"

She nearly went cross-eyed trying to follow dim shapes moving between the trees. "It's not like that. This is not a family."

The words sounded strange spoken aloud, but it was true and fine with Finder. She'd never had that kind of family. It was just her life. It was Mother Mab, who ran the house and cooked the meals and corrected anything that Finder did. It was the Ossifier, who'd changed alongside Finder since she arrived, already grown when the basket appeared on the porch. He at times seemed ageless to her, unknowable, an animal that walked on its hind legs and ate at the table with them. He helped Mother Mab when a task required it. Otherwise, he remained confined to his chair, whittling and working away at some scrap of cartilage to add to Mother Mab's working collection, foraged from the line of trees or the skinned body of a hen.

She didn't ask many questions these days. Not after her punishment and the stolen sun. Not after her world changed and the proof of it was denied to her. But once she'd been blessed by red light, and the boy remembered the sun too, didn't he?

The ground sloped down. Deeper in the woods the air was syrupy and warm, jam spooned from the sky. An echo resounded in the delayed thump of their footsteps, like their past selves were following in the outlines of their shadows. Finder wondered, not for the first time, if she'd ever been alone in this world before, or if she was doomed to be stalked by the night for the rest of time. It was a chilling thought. She banished it just as quickly as it came.

"Ossify," the boy said into the dead air. "It means to turn to bone, right? Did Mother Mab give him that name?"

Finder fell silent. Origins. How was she supposed to know? She'd only ever known the names of creatures raised by Mab. Sofia had been cagey about her life, choosing instead to focus on the minute details of the other universe. Finder lived in a world that didn't trust her with stories of beginnings.

But roots didn't matter after all, because the trees broke apart, one last bone doll pinned to a poplar at the edge of the woods. There was the lake before them, a wide expanse that shimmered like tar under the pale glow of her lantern.

"Wow," the boy breathed. He felt for her, fingers landing at her elbow. In a way the touch was grounding, and she found herself suddenly grateful that she wasn't alone.

It'd been years since she'd heard the steady rocking of the rippling water, the scant buzz of insects among the reeds. She remembered wading and laughing, Sofia's joy amplified by miles of quiet. But in the dark it was a boiling pot. Black as the day. Carefully, she stepped closer to the water. Muck clung to her boots.

"Watch your step," the boy called, like Finder had half a brain and no good common sense. She hoped that even in the dimness he could make out the angry twist of her mouth.

The water sloshed. Finder squinted, trying to get a better grasp of her sight. The lantern could only do so much—the air here was too oppressive for its beams to stretch far.

"You heard that, right?"

"It's a lake," Finder said. "There are animals." But anxiety built a nest in her body. She could feel it too; something bigger than them, looming, watching. In her head, she saw the lantern radiant against the body of a bone doll.

"We need to build a fire," she said.

Once, the sun had shone overhead, a cherry ready to be plucked and eaten. Once, Finder had seen under the brilliant light of the world. She was not powerless. She would choose to see.

They gathered as much dry kindling as they could find. She cracked open the door on the lantern, cupping her hands around it for protection, and ignited a bundle of dry grass, placing it snug inside of the pyre they'd built. It caught quickly. The glow that emanated was orange and full, and she felt safer at once watching it grow.

"Are you sure this is smart? What if something sees us now?"

Finder raised the lantern, relishing the magic of fire. "*You* wanted to find it, didn't you? Don't you have some grand plan of destruction?"

He didn't answer. They stood like that for a long time. The mud beneath her boots was cold and dank, and her feet felt nearly frozen despite the heat from the fire. The boy fed it beside her as they watched the water, listened to the trees, waited for change.

"I don't think there's anything out here," she said after a while, her voice catching in her throat.

"Then what were those dolls for? They led *here*, Finder. There has to be a reason for that."

"I don't claim to understand the Ossifier," she snapped, "and I don't think you should either. Maybe it's false magic. It's a ward against nothing."

"Something killed the chickens," the boy said.

"A wolf killed the chickens. A bear killed the wolf. The bear drowned in this very lake, suffocated by river reeds. I don't know what you want me to tell you, Creature, but I don't have the answers."

The fire lit the boy's face, scarlet with embarrassment. Guilt crept over her. Finder should have never called him Creature, should have known better, but it was done now, and it was the natural order of things, after all.

"Let's just go back," he snapped.

Finder gave the smoldering wood a harsh kick. Coals glowed on the ground. She was full of sudden and debilitating hate, with nowhere to place it. So she shoved it inward and let it fester.

Finder faced the water, tipped her head to the sunless sky. "Show yourself!" she bellowed, raw with effort.

"Finder," the boy hissed. "What are you doing?"

"Come and get us!"

"Stop it. Now."

There was a shape in the water. She held the lantern at eye level, a trick she used to pull when the night was still a marvel to wonder at. With the light glowing against her iris she could see every insect eye, know where the spiders waited in the grass. She peered forward. There, glinting on the water. Something wriggled, an intestinal blur of rippling matter. She could taste embers.

"Come on!" she cried again. "Here I am!"

It rose from the water like a drowned body bobbing to the surface. Tendrils pulled from cresting waves—great roots, a plant blooming toward the sky, seeking earth. Liquid rushed as the creature pulled itself from the black lake, the form of it barely distinct against the lightless world. Her lantern shimmered on fragments of spun dust in the air. She stumbled over burning remains, fear seizing her by the neck.

"Run!" Finder shouted.

It crashed after them. She heard the last of the fire hiss out as a wall of water followed the creature. It released an inhuman screech like the wail of a catamount, the terrible sloshing of its dripping roots tearing through the trees. She could feel it more than she could hear it—the ground reverberating as its body slammed down against earth, the shuddering of the brush under felled trunk after felled trunk. She imagined the forest, leveled. Every hovel pried open, every animal set free. The sky dripping down on her shoulders and hardening her into stone. She ran harder. Her feet barely hit the ground. The boy panted, shoes slapping dirt, his panic louder than his desperation. Behind them branches cracked and brush flattened and the creature hissed, that extinguished sound, that released breath.

"Faster," she cried, "you have to go faster!"

Puppets waved and mocked from the shivering trees. The boy stumbled, screamed, and disappeared from her sight. *I can't,* she thought, one desperate plea, and then she spun to pull him from the ground.

Finder had read every book on Mab's shelf. She'd taken painstaking notes. She'd dreamt of every fear until it felt real as the image of a girl pushing past the water—horned beasts tunneling down to the core of the earth, goat women born from fires left untended, blood sacrifices passed from one mouth to the next, tongues twisting them to life.

But this was unlike any horror she could have thought up. The creature towered past the heads of trees. It was featureless and wrong, like an ancient tree torn from the ground, rooted head raw and exposed. It flickered and warped, particles of matter feeding and seeping, the body never completely solid yet its form never faltering. It reared back with a resounding crash of foliage. It screamed again. It bent to face her, wind whipping, trees bending low to the ground.

Finder dragged the boy to his feet, nearly falling to her knees in the process, and ripped him forward.

They ran, ducking low, weaving through the trees as if the path might hide them from the coming force. It felt foolish, insignificant. But Finder, above all else, was not prepared to die.

She could see the fence, the coop, the crooked foundation of the house. A sob rose in her chest. Relief. Palpable, wanting, desperate.

Let it be safe, she incanted, *let us make it.*

The boy barreled into the gate, collapsing into the tall grass, crawling forward and pressing himself low to the ground. She stumbled after him. The gate banged in the vicious wind, whipping like a cyclone.

She fell beside him and covered her head, bracing for impact, the beast circling and screaming, its cry like a hundred voices wailing at once. She waited. But—nothing.

Finder finally looked behind them and found the creature snarling and stalking the boundary, rooted head bending low to the ground, body writhing past the path and over felled trees. But it couldn't follow them. It couldn't pass the fence.

"The ward," Finder whispered.

"We're dead," the boy said, frantic, "we're dead we're dead we're dead."

"We're not," she ground out.

He looked at her, mystified, and then back at the creature. His eyes were full of horror. She staggered to her feet and pulled him after her. "Inside," she said raggedly, spent. "Now."

Finder eased the door open and crept into the house. The boy closed it with a creak behind him. The air was still, the house asleep.

And then a shift in weight, a gentle groan of the floorboards.

She peered down the dim hall that led to the kitchen, where a figure stood silhouetted against the low flame of a single candle. There was a moment when her mind fractured and took the scene apart. The creature had followed them inside, and now this really was the end.

No—it was the Ossifier, stepping out of the basement and clicking the door shut behind him. His eyes fell on her. They sized each other up.

"Where have you been?" he said, and his voice crawled down the hallway on its hands and knees, chilling and raw.

Finder willed herself not to falter. "I could ask you the same thing."

The candle lit up his face. When he bared his teeth, the flame shone against the exposed bone. Slowly, he held a finger to his lips, a *hush* motion that chilled her entirely.

"I won't tell if you don't," he whispered. "But you should go upstairs before someone else catches you out of your bed."

They hovered in that moment. She wondered if he could feel it too—the residual haunt of Sofia darting out the back door, dashing for the trees, Finder screaming for her to run until her throat went raw and Mother Mab successfully caged her back in her room.

He gleamed at her in the dark. "To bed," he said again.

Dutifully she climbed the stairs, the boy left behind to his cot, the Ossifier's rhythmic steps following behind her. She clicked her bedroom door shut. Alone at last, she stripped down and struggled into her nightgown, shivering all the while.

When morning came, she found that she was still shaking.

30

WHOM YOU PROMISED DOMINION

They slept in Frankie's room, Poppy and Cass in the bed, Marya and Frankie in a mess of blankets on the floor. With Frankie's mattress soft beneath her, Cass could almost imagine that nothing had changed—that she was still the same as she'd always been, that she'd wake to find Sofia lying to her left, that the sun would come up on their shared history.

But she opened her eyes to stale memory, mouth dry, hand pinned under the pillow where Poppy slept a fitful corpse rest. She propped herself on her elbow until she could spot Frankie and Marya on the floor, Frankie with her wrists over her head, Marya with hers over her heart, both stirring under morning light.

I want this forever, Cass thought. *I want them down the street. I want them in this room until the end of time. Just them, and this moment.*

A burning scent carried up the stairs, someone's breakfast long forgotten. Cass rolled over and faced Poppy, forehead furrowed in a dream. There was a pervasive fear that yesterday had been the start of something worse, that there wasn't enough rest in the world to keep Poppy safe, that Cass was spiraling desperately out of control.

Poppy blinked awake and pushed deeper into the pillow. Cass smiled. "Smells like it's time to eat," she said, trying to sound like the world hadn't ended.

It took another thirty minutes before they were all awake enough to gather at the dining room table. There was a candle burning somewhere, likely meant to obscure blackened bacon. Tension strung throughout the house. Cass watched Frankie shrug off Sissa's hand and avoid Oph's concerned expression until the women finally left them to eat.

But things between the four of them had been different since that moment in the kitchen and the subsequent ritual. The fault lines didn't seem to matter so much anymore. That was something, right? That had to be enough.

Cass picked at too-crisp toast and Marya took the seat beside her. Frankie poured coffee for each of them except Cass, who already had iced tea sweating beside her plate. It was stiflingly hot. The oven ticked on, sun cosmic through the windows, and still Cass watched Poppy warm her hands around her mug.

"We need to go back to the house," Poppy insisted, when the quiet had dragged on for too long.

"It's not safe," Frankie said. "How do we know their ritual worked and it won't happen again? I don't want to see you get hurt."

Poppy's face shuttered and closed.

"You know we all want to make progress," Frankie continued, softer now. "But we need to be careful. Especially after . . . what we dealt with."

"The magic," Marya answered.

Frankie frowned but didn't snap back like Cass had expected. That felt like progress.

"So, what do we do?" Cass asked. Beads of condensation trailed down her glass onto her skin.

"I guess we should—" Frankie started. "Fuck. I don't know. I'm not willing to risk any of you. As much as I hate to admit it, I think they were right. We have to leave the house alone."

Poppy's hold tightened around the mug. "We can't just give up."

Cass couldn't resist. She tipped to her right and let her temple rest on Poppy's shoulder. Poppy cupped the back of Cass's head with a gentle palm and Cass felt her heart sing, higher than magpies in the sky.

"I agree," she said, fueled by the warmth of Poppy's reciprocation. "We already found stuff the police missed, and it's clear that they're not going to put any more effort into the case."

"Frankie is right," Marya said. "We don't have to give up, but maybe it's best if we all take a break until we can sort out where to go next."

Frankie looked annoyed to be agreeing, but she said, "Exactly, a break."

"Whatever," Poppy said finally, exhaling across the top of Cass's head.

They split that night, returning to their own beds. At home, Cass couldn't sleep; she had vivid, awful dreams, nightmares where Poppy was torn apart by phantom hands, where Marya's mouth sprouted vines, where Frankie's skin smoldered and cooked. In each of them she was a stone corpse, unable to save them.

Cass blinked awake in the frayed fingers of dawn. She was afraid to be alone in her body and ashamed to fear the dark.

A week passed like this. She obeyed the rules. No hunting, strictly mindlessness, just bingeing shows in her bed or spending afternoons in the studio watching Frankie work.

But living with her parents again had consequences that stretched further than she'd previously imagined. Coexistence with her dad was a thorn that pricked her finger with each unfortunate meeting, every awkward dinner. Cass saw him and thought: *she was out there, alone in that tree, and no one came.*

An itch crawled across her skin, that restlessness returning, the need to do *something* before she thought she might explode.

It was a Thursday when she decided to follow Lucas alone.

She found him leaving the hardware-store parking lot on the other side of town. His truck shone pristine among the muddy ones passing on the roads. Yesterday's rain had churned the earth, but nothing seemed to touch Lucas, not even nature. She trailed him slowly down winding paths until they were close to his house again, afternoon sun making stark patterns against the road. She wondered if he knew he was being followed, if he recognized the Ford by now, but found that she didn't really care.

Until Lucas pulled over on the side of the road in the same place Sofia's car had been found all those years ago. Cass hurried to stop, fumbling with the gearshift. What was she doing? Why was she giving herself away like this?

She wanted to see his face. She wanted him to know that she would follow him to the ends of the earth if it meant keeping Sofia's memory sweet.

But her vision sputtered as she tried to make sense of it. From her spot on this overgrown stretch of highway she saw Lucas open the driver's door. As her mind reset, the passenger side swung open. Her brother slid from the truck.

Alex looked small and different, the outlines of his body not the same ones she remembered from that morning. But it was her brother, unmistakably. Driving around Loring with her best friend's potential murderer.

Fuck me, she thought with venom. If there was a chance that Lucas Glasswell killed Sofia, there was now a chance that her brother knew something about it.

She reached for her phone. Dropped it again. The song on the radio clashed metallically with her thoughts so she turned it all the way down. Something caught her eye in the rearview mirror, a quick shape, but when she looked again there was nothing but the green and empty road behind her. And before her, her brother followed Lucas as they walked over to her window.

Cass tried to steady her thoughts. She'd blown whatever cover they had pretended to have. Frankie would be furious at her for going out alone, and things were just starting to get better between the four of them. How could she have taken it upon herself to throw everything back into a spiral? What proof did she have to panic about?

All they had were splintered theories to roll around in their heads. A symbol and a feeling and a haunted house. And Alex would never hurt someone, would he? He'd always been soft, cowering away from Cass's pinches and prods and shoves. Never the type to fight back. Alex couldn't, wasn't capable, was never that kind of boy.

Lucas rapped on her window. She slowly cranked the lever, watching the glass slide down inch by inch. Alex stood beside Lucas—the top of his head only reached Lucas's shoulder, every inch of him brown and summery against Lucas's ghostly and imposing stature. They were both short, those Sullivans. Cass liked the thought, that she and her brother shared something coded into their bodies.

"Can I ask why you're following me?" Lucas said, his tone easy.

Cass cracked her knuckles in her lap, a nervous habit. They popped like snapping twigs. "Hey, boys. What's up?"

"Cass," Alex said, taking on the kind of admonishment that should have belonged to her alone. When had his voice gotten so deep? He'd grown up while she was gone. And apparently, he'd gotten closer to Lucas Glasswell than she expected, closer than he should have. She knew that Alex had always had some guileless obsession with Lucas and Tommy and the rest of the boys they'd grown up with. She hadn't realized how lasting those friendships had become. How deeply the claws of their influence had hooked into her brother's susceptible heart.

"I asked you a question," Lucas said, bitterly. "I'm not clueless. I've seen your truck following me for the past few weeks."

What did she think, that he wouldn't notice the Ford's rusted body, the wheezing sound its engine made when she begged it uphill? It was foolish to even hope. But she had been *so* hopeful, and *so* foolish.

"You didn't kill her," Cass said, a statement without a question mark but in need of an answer. She expected anger. But his face only fell. His eyes went blue and heavy.

"I didn't kill her," Lucas repeated.

Cass tried to crack her knuckles again and ended up kneading them together instead. "I need you to prove it."

"Cass," Alex said again. "This is ridiculous."

"I don't have to prove anything to you."

Sure, maybe he didn't. The sheriff's department had already cleared him, and the case wasn't big enough to warrant state involvement—her dad had told her so himself, and laughed when she suggested reaching out to federal law enforcement. If Lucas had truly played a part in the whole mess, he wouldn't be standing here now, would he?

"I'm asking you," Cass said. "Please."

"Why should I tell you anything?" Lucas's face shuttered, his whole body made of angles. It was hard to remember that Sofia chose him for a reason—that Cass had watched the two of them be affectionate in between their rocky break-ups, that she had witnessed dinner dates and school dances and parties where Sofia fell into Lucas's arms at the end of the night.

"Fair," she admitted, avoiding Alex's crestfallen face, "but I'm coming to you as—an ally. I want to find who did this and bring them to justice."

He watched her. "Okay. So do I."

Cass's hands stilled in her lap. "Tell me what you know about the end."

Alex's eyes burned into her. Lucas's chin tipped back in defiance when he finally answered.

"Fine. Follow me. I know you remember how."

Lucas led Alex to where the dirt path blended into foliage. When he glanced back at Cass and the Ford, his eyebrows raised a question at her.

"Fuck it all," she said, and she slammed the door behind her.

He led them through the trees. It was the same path they had taken to the barn—a new fear struck her heart, like the forest was watching her. She kept her eyes trained on her brother's back. A domineering part of her wanted to command him to get away from this, to go back home, to leave it all behind and let her clean up the mess.

"How do I know you're not leading me somewhere to finish me off?" Cass said, nerves climbing from her belly to her throat.

Lucas jabbed his thumb in Alex's direction. "Would I really let your brother tag along as a witness?"

Cass scoffed. "Maybe he wants me dead, too."

"Not yet, but keep it up and we'll see," Alex muttered.

They stopped at the edge of the Glasswell property, where the barn stood among verdant grass. Lucas used the weight of his shoulder to lift the bar across the wide door, pulling it open. Past the wooden frame Cass could see pockets of sun filtering in from small windows along the stalls, illuminated dust snowing down over their heads.

"After you," Lucas said with a wave of his arm, and they stepped inside.

"What are we doing here?"

Inside it was quiet, the only sounds the muffled thud of a horse's hooves against hay, the low bleating of a goat. Cass rubbed up and down her biceps, suddenly cold. She watched in frozen fear as Lucas walked to the center of the barn, where the packed dirt floor was the only clear path. He stopped at the stall door. The symbol was so clear now that she'd seen it up close. He paused, staring at it, and she waited for him to turn and put his hands around her throat, to slam her up against the wood, finish her off. Maybe he would ask Alex to watch.

"This is where I found the ritual," he said.

Cass's pulse began to pound. "What the hell are you talking about?"

"See, I thought you knew all about it," Lucas said. "I thought you told her to do it."

"Elaborate," she said, impatient. She peered at the twining snakes as if they would give a dead girl's secrets away.

"She had tried to break up with me the day before. Said it wasn't right, that we weren't meant to be together. I mean, it came out of nowhere, so clearly I was shocked. I asked her to think about it and not to rush into any decisions, but she was a mess. She said that she was sorry, but she couldn't change her mind."

He ran a hand over his scalp, mouth twisted. "My family was supposed to go out of town that day, a vacation before graduation. I'd even invited her, but she shut me down. Then there was that storm—you remember, half the power in Loring went out for a night—and the flight was postponed. My dad turned the car around and came back and I went to feed the horses. She was there," he said, gesturing to the dirt, "bleeding over a candle. Her eyes were all white, no irises."

Cass pressed a palm to her mouth. "What did you do to her?"

"What did *I* do to *her*? She was fucking hexing me, Sullivan, I don't know. She was speaking to something—this huge, dark figure. It looked like a goat standing on its hind legs, with big horns. Don't look at me like that, okay, I'm not fucking crazy. It had a hand on her head, but the fingers were more human than anything else, and it was dark enough that I couldn't see anything behind it, just this massive gray shape. And she . . . I don't know what I saw, but it looked like her shadow was stretching out across the floor. Like—spilled ink." He stood pale and stiff. "I scared it, I think. The door slammed behind me and it let out this *scream*. It crouched and started clawing at the ground and when she turned to look at me, it faded away."

"Jesus," Cass whispered. "Weren't you terrified?"

"Of course! But she was still my goddamn girlfriend. I wrapped my shirt around her hand—there was blood everywhere, I never realized that much could come from such a little wound."

Alex went green as Lucas continued, "I didn't know how to help her. She shoved me away from her and said I had ruined everything by interrupting. I didn't recognize her. Her voice was different. Rougher."

"Why didn't you tell anyone?" she whispered, her heart in her throat.

"Her sister would have told me to eat shit," he answered immediately, and Cass couldn't deny that. His expression went sheepish. "But I told my mom. And Alex, eventually, a few years down the line."

"Seriously?" she muttered. She wanted to snatch Alex by his collar, demand to know why he had never told her, but that could wait. "Okay. Cool. You told your mom. What did she do?"

"She prayed over me for a long time and told me I was never allowed to see Sofia again. But we spent years together, Sullivan. Whatever assumptions you have of me, go ahead and have them, but I loved her." His face fell, wounded by something she couldn't see. "I just—she was hurting. I wanted to help her and make everything right before we had to go. But she disappeared the next night."

Cass pressed a hand to her forehead, thoughts running a mile a minute.

"It was like she didn't even recognize me," he said, fists shoved as far down into the pockets of his jeans as they would go.

Cass thought about Poppy in the kitchen, her expression all wrong for her face, gaze unfamiliar.

"Does that mean anything to you?" Lucas asked, watching her intently.

"Yes," she answered. "It does."

She could go home and tell them. She could sit Frankie down and explain everything that Lucas had told her. But Frankie would never forgive her for going behind her back—she might not even believe what Lucas had said. Her distrust and hate for him were hardened things, buried low in her heart.

"What about the bonfire?" Cass asked. It was hard to breathe. "You were with her, weren't you? You were the last one to see her?"

He shook his head. "She ran into the woods the moment my dad showed up. Last thing I remember was seeing her take off toward the trees and Tommy telling me to get inside the house, right before the porch collapsed under him. I should have stayed with her."

Cass bit down on her cheek and tried to look at anything but the writhing shape on the stall door. The patch of dirt where Marya's hands had pressed seemed to pulse, like it was sensing Sofia there, some distant echo.

She remembered the videos of that night circling online, Tommy's leg shredded and gory, the collapsing house lit up in siren hues. Lucas nowhere in sight despite his claims. Remembered lying in the dark with the trees whistling overhead, praying that Sofia would come stumbling down the hill after them.

They had all left her behind. But Sofia had left them too, in one way or another, hadn't she?

There was no way to win, only further abscesses to spiral into. It was an impenetrable dread that told Cass she had dug her heels in too deep, and that maybe she hadn't known who Sofia was at all.

It was late when she slid back into her truck, phone buzzing between her back pocket and the leather seat. She flipped it over, luminous blue screen turning her fingers ghoulish and strange as she read Frankie's text.

break's over. meet at the styx.

31

Conceive of a Vile Hope

The Styx was little more than a trickle from a storm drain, summer sucking it up through a straw. It cut its way under a narrow bridge—only wide enough for a car at a time, every crash said to summon a woman in white—and slipped through the lowing trees.

When Poppy was a kid, the four of them had loved that gouge in the earth. It was ancient with moss, peppered with jagged stones that clawed their way through the slow current of the water. The water always smelled of copper and heat—hurt waiting to happen. They would bike there when the sun was too much to bear and the lake felt too close to home, when it was preferable to strip half-naked and lie in what must have been the remnants of April's last snow carving its way down the mountain.

"Why are we here?" Poppy called as she stepped sideways down the embankment, trying to prevent slipping into the craggy mess that waited at the bottom. She was suddenly grateful for the night. For how it softened the blow of remembering.

Salamander in her hands. Grapes pulled from wild vines, sharp and sour, crushed between her teeth. Sofia brushing Poppy's braids from her face, leaving berry stains on her temples, the earth so thirsty it splintered open beneath them. Hot always. Even when the leaves began to fall, even in the dark.

How to describe it, the unbidden memory? How to describe them among it? Holy place. Sinless. Sofia standing in the rising creek after a fast and hard rain. The coming of her heart over a distant hill. How to say it? Perfect, in some ways. All she had ever wanted.

Now Frankie waded ankle deep in the thin current, looking like she'd just stepped out of a painting. Her hair draped over her shoulders. Her pale tank top was splattered with creek water. It was just night enough to turn her eyes into two black pockets, as if summoned incomplete from Poppy's head.

"Security reasons," Frankie answered when Poppy was close enough to hear. "No eavesdroppers."

So, things were still bad with Oph. Poppy was hesitant to speak on the subject. Oph and Sissa had tried to help her, hadn't they? Who was she to deny them?

No, that wasn't it. They hadn't tried. They *had* helped her.

Marya waited on the bank, less eager to stand in the creek. Poppy joined her. Her shoes sank in damp loam. Her head ached with a penetrating buzz and there was a drag to her movement that made her want to sit down. She swatted at her ear like it might shoo whatever was bothering her, but the hum only deepened.

The ritual had helped. She felt better. She felt fucking amazing. That was that.

Headlights flooded the woods around them, then died just as fast. Cass came stumbling down the hill a second later. "Christ," she said, huffing, "you couldn't have picked somewhere less likely to break my ankle? What are we doing here?"

Something prickled along the nape of Poppy's neck. She cleared her throat, rolled her shoulders.

"If we're not going to the house, then we can go back to the barn," Frankie said. Her foot arced in the water, droplets following. "I want to know exactly what that symbol meant. I don't care if that means confronting Lucas."

Cass looked green, surprise and discomfort warring on her face.

"I don't see how that's going to help Sofia," Marya said hesitantly.

Poppy's temple panged. She winced, pressed a fingertip to the spot. The skin was too warm. She couldn't tell the difference between a headache and the loss of her mind. Her heartbeat was too close, too loud, boiling under her skin. "What would you know about helping her? Your last suggestion only left us with more questions. We need answers."

It came out like an accusation, and it was only after asking that Poppy realized she meant it as one, though the intention made her feel dizzy. Her words seemed to transform once they left her mouth, against her will. Cass gave her a warning glance.

"I—" Marya started. Her eyes flickered between them. She touched the nape of her neck and swallowed. "I know Oph said it was dangerous. But I have a friend who might be able to help us perform mirror magic. And I think they could contact Sofia in the Fissure."

"Holy shit," Cass said, immediately. "You could have led with that, you know."

"It's not a guarantee," Marya answered. "It's just . . . a possibility. But she kind of hates me right now, so if she shuts us down, then that's that."

"What'd you do, ruin her life?" Poppy asked, trying to turn her direct suspicion into a joke. Marya's expression flattened and closed itself off.

"Hopefully not," she said, vague and stiff.

They turned to Frankie for direction, radiant in the dark. There was so much excitement on her face that it embarrassed Poppy, left her reeling, afraid and wanting and awake.

"We're going," Frankie said. "Tonight."

Sofia lived in a mirror world, so they would enter a mirror. Simple as that.

It was easiest to follow someone when you loved them, and even when it seemed like the world might be ending, even when years of tension had split them down the middle like a sloppily sliced fruit, Poppy loved Frankie undyingly. Once, she'd loved Sofia like that, more than that, with a natural affection. Loved her still, with a kind of reverence that terrified her.

They piled into the Ford. Poppy pressed her forehead to the cool glass of Cass's passenger-side window, relished how it soothed her skin.

Poppy and Cass sat in the cab of the truck, radio blaring into the night past Cass's rolled-down window. Crickets sang like music rising from an orchestral pit. It was summer. Poppy was a woman who loved, in a car with the people who loved her back, on her way to save a girl she'd once held in her unknowing arms.

Those arms prickled now, like a limb halfway to falling asleep. She leaned her head back against the seat. Her lashes fluttered against her cheek and her breath lagged in her chest.

Frankie and Marya sprawled out in the bed of the truck, blankets tucked around them to make the long drive more comfortable. Cass's key chain bumped against the dashboard every time the road became uneven.

"What do you think they're doing back there?" Cass said.

"What?" Poppy asked, eyes still closed. She pinched her thigh just to ground herself with the sting. She used to have panic attacks all the time, back at college and around the time she'd left Loring. It had been a while since the last one. Her heart felt swollen, her tongue heavy.

"You know. Frankie and Marya."

"I think they're riding in your truck like the rest of us, Sullivan."

Cass drummed against the wheel. "I don't know," she said breezily. "Gays these days." And it was such a stupid thing to say that it shook her out of her own head. Poppy choked on a laugh, her head tipped back, eyes crinkled at the corners. Cass's laugh echoed back.

And Poppy was suddenly so grateful that she'd always been accepted by them and she'd always accepted them right back, so thankful that they'd found each other and the ties between them were the unshakable kind, the redeemable kind, the understanding kind of soul bond that couldn't be erased.

"We're lucky," Poppy said.

"*Lucky*? That's rich. We're fucking hexed."

"No," Poppy interjected. She watched the road, the yellow lines winding like twin snakes down the center—she was too afraid to look at the pockets of foliage along the shoulders. Her heart was still beating too fast. "I mean—I've never had another friendship like this."

"Come on, you had to have made some good friends at college." Then Cass's voice went uncertain. "I mean, did you? I don't really know anything about your time away."

Because Poppy had been so terrified. Because she had missed them so badly that it was easier to close herself off. Because she had wanted nothing more than to go home for months, had cried in the communal showers crouching under the spray. Because she had answered the phone for Cass once—just one time—and the sound of her voice had been enough to make Poppy unable to eat for a week.

"It wasn't like this," she said.

She meant: *They weren't my family. They didn't watch me shift and change, didn't know me in my most vulnerable time and still love me in the end.* Cass had been the first person to see her. Frankie had taken care of her, knew exactly what she needed in their silent moments. Sofia had loved her more than Poppy thought herself worthy of being loved.

"I guess you're right," Cass said, wistfully. "We're lucky."

Poppy looked at her, cheek rubbing against the worn leather headrest of the bench seat. Her heart was beating so fast. It was just anxiety—new places, new people, the strange feeling clinging to the back of her throat.

"I love you," she said.

Cass's profile was just a shadow, but the line of her mouth tilted down. "Don't say it like that."

"Like what?"

"Like you're afraid something bad will happen."

Poppy blinked. There was a moment where her eyes took too long to come back to her, where the darkness stuck around for too long. She remembered the jerk of her body in Oph's kitchen, her joints no longer belonging to her bones. A complete lack of control.

"Something bad already happened," Poppy said, almost too quietly to be heard over the radio. "What's so wrong with being afraid?"

Cass glanced at her. One hand searched blindly while the other clutched the wheel. Poppy found it, took it in her own. They sat together in the quiet. Pale headlights danced across her eyes.

An image of the old house in the middle of the woods flashed across her mind. The empty tree, waiting, ink spilling from its hewn-open trunk among the impossibly sprouted flowers. *Mother.*

No. That wasn't right. Was it?

Her cheeks burned with the parasitic creep of fever. Anger stoked deep inside her, a foreign feeling hotter than she could make sense of. It cooked its way up to her mouth.

Cass's grasp felt too tight in her own. And that was the problem, wasn't it? She was always anchored down, drowning in being known. Maybe it wasn't meant to comfort Poppy but to keep her locked in place. The others were fearful when they looked at her, weren't they? Good. They didn't trust her regardless. Frankie hated her. Cass pitied her. Marya thought her an experiment.

No. She flared with heat, banished the psychopomp of a past self. She didn't actually believe that, did she? Frankie and Cass loved her, and Marya wasn't so bad. Poppy actually kind of liked her now, with the layers peeled back.

THE WITCH WILL BURN.

The thought thundered through her head, the same grinding sound that had crawled from her mouth back in that decrepit house. The cadence made her wince. The sound was excruciatingly familiar—it was a part of her, like a finger that had lost its feeling and was finally waking up. Cass glanced over at her, feeling the pressure of Poppy's tightening hold.

"Stop looking at me like that," Poppy mumbled. The sound of the words hadn't exactly hurt her, but it felt like her mind was rattling around in her skull. Her thoughts had gone malleable.

"Stop acting so strange then," Cass said lightly, but Poppy could hear the worry despite how hard she tried to disguise it. She wanted to apologize, say that she hadn't meant to scare her, but—

THEY WILL BURN AND YOU WILL LIGHT THE MATCH. IT WILL MAKE A LOVELY PYRE.

"*Stop* it," she whispered out loud.

"I'm not doing anything," Cass said.

"No, sorry, not you." Poppy pressed a hand over her eyes. When she opened them again, she almost expected to see a shadow where her skin was supposed to be, the brown of her arm replaced by ink and soot.

"You're being weird," Cass whispered. "Why didn't you tell us that something was wrong in the first place?"

"I didn't know," Poppy gritted out.

But maybe she did. From that very first second, her skin grazing white petals, her pupils blowing wide. There had been no other possible understanding—just the before and after. And now her pulse was different. She saw shapes in blurred corners, always gone when she turned her head, like looking through a clouded haze of smoke.

But there was a small part of her that said that she felt *powerful.* She would contain all that enormous energy, she would control it, she would make it tell her what happened to Sofia and she would make things right, she was going to—

GO TO THE HOUSE ON THE HILL WITH THE TREE FOR A HEART, WHERE YOU WILL SLEEP AND THEY WILL DIE AND YOU WILL BE MINE.

Her mouth moved against her will. It was a smile, then a snarl, then a smile again. She felt like she was going to cry. She felt nothing at all.

"Poppy," Cass said. Her voice was too loud in the cab of the truck. "Tell me what's going on. You expect me to watch you get possessed and just think everything's going to be okay?"

Poppy's jaw was wired shut. Her bones pulled in every direction, like her body was attempting to make itself a new shape. She made her free hand into a fist, then unclenched it, nails leaving angry little divots along her palm. Lunar phases spelled out in the unbroken skin.

And this feeling—this knowing—it made a sick thought crawl up her throat, made her question everything she thought she knew about the natural shape of the universe. What if Sofia hadn't been murdered by someone, but some*thing*? Was it possible that this thing itself had taken her to the tree inside of the house? Could a shadow, a projection of blocked luminance, really kill a human being?

It was no longer a question of possible or impossible. Everything Poppy knew about the natural world no longer held up under scrutiny. The only thing that mattered now was the question of true or false, and the answer that lay in between those options, the *maybe-so*, the midpoint where her understanding faltered.

It was just that—if Sofia had been killed by something bigger than reality, then that meant there was something very wrong with Poppy too. Because she'd touched the tree and she'd opened herself up to the terrible and wanting world. There was a soul-splitting moment where she thought that maybe, regardless of the rising sun and the lake-water baths, she'd never be free of this untethered feeling.

Her thoughts sluiced through the pool of her mind. The thing inside of her thrummed with power, and she could feel tendrils of it crawling up her spine. It moved her eyes for her. It took her name from her throat.

"I'm fine," she said at last. "I'd tell you if I wasn't."

Cass was quiet for a long moment. "And I'll tell *you* when I believe that."

Poppy stared ahead as the truck made its way down the empty road, trees lit up by the wash of the headlights. Her hand lay empty in her lap.

32

Even the Beasts Could Barely Find It

The sky was speckled as a bird's egg. Satellites stuttered and blinked. Marya lay on her back, blankets softening the hard bed of the truck, Frankie's arm warm against her own. It was a three-hour drive to Raleigh—by the time they got there, it would be nearly one in the morning.

Marya had never felt like this in all her life—alive, and unafraid.

"We could play twenty questions," she said to Frankie, yelling over the wind.

"I'd actually rather die," Frankie answered. Open fields littered with cows whizzed by them. They were speeding.

"I spy?" she tried again.

"What about the quiet game?"

"Someone's in a bad mood," Marya said. "I thought we were friends now."

She liked that Frankie's temper showed when she prodded, that it could exist as something familiar—it prevented her from spiraling down into the pit of her thoughts. She pushed away dread when she thought about Nina's grin, shared gin and tonics, neon signs glowing a radioactive red.

"Okay, new game. Secret for a secret," Marya said, arms folded across her chest. "Here's mine—being in Raleigh again makes me nervous."

Surprised silence answered her.

"The game requires your participation to work. I want to know why you were fighting with Sofia before she disappeared."

"I told you already," Frankie said. "I wanted her to choose me."

Marya tried not to turn her head and catch Frankie's gaze. The task was herculean.

"Over what?"

"Not what, who."

"Lucas?" Marya asked. Her cheeks were hot, wind-whipped.

"Sometimes," Frankie admitted. "Not always. She barely spent time with any of us in that last year, but if she wasn't with Lucas, she was with Poppy. The two of them had something else, I guess. I didn't pry." She squinted, like the action might ward off emotion. "I don't know. I just wanted us to be together and I didn't want to pick sides. I said some things I regret, did some equally regrettable shit, alienated everyone. I told her—I said that one day none of us would put up with her and that she would find herself alone."

Marya wasn't sure how to respond, so she chose to wait. In the silence, Frankie fidgeted, until the pressure became too much.

"She said she thought it was embarrassing how I acted like I was in love with all of them, and that I needed to get over it and stop pretending like I could convince them to stay. But I wasn't trying to convince them, I swear. I didn't need them to stay. I just—I wanted them to come back one day. That's all. I just wanted to know that they would come back."

"Well, you do love them," Marya said, because saying it felt like manifestation. Like speaking it aloud might take her a step closer to their orbit.

"Of course," Frankie mumbled. "She was mad, and we were already in such a bad place. She knew I wasn't *in* love with them, not like that at least, it's just—it's always been bigger than friendship. That word is insignificant. With us"—she paused, looking at Marya—"it was family from the beginning."

"Sounds incestuous," Marya said, because she needed to turn this whole mess into a joke before she found herself reaching for Frankie, just for the natural comfort of holding a hand in her own.

When Frankie scoffed, Marya laughed, tipping her head back against the bed of the truck and feeling the rumble of the road in her stomach.

"You know, friends can tell friends when they're being incredibly annoying," Frankie said.

"Am I annoying you now?" Marya asked.

Frankie had a twisted little smile on her face. "You're always annoying me."

"So you admit it."

Frankie pressed her cheek into the cushion of blankets. "Admit what? That you're annoying?"

"That we're friends."

Frankie narrowed her eyes. Freckles stretched across the bridge of her nose in sweet patterns. Marya knew she was staring, but there was something entrancing about her like this, agitated and intent.

"We won't be for long if you keep this up," she answered.

"I told you," Marya said, turning her face back to the cloudless expanse over them. "I can bear it."

She wondered if Sofia could see them now.

They stopped once for coffee and hot french fries shared between them, sitting in a parking lot while they ate. Cass passed bites through the sliding rear window. Frankie accepted them with her head against the glass, only pretending to snap at Cass's fingers once. The laugh that bubbled out of Marya surprised her. There was something so intimate about it, the casual tenderness between them, even as doubt clouded Cass's eyes and Frankie's face creased with frustration and Poppy was quiet, so quiet. Marya still found herself jealously longing in the face of it. How special it was, to care about another person on purpose. How massive and strange.

Marya had never really had something like that. Once, she thought she might have, with Nina. They had only ever been able to choose each other until they hadn't.

It was another hour before they entered the city. Streetlights ate the stars. Cars blew by and laughter spilled into the street. By the time they found a place to park, the moon was an unblinking eye high overhead, and Marya shivered beneath its gaze. What would Nina say, when she saw her? Would she feel like Marya did now? A little yearnful, unnervingly resentful?

"It's just around the corner," Marya said. She jumped down from the bed of the truck with an asphalt thud. Everything was familiar and foreign to her all at once. Even the air smelled like the past.

"What if she's not there?" Cass glanced around the road as if she expected something to leap out at them. Evening heat rose molten and the night was heavy on their backs.

"She'll be there," Marya answered.

The bar emerged down the block with a dim windowed front that read *Syndicated* in scrawled Gothic font. It gleamed like polished silver. People smoked in clusters under the awning as music poured from behind them. The sign over the door had fake horns glued to it, the ends painted a red that was too bright and gooey to emulate blood. It gave a nasty effect, nonetheless.

"You worked here?" Cass asked, dumbfounded.

"It paid the bills," Marya said. She pulled the door open. They followed in after her.

Everything was a pulsing red. Marya's head felt like it was unattached to her body, weightless and buzzing, overwhelmed by the sudden wash of nostalgia. People danced close to one another with drinks in hand. Two girls leaned against the bar and into each other. She blinked at them for a moment, foolishly thinking that maybe she was looking at a residual haunting of herself and Nina, wrapped up in each other and the possibility of forever. She squinted and they were just two girls again.

Marya pushed her way up to the bar. It was easy to walk like she fit right into this space when she knew from experience that it appeared that way; as if she were ghostly and alive all at once, the lights turning her hair the color of pale cherries.

Nina stood behind the bar, cleaning glasses. The cropped cut Marya remembered her having now fell in black tendrils, stark against her white throat. Muddy makeup smudged around her eyes. Jewelry glinted in her nose and along her ears. She had a new piercing, a hoop in her left nostril to match the right.

Marya leaned up against the bar. Nina found her immediately, and Marya watched the other girl short-circuit in a way that was all too familiar—a seize of the heart. She set down the glass she'd been cleaning and her face lit up with surprise.

"What the fuck, Masha," she said in lieu of hello. Marya just barely heard her over the roar of the music. There was a fluttering lilt to her deep voice, music of another language no longer spoken. "What are you doing here? Where the hell have you been?" Her eyes jumped to the rest of them. "You brought friends?"

Marya felt unknowable. "Nina, everyone," she said, waving between them. "Everyone, Nina."

"Awesome introduction," Nina said, scathing. She spoke with impatience—the syllables were a tapping foot, in a terribly comforting way. Her deep-set eyes were wicked, caught up in a joke that Marya could no longer follow.

Nina turned to Poppy and tucked the rag in her hand into a back pocket before extending it to shake. "Nina Golubeva." She moved down the line and they introduced themselves to her one by one. Marya didn't miss the firm grip Frankie gave Nina, even through her bandages.

Nina filled a row of even shot glasses and slid them across the bar. Marya tipped hers back with a searing burn and glanced at the others to gauge their reactions. Cass's face was open and thrilled, taking it all in, dancing a little to a vaguely familiar pop song. Poppy hung close behind with a shuttered expression nailed in place. Frankie's face was a cautious mask, and it stayed trained on Nina behind the bar.

Something thrilled in Marya's stomach at the sight.

A palm pressed against her lower back as someone passed behind her. Another shoulder brushed hers. Her skin buzzed; she blinked and savored the dark behind her eyelids in the split second of peace. Nina was liquid behind the bar, flowing from one end to the other, taking orders with an electric grin. A man joined her and started filling drinks. She spoke to him too quietly to be heard over the music, and Marya caught his eye as he glanced up at her. She grinned back, baring her teeth.

Nina angled away from him, passing a drink to someone down the bar. "Masha, you won't believe how much has changed around here. Dominic has a girlfriend. A *girlfriend*. Who would have thought he could shut his mouth long enough to convince someone to stick around?"

Her heart seized and stuttered. Somewhere, in the back of her mind, she'd thought the life she'd left behind would have died without her there to experience it. "Sounds like things have been pretty entertaining," she answered.

"This place misses you. We're still adjusting," Nina said. Marya heard the unsaid bite in the words.

"So you met here, huh?" Frankie cut in. Marya glanced at her, surprised. Frankie's mouth was a serrated line. Flashing neon made her skin gleam. When Frankie felt Marya looking, she glanced back and softened her mouth. Marya's pulse skipped. She was dangerously pleased by the feeling.

"We grew up together," Nina answered. "Our parents lived next door to each other until mine carted me south. When Marya left the city, I got her a job here so we could reconnect." She smiled at Marya then, knowing and bittersweet.

"Your family still lives here too?" Marya said, trying to veer the conversation toward anything other than their "reconnection." She set down her glass. It made a wet ring against the surface of the bar.

"My mom," Nina said. "Moved apartments though. She's living in the same building as Dom, and they had a break-in a few months ago. I tried to call you and tell you about it."

"Reception is bad in Loring," Marya said, feeling like a supreme bitch.

"I thought you were dead," Nina continued lightly. Wide silver rings adorned most of her fingers and they made resonant sounds against the glasses she collected. "An entire year passes by, and now you just show up without a word." Hurt had etched itself into her face, barely disguised.

"Well, you know," Marya answered. She sipped from the sweating glass, unable to keep her hands still. "I had to follow an opportunity to make better money."

Frankie laughed.

"Don't we all," Nina said, too lightly. For the first time since they'd entered the bar, she went still. Her eyes swept across them and landed on Marya. "So. How long are you in town for?"

"That's the thing," Marya said. She kept her voice casual, drawn out like a sunning cat. "We need your help with something important, and we only have tonight to get it done."

"Ooh, a mission," Nina said with delight.

"It's serious," Marya said.

"I can be serious," Nina answered, but the smile on her face remained.

Marya's fingertips rested against the bar. She spent most of her energy focusing on not letting them tremble.

"Listen, this is—" Frankie started, already rearing back, but Marya gave her a pleading look. *Let me handle this,* she willed through her gaze. Frankie grimaced back.

Haltingly, Marya said, "I need you to look in the mirror."

Nina faltered. She cleared her throat. "Come on. Go easy on me."

"I wouldn't ask if it wasn't important," Marya said.

The casual expression flickered back into place on Nina's mouth. "You always say that."

Nina took them to the back. The bar filtered into a larger room lined with speakers and she wove her way through grinding couples and sloshing drinks. Everything was familiar to Marya: the scent of sweat and tequila and cloudy perfume, the humid air, the sticky floor. She reached her hand behind her for Frankie's, linking them in a chain that snaked through the crowd, and felt goose bumps rise along her arms when the other girl took it.

It was like she'd stepped out of the body she once had and now watched it move from the sidelines. This was the same place where she'd spent a year working, the same dance floor she'd mopped endlessly, the same room where she'd drunkenly danced with Nina tens of times when Dominic took over her shift at the bar and they'd pressed close, lost in a thrumming beat.

Marya glanced back at Frankie, the two of them still knotted together. Poppy's and Cass's heads bobbed behind her. Under the haze, Frankie looked beautiful, all shades of crimson and maroon and the palest pink among the swirling mix of red, blue, green, red again.

Selfishly, Marya wished that for just a moment, she could stop pushing her way through this crowd and pull Frankie up against her. They could dance. She could press her cheek to Frankie's wild hair, made molten under the lights. Dangerously brush her lips against an ear. Shut her eyes, feel a hand clutch at her waist.

Just for a moment, they would act like two people who found each other interesting, and she could shed her usual sort of skin. Slip into something more comfortable.

Outsider. In her mother's voice, she heard the admonishment, felt the sting of shame. As long as she remembered drunken kisses behind Syndicated with Nina and stole furtive glances at Frankie, she would wear that brand. It clung to her like spider silk, caught itself in her hair, in her mouth. She couldn't shake it off.

It was like she was in that room again. Like one memory led to another and she couldn't stop tumbling into the mess. She could see her mother in the doorframe of her childhood bedroom, mouth curled in disgust. All the magic in the world, all the twisted and lurid apparitions, and her mom thought *this* could be the worst thing about her? That Marya could disappoint her desperately enough to no longer be worthy of love? That she herself could be an abomination?

Marya had let that feeling rule her for so long. She'd carried her shame like an egg in the nest of her heart. She'd run from every reminder of that former life, Nina included—abandoned the bar and the kisses and the desire without a goodbye, just her shit packed in a suitcase and a bus ticket screenshotted on her phone. It left her exhausted. She was out of masks to hide behind.

But Frankie's hand was warm in her own, winching her from the deep pit of her shame. There could be nothing wrong about this, the sure grasp of a beautiful girl.

"I haven't done this in a long time," Nina said, words carrying over her shoulder and down the line as they slipped into the dim hallway. The sight of it filled Marya with uneasiness, too much work association in her memory for comfort.

"No one is judging how skilled you are," Marya said. Her voice bounced off door-lined walls. "But we kind of need you to succeed."

"Kind of?" Frankie muttered behind her.

"This one has no faith in me," Nina said, pointing her thumb over her shoulder at Frankie. She tugged a ring of keys from the apron around her waist as they approached the last door in the hallway. Overhead beams buzzed in sync with the echo of pounding music. She tried a few keys, cursing loudly until the correct one fit the lock. Nina flicked a switch and the room filled with milky light.

"Is this a closet?" Cass asked, nose wrinkled in surprise. It was barely big enough for all of them to stand in. Shelves lined the walls, littered with cleaning supplies and countless bottles of alcohol, glass rattling along to the beat. In a corner, a tall mirror was propped up against the wall, splotches staining the edges where rust and time had eaten away at it.

"It's technically a break room," Marya said, embarrassed before the words finished leaving her mouth.

Nina crossed her arms. "Would you rather we did this out in the open, where everyone else can watch?"

Marya just closed the door behind them and stepped closer to the mirror.

"What am I supposed to be looking for?" Nina asked.

"We need you to find someone," she answered. Everything smelled antiseptic and cool. The scent went right to her head.

"Dead or alive?"

The question sucked the air from the room. "Dead," Frankie said, flat and cold.

"Alright, alright," Nina said. "It's an important thing to know."

"What do we need to do?" Poppy asked. She ran a finger along the edge of the mirror, where the glass beveled. Marya tried not to look too long at the reflection of the two of them; something seemed untrustworthy about it, like it might steal her sight from her head.

"*We* do not do anything," Nina answered. "I go into the mirror. You sit beside me and make sure I'm not in there for too long. If more than ten minutes pass and I'm still gone, you pull me back out. Got it?"

"Fine," Marya said, still trained on the mirror. If this went wrong, it would be her fault now, putting people she cared about in danger like she was a curse hanging over them. She turned to meet Frankie's eyes. "Are you ready?"

Frankie nodded. Cass stood by her side, pinky finger looped in Poppy's hand.

Nina pulled the mirror to the middle of the room and propped it up against a row of shelves. She kneeled, fists against her thighs.

"You'll have to sit on either side of me," she said. They obeyed, though it was a struggle in the cramped space. Marya tried to scrunch herself to Nina's left in the small amount of room that was allotted to her. Still, she left a generous inch between them, attempting not to let their skin touch if she could help it.

Nina splayed her fingers against the mirror, eyes downcast and half-lidded, intent in the reflected surface.

"Tell me about them," Nina said. "I need to know exactly who I'm looking for."

Marya closed her eyes, saw blue skin.

"Her name is Sofia," Frankie said. "She looks—she looks just like me. But her hair is shorter. She cut it herself." On the last word, her voice cracked, and the sound left a slice in Marya's resolve.

Cass swallowed, hard. "She's part of our family."

"There's something inside of her, trying to take over her body," Poppy added. "Coming after us."

"She's trapped in some kind of purgatory," Marya said. "A Fissure."

The mirror's surface clouded around the condensation of Nina's warm skin. She drew her shoulders close into her body, jaw clenched.

Nothing happened.

A minute went by. Marya shifted anxiously. Beside her, Nina was impossibly still, watching her own reflection. Maybe it was wrong to ask her to do this. She heard Cass clear her throat, jarring in the silence.

"What do we—"

Marya pressed a finger to her lips. "She's already gone," she whispered, though she was only halfway convinced that she was telling the truth. "We have to wait."

She shifted again. Her legs were starting to fall asleep. Poppy was statuesque, Cass fidgeting with a ring around her thumb, Frankie's gaze trained on the group's reflection. Nina's breath fogged the glass. Marya glanced at her watch. It ticked on, and on, and on.

"It's been ten minutes," she whispered.

"Do we try to pull her out now?" Frankie asked. "Will that mess it up?"

Marya hesitated, glancing at the mirror, then back to Nina. She worried at her lip. In the reflection, Marya's expression was a question mark, neatly dotted.

Another minute passed. It felt impossibly long. If Nina died—if she killed someone with her selfishness, her own cowardice—

"Fine," Marya said. "Pull her out. We do it on three. One, tw—"

Poppy touched Nina's arm before Marya could get the words out. The rest of them scrambled to follow her. When Marya's hand landed on Nina's wrist, she felt the *burn*.

The world hurtled into darkness.

33

Uprooted Soil Then at Last Glimpsed the Sun

Cass opened her eyes to find impossible water. It was everywhere, impenetrable, cold seeping into her skin. Above her the surface simmered. She kicked, legs tangled in reeds, gulping down mouthfuls of choking liquid.

Her head broke the waterline. She coughed viciously, thrashing, struggling to keep herself afloat.

She'd never seen darkness like this. As her eyes struggled to adjust, she thought she could make out the beginning of trees wavering in a chilly breeze—shoreline. It reminded her of the lake in Oph's backyard—but where was the house? Where was the life? There was a moment of stark adjustment where her eyes met only forest and reedy growth.

The sky above was starless and blank and the air around her pitch black. She swam toward the bank, pushing through the current like moving in a dream. If she could just reach the shore, pull her heavy body from the water, everything would be—

Something yanked her back under.

The grasp was firm around her ankles. She fought the hold, gasping, water closing in tighter. It was too clouded to see what waited beneath her. She was going to die like this.

Her kick met something flesh-soft, and the weight on her ankles disappeared. She shoved forward with a pent-up scream, the sound tearing out of her chest. Her feet hit the slimy bottom of the lake as she fought closer to the shore, heaving, stumbling, falling to her knees in the shallow water at the edge.

Cass pushed herself up on shaking arms, struggling to catch her breath. Black water lapped around her wrists. The trees bent and whistled as a harsh wind whipped, a bloody current. Each breath she sucked in was wet. There was a soft clattering sound in the distance, like wind chimes.

There was no moon here. The world was vividly absent. She struggled to her feet and stood dripping on the path, squinting into the dark, trying to consider her options. Where were the others? Why was she alone?

"Poppy?" she called, the world too silent, her voice too loud. "Frankie? Marya?" She hesitated and listened for movement before stepping forward, where a faint tinge of white stood stark against all the darkness.

There, pinned to a tree. She peered closer and attempted to make out the shape. There was a little doll the color of hide nailed to the trunk. Cold bled through her at the sight.

"Cass!"

She turned at the sound of her name. It echoed across the water with a boom. "Poppy?" she tried, and when Poppy answered with her name again she rushed across the shore to where foliage met water. Poppy kneeled there, coughing, her head clutched in her hands.

"Shit," Cass said, crouched to help Poppy to her feet. "Are you okay? Can you walk?"

Poppy shook her head against Cass's shoulder, a pained moan falling from her mouth. Her palms slid over her ears and pressed down hard. "It's so fucking loud it hurts."

Cass didn't know what the hell that was supposed to mean, her ears muzzy with water and prickling in the silence, but she just held Poppy tighter. "Okay, it's okay, I've got you. We need to walk, I don't think we're safe here."

She looked at the white glow of the doll, the sight of it horrifying enough to raise the damp hairs on her arms. Still, it seemed a marker of civilization—she guided them toward it with an arm hooked under Poppy's, and followed the next one, and the next, as they led through the woods.

Something about this was eerily familiar. She had been here before—she was sure of it.

There. Over the top of the pines she saw it, framed by a faint gray glow along the horizon. A cross, perched on the steeple of a church, tilted precariously. They were near the abandoned house and the church in the old woods. She hurried toward it, trying to support Poppy's weight all the while, but she barely came up to Poppy's chin on a good day and this was the most exercise she'd gotten in months. They'd been walking for only a few minutes before she started to pant with effort, Poppy's head lolling with her teeth clenched in pain.

There was a distant, sluggish pull, like a body unsticking itself from the blood it had spilled. Dread prickled over her, turning her skin rigid. There was no time to contemplate her fear.

"We need to run," she whispered in a rush. Poppy whimpered. "Can you do that?"

Cass doubted it was possible, but Poppy just nodded. She stumbled as Cass pulled them forward. Cass picked up speed as quickly as she could force herself to go—but she was exhausted already, and her wet shoes kept slipping, and Poppy lagged a step behind. The sound grew louder until it was cascading nearly beside her. She refused to look. A scream threatened to force its way out, but she was breathless, unable to make a sound.

"Cass!" Another voice cut through the crashing as Frankie stumbled out of the woods beside them. Her hair was dark with water and plastered to her cheeks, a scratch beneath her eye. Her face was lined in desperation. "You need to go!"

Frankie's words were almost drowned out by the cacophony of sound as Marya and Nina burst past the tree line behind her. Marya faltered and Nina caught her with a strained curse, yanking her back to her feet. "Hurry!" Nina called, the word falling ragged from her mouth.

Cass urged herself faster, dragging Poppy close behind her. Frankie leapt over fallen trees ahead of them, her shoes loud against the packed dirt. Her head kept whipping back to make sure they were still there. She broke out of the forest as Cass scrambled to catch up, Marya and Nina keeping pace.

The crunch of brush grew louder. "Please," she whispered, "please just let us make it. Please. *Please.*"

Together they slipped through the line of trees.

In the distance she could just barely make out the shape of the house. A little glowing eye illuminated its porch—the first light she'd seen, red and ominous. The house was a crooked thing, angled and lively, like it might get to its feet and leave her stranded on the ground. She heard the distant honking of geese and the steady thump of footsteps. Behind her, twigs crackled and hissed and the leaves on the trees murmured to each other in warning. The whole world was afraid of what followed them.

She turned, just for a second. At the edge of the trees she found the source of the sound.

Something burst past the black foliage, a massive form pacing the perimeter of the forest. Tendrils snaked from the top of its—head? Something like roots, pulsing, coagulating. Teeth gnashed in the slit across what must have been its face. Long-fingered hands yanked at overgrown grasses, and it let out a scream that echoed like shattering glass. It reminded her of her most awful nightmares—shadows in the dark standing up and turning to face her. It was the same thing that had slammed down against the hood of her truck, now swollen with space and mass. Cass's heart slithered up into her mouth. She swallowed it whole and burst through the fenced-in yard, pulling Poppy past the boundary.

Someone stood on the house's porch, illuminated by that red lantern. Cass couldn't tell what she was seeing—another monster? Sofia?

But as she neared she saw—a girl, hair long and wild and gleaming black. Skin rusty and deep where the light caught it. Dress pale and stained, corset tightened around her chest like the garb of a corpse.

She felt the moment when the others saw her too, Frankie nearly bumping into Cass as their steps finally matched and Marya and Nina halting beside them. Poppy leaned heavily into Cass's side and the girl raised her lantern higher. The glow painted the shape of someone beside her, and the boy's lips parted as if preparing to speak.

"Inside," the girl said. Cass just barely heard her over the groaning of the creature behind them.

They thundered up the porch steps and the girl pulled the door shut behind them. Cass crossed the threshold into a new understanding of the world.

"You have to help—" she started raggedly, but the girl held a finger to her lips. It was an eerie sight, with her snarl of a mouth. She nodded at the boy beside her and pointed across the room, and Cass followed the outstretched finger.

There in the mind melt of the mirror world, everything held a hazy quality, like glass gone milky with age. They were in a sitting room connected to what seemed to be a kitchen. It took a moment for the realization to sink in, but it was impossible not to see once her mind made sense of it; it was the exact same layout as the old house where Sofia's body had been found.

And in the center of a kitchen illuminated by the glow of a burning woodstove, a tree split through the floor, emerald leaves curled against the ceiling.

The world went wooden. Stained knots in the floorboards glowed gold in the lamplight, and everything had the worn nature of centuries of use, save for a tall white chair that stood at the end of an old dining table. Cass stepped toward it, sickeningly mesmerized. Her footsteps creaked on the floor.

"Stop," the girl hissed. She pointed to her right. "Follow him."

The boy looked at Cass and gave her an attempt at a smile.

She categorized her options. Remembered the hurt sound Poppy had made as she dragged herself from the water. Pictured that *thing* circling them through the woods and swallowed hard around the tossing of her stomach.

This was a mistake.

But they followed him, creeping past the tree in the coal-red kitchen and down a narrow hall. He carefully pried open a door and, after nervously glancing over his shoulder, led them down a staircase.

Cass did a quick inventory of every absurd decision she'd ever made and decided that heading into a basement inside of a mirror world would unfortunately top the list. Maybe this was the punishment she got for betraying their trust. Frankie had asked her to wait. To rest. To give them some time to understand what they were dealing with. And she had gone to Lucas and opened up to him instead.

She heard the door close behind them and the girl's lantern fell across the stairs, illuminating their steps. Sick anxiety seized her at the memory of the last cellar she had descended into. She could smell her own fear, an earthy gasoline curl. Cass counted heads to calm herself, her family lined up in a row, all of them still together, still safe. She kept her hand close to Poppy's back, as if waiting to catch her.

At the base of the stairs the floor was packed smooth. Overhead, roots rippled and stretched, warping down into the dirt, disappearing beneath the surface. In a dark corner of the room, past the roots and vines, Cass saw a worktable piled high with little objects.

The girl set the lantern on the floor. It bloomed beneath her chin and against her deep lashes, painting her face like a mask. The impossibility of her was difficult to look at directly.

Then the girl shoved Frankie as hard as she could.

Cass watched Frankie stumble back, her face slack in surprise. She moved forward to put herself between them, but the girl was already advancing, too quickly. Cass looked to the boy, suddenly fearing that they were standing in the center of a trap. But he appeared just as stunned as she felt.

"How could you?" the girl hissed as she got up in Frankie's face. "You—you—how could you not come back, how could you just—" Her voice shattered around the words. She shoved Frankie again. "You left!"

But Frankie, who Cass had never known to be speechless in all her life, just stared at the girl in shock. Her mouth floundered. "I don't— I've never—"

"I waited for you," the girl whispered, but now there was doubt in her face, and she wrapped her arms around herself as if she could hold the pieces together with will alone. "You told me you would come back. You told me you would be okay."

"Oh fuck," Poppy said roughly, as the pieces clicked in Cass's mind.

"You knew her?" Frankie asked. "You knew Sofia?"

Cass watched her morph and change. The girl's expression, at first a wound, grew heavy with fury. Then understanding expanded and the anger dissipated, replaced with despair. The boy lightly touched her shoulder, but she shrugged him off. When she turned, her eyes were hard. Cass thought she was going to hit Frankie again.

Instead, she pulled a curved blade and pointed it directly at Frankie. It glinted in the lamplight with a vile waver. The boy started to interrupt, panic clear on his face, but she hushed him just as quickly.

"I don't know who you are," the girl whispered, "and I don't know who or what sent you here, but you have no more than a moment to explain yourself before I gut you."

Nina held her hands up in surrender and waved them, trying to pull the girl's attention. "We—ah, we, um, came through the mirror. We're not here to harm you. We're just looking for someone and the search led me here." She was frantic now. "And I don't know how *they* managed to follow but—"

"What mirror? Who are you looking for?" the girl hissed, cutting her eyes at the boy. He shrugged.

"Same person that you are, it seems," Frankie said, sharp enough to cut.

"I came from somewhere along the lake's edge," Marya said, and Cass caught the sound of uncertainty. "I guess the water served as a mirror for us to pass through."

The girl clucked her tongue. Cass didn't understand the reaction, but she could see the emotion—a deep-set hurt clinging to every angle of the girl's body.

"You're wearing Sofia's face," the girl said, more of an accusation than a question. She held the knife steady.

"It was mine first. She's my sister. My twin." Frankie's voice was sensible where Cass's would have been all fear. In the pale glow of the lantern she made out the strained lines around Poppy's face. She looked a little less pale and pained compared to how she'd been when they first emerged—but she kept a fingertip pressed to her temple as she met Cass's eyes.

"What about the rest of you?" The girl gestured. "Why would you try to find her here? Sofia hasn't returned in five years. Have you—have you seen her since?"

"Returned," Frankie said slowly, tasting the word. She avoided the girl's pointed ask. "How often would she come to see you?"

"I'm asking the questions," the girl snapped.

Cass glanced at the others, blood racing desperate as a caged bird. Poppy's eyes aching, Marya's mouth thin, Frankie's arms crossed over her chest.

"We're here because we asked *her* to look in the mirror," Frankie said, pointing her thumb in Nina's direction. "We followed when it seemed she was trapped."

The girl had a vicious mouth, taut like a wound slashed into her face. When she spoke, Cass watched for blood. "That was foolish," she said at last. "Take off your shoes."

"Excuse me?" Cass said.

"Check them," the girl said, nodding to the boy. "I won't be the first to bring a shapeshifter into this house."

"What are you looking for?" Poppy asked, and Cass appreciated the question, feeling naked and nervous as she toed off her sneakers. The floor beneath her feet was warm, like sunbaked dirt.

"Foot fetish?" Cass whispered to Marya in an attempt to break through the scrutiny. Marya scoffed in response, and it earned them both a glare from the girl.

"Hooves," the girl answered, as she peered down at them with the lantern held beside her face.

"Oh, sure," Nina said, kicking off her boots.

The girl waved at them, dismissive. It seemed they passed her inspection. Cass shoved her feet back into her shoes.

Where was Sofia? Had Nina brought them to this house because of the tree? Had this girl led them to her somehow? She had known Frankie's face. She had thought it was Sofia, alive again. Cass thought of the fear in Lucas's face, the way he'd said "this is where I found the ritual."

Overhead, the floor creaked. They fell silent and looked up at the ceiling. Roots had twisted and gnarled themselves against slotted boards.

"It's not safe for you to be here," the girl whispered. "It was a terrible idea for you to come in the first place."

"We're not leaving until we find her," Frankie said, too loud. The girl hushed her. The boy looked sick to his stomach.

"Then you'll die here. I've been waiting since the day she ran."

"Oh," Marya said softly, a pitying sound. So this girl didn't know.

"Who was she to you?" Frankie asked.

The girl's face locked itself up. "We were friends."

Frankie nodded, once, twice, three times, until Cass thought she might not stop. "Then I guess you should know that she's dead."

Cass remembered standing in that same carved-out moment, in a life that felt decades and worlds away from her now. The way her stomach had bottomed out. How strange the daylight had become, a foreign creature that didn't understand the life it graced. Cass standing on a porch that had raised her, waiting to be told what to do next.

The girl slackened, the hand holding the knife now hanging limp at her side. "And you think what? That she's here somehow, strung along?"

"Yes," Marya said simply.

Poppy winced, pain evident in her stiff shoulders. Cass wanted to reach for her and found herself scared to do so, thinking of their hands laced together in her truck, Poppy's words not quite matching what she intended to say.

"Finder, maybe we should—" the boy started.

Finder, Cass wondered, rolling the name around in her head.

"Stop! I'm thinking." Finder locked eyes with Cass. Her lips downturned in annoyance, cheeks the ruddy brown of crushed roses. Her hair escaped in wild strands away from her face. There was a certain strangeness to the edges of her skin, like she was constantly in movement, like Cass couldn't pin her in place.

"It's not safe for you here," she repeated, low in her throat, "so I'm going to help you leave, and then I'm going to look for Sofia myself."

"I'm not going anywhere," Frankie answered immediately.

"What reason do we have to trust you?" Poppy asked, as if Frankie hadn't spoken.

"I can't force you to do anything. It's your choice whether you live or die." Strangled, Finder turned to the boy. "Mab is going to skin us and tan our flesh for hide. We shouldn't be down here."

The ceiling gave a low groan. The doorknob at the top of the stairs rattled. The boy and Finder passed a fearful look.

"I'm going to retrieve a mirror," she said, intended for him alone though Cass heard the words ring around the room, "and you're going to distract them."

"Me!" the boy squeaked. His eyebrows disappeared beneath dark hair. "You think they'll pay attention to *me*?"

"We don't have another option," she hissed.

Cass found Poppy across the room. Despite the dimness, she could feel when their eyes met. Her hands were shaking. She wondered if Poppy's were too.

Finder faced the rest of them. "You'll wait here," she commanded. Even with her voice reined in, she was firm, powerful. "I'll be back."

Finder took the stairs two at a time, her steps nearly silent, and the boy crept behind her. Cass watched them go, a sharp argument rising the moment the doorknob turned. In that dark pit the world warped around her, and she felt that this was the point where her universe revealed a brand-new face.

In the sightless basement, Nina said, "This is the last time I do you a favor, Masha."

"Fair enough," Marya answered.

"What the hell are we going to do?" Poppy asked.

Frankie cleared her throat. The room pulsed around Cass like it had lungs of its own. She breathed with it, in and out, in and out.

"We'll wait. Like she said," Frankie answered. "What other option do we have?"

34

LONGING IS THE DREAM KILLER

Finder deserved the harsh words. She deserved the quick crack to her cheek, hard enough to leave the bone bruised and aching. She deserved the bucket shoved into her arms, the rags piled in it like fallen feathers from a skinned animal.

She'd been foolish. Utterly, supremely vacuous. What was she thinking, letting those people into her house, just because she'd lain awake in her bed, just because the geese had called her to the window before the unfolding and resounding brute roar, just because she'd risen from her bed with the small hope that it might be *her*, returning at last?

Hadn't she learned enough the first time, with Sofia? But Finder had been different then. Entirely too eager for beauty and intrigue. Passing years in isolation had given Finder no option but to harden herself. The tally marks burned into her thigh were painful and plentiful enough to prove that.

And the second time? The boy running behind her, Finder yanking him past the ward? It was easier to pretend it had never happened at all.

Compelled by some sick impulse to be useful, she began washing the kitchen windows as instructed. The boy had his own bucket and rags. He'd been banished to the front room, where the windows were dirty enough to go opaque among all the lightlessness. She wished they'd at least been sentenced to the same room, where she could will him to keep his mouth shut. *There is no one beneath us,* she thought, mostly to convince her heart to slow its frantic beating, *there has never been anyone beneath us.*

But there was a giddy part of her, too, at the acknowledgment that Sofia hadn't been a wistful dream. She had been real. *And now she is dead,* Finder remembered. The thought was as continuous and sudden as a burn.

Dead. But dead was an answer, wasn't it? Dead was something in the Fissure. Dead was buried in one world but maybe walking in the next, head screwed on askew, the edges of you fizzy and warm.

In the sunless days, among the books and the notes and Mab's concoctions on the stovetop, Finder had come to understand that there existed more than just their little house. Creatures died in every world. Energy, with no bounds, had to take on another form. So it fed on shadow. So it grew and expanded, so it had two legs, so it walked the same woods that she and the boy had traversed. She had read about such manifestations—those beings culled power for their own, demanding a place to go. Such spirits were drawn to one another and when lost in the murk sought each other out. Expended energy could serve as a sort of fuel for such formless creatures to eat.

And it was what all the stories fell back on, wasn't it? Don't seek the spirit that howls your name. Don't followed the horned beast past the trees. Don't go into the dark because a witch waits to eat you up. Well, here Finder was, in the dark, a witch. Would it be her turn to feed next?

"I told you to stay out," Mother Mab hissed as she prodded at the stove and frightened Finder out of her thoughts. Her silver hair was swept up into a bundle on her head. She clutched her shawl around her shoulders with a gnarled and ashen hand, a terribly human gesture that reminded Finder that Mab was made of meat, just like herself. "You have no business being in the cellar."

"And I told you, I thought I heard something down there," Finder argued. Her jaw hurt when she talked. "After what happened with the chickens, I wanted to make sure everything was alright."

Why had she helped them, anyway? Because she had held the lantern up beside her eyes and seen that girl wearing Sofia's face and thought, *there she is*. Because she was always the one cleaning up a mess. Because she would rather hold the problem in her hands than deal with an aftermath that would come to haunt her.

"What happened with the chickens, *hah*, chick, you say it like it was just another day. That was our dinner, Finder. Our dinner's dinner. Enough bones for stock to keep you and Creature fed and out from underneath my damned feet."

Finder scrubbed, one-half of her brain tuning Mother Mab out to listen closely to the music of the house. The floor creaked in the sitting room where the sound of a cloth on glass rippled. Overhead, footsteps meandered in the Ossifier's room. The stove crackled with life and Finder's head throbbed.

She watched the window as she washed, hunting for a glimpse of gloom come to life. It was a tenebrous reminder of the boundary between her reality and her death. She could feel it waiting in the forest, drawn out by the promise of fresh blood.

Now there were people in her house, something new she'd have to fret over. Sofia was dead. And Finder had lived all her life knowing that the Fissure held a certain strangeness to it—a sticky quality, a clinging. It was hard to walk through your death and make it to the other side. Some got lost along the way.

They called it the Fissure because it was a rift—a splice down the middle, a split in the natural order of things. She'd only ever been able to tell one person that story. Her first girl, who had demanded so much of her but always returned the favor with a thumb against her cheek or a smile bright enough to rival the dead light. In the end, she'd brought Sofia into her home with the hope that she could keep her safe.

What made Finder think she could succeed now when she had only ever failed?

"I don't know what I'm supposed to do with you," Mother Mab continued. The kettle whistled and she eased the steaming water into a pot of chicory. "This is not how I raised you to act."

"What's all this?" the Ossifier said.

He was barefoot; that's why Finder hadn't heard his boots on the floor, the betrayal of sound. The white bones of his ankles were exposed and cruel.

"These children," Mother Mab spat. She poured the fragrant dirt-colored liquid into ceramic mugs. The Ossifier took one and cupped it.

He looked at Finder, a knowing glance, the type that said *I know what you are and where you've been.*

How smarmy would he be if he knew the rest of it? That she might not understand how the sun had been stolen from the sky, but she had experienced things of magic, that she had corralled people into the cellar for her own safekeeping. That there was something else burning inside of her—hope that she might see Sofia again, even if it meant letting her go.

As if sensing her thoughts, he glanced at the cellar door. The wood shone oiled and firelit. She wondered if the same image from nights before passed through his mind as it did hers; the dark hall, their knowing eyes landing on one another, a wail tearing through the woods. The Ossifier coming out of the basement that Mother Mab had banned from their use, and Finder and the boy tumbling in with soot on their cheeks and mud on their boots.

As long as Mother Mab was near the basement door, the Ossifier wouldn't try anything, would he? Finder just had to steal the perfect moment to slip past them, mirror in hand—the little one with the ornate bone handle she used to brush her hair each night, fingers curled into lines carved by the Ossifier. Sure, he had some hold over her. Over the boy, too, and maybe even Mother Mab. But she was smarter. Faster. Once touched by crimson resplendence.

In her mind she held an arrow notched in a bow, aimed at the Ossifier, ready to fly. *Got you,* she thought.

As long as her arrow found its target, she would be safe, and she'd make the women vanish and find Sofia. She would set her free from whatever horror the Ossifier had caused. She would find out exactly how he had done it, and she would give that same pain to him, tenfold. That was how she'd earned her name, after all.

Finder dipped her rag in soapy water and went to work.

Mother Mab had an endless list of punishing tasks for her to complete. Her chores were relegated to the kitchen while the boy was sent out to the yard to feed the geese. She could see the fear caught up in the tension of his shoulders, the memory of running still alive in both of their minds. While Mab stirred soup on the stove, the Ossifier whittled in the sitting room, and the boy gathered the grain basket, Finder flashed him an apologetic look. He answered with a rude gesture.

Sweat gathered along Finder's brow, stinging the corners of her eyes. She slid suds across the floor and imagined she could see through the wood; that beneath her the women were sprawled against the dirt, staring up at her like she was a constellation mapped across the sky.

"I'll be back in an hour," Mother Mab said, lifting the soup pot from the stove and carrying it to the dining table. "Eat if you'd like. Or don't. But the floor needs to be finished by the time I return."

"Where are you going?" Finder asked, sitting on her heels. Her corset was too tight. She inhaled until it hurt.

"Someone has to go beyond the fence and stock the herbs," Mab answered. "I can't trust you to do that anymore now, can I?"

An image—Sofia kneeling before the tree, sassafras root bundled in her hands.

Mother Mab disappeared down the hall. Finder heard the hard slam of the door. She rose on her knees and waited. Only the settling house and the distant scrape of the Ossifier's knife answered her.

She'd go upstairs. Passing through the sitting room would be necessary, but she could explain it away. Maybe she needed a ribbon for her hair, to pull it away from her face—that would do. She could grab the mirror and tuck it into her corset, then be in and out of the basement as quietly as she could manage. The Ossifier would never notice, as long as he kept working at his whittled bone.

Then, distantly, footsteps—the boy returning from the yard. He let the back door swing shut behind him and made his way through the dining room. The basket bumped limply against his thigh. "Still scrubbing, huh?" he said, when he spotted Finder hovering in the kitchen.

She held a tense finger to her lips and nodded at the wall between them and the Ossifier. "Of course," she answered, and beckoned him closer.

He went to her. When he kneeled near enough for his hair to tickle her cheek, she whispered in his ear.

"Wait here," she said, "and don't let him pass the basement door."

She was on her feet before the boy could so much as nod. In the sitting room, the Ossifier was curled up in an armchair, one leg thrown over an armrest, little blade glinting in his hand. He twisted his head in her direction before she could make it to the stairs.

"Aren't you supposed to be cleaning?" he asked. His voice was a wind chime of glass, glittering dangerously in the air.

"Forgot something," she answered, taking the stairs two at a time. "I'll be right back!"

She slipped into her room. The loose floorboard where she'd buried Sofia's necklace gave a low creak underfoot, and she hesitated—she could almost imagine it beating beneath her like a wet heart, freshly torn from the body. Finder considered bending to pry the board up, considered notching the chain and clasping it around her neck like it might be able to protect her from the inevitability of disaster. But she was afraid of making herself evident. With her hair swept up, the Ossifier might spot the glint of gold shining against her throat.

The mirror lay waiting on her bedside table, barely bigger than her hand. She tied up her hair in a rush and stuffed the mirror down the front of her dress. The glass was cool against her stomach, bone handle sharp where it pressed between her breasts.

When she reached the bottom of the stairs, the Ossifier's chair was empty.

Voices rose from the kitchen. She slowed to a creep, hesitating in the doorway. The boy stood in front of the cellar door. He had Finder's wash bucket clutched against him, the water almost sloshing over the edges. The Ossifier leered close with his hands tucked behind his back. Finder saw the blade there, cool against the meat of his palm.

The boy looked at Finder. His eyes were wide with fear.

"Why won't you let me pass?" the Ossifier asked, head cocked in question.

"Mother Mab says we're not allowed to go into the basement," Finder answered.

The Ossifier faced her, his hungry stare hot as a coal in the wood-stove. There was a raw look to him. His skin seemed uncooked, trans-lucent and thin.

"We're not," he agreed, "and we're also not allowed to leave the house after the last candle is blown out. But you two did, didn't you? Where did you go?"

"Why were you in the basement?" she challenged.

"I'm working on something," the Ossifier said. "It's a surprise."

The mirror was so cold against her skin.

"It has to be made in the basement?" she tested.

"The point of a surprise is that no one sees it until it's time for them to be *surprised*," the Ossifier said. He looked at the boy again and waved dismissively. "Move aside."

"No," the boy said quickly, then paled.

The Ossifier tipped his head, eerie face full of barely concealed irritation. "No?"

"You can't," Finder insisted. "Mab will be back soon and then we'll all be punished."

The Ossifier laughed, high and piercing. "I'm terrified. Get out of my way, Creature."

"No," the boy said again, and Finder was suddenly filled with appreciation for him, this person who barely knew her and yet entwined himself in this battle.

The Ossifier shoved him aside. The bucket sloshed against the boy's legs, splattering on the clean floor. Finder watched it puddle as the Ossifier turned the knob.

He opened the door. Panic burned up inside of her. With the mirror cool against her stomach, her breath tight in her throat, she made a decision that would come at a cost—she would choose to act.

She tackled him.

They went head over heels down the staircase, tumbling together, landing with an awful thump against the dirt floor. The mirror cracked and splintered against her chest. Spots bloomed at the corners of her vision and she gasped hard enough for her lungs to protest.

A collective cry rose from the group. The Ossifier roared. He staggered off the ground, clutching his skull. Pale oven glow filtering from above spotlighted him at the bottom of the stairs. His head snatched up and he gaped at the women staring back at him, frozen in fear. "What is this?"

Finder staggered to her feet and hit him as hard as she could. His head snapped back and her knuckles screamed. Blood gushed from his nose, red even in the dark.

Hands shaking, she reached into the front of her dress and pulled the shattered mirror from its hiding place. Bits of glass scraped against her skin, and she cried out when she saw the empty frame. Pieces of the mirror stuck to her stomach and fell from the bottom of her dress, twinkling on the floor in a pile of her last hopes.

But—maybe if she could just—

The boy stood at the top of the stairs, paralyzed in fear. The woodstove illuminated him from behind and spilled into the black room. "The bucket!" Finder screamed as the Ossifier lunged at her, his fingers around her neck. She fought and tore against him. "Dump the water!"

The boy didn't question her, and she loved him for it. Water cascaded down the stairs, soap clinging to the steps and liquid pooling at their feet, and then the boy was running after them with thudding steps. The Ossifier shoved Finder again and spat somewhere unseen.

She pushed back. She'd been hit before—this was no new battle.

"It's a mirror," she choked out to the others, "the water is a mirror!"

The women watched it happen, gathered in the middle of the dank room, hands around one another. Finder locked eyes with the pale-haired one, who stared at her in horror. "Use it! Now!"

"I'm going to kill you," the Ossifier said. He grinned at her—blood collected between his teeth. "I'm going to tear you apart. You know how many witches I've seen walk through mirrors? How many before you thought they could master a world they didn't understand? You think yourself so clever? You know *nothing*."

Shrill voices warred around her: the boy, calling her name, fighting with the Ossifier, the women's high screaming, flitting words that passed back and forth—*I won't leave without Sofia, we can't abandon her, we have to help her, we need to GO*—

Finder pushed desperately against his face, digging her nails into any soft flesh she found. She spared a glance. The one who'd led them to the Fissure, broody and metal-pierced, kneeled in the dirty water with her palms pressed to the floor. The others rushed around her, a body cocoon, grasping at her hunched shape.

Good, Finder thought, as she watched them blink from the world.

It was a miracle to witness it happen. All this time, she'd only seen Sofia sink beneath the still lake. She'd tried a hundred times to hang under that water, begging to mirror-walk, wanting only to find her first girl. In the years after, she had read everything she could get her hands on, scanning for any mention of the word *scry*. Mother Mab refused to teach her, so she taught herself. But she failed every time—the lake stayed a lake. Sofia stayed elusive. Lightlessness stole her hope from the soft meat of her heart.

Then the Ossifier released her throat, and she took a last gasping breath.

When he knocked her into the stairs, the boy hanging around his neck, she felt the crack of her skull reverberate through every bone in her body.

35

THE ANCIENTS CALLED HER CHAOS

Frankie had thought she understood her own capacity for horror. In the face of shadow figures and creatures tracking her in the night, she lived in a world without limits or expectations. But then the man came tumbling down the stairs. Then he put his hands around Finder's throat. The girl who had known her sister, who had seen her face and recognized its mirror.

Frankie was so afraid, and so close to more.

The room flickered with chaos.

Nina kneeled before them. The water shone on the floor, light from above reflecting a carved-out square. Frankie could just make out the distinct outline of Nina pressing down into the murky water and the reflection of the unfurling brawl. The man, long and pale and sallow as a nocturnal animal, seemed human only in technicalities. He throttled Finder as she clawed at him.

Marya yanked Frankie down to the floor, any remembered gentleness abandoned.

"I can't," Frankie said. "Please stop—" Her knees ached, head pounding, hands like two open wounds. "I can't leave without Sofia."

The frantic rise of voices, the strangled sounds of the fight happening before them. "We have to help her!"

Marya cut in: "We need to *GO*—"

"Hold onto me!" Nina cried, her stare trained down into that rippling puddle. Cass crouched beside her, Poppy clutching her arm.

"Frankie!" Poppy cried. "We don't have a choice."

"I can't," Frankie whimpered, but Marya had a firm hold on Frankie's wrist. It sent a spark of pain traveling through her, and with their bodies linked she placed Frankie's hand on Nina's arm.

The world shifted. The last thing she saw was the tangled spider of the boy, the girl, and the monster, each fighting to save a different life.

Everything was the blurred-out red of sun shining through skin. Frankie couldn't make sense of space or time, object or place. There was a moment where she felt nothing, and then the fierce cold hit. Bits of sediment choked her, crawling down her open mouth. The air spun into smoke and ash. She could smell the start of the world. Innards, cedar split, blood swelling to the surface. She was falling. She was—

Kneeling, the ground solid and cool beneath her. Her fingers pressed into the cement floor as her universe fell apart and pieced itself back together. She bent, arms around herself, palms stinging. The urge to throw up racked through her, but she coughed instead, head spinning. She reached for feeling and found a void—maybe some important and distinct piece of her had been lost in the shuffle.

"What the fuck was that?" Nina snapped, whirling on Marya. They were tangled together. Frankie blinked at the pile of limbs, instinctively reaching for Poppy and Cass, for the reassuring warmth of their life. Cass drew in a labored breath. Poppy pressed her knuckles to her forehead.

"Do you think I know?" Marya started. Frankie had never heard her sound so uncertain.

"You brought me to a godforsaken death trap." Nina glared at them all as she staggered to her feet. She stumbled, nearly collapsing back into their intertwined pile. "I need to get out of here," she muttered, trying to stretch a leg over the rest of them and escape the room.

"Wait," Marya said. Her voice raked over Frankie. Nina shoved her way through and out into the hall.

With the door open, only silence answered.

"What time is it?" Poppy asked. She sounded like she'd been screaming. Marya looked at her watch.

"Oh shit," she whispered. "It's morning. Almost eleven."

"What?" Cass's head perked up, her arm warm against Frankie's. "We were in there all night?"

Frankie's pulse thrummed. Images from the mirror world played on a loop in her head. The creature, the girl's distrustful face, the dank basement with its root-covered ceiling, the blooming tree in the kitchen, the bone-hued man with blood running down his chin. Blinding anger burned to life in the sour pit of her stomach.

"You shouldn't have brought me back," she said.

Marya blinked at her. "What are you talking about? You would have died there, Frankie. You saw what that man was doing to her—"

"You should have *left me*. What can we do now? That could have been our one chance to look for Sofia and we fucked the whole thing up. Now that girl is probably dead because of us, because of *me*, another corpse to rot, right?"

Cass was stern. "We couldn't do that."

Marya reached for her, placating. Red flared at the corners of Frankie's vision and she bent away from Marya, pointing at her instead. Her hand shook with fury. "I'll never forgive you for that."

"It's not her fault," Poppy cut in. "None of us would have left you behind."

"Oh, now you want to defend her?"

"*Frankie*," Cass said sternly. "That's enough."

Frankie got to her feet and stumbled out into the bar, now a forlorn mausoleum in the yellow regularity of day. Nina sat on a stool, elbows propped against polished wood.

"We need to go back in," Frankie demanded.

Nina scoffed. She kept her head pointed down, palms pressing against her forehead. "Are you out of your mind? We'd die the moment we stepped inside. We shouldn't have tried it in the first place. That was the most ridiculous thing I've ever done."

"I've done worse," Frankie said.

"Ha! I'm sure of that." Nina slid off her stool and faced the wall of bottles, poured out a shot and knocked it back. Frankie grimaced.

"It's eleven o'clock," she said.

"Is it?" Nina asked. She slammed the shot glass down against the countertop, and Frankie was surprised that it didn't shatter. "You know nothing about the mirror, or how hard it was to bring all of you back here without leaving one of you blind or, I don't know, fucking spliced in two!" She poured another shot. It went down like water. "You shouldn't have even been *able* to follow me in there. Time means nothing! Reality means nothing! We could be in mirror limbo for the rest of our lives! This could all be some otherworldly dimension! You. Don't. Know. How. It. Works." She punctuated each word with a tap of the glass on wood.

"Isn't that why we came to you? Marya said you were an *expert*."

"I'm not an expert, I'm just—I'm her friend. If she's in trouble, I want to help." Nina faltered as her eyes landed on something, and Frankie turned to find them gathered behind her. Cass kept her face averted. Poppy's dark circles had deepened and she looked gaunt. Marya was unreadable beside them, brooding, a ghostly image.

Frankie had never felt so many conflicting emotions: comfort, at seeing them standing there, her people all gathered in one place. Fury at meeting Marya's wounded eyes. And something else that worsened her mood, an immediate sort of hesitation flaring at the way Nina said *friend* without explanation. Rage. Discomfort. Envy.

"So, is it a dream?" Poppy asked.

Nina squinted at her. "What."

"Are we still trapped in the mirror realm, or is this reality?"

Nina snorted. Her cheeks were pink. Frankie wondered if it was embarrassment, anger, or alcohol that made them that way, and settled on a combination of the three. "Fuck if I know. The sun is out, isn't it? That's gotta mean something."

As if on cue, there was the familiar sound of a key turning in a lock, and then the front door swung open and spilled morning across the room. A boy, tall and lanky, followed it inside.

"Whoa—is that you, Sokolova?" Frankie caught the flicker of joy as it tore across his face.

"Dominic," Marya said. Frankie caught the lilt, the fragmented pieces of a name. Even as her stomach sank, she refused to feel guilty. She held on to the anger, squeezed it tight between her fists.

He dropped a bag behind the bar and stopped beside Nina. With the door shut and the morning light muted again, Frankie could see that the two of them made a sensible pair for their environment—dark clothes, dark hair, fair skin and sharp features. He patted her shoulder and Frankie caught Nina's flinch, felt it in her own body too. Her head ached. Her hands burned. She wanted to go home.

"You left me with a full bar last night, asshole," Dominic said, poking a finger into Nina's side. She scowled, and he turned to Marya. "You couldn't stop by and say hi before tearing off somewhere? You and Nina spend the night *reconnecting*?"

Electric currents commanded Frankie's heart. She fought the tug between longing and rage.

"Shut up," Nina muttered, but she leaned into Dominic's side like she was seeking protection.

"Well, are you going to introduce me?" Dominic asked brightly.

"No," Frankie said, curt before she could iron the emotion out.

"We were just going," Cass said.

"Right," Marya answered. "We needed help with something and now we really have to get on the road."

"Already? I've only seen you for what, thirty seconds? It's been a year since any of us heard from you. We thought you were kidnapped, or like, dead in a ditch. You *disappeared*, Marya."

Cass raised her eyebrows. Poppy looked at anything but the rest of them. Frankie stared pointedly at the mirror above the bar.

"Yeah, well, I had to go," Marya said, impatience filtering through her even tone.

Nina looked seconds away from an argument. "I really would have appreciated a heads-up that you were going to pop back in, use me for a *favor*, and disappear all over again."

Marya balked. "You know if I could have done this any other way—"

"You would've what? Called me to say hi? Maybe tell me you were moving away in the first place?"

"I'm sorry," Marya said. Frankie couldn't look at either of them without her face going hot. Her gaze kept bouncing around the room, scalding each time it stopped for too long.

Nina leaned against the bar, watching them with a downturned mouth.

"We really have to go," Cass pleaded. "It's not because of y'all. This is important."

"They always say that," Nina snapped. Dominic sighed and rubbed a palm down her back. Something about the way he did it, casual and kind, made Frankie's eyes burn.

"Call us sometime," he said.

But Marya was already heading for the door. She brushed past Frankie with the lightest of touches.

With one last glance at Nina, who glared back with vitriol, Frankie followed.

Outside, the air was clean and bright. Marya hurried down the block toward the truck. Cass jogged to catch up with the rest of them, Poppy's long legs carrying her to match Frankie's pace. Frankie nearly jumped when Cass grabbed her elbow, her hands cool.

"Stats," Cass commanded.

It was something they used to say as kids. It meant *I'm here*. It meant *tell me all about it*. It meant *reassure me that you're okay and I'll keep breathing*.

"Good as gold," Poppy said drily.

"I'm fine," Frankie answered.

Cass huffed. "You're both goddamn liars. And I'm starving. Marya, wait!" She pushed past them, her sneakers slapping the sidewalk. "I'm the one with the keys!"

Cass unlocked the Ford and Poppy hauled herself into the bed without asking, Marya beside her. Frankie, grateful even as she burned, slipped into the passenger side of the cab.

"We're getting food and then we're talking about it," Cass said into the sliding rear window. "If y'all can wait, I know the best diner, a few miles outside of Loring. No arguments, okay? Promise?"

They fell silent. The city rolled away.

36

THE STARS SUNK BENEATH THE EARTH

Poppy had never been so glad to see a shitty diner before. The windows glinted, all chrome and gleam, steam pouring into the cornflower sky. Afternoon outlined the mountains while swooping power lines cut into the silhouette. It was all too bright, too blue. In comparison to the horror of the last twenty-four hours, Poppy felt as if she were living in a simulation, a world that no longer existed anywhere but in her head, exhausted, distant, untethered.

Cass pulled the truck to a stop and Poppy lurched forward with it. Outside of town, the only sounds were the chirping of birds and tires on distant pavement. Poppy let the sun cook her bare arms and drank in the hush. Compared to how loud the mirror world had been in the confines of her mind, any kind of lull was a respite.

· Now her head ached. The moment she'd opened her eyes, peering up at that wide expanse of darkness as she'd hauled her way into it, the world had boomed back at her—

OH IT WILL BURN AND IT WILL HURT AND I WILL CATCH YOUR SCENT ON THE WIND AND CROSS THE THRESHOLD OF DREAM, WON'T I? AND I WILL RUN AFTER YOU BECAUSE A FASTER HEART IS A HARDER HEART AND

ONCE YOU ARE HARDENED YOU WILL BLOOM FROM YOUR COCOON.

The words had played on a loop as something crushed fauna around her, as she ran after Cass, as she tore her way through forests and across fields into the house shaped like the place where Sofia had died. In the basement it had been only a constant whisper, picking at the fine threads of her mind until she buzzed with sound.

A bell chimed overhead as the diner door swung shut behind them, enough to make Poppy jump. She looked down at the pads of her palms. Beyond her wrists they were numb, like they'd fallen asleep. Her body was disconnected from her mind.

"Poppy?" Cass called. When she looked up, the others had already crossed the room, heading for an empty booth. "Coming?"

"One second," she said, the roughness of her voice surprising her as it came out. "I'm just gonna use the bathroom."

With the door shut and the rest of the diner sealed out, Poppy splashed water on her face with a concentrated effort to not look at the mirror. It was harder than she'd expected. When she caught a glimpse of the glass out of the corner of her eye, the edges of her reflection were blurred and shifting.

She nearly jogged back to the table where the others were gathered around cups of coffee and orange juice. When Cass saw her, a warm grin split across her face. "I got you one of each," she said, pushing a few cups Poppy's way, "and water, too, in case that wasn't enough."

Despite her churning stomach, Poppy smiled back and thanked her, taking a long sip of the coffee. With her forearms pressed against the cool metal table, hesitant warmth spread through her chest. Frankie slumped in the corner of the booth, Marya across from her, staring out the window at the lined-up cars.

"We're in a predicament," Cass said between mouthfuls of orange juice. She jabbed Frankie in the side when the silence stretched on. Frankie remained frigidly still.

"We wouldn't be in this position if you'd left me there," Frankie said.

"Oh, grow up," Marya said.

They stared back at her in surprise. Even Frankie finally met her eyes.

"You're grieving, I get it," Marya said. "But if you thought for a single second that we would have left you in there to fend for yourself, you don't know any of us. At all."

Frankie opened her mouth, but Marya kept going. "Look where you are! You're surrounded by people who care about you, who crawled through a *mirror dimension* to try and help you. And you're going to lash out at us now?"

Frankie was silent. Poppy glanced around at the other booths, checking to make sure no one was listening too closely at the immediate turn their conversation had taken.

"Be angry if it makes you feel better, but don't make us out to be who we're not. I mean—I barely know all of you, but I'm willing to bet anything that Poppy and Cass wouldn't have left you in that mirror even if you begged them. And I would like to think they'd believe the same about me."

Frankie chewed on her bottom lip. Poppy pretended not to notice the falter in her resolve.

"Sorry," she said at last.

"It's okay, we all know you're a drama queen." Cass swung an arm over Frankie's shoulders and pulled her in close. Frankie cowered away.

"So, what are we really going to do about it?" Cass asked, absently stirring her orange juice with her straw. "Nina won't take us back into the mirror. I mean, not that I ever want to go back there again. But we left Finder behind, and we don't even know if she's still alive or if . . ."

Cass faltered and chills rose along Poppy's arms. She'd never forget that man tumbling down the stairs, wicked teeth flashing, his eyes slitted and furious. The long white lines of his fingertips, like exposed bone. A voice like sifted sand filtering through her mind.

"Oh," Frankie breathed, sitting up.

They looked at her, waiting. "Frank?" Cass urged.

"I think—I mean, I didn't put the pieces together before, and this might not mean anything, but—" She paused and chewed absently on a fingernail.

A waitress interrupted her to take their orders. Pancakes for Cass, toast and eggs for Frankie and Marya, waffles and a side of bacon for Poppy. They waited patiently for her to walk away again before Poppy tucked her hands under her thighs to stop their trembling and pushed Frankie further.

"What didn't you put together?"

"When Oph and Sissa performed their ritual, I was, um, transported? I think? Into some kind of vision where I was in the cellar with Sofia. I saw her down there, an apparition or whatever you want to call it. I tried to speak to her, but she couldn't answer me."

"You were *mind-teleported* and you didn't tell us?" Cass gawked at Frankie.

"Well," Frankie said. Her cheeks flushed pink. "I told Marya."

"Oh great, that's super helpful!"

"I'm just trying to say that I think it's strange that we show up in the mirror world and instantly we end up shoved into another basement."

"In a replica of the abandoned house," Marya continued for her. Frankie nodded back.

"It just seems like too many similarities to be a coincidence." Frankie rubbed absently at her gauze. "I think, maybe, Sof is trying to tell us something."

"I might have something that will help us," Poppy admitted. Her breath was unruly in her chest. "That night when I fell asleep on your porch, I saw Sofia in my room."

"Oh my god," Cass moaned.

"I tried to drive to your place, but something came over me, and when I came back to my body I was standing in the woods near the Glasswells' house. I saw someone drive past me, a woman, and she looked at me like she knew what I was doing there." The memory traced its fingers along her spine. "Not saying it means something, just that it was weird."

"Okay," Cass said, "fine. Maybe Sofia is trying to talk to us in her own way, if something isn't allowing her to speak directly with us." She took a long breath, eyes fluttering shut. "While we're on the topic of strange encounters, I might as well share. Poppy already knows this, but on the day of the vigil, I saw something in the cellar. Well, ran into it actually, full force, like, I'm talking real-life, human body standing in your dank-ass basement."

Frankie gaped. "Okay, you do *not* get to be angry with me for not telling you about seeing Sofia when you run into a creature in my basement and hide it from me."

"You were busy!"

"I think you could have interrupted me for *that—*"

The waitress returned with their plates. They gave her a chorus of thank-yous before turning back to each other.

"Alright, alright!" Cass said, tapping her fork against her plastic juice cup. "Marya? Got anything to add to this confessional?"

Poppy looked at her. With the afternoon light streaming through the clear windows, Marya's profile was outlined in white, peach-fuzz hairs on her cheeks glowing. She swallowed a bite of toast, mouth working. There was something grave and fearful about her mouth.

"Nothing," Marya said.

"You sure?" Cass asked.

By now Poppy knew that sharp edge in her tone, the inquisitive catch. Marya stared out the diner window, carefully avoidant. *Strange,* Poppy considered. Cass turned to her for a split second and Poppy caught the glance passed her way.

"We just need to keep at it. Don't give up so easily," Marya added, lips quirking just slightly. "The world has several corners and a hundred faces. Maybe we're just looking at the wrong one."

They picked at their food in silence. Poppy finished off her coffee.

"Well, anyone wanna try these?" Cass asked, gesturing to her pancakes, which had been butchered by her fork and smothered in a lake of syrup. Poppy wrinkled her nose and cut a neat square from her waffle.

"They're good, right?"

The voice stopped beside their table. Poppy looked up and froze with her fork an inch from her mouth.

Lucas had his hands in his pockets, shirt straining against the muscle they had watched him earn in the past month. It was funny how Poppy always expected time to ease emotion, how one moment she could tell herself *you will see him and it won't hurt. You will look at him and you won't think of what you lost. You will hear him and you won't hate him—you will go on, and you will keep the memory of her where he'll never find it.*

She had never been jealous of Lucas and Sofia. But she had wanted to be wanted, to be chosen. And even in her kindest longings and intentions, Sofia had always, always held that satisfaction out of her reach.

Looking at him in the aftermath of all that she had learned and done and felt, Poppy could almost imagine she had just punched him the day before. She would never be free of this feeling—the feral and debilitating desire to be seen.

"Can we help you?" Frankie asked. Poppy could have sworn Lucas's expression cracked—a chip in glass. She watched horror bloom across Cass's face.

"I saw your truck outside and thought I would say hello," Lucas said, tilting his head in question as he spoke directly to Cass. "Have you made any progress? Did my ideas help you?"

"What the fuck are you talking about?" Frankie said.

Lucas pressed his mouth into a crooked line. "Oh, you didn't tell them." His gaze bored into Cass, blue and insectoid. Poppy watched her swallow, once, twice.

I HAVE A DAUGHTER AND I PRAY SHE MAY OUTLIVE ME—

Poppy pressed a finger to her temple. *Not now,* she thought desperately, *please.*

"Tell us what?" Frankie insisted, her voice low and heavy with threat. Poppy, pathetically, found that she was relieved the vitriol wasn't directed at her.

Cass paled. "Listen, I ran into Lucas the other day and we—"

Lucas laughed. "Ran into? That's a funny way to say *stalked.*" The words were good natured. "Seriously, no problem though. It was actually kind of good to see you, Sullivan. Next time we can meet in public like two regular people."

"Frankie," Cass started, pleading. She reached across the table and tried to touch Frankie's arm, but the other girl yanked away. Poppy knew her too well not to see where this was going—Frankie was furious. She would retreat inside of herself until the emotion exploded.

"We're being seated, dear," a new voice said, and when Poppy faced Lucas again she found his mother standing beside him.

Poppy could smell the darkness. Barefoot in the dirt. Cool air pushing through the flimsy fabric of her pajamas. Tree blood and root rot and churned earth. It was a strangely familiar face, that had once met Poppy's through the warped glass of a car window. Now something ill fitting clicked into place, and as she looked at Lucas Glasswell's mother, Poppy had the sudden sensation that maybe she was just a fractured piece of an already shattered dream.

Cool eyes leveled her, a prim purse looped over a shoulder. A sensible blue dress fell just below her knees, hair slashed at the edge of her chin.

"I didn't realize anyone else in Loring knew this spot," Mrs. Glasswell said. "It's always been a special getaway for Lucas and me when his dad is busy at work." When she smiled, it was rigid, her teeth like a fenced-off yard. Poppy counted the beats of her heart.

"You're her sister," Mrs. Glasswell continued, warm as a corpse. "Frances, is it? What a shame it was to lose Sofia, Lucas was destroyed over it. But you know what they say about first love," she added, sighing. "It's devastating. I mean, you probably already know this, but the sheriff and I were high school sweethearts just like those two, and when we went to college, I just about tore myself apart with my boo-hooing."

She squeezed Lucas's shoulder with a pallid hand. "It's different in your case, honey, I know. But I have to say that I'm so proud of the man you've grown into over the years. You're resilient, aren't you?" To the rest of them, she said: "Isn't he just as handsome as can be?"

The table stared back at her, dumbfounded. Lucas had enough couth to look ill.

Poppy let her fork rest on her plate and focused on Frankie—on the halo of her hair, the storm of her mouth, the cavern of her eyes. If she kept her composure, maybe she wouldn't have to feel herself crumbling, remember the sensation of her body belonging to something other than her mind or the sight of a body curled in the center of a tree.

"Is there something we can help you with?" Marya asked.

Mrs. Glasswell's head cocked. "I haven't met you before, have I?" She offered a hand for Marya to shake, leaning over their half-eaten food. Her hair fell from behind her ear and shadowed her face. "Marcia Glasswell. Lucas's mother and wife of Loring's sheriff."

Marya took the hand, her own limp and frigid. "Okay," she said.

"And you are?"

Marya was silent for a beat. "Marya Sokolova."

Mrs. Glasswell tilted her head. "Ooh. That's not a Loring name, is it? Our little town loves transplants. I hope you've been enjoying it just as much." She leaned against the surface of the table. Her manicure was long and rounded at the corner of Poppy's vision. "I have a question that I think your group might be able to answer. The truck outside. Who does it belong to?"

"It's mine," Cass answered.

"I thought it might be," Mrs. Glasswell said. "My son mentioned to me that a junkyard Ford had been tailing him the past few weeks. A pretty rusted shade of red, dented hood. And I happened to spot the same thing circling near our property a few days ago. Sounds familiar, right?"

"Mom. We handled this."

She ignored her son, even as he tugged on her forearm.

"I'm sorry, but is there something you need from us?" Marya cut in again.

Poppy blinked away spots from the edges of her vision, felt the ground slope beneath her shoes. Warm light reflected off the diner's polished chrome and left her disoriented.

"There is, actually. You can stop harassing my family or I can go to my husband, share your license plate with him, and file an official report."

"We could contact the state police and let them know their sheriff's son was last seen with my sister," Frankie said icily, "and that we found something of hers on your property. We could tell them all about the exemplary job your husband has done on Sofia's case."

"You're a sweet one, aren't you?" Mrs. Glasswell said, pleasant again. "I welcome you to do so, honey. I'm sure they would love to hear from a trespassing spitfire like you, but you'll find that my husband has already given them all the information he has." She tucked her hair behind her ear and smiled, demure. "And that information has provided them plenty to work with."

YOU WILL CROSS THE BOUNDARY OF WORLDS AND TOGETHER WE WILL GROW, VINES FROM LOAM.

Now Poppy looked at her and let mirth bleed through, teeth bared. Mrs. Glasswell met her challenging stare. "Is that clear?" she finished.

"Perfectly," Poppy said, and when the rough grate of her shifting voice came with it, she relished the change. Treasured the sudden sensation of power humming like a hive in her head.

Mrs. Glasswell leaned away. "Good," she said, a little shakily. "I'm glad we could have this chat."

Lucas pulled her from the table. He looked over his shoulder at Poppy as they walked away, and she would swear that she could feel the fear radiating off him. Let him be afraid of her. It wasn't the first time, and it wouldn't be the last.

"For someone who claims to not want secrets, you seem to have a lot of them," Frankie snapped at Cass.

"It's not what he made it sound like," Cass insisted.

"Oh, okay, cool! Then what the hell was it? What was any of this?" Frankie asked, and she looked at Poppy when she said it.

Poppy was glad her hands were still trapped between her thighs and the sticky plastic of the booth. She could feel them trembling, electric, while her heavy head drifted with the presence of something larger blending with her own awareness, a filter over the world as she saw it. She watched her reflection dance and shimmer in the surface of the table.

"It's just another insignificant hurdle to cross." Marya's fork clattered against her plate. She eyed Poppy carefully, and Poppy stared back. Let her wonder. "Could we get out of here now?"

"Gladly," Cass mumbled. There was a split second where she was illuminated with a done-up mask of joy. Some monstrous part of Poppy fought the urge to snatch the look off her face and devour it whole.

Frankie caught Cass's wrist before she could get up from the table. "We're not just letting this go. Why did you go to Lucas when I specifically asked you not to?"

Something in Cass's easy demeanor snapped. She yanked away from Frankie. "Who says I have to obey you?"

Frankie stared back. "Excuse me?"

"It's not like I planned for it to happen," Cass said. "I wanted to do something, okay? She was my friend too, and it's impossible for me to just sit around my house watching the fucking deputy talk about her like he knows anything about her and just having to pretend like it doesn't affect me. I wanted to be productive, so I followed him." She trailed off, hesitant. "But—I saw my brother get out of his truck."

Poppy blinked back at her. "Alex? Why?"

"That's exactly what I wanted to know. I stopped when they did, on the side of the road, and we . . . talked."

"You talked," Frankie repeated.

"That's it. I asked Lucas if he thought Sofia was keeping anything from us."

"And?"

Cass's frown quivered, just for a moment. "He led me to the symbol and told me that the day before she went missing, he found her performing a ritual in his barn, bleeding over an open fire. He said that she tried to break up with him, and that she seemed possessed. There was . . . a shadow figure there too, touching her. He said that he didn't recognize who she had become. That everything about her was different."

Poppy watched Frankie, waiting for her anger to burst open like an overripe fruit splitting in the sun. Instead, Frankie's hand fell away and rested on the table. Her eyes were blank, her mouth trembling.

Then she began to cry, silently and all at once. The tears fell across her cheeks before she could swipe them away.

Cass reached for her immediately, but Frankie shoved past her out of the booth. She was across the diner before any of them could stop her, and the door swung shut with the grating sound of bells.

"Shit," Marya said under her breath, and then she got up and followed Frankie, just as she always had, just as Poppy was beginning to suspect she always would.

Poppy didn't watch her go. She focused on Cass instead, who caught her looking and made a pleading face.

"He's a liar," Poppy said roughly. "He'll say whatever he can to get the blame off his back."

"You weren't there," Cass said. "You would have believed him, too, if you could have seen how afraid he was."

Poppy didn't feel that she knew herself well enough anymore to argue. Instead, she said, "I told you this would be too much for her. If this ends badly, it's going to fall on our shoulders."

Cass's eyes followed Frankie out in the parking lot. The mournful look dropped from her face as the waitress swished by and replaced itself with flat politeness. "Hey, love, could we get the check?"

37

THE SWEET BLINK OF VERTIGO

Marya found Frankie in the parking lot, rolling a rock around under the toe of her sneaker. "You can't walk home from here," she said. Frankie didn't turn, though Marya had hoped she would. A secluded, selfish part of her wished that her presence might be enough to comfort by now.

"I can try."

"Cass would never purposefully hurt you," Marya continued. She picked at her thumbnail and watched Frankie's rigid back. "I'm sure she was just scared of what Lucas said, and she knew it would be upsetting. She was trying to help."

Frankie kept looking at the sky, and Marya waited. Frankie shook her head and laughed, finally glancing over her shoulder and showing Marya her damp cheek. There was mirth all over her mouth. It somehow made her face even sadder.

"You know, they think I tried to die."

Marya balked. "What?"

"The year before Sofia disappeared, I went out too far in the lake. Poppy pulled me to the shore and pumped the water out of my lungs." She turned fully and squinted, thinking. "Pretty sure I was technically dead for a few minutes. I spent two weeks in the hospital. Good thing she was a lifeguard one summer, right?"

"Did you?"

"What?"

"Do it on purpose," Marya said, her mouth dry.

Frankie shrugged. Everything about her was posed nonchalance—but her eyes were still wet. "Sofia was so different. She wouldn't talk to me anymore, and Lucas was such a dick, and I just wanted someone—I needed to know that it was going to be okay before she left for college. I was trying to understand her. My mom used to stare at the water for hours, lose herself in a mirror. I thought that maybe if I could do what she did, I might be able to talk to my mom wherever she'd gone and ask her how to help Sofia. I didn't want to lose any more of her than I already had."

Frankie shook her head once, bitterly. "Of course it didn't work, and I nearly drowned instead. I didn't want to come up out of the water until I got it right. They all thought I was just trying to die, and I let them think that and dance around me like I was breakable, because I felt so fucking ridiculous for believing it might work in the first place." Finally she turned—her eyes and nose were red. She tucked her hands into her pockets, but Marya imagined those were red and aching too.

"Frankie," she murmured, as soft as her voice could go.

"When I'm with them," Frankie said, "all I can think about is how she isn't. And god, she hated to be left out. She always wanted to know where I was going. I can count the number of times I left the house alone on one hand, up until that last year." She smiled. Another quick tear fell, and she swiped it away with the heel of her palm. "I love them like nothing else in this world. And I don't really want to be around them anymore because I see us standing there, and I see her absence. It sucks being here without her. It really fucking sucks."

"We'll figure this out," Marya said.

Frankie bit her cheek. "Maybe. But when this is done, so am I."

"Done?" Marya asked.

"Things aren't just going to go back to the way they were before she died," Frankie said. "We're different now. When we catch whoever did this, we can all return to our lives and pretend none of it ever happened and go our separate ways. We've wasted enough time already."

"You don't mean that," Marya said.

The bell above the diner door chimed an exit, and Marya turned to see Poppy and Cass. By the time Marya faced the Ford again, Frankie had already climbed into the back, and the rest of them ended up crammed across the bench seat of the truck while she slouched into silence.

Marya, pinned between Cass and Poppy, felt the intricacies of their deceptions, the tangled mess of their threads. Her mind replayed the moment Frankie's face collapsed—no anger left to sear. That was the issue with weaving secrets: somewhere down the line, a mistake was inevitable. A knot in the fabric of the future. The slow and steady unraveling into a familiar sort of madness.

It'd be so much easier to spread her furtive thoughts out in front of her and allow the others to pick at her, carrion birds, her heart a meal splayed in the dry rolling grass. But it was sickeningly simple to be afraid.

Cass's Ford crossed the town lines into Loring and the sun burned star-heavy overhead. Marya's knuckles pushed into hot leather as control spun away from her into a supernova. She wanted to tell them, *but*—there was hesitation, and the loose-limbed sensation of her loss. The private bird of her body hungered. Secrets demanded secrets—the others had offered theirs, no matter how reluctantly they'd been plucked free, and in return she'd locked herself away. When she thought about it like that, prodded it like her tongue to the back of her teeth, she trusted them. But she'd seen Cass's look across that diner table and sensed the cool stillness of Poppy's disregard. Had watched Frankie shatter from the pain in less than a second.

If this was going to work, if they were going to find Sofia and her killer, Marya needed to be vulnerable, or else she'd wind up on the other side of all that hurt.

Once, she'd opened herself to Nina, to the lake-glint and sky-light of her, spring-young and new to love, gave herself over to the type of girl who craved and desired and dreamt. A year of wildness. No one loved like a girl.

Marya had never denied herself that desire; she'd been aware of what she wanted from the beginning. When she saw Nina for the first time, just kids then but alive enough to understand longing, she'd felt the pull; that cosmic dreaming preceding the fall. When they kissed, Marya had never been surer of what she wanted.

Seer, at first, and then *seen*. She'd always been a private person and what was hers belonged to her alone. Her mother was the one who invented the shame, hammered it in place with thin nails. It was easier to take flight and follow the roots of someone else's growth, drawn to cigarette smoke and Nina's hungry mouth. When it became too real, she could run again.

Admit it, she thought, her own personal persecution. Poppy slumped beside her, sun making trapezoids across her closed eyes. Cass kept her hands tight around the wheel and music unspooled from the radio. *You're not keeping secrets because you're afraid they won't like you. You can handle the anger if you try.*

Though, surely, that was a piece of it, that fear of being seen and then hated, the perpetuation of her own self-immolation. *Admit it. You'd rather not be known at all.*

"You should have told us," Poppy said, and Marya felt the thin shock of being found out, before Cass sighed.

"I know," Cass said, "I'm sorry. I was trying to figure out how to keep it from hurting you."

Marya looked at Poppy. There was something hazy about the edges of her, an unreadable fuzziness.

Poppy picked at a loose thread on the hem of her shirt. "I've been trying to stop hurting all of you this whole time. I know it's not easy."

Cass laughed. "Yeah. I guess you could say that. Thanks for not hating me or anything. Do you think—did I fuck it all up?"

Marya pressed her cheek to the hot glass of the rear window. Frankie stretched out under the clouds, her hair in a fan around her, tossing in the breeze. Her eyes were closed.

"Give it time," Marya said.

Cass paused, then glanced at Marya before turning back to the road. "Are you both okay?"

Warmth spread in Marya's chest, as delicate and moony as a night-blooming flower. "I should be asking you both the same thing. But I'm fine." She picked at the frayed hem of her shorts. Poppy hummed in response, her eyes fluttering half-shut again. Marya wanted to say something meaningful, but they went over a bump in the road where the pavement gave way to loosened gravel and it knocked the words from her head. She recognized the long driveway now, the warped road curling through overgrown greenery.

They were home, a word that tore into Marya like a parasite.

Honeysuckle and forsythia warred to claim the lattice beneath Oph's porch. Birds called high in the trees. The wisteria was so purple. The daffodils so gold. Everything brighter and oversaturated with summer, save for an unfamiliar black car parked in the driveway near the carport. Cass pulled the Ford up to its right and hesitated behind the wheel.

Maybe, Marya thought, it didn't matter if she told them or not. She could wait out this whole mess. Learn from the fractures already forming. When was the last time she'd been able to see Sofia, anyway? Had it been the lake bath, that flicker of shadow looming past the blur of Poppy's dragging head? Maybe it was the house and the dark shape curled up in the crux of that tree. Maybe Marya was just a fraud after all, one of those psychics her mom went to back home with trick cards up her sleeve. So why tell them that she'd seen Sofia, that now she'd lost her all over again; what good would that be?

Because she was supposed to be helping, not hurting. Because keeping it in made her feel like all she could do was inhale until her chest threatened to split. Because maybe she'd never seen anything at all but the projection of her own desires.

So why did it feel like her mind was sliding liquid through her fingers?

She watched as Frankie stepped down from the back of the truck and headed toward the house without a second glance in their direction.

"I'm not going in there," Cass said.

"It couldn't possibly get any worse," Poppy suggested.

Cass scoffed. "Don't say things you don't mean."

Poppy tugged the car door open and slipped out.

"Wait!" Cass started, but after a pause she killed the ignition and slid from the truck. "God, this sucks."

Marya could have agreed, but she kept her mouth shut. She didn't trust herself to keep the truth from spilling out.

They made their way up the porch steps. Inside, the afternoon light turned everything eerily quiet, save for a man's voice carrying past the kitchen. Frankie stood in the living room, her shape just a silhouette. They stopped behind her, and they waited.

"I appreciate your cooperation," the man said, the sound of him so strange in the house that Marya had to fight the urge to conceal herself and disappear.

He stepped into the hall where the four of them waited, staring back like a herd of hunted animals. "Oh," he said, and that's when Marya made note of his suit, and the badge pinned to his lapel. "Excuse me."

He brushed past them and out the door, dress shoes thudding down the porch steps. Oph emerged from the kitchen, looking rumpled and hollow-eyed.

"Where have y'all *been*?" she breathed, exasperation like a sigh of relief.

"Who was that?" Frankie asked. "Did you report us missing?"

"Don't look at me like that, Frances—no I didn't, though I rightfully should have. If you really want to know, that was an officer, and he was here to let me know that they're investigating the possibility of my involvement in the ritualistic nature of Sofia's death."

Marya froze, blinking back at Oph. "What?"

Oph laughed, a thin sound seconds away from shattering. "Unfortunate, right?" She clutched the kitchen doorjamb, then gave a wave as if brushing away the whole thing. When she spoke again, it was easy and careless. "With all the murder and demonic haunting going on, you could have—oh, I don't know, told me that you were planning on running away for a night."

Frankie paused, her mouth a fragile line. If Marya couldn't share her own secrets, maybe she could take the blame for another. "It's my fault," she admitted, her mouth tasting sharp and coppery around the words. "I took them to a friend of mine who does mirror magic, to find Sofia."

The apples of Oph's cheeks reddened; her pupils were huge and blown out, fear or anger or both at once staking their claim across her face. "You didn't," she whispered.

"We had to," Poppy answered beside Marya. It was the *we* that did it; she could try to take the fall for them, but they waited like a net beneath her.

"Really, it was my idea," she insisted, arms crossed over her chest to disguise her trembling. "I convinced them to go."

Sissa crept into the hall, called by the shake in Oph's voice. "We're in danger now," she said, heavy lashes blinking like frantic insect wings. "There are too many open doors."

"We can salvage it," Oph said immediately.

"This mess is unavoidable," Sissa said. "You can't turn back time. All we can do is move forward."

Oph was firm. "We can't. She'll never forgive us."

Marya was unnerved by the blank dark of Sissa's eyes. "The boundary has been crossed, all rooted things ripped from the ground, life in the air like migratory birds—"

"Stop! Please, just, let me think," Oph commanded. Sissa ran a hand across her back, humming low in her throat. "I can't understand why you would do something like this," she said to Frankie.

"What are you talking about?" Frankie pleaded.

"You won't understand," Sissa said low in her throat. "Not yet."

"Of course I don't understand! How am I supposed to?" Marya watched the glassy sheen of Frankie's eyes. She remembered the tears. How quickly they fell, as if trying to sneak their way out. "My mother never told me anything, *you* never told me anything. Everything I know about magic has been the destruction I've seen from the sidelines. Obviously I'm going to be suspicious, you've never given me anything to believe otherwise. You've only ever drilled this fear in me and expected me to respect when you play with candles or tea leaves or whatever else your current fixation is."

Frankie crossed her arms over her chest. "I'm not sorry about any of it. We finally got real answers that would have never come otherwise. We found people who knew her."

"They helped us," Cass cut in, and Marya watched Frankie's jaw harden. "In a house where a tree grew through the floor, with roots that filled a basement."

"We think that Sofia is trying to tell us something," Poppy added roughly. "That there could be something in the cellar that would help us find her. It's all a mirror."

Oph and Sissa watched them, newly aware. Suspicion clung to them in spiderwebbed lines.

"I know you know more than you're saying," Frankie whispered. "What does all this mean? Who was that officer? No vague spells or hints or any other bullshit. Just be honest with me."

Like an arrow in Marya's heart, loosed from a sure hand.

Oph stared back at them, vacant and furious all at once. Marya was afraid to meet her gaze.

"Clearly you're not listening to me, so you're grounded," Oph said. "I'm throwing every mirror in the damned lake. Don't go near them. Don't leave this house. And do not ever go into the cellar. In fact, go to your room."

Marya watched Frankie freeze. Then she started to laugh. The sound bubbled out of her, heady and hiccupping and bending her in half. She crouched. Marya touched her back gently, and Frankie laughed harder.

Oph pointed at the stairs. "I said, go to your room!"

Frankie darted for the cellar door.

38

EVERYTHING IMAGINARY, EVEN IF LOVED

The house erupted. Oph lunged after Frankie and knocked into Sissa in the process, who let out a little shriek of surprise. Marya, Poppy, and Cass stumbled close behind as the narrow hall swarmed with a cluster of frantic women and raised voices. Just past the kitchen, the cellar door waited, a cutout in the patterned wall. Frankie clutched the knob hard enough to hurt as Oph slammed her shoulder into the door and pinned it shut.

"Move!" Frankie shouted, yanking on the little glass knob, her bandages slipping.

What was down there that her aunt didn't want her to see?

"Stop it!" Cass cried, but Oph held fast. Frankie pulled harder with a frustrated snarl.

"Move," she howled again, "now!" and Oph was trembling, forehead digging into the doorjamb.

"I can't," Oph sobbed. "I can't, I can't, I can't." She sank to the ground with her weight pinned against the door, weeping.

"Enough," Sissa said. Her voice barely rose above the din—but it rang like a church bell. Her mouth twisted sadly and turned her beautiful face into a tragedy. "It was a ritual."

"No," Oph wept, "please don't, we can't."

Frankie's heart crawled into her mouth. She kept swallowing, kept trying not to choke. "What was a ritual?"

Sissa stepped forward and tucked a strand of hair behind Frankie's ear. She felt the touch take root in her, somewhere dark and waiting. "You have something special here, you know that? It's bigger than friendship. This kind of love is pure—it's family. There aren't many people in this world who get that lucky, who find the other pieces of their souls. But people like us need that kind of family, don't we?"

"Like us?" Frankie whispered, meeting Sissa's gaze and feeling small, like a resurrected past self.

Sissa smiled at her. "Strange and unfettered, queer and encompassed by magic. It is different for us—you know that. You always have. Your mother raised you to know."

Frankie's face collapsed, but Sissa pushed on. "It was the same way with the three of us," she said, distantly. "It still is, of course, but with your mother gone, it's different. Just as I imagine it must be for you with Sofia. It's a lingering quiet, loud enough to be a person of its own. You can be together, all of you, but you're always going to feel that space—the echo of energy left behind."

Cass sucked in a breath beside her, the shredded sound of someone trying not to cry. Frankie kept trying to summon feeling, to ground herself in the moment.

"She begged me," Oph whispered. A shaking hand over her eyes shielded her from Sissa's story. "She was my sister."

"What are you hiding?" Frankie asked.

Sissa's palm flattened against Frankie's cheek. She leaned close until they were only a breath apart, like Frankie was a child in need of soothing. "You still feel your mother here, don't you?"

"I mean—" Frankie whispered, resetting. "You told me ghosts were real, didn't you?"

"Nothing with life ever leaves. What you get, you might be forced to give back tenfold. It's bartering. It's an exchange. You cannot beg something of spirit and expect it not to demand in return. You've seen that price, been touched by it, with Sofia gone and this haunting's claim on Poppy."

At the sound of her name, Frankie watched Poppy reach for Marya, fingers encircling her wrist for stability. She looked gray and sick, unsteady on her feet.

"I saw her once," Frankie said, hoarse with fear. "When we were kids. She spoke to a shadow figure. She said, 'I have a daughter and I pray she may outlive me.' She didn't realize I was there." She'd been too terrified to confront her mother. Too sick to ask which daughter she intended to keep alive. If Frankie had had a say, she would have told her mother to make it Sofia. She didn't want a say. "She fucked it all up and she left me here alone."

Poppy rocked. She let out an aching gasp and her knuckles went white around Marya's arm.

"Do you know how old the world is, Frances?" Sissa asked. "Do you know how ancient magic is? How big and blue and bright? It's endless. We are pinpricks in its timeline, grains of wheat in a giant's silo. Your mother made a bargain she wasn't equipped to fulfill."

Oph held her head and wailed. She was a stranger. Frankie kept trying to summon the anger, the hate, but her tongue was fuzzy and dead in her mouth.

"When you ask something of a demon, you invite them to eat. You open yourself up to devouring. Your mother wanted to world-walk. She found the Fissure and she loved it—a pure love, free of conquering. She just wanted knowledge. She was so smart, Frances. She was so good. Our magician. When she made the bargain, she thought she was offering herself. That she would be the only casualty when things went wrong." Her eyebrows furrowed, a crumpled expression.

"I tried to tell her," Oph said. Sissa dragged her palm over Oph's head, soothing her. Frankie kept one limp hand on the doorknob.

"Ophelia," Sissa hummed, "you did everything you could. You can only want goodness for someone for so long. We asked her to leave it alone. But sometimes you can't know how empty that desire will feel until you've already lost it all."

Frankie started to shake her head and now couldn't stop, a silent *no, no, no.*

"She came to me in the last few weeks of her life. It took something crucial from her, she said, and it left her drained, a transparent version of the person she had once been. It split her in two—she was our Fiona, but she was a part of the Fissure, too, a shadow self that the demon could use as a physical form. The creature she bargained with told her that she hadn't given enough, and that when it used up the rest of her, it would move down her family tree until it finally died out. She was so scared, Frankie. She told me that she made a new deal—if she offered her death and gave it everything she had left, you and Sofia would be spared."

"We promised we wouldn't tell," Oph whispered.

"This creature," Sissa said, "it's a devouring thing. It is a black wind, a parasitic root. It comes like a storm and it eats everything in the sky. It will not be satisfied until it eclipses the world, and it feeds on the thin places first, the boundaries and the people closest to its veil. It uses a body as a vehicle. We hoped her sacrifice had sated it."

"It takes, it takes, it takes," Oph wept.

"We buried her ourselves," Sissa said, voice shattering around the words. "Hands bound, face down. Those were the terms for feeding. It was an awful way to die, suffocating alone in the earth." Frustrated tears threatened to spill from the silvery corners of her eyes. "She crafted a tincture, and I had to tip it into her mouth—it left her sleepy and vacant as a doll. She was laughing the whole time, so happy in the end, Frankie, because she was keeping the two of you safe."

"We thought it was finished," Oph said. "We thought it couldn't ever come back."

"What went wrong? Why are we being punished now for what she did?" Frankie asked, trembling. Why was her life always the cost, when she made a boundary between herself and that end, when she'd only ever been the one left behind?

"There are two possibilities," Sissa said, the words distant as an echoing cry in a forest. "Either you or Sofia voided the terms of her agreement with the demon, or something disturbed the burial."

The room went silent. Even Oph's breath stopped heaving, tears caught along her lower lashes. "I told you, it's not possible," she said.

"You know as well as I do that you've felt her here," Sissa said. "Haven't you ever wondered? Why there's this block between us when it has been so easy for us to conjure spirits in the past?"

Frankie let go of the door as if it had burned her. Her hands pulsed with pain. "Please don't say that."

Oph looked up at her from the floor. Everything went red and wounded, the faint lines of her face simultaneously carving her old and young. "Frankie," she whispered.

"You didn't. You can't tell me that—" Frankie pressed her fists to her eyes. Her heart heaved in her chest. She thought about striking a match and illuminating her sister's apparition, about the earth under her bare feet, the room pulsing with life. "Don't tell me she's buried in the basement."

"Okay," Sissa said, "we won't tell you, then."

Frankie couldn't catch her breath. She turned and stumbled into Cass, who caught her like a funeral pyre and held her just as hot. "What else is a lie? What else have you kept from us?" she asked, righting herself and backing away from everyone, everything. "Maybe you really did do something to Sofia. How would I know?"

Oph shook her head, knocking the accusation away. "Don't say that."

The roots of Frankie's system were rotten. Oph had raised her beneath a falsehood. Omission was still a sharpened dagger, ripping into her tender heart.

And she had always believed Sofia to be the better half of her. A crucial part of Frankie's mechanics. Now she was afraid that Sofia had presented Frankie with a mask and kept the reality of herself nailed beneath a floorboard, cloistered in another world. *Coyote,* she thought, *why didn't you tell me something was wrong?*

Frankie already knew the answer—she had turned herself into an implosion, left wreckage everywhere she went.

"Sofia made a deal," she said, mouth twisting bitterly as she looked at Cass. "Didn't she? Isn't that what *Lucas* claimed?"

"Frankie, please," Cass started.

"Tell them what he said to you."

Cass wouldn't meet Frankie's eyes, no matter how hard they burned into her cheek. "He said he found Sofia with her hand bleeding over a fire, looking at a dark, horned figure."

Sissa shared a look with Oph, until Oph's eyes fluttered shut.

"If all of this is true, then why is it attacking Poppy now?" Frankie demanded. "Shouldn't I be next in line now that Sofia's gone?"

"The burial was supposed to force the demon dormant. We thought we at least left it weak enough that it couldn't permeate past the Fissure." Sissa's eyes were vacant with fear. "But if Sofia was the one to make contact again, then the offer we made with your mother is negated. Sofia's removal from the tree could have severed whatever your sister dealt, but there's no way to really know the terms of a bargain like that without witnessing it. It's possible that it chose Poppy because it knew she was mourning, and because it could punish Sofia by doing so. Besides," she finished, face softening, "she's your family too."

Poppy's knees buckled, Marya's weight no longer enough to support her. "I need to sit down," she gasped, "I'm sorry, I don't know what's wrong with me."

"Don't be sorry," Marya urged, bending to keep Poppy supported. Frankie hurried to their side and Cass was quick to follow. Oph reached to help, but Frankie stepped out of her grasp, the place where her aunt's fingers grazed her arm stinging with heat.

"Enough," she said. "This is finished."

She slid one arm under Poppy's and Marya took the other. Together they lifted Poppy and helped her to the stairs, Cass leading the way.

"Wait," Oph called after them. "We need to talk about this!"

Frankie glanced over her shoulder and found Oph staring back. There was something otherworldly about her aunt; prophetic, exalted. Her hair twisted over her shoulders in wild ringlets, cheeks flushed pink. Her back pressed harder into the cellar door.

Frankie needled Oph with her eyes, wishing that for once something dark would reveal itself to her so she might make sense of its secrets. They shifted Poppy between them and took her up the stairs, each step slow and sure until they reached Frankie's room.

"Lock the door," Frankie said. Downstairs, voices rippled and swayed, hushed arguments unfolding beneath them. Cass shut it and turned the lock. They placed Poppy on Frankie's bed and assumed positions around her, knights frozen in place.

"What happened?" Cass whispered, perching on the bed to Poppy's right. She brushed a hand across her forehead. Poppy's eyelids fluttered.

"Just need a minute," Poppy murmured.

"You were supposed to tell us if something was wrong," Frankie whispered. "You can't just go and martyr yourself for no damn reason."

She looked so small there among Frankie's sheets, her lashes heavy and low. Poppy's grimace faltered. Her skin was clammy, her knuckles bright where she gripped the sheet beneath her. "Hey, got you out of that awful conversation, though, didn't I?"

"Should we, I don't know, take her to the hospital or something?" Cass whispered.

Marya leaned into Poppy's side, eyebrows furrowed. "And tell them what? She's possessed? That a dead woman or some ancient demon passed a curse to her?"

Frankie's jaw trembled. "No hospitals. We're not letting her out of our sight."

"We are so fucked," Cass said, shoving the hair away from her face. "Did you hear what they said? Do you think that demon is what chased us in the Fissure?"

"I don't know, Cass." Frankie turned to the mirror over her dresser and avoided the sight of its reflection, afraid to see her feelings apparent in her face. Poppy's eyes flitted behind their lids, slipping closer to a fitful sleep. Marya brushed her cheek with the back of a hand.

"How the hell are we supposed to fix this? What if there's no way to protect her? Clearly Sofia got mixed up in something we don't understand, and now she's dead and we're losing Poppy to something equally terrifying. What do we do?"

"I don't *know*, Cass," Frankie snapped. Her hands ached. She folded her arms and tucked them beneath her armpits, pressing down to let the pain anchor her in place.

"Frankie," Cass started. "Can we talk about it?"

Frankie sucked in a ragged breath and deflated—the fight had seeped out of her, nothing left to bite back. Cass waited.

Everyone wanted to *talk*. But Frankie wanted to crawl into that bed beside Poppy, wanted to press her nose to her shoulder and breathe in the scent living there, coconut lotion, linen detergent. She wanted to shut her eyes. Feel the bed sink under another weight, until it was heavy with them, until they sat suspended in that moment forever.

She wanted to trust someone wholeheartedly, and she couldn't. Her aunt had lied to her all her life. Cass went behind her back and listened to the one person entirely capable of killing her sister. Frankie hadn't thought friendship could break her heart like that. But here she was, in pieces.

"I can't," Frankie said finally.

Cass's eyes welled up immediately, but she shrugged it off, trying valiantly to smile. The shape of it was all wrong for her face. "Fine. Okay. That's fine." She sucked in a heavy breath. "Do you, I don't know, have some trick of Sofia's or your mom's or something that we could try? I know you said no magic, but this is bigger than painkillers."

Wind pushed past Frankie's open window, ruffling the curtains. They all stared and thought.

Carefully, she said: "I had this box of stuff that was Sofia's, and she had tinctures in it that our mom taught her how to make."

"Do those expire?" Marya asked. Frankie shook her head weakly. How was she supposed to know?

Poppy sighed between them, a gritty sound that sent a shiver along Frankie's spine. Her eyes remained half-lidded, chest rising with slow breaths.

Frankie bit down on her cheek. "I used to keep the box under my bed, but I haven't seen it in years," she muttered, and hunched down to peek beneath the layers of blankets and box spring. "There were journals too, but I didn't read them. I thought—I was trying not to invade her privacy."

Her eyes met a black swath of space, a binder stuffed with old school papers, and a lone rolled pair of socks. She pulled back, crouching, and said, "They're not here."

"Where are they then?" Marya asked.

Frankie glanced at her bedroom door. "Maybe Oph took it. Clearly I don't know who either of them are anymore."

"Maybe she just needs to rest," Cass said, looking down at Poppy.

"Maybe," Frankie whispered after a beat. "I just don't want them near her ever again."

Marya touched Frankie's shoulder. "They won't be. We'll make sure of it."

Frankie didn't shake her off, but her body went rigid. The feeling lit up every nerve. She kept her head down, the truth of her heart written all over her, wishing something could be different, that they could go back to a past life.

"We should try to get some sleep too," she said to the floorboards.

But they were wired with anticipation. They watched the door until night crawled across the sky. Once, Sissa knocked and pleaded for Frankie to talk, but she stayed quiet. Poppy's chest rose and fell, lashes fluttering like insect wings. Finally, Frankie closed the window, lay down beside her, and shut her heavy eyelids as they made a nest there among the blankets.

Moonlight made thin slats across the comforter. Cass threw an arm across Poppy's waist, and Frankie became distinctly aware of all the places where her thigh stuck to Marya's knee. She shuffled close until her face was inches from Marya's, lulled by the heat of her shoulder and the grassy cling of Marya's skin. She wondered if the others could feel her heart pounding through her body, wired awake by the threat of a kiss.

In the end, the plush bed claimed her. Marya, Poppy, and Cass kept her warm through the daze of the night.

A breeze woke her, soft rustling, fabric against fabric. She sat up and stretched, neck sore from spending hours scrunched in the bed. The room was still dark. Poppy was gone.

Poppy was gone?

She blinked, straightening. The window sat open. The rustling sound had been the curtains, brushing against one another in the wind.

Frankie shook Marya and Cass, her heart starting to pound. Marya blinked awake like she'd never been asleep at all and Cass curled like a cat, back arching as she yawned.

"She's not here," Frankie whispered.

Marya slid off the bed immediately. Cass sat up and yawned around her words, picking sleep from her eyes. "Maybe she woke up and had to pee. Don't freak out."

But Frankie tried the knob, still locked, and felt the fear dawn on her face. They stared at the open window. The curtains wisped through the air again, two spinning ghosts in the night.

39

Her Heart Bound with Ivy

Something had carried her to the tree. But first she sought it out.

The call rose tectonic from the earth. It pushed the window open, stirred the curtains, tugged her ankles until she slid, boneless, crawling, from the bed. She recalled falling. Remembered hitting the ground hard, feet first, stones cutting into her palms when she tried to catch herself and specks of blood seeping from the meat.

She walked a long time, until she wasn't so much a woman as something that went on and carried itself. The house shuddered and opened its mouth for her. She went barefoot up the stairs, splintered and wanting, and found the tree waiting. White flowers rose to meet her. The roots roiled and lashed.

She stopped in the doorway.

Maybe she'd never left the mirror world at all. This was just awareness, a dream in which she was the primary performer. That moment in the kitchen could have been an invention of her mind—the fever pitch of her heart, Oph's broken wail, the demolition of Frankie's haunted face.

Already the images slipped away, the room close as the inside of a heart, red and warm and heavy all around her. She was achingly tired.

It was hard to tell where her body ended. What was once flesh had begun to scale over, harden, blend with the things that she touched. Calcify. Ossify.

Or maybe it hadn't. Maybe she was still just flesh and blood after all, and it was the sensation of loss that convinced her otherwise. Maybe she wasn't even that but mist to be looked through, matter to be dissipated in one great gust of breath. When she blinked, all she saw was refraction eating across her skin, working her apart like termites on a dead tree.

Speak of trees. Speak of rotting trunks, crumbling bark, smell of earth, heinous dark. The one in front of her with its girl-carved cavern yawned wide, newly alive. She remembered it barren. Now the leaves glowed and trembled against the ceiling, making lush sounds as they brushed against each other in the summer-wet night. The flowers bloomed and fractured, sickly pale against all the new growth.

The soles of her feet cut into earth beneath her. There was no pain as her steps crunched, only lightness, only living things rooting in the ground. There was a part of her that sprouted panic up through her throat and thought: *someone help me, I'm afraid . . .*

But it dissolved as quickly as it spilled into her, sugar stirred into warm water. A sound came bounding into her mind.

COME HOME.

Home. A spineless word that held no meaning. There was a clawing sensation inside her skull, the kind of dream that couldn't be scratched away. The exhaustion that plagued her was nothing more than an itch now. It melted to liquid under her skin. Now she would turn the world to sinew between her teeth.

She felt free for the first time in—forever. Somewhere in the world where her old body had lived, women knew her name. But they didn't trust her, and she didn't trust them in turn. They were going to find the truth in that cellar, and they were going to pull her apart and make spells out of the strands of her mind.

A distant whisper tickled down the nape of her neck. A familiar voice. A feral sound ripped its way out of her mouth in answer. She stepped closer to the tree. All around the house cicadas screamed.

COME HOME.

Yes, she was going home. She had a higher purpose to serve, a greater animal to feed. No more agonized dreaming. She would be free from the things that plagued her, free from the scathing glances the other girls gave her. They didn't trust her. They didn't care. She was better off without them.

The air itself was thick as sap. She felt she could reach out and grab strands of atmosphere, so she did. It slipped past her like silk. Leaves rustled and whispered to one another and owls overhead called warnings.

All her life she had watched power expand beyond the confines of her body. She had never thought herself to be magic—it was a bird-boned word, not big enough for the feeling, for the immensity of it, the possibility of it, the hard heat curling from her fingertips, turning everything she saw to gold. She'd never been privy to anything that had happened to her. She wanted to choose her end.

COME HOME.

There was no one left to halt her. Just the trees and the ominous things that wove between them. She was unburdened as the wind.

Beneath her the earth rolled and tilted, and she struggled to find solidity. She had felt this way before, something like it at least, a few times with Frankie and Cass and even her, even then, even Sofia. The memory of those names boomed like night-falling rain and she felt it again. Drunken, stumbling, fuzzy all over. Falling into a bed, a nest, a den. Allowing the dark to wash over her.

But that feeling couldn't quite match this kind of detachment. She floated, breathless, unscathed, unbroken. Her body wired to every star in the deep black sky. There was something inviting about the gaping slash in the tree, the one made just right for her.

She saw them in her mind, the ones who prodded at her, poked, sliced, probed. At the root they were a part of her world, where she danced in the dark, where her body was dust and to dust it would return. The tree awaited with open arms. She was nameless. There was a part of her that knew the feeling hadn't always been true, but now, in the darkening room, names whispered away on the wind.

A NAME IS A REPLACEMENT FOR UNDERSTANDING.

It didn't matter anyway. Pointless to try and remember.

There was a touch along the skin that must have once been her neck. The feeling seized up in her stomach. She reached for something to anchor herself, anything, the edge of a table, the smooth bark of a tree. Each grasp was useless. Her fingers, only minutes ago hardening like a beetle's exoskeleton, now went transparent.

Had it been minutes? Seconds? Was she to be condemned to a forever of moments?

The shadows dancing around her started to cower away from something. The drunken feeling buzzed in the blur of her mind.

"It does not control you," a soft voice said.

She turned to find it. Some part of her keened, desperate to put the pieces together. The thing in her chest that had known the sound immediately was a traitor, a beating animal that said *Sofia Sofia Sofia.* It remembered her when Poppy had not.

Yes, that was her name. The thought came like a punch to the teeth. The room wouldn't right itself. Haze burned around her like the beginning of a house fire. She tried to steady herself again, with a hand over her heart.

"It does not own you. You made no bargain."

Sofia, her chest screamed, *Sofia Sofia Sofia Sofia Sofia.* She'd thought about that name beside hers for a long, long time. How the syllables sounded together. She'd thought about a clumsy kiss against cool bathroom tiles, in an unmade bed, over the center console of her car, Sofia's breath becoming her own.

There was a hand against her cheek. It was barely visible, like dust caught up in sun-drenched air, but the feeling was real. The warmth of it was vivid against all that shadow. She leaned into it, savored it, craved more.

"Listen. You remember this," Sofia said. Her voice was an anchor in that rocking room, despite its waver. "You remember, and so do I. Even when the rest of it washes away, you will remember this."

She could *taste* how true it was. Her body might be changing, but she could still feel the bare skin along her skull, how the air conditioner in her bedroom breathed across it, the stifled sound of music on the television, the press of lips against her own. If that was the only kiss she ever had in her life, she would be okay with the rest slipping away.

"I'm sorry," Sofia said. "I tried to keep you safe."

Poppy pushed her cheek deeper into that faint feeling and shook her head.

"It's been a long time," Sofia whispered.

"Yes," Poppy said.

"I missed you."

"*Yes*," Poppy agreed.

SHE MAKES YOU WEAK.

"You will have to fight if you want to stay alive," Sofia said, sweetly gentle. "You will have to be very brave."

Poppy felt panic rise inside of her. "I don't know if I can," she admitted. Her voice felt like it had been spliced open, like the sound of the other baritone that dwelled inside of her was slowly cutting her apart.

SUBMITTING TO THE DEAD DOES THE POWERFUL NO GOOD. DO YOU WANT TO BE WEAK?

"Braver than I was," Sofia said.

Poppy wished desperately that she could see her. The air remained empty and dull, the touch steady and comforting. "I'll try," she said finally, eyelashes heavy against the top of her cheekbones. Everything was syrupy around her. Like the world had melted away and she had been tossed into the pot to be cooked along with it.

"Good," Sofia said. A thumb brushed across her lips. It sent a shock down her spine, a reminder that she had skin and bone and muscle and that she was here, real, alive. She wished there was more time, that her body felt more like her own, that this godforsaken thing would get out of her head and just—

LIE AMONG THE WEEDS, LET THE ROOTS SWALLOW WHAT THEY HAVE GROWN TO DRINK.

She scrambled sluggishly, hoping to grab onto Sofia, pull her close, collapse there in the haven of her. Panic rose. She wanted to go where Sofia went. She was so afraid to be left behind. What was rest if she was still alone when she woke? All she'd ever done was wait, and hope, and wish, and crave. Time made nothing better. It only scraped her hollow.

But if she could go where Sofia went—

SHUT YOUR EYES TO FIND HER IN A RED LIFE AND FEED THE ONE WHO HAS CARRIED YOU HOME.

Something lifted her into its arms, nearly tender. But it lacked all the sweetness of Sofia. It was harder and colder, holding her fetal and forlorn. It placed her in the hovel made for her, the cavern of her heart.

"Don't go," she whispered to Sofia. Had she spoken the words aloud, or just thought them into the murk? She exhaled against the body, needing reassurance to radiate down to her bones.

GIVE YOURSELF OVER AND BE GRANTED DOMINION. YOU WILL SERVE AND I WILL RISE AND WHEN THE WORLD RIPS OPEN YOU WILL FIND HER THERE WAITING IN ITS CORE.

"I'll be beside you," Sofia said, further away now. "I'll be waiting beneath the water. I'll be here, when it takes you, as long as you remember." The voice slid away. Her ears were so hot she thought they might be wet. Waves of feeling slammed against her, tidal, destructive, pulling her down to the crux of the world.

Poppy Loveless, she thought. *That's my name.* If she could just recall that one simple fact, cling to the syllables.

There were tears in her eyes. She flickered and changed.

40

PRELUDE TO THE CRASH

This was her first madness. The rest had all been practice; now, Cass was truly and properly out of her mind.

She shouldn't have gone to Lucas. She shouldn't have allowed it to come out like it did. She should have told them, should have fixed it, should have made it right. Now Poppy was gone all over again, and Frankie wouldn't meet her eyes. It all seemed to come back to her, didn't it? She kept trying to be the right friend, kept fucking herself and the rest of them over in the process. She'd thought love was supposed to be good. But hers kept making her fail.

"Maybe she went home," Cass said, feeling like a fool. She pulled helplessly at a loose thread on Frankie's bedspread. Marya stood by the window. Frankie crouched on the floor, hands over her face.

"How did she leave when she was lying between *three of us*?" Frankie said roughly. "Are you sure that no one heard anything last night?"

Cass's teeth threatened to chatter, anxiety building and needing an escape. "I was dead to the world."

"Don't even joke," Marya muttered. Morning washed her out, T-shirt hanging off her shoulder. To Frankie, she said: "At this point, anything could be real. She could have jumped out this window.

Someone could have taken her. Is it possible . . . would they have come into your room?"

She didn't say who, but the message was clear. Frankie's hair draped over her shoulders, shrouding her until she appeared impossibly small. She stared at the locked door. Cass wanted to smooth a thumb along the wrinkle in her forehead, soothe with touch, but it all seemed impossible. Before she could decide how to act, Frankie rose to her feet and began to fumble with the lock.

"Let's work through this," Cass whispered. "There are options, right? Everything has options."

"Option one: I demand that they tell me where she is," Frankie said.

"I deny option one," Cass said quickly. "You know, maybe she just left and went home. When I'm not feeling well," she added, weakly, "I know I'd rather be in my own bed."

It was something Poppy would have done once, leave rather than ask for help. But maybe she didn't know Poppy at all. Maybe Poppy had become something new.

"You think she'd pass out cold and just get up and go home without saying anything to us?" Marya asked.

"Another option, then. She did walk out, but it wasn't Poppy in control."

Frankie wouldn't look at her. Cass felt something inside of her go brittle. After everything, and they couldn't repair the crack between them? Cass wanted to reach for her. Wanted to fall to her knees before Frankie and beg for an easy smile. She even wanted anger, if it would come. But Frankie stared at the billowing curtains, the fight all snatched from her face.

"I guess it's possible," she murmured.

"It's very possible," Marya said. "We know this monster exists, and that it's somehow harming Sofia too. So if that's the case, where do you think it would take her?"

She gave them a pointed look. Cass felt her heart sink through the floor.

"I can't go back to that house," she said quickly. "We *can't.*"

"Well, I'm not going to let her die," Frankie insisted. There was an unspoken word tacked onto her fear—*too.*

"You know I didn't mean—" Cass started and faltered. She balled her hands into fists until keratin cut into palm. "You know what, fine."

Marya gestured toward the door. "What do we do about them?"

Frankie's mouth pursed with hurt. "We're wasting time already. It will have to be dealt with later. If something happens to Poppy, I'll . . ." She trailed off, closed her eyes. "We can't let anything happen."

Cass slid from the bed. She pulled her overalls back on, tucking her T-shirt into them in one slick movement. She stuffed her feet into her sneakers and slung a leg over the windowsill. "Alright. Let's get this over with."

"Wait!" Marya called, but Cass launched herself down the lattice and hit the earth with a solid thump. When she looked up, she found Marya's panicked face jutting past the windowsill.

"Just climb down," Cass called. "We used to do it all the time."

Marya stared down at the drop. Cass waited patiently, wondering if Marya was crushed by the confrontation of heights, or if it was something more—the impression of years spent sneaking out and exploring. Cass had had most of her life to build these friendships. She couldn't remember who she had been before them. Marya's face sat open, as if the idea was dawning on her too. That these people, somehow, in the grand scheme of things, had become her friends. That Cass cared for her. That she wanted to give her this—a memory come back to life. The vine-covered lattice, angled footholds, early sun speckling the white with light.

Marya swung a tentative foot out, and when she reached the bottom, Cass offered her a hand.

Frankie made quick work of the lattice, just as she always had, and they darted for the Ford before anyone could spot them. Cass jammed the key into the ignition and the engine purred to life, loud enough to wake a grave. If Oph hadn't realized they were leaving yet, she was sure to know now.

But Cass tore down the driveway before anyone could step outside. Marya sat between them, knees swaying open with every bump. Frankie leaned against the passenger-side door. Her freckled arm hung out the window in a way that tugged at Cass's heart, the familiarity of it, the Frankie-ness of the action. But there was an ocean between them. Cass felt like the worst girl on earth.

She focused on the road instead of her building fear. For a moment she thrummed, alive, powerful, hungry. The wheel was molten leather under her hands. Spent forsythia lined the two-lane highway, its fallen blooms an echo against the muted greens of the world. The Ford seemed to have a memory of its own. It carried them past landmarks she'd known all her life, past the clearings and Main and the Styx, deeper into the country until it reached the break in foliage where a dirt path led to the abandoned house and a steeple jutted past the trees. She angled the truck off the main road and let it follow its natural instincts.

They snaked across the world.

Then the siren sounded. When she glanced in the rearview mirror, she saw the sheriff's car close behind her, lights ablaze. They let out a united curse. Cass pulled the Ford to an obedient stop.

Here the woods were ominous, even more so than the day they'd gone hunting through the umbrage where Sofia's car had been abandoned. Cass lifted a glance to the mirror again. The sheriff's vehicle was dark despite the brimming morning, and she imagined him inside of it, hat pulled low over his eyes. She jumped when someone rapped on her window and found the sheriff looking back at her. When had he slipped from the car? When had he stepped up beside her?

Staring through the smudged glass of her window, his eyes were the vacant blue-black of a frostbitten limb, beard trimmed blunt against his skin, cheeks lined with age but rounded with the youthful pudge that Lucas's had too. Cass swallowed as Marya tensed beside her and slowly rolled down the window. It took several moments, despite her practice with the crank.

"Hey, Officer," Cass said brightly, flashing him her widest grin. She wondered if he recognized her from that evening when he'd almost given her a ticket. Deep down she knew, from personal experience, how the dimples that formed on her cheeks could make a man go soft. But the sheriff stared at her, blank and cold.

"I need you to step out of the car, please," Sheriff Glasswell said.

"Sorry," Cass said, feeling anything but, "could you tell me what exactly I did?"

"Step out of the car," he said again. His jaw tightened just a fraction. Cass felt her skin prickle.

"You don't have to do that," Frankie said to Cass.

"All of you. Out, now."

"Why?" Marya pushed.

There came another rap, insistent and metallic, against Frankie's side of the truck. When they turned, the blood rushed from Cass's face and pooled in her stomach, acidic.

Mrs. Glasswell pointed the barrel of a shotgun at them. Shadows made the sharp planes of her face indistinct, obscured by the curtain of her hair. Her voice rang loud and even.

"Get out or I shoot. It's your choice!"

They got out. With the gun pointed at their backs, the sheriff and Mrs. Glasswell urged them deeper into the woods, where the brush swallowed them whole.

41

A WOMAN WILL BUILD A NEW WORLD

Finder woke to darkness. Her tongue was a fat insect in her mouth, heavy and crawling, and her head spun, that way and that way and that way and that—

"Oh," she said, more a groan than a word. She was on her back. The floor was hard and cold, even through the bunched-up layers of her dress. She pressed against it and closed her eyes, trying to stop the turning sensation that claimed her.

For a moment she forgot where she was, and fear took over her body. The feeling was too painfully familiar—her jaw stung just as it had the night Mother Mab caught Sofia in the house. Finder felt the rush of blood to her head with the rise of desperation. *Run. Don't let them catch you.* Then the slap that spun her thoughts like a clockwise ladle in a pot of herbs.

She let out a wounded sound.

"Thank you," came a voice to her right, "thank the spirits, thank the earth, thank the sunless sky." Hands cupped her face, fingers careful as they pressed along the bones of her jaw. "Finder? Can you hear me?"

"Obviously," Finder answered, though her head was ringing with the kind of buzz reserved only for insects. Beneath it came a rhythmic beat. Was that the calling of a bird, far in the distance, or the recollection of her brain crashing around in her skull?

"Still rude," the voice answered. Her eyes started to adjust. The soft line of the boy's jaw outlined itself in the gloom. She reached for the skin of his cheek to prove that he was real, but she faltered and snagged on his sleeves instead.

"Where is he?" Her hair was stiff, drying to her cheek and her throat.

"The Ossifier is upstairs, I assume," the boy answered easily. "He locked us down here. Got me good in the chin." He tapped for emphasis. The movement was molasses slow as Finder tried to catch up to it. "I'm glad you got to sock him before he left, though. That was incredible. Top-notch."

She laughed and then cried out, the tightening of her stomach pulling on the raw wounds the glass had made against her abdomen. She twisted her head until her cheek pressed against the ground. With her eyes shut, the spinning slowed. Her ears rushed with the pounding of her heart, so loud that she thought for a moment it might be coming from the ground itself. She pushed herself up onto her elbows and fought through the pain.

"No rush," the boy said. "It's not like we have somewhere to be."

"Why didn't he kill us?"

"Oh, he gave it his best shot." He rested his chin against his knee. "I tried to hold him off you after you conked out. But Mab returned when he was, um, well, thoroughly choking me. He told me to stay in the cellar or he'd kill both of us and went up to meet her. I figured I'd hang down here. They fought for a while, until it went quiet."

Finder felt dread pool in her stomach, hot and violent as it mixed with her appreciation. Quiet didn't seem to be a good sign. "Thank you," she said, quickly.

He smiled. "For what?"

"You didn't have to protect me."

He scoffed, the sound passive. "I wasn't going to sit here and watch you die. Besides, he would have killed me, too, eventually, if I didn't try."

"Still. You defended me." She smoothed over her dress, imagining what hurts hid beneath the stained fabric. "I know it's not really my place to give you one, but I think you deserve a name."

"Oh, great and mighty Finder, thank you for bestowing upon me this gift that I am undeserving of—"

"Don't make me regret it," she said, unable to prevent herself from smiling back, even in the basement's blanket of dark. "I think you should be called Keeper. You've protected me and this home. It's only fair."

"I guess it's better than what they gave me when I was born," he said, wry.

"Don't sound so excited about it."

He nudged her shoulder. "Really. I like it, I think I'll keep it. Ha ha. Get it?"

As a response she rolled away from him and his laughter, stomach soothed by the cool dirt. With a heaving push she got to her knees, only crying out when her abdomen bent. A success in her book.

"You shouldn't be moving around," he said.

"Like you said, I'm not going to wait for him to come finish the job." The thudding sound continued even as she raised her head. She felt along her scalp, the hair matted and dried with blood, and sucked in a hurting breath. "We have to get out of here."

"I mean, yeah, that would be amazing," Keeper said.

She got to her feet. Took a few wobbling steps. She listened, closely, for any kind of movement above them, but the house remained quiet. "You don't happen to have a lantern, do you?"

Keeper's teeth gleamed. "'Fraid not."

Finder grimaced back, the muscles in her cheeks pulling at her tender skin. Above them roots twisted through the air, snaking across the beams of the ceiling. Finder felt her way along the walls. The room seemed bigger than she remembered it. Over time it had warped and changed in places, but the walls remained cool, the floor packed and hard as stone, all radiance leached away by hungry earth. Her fingers dragged along the dirt until she reached the table at the back of the room, vines digging into the wood and curling around the unsteady legs. Keeper stumbled over to where she stood.

Bone piled high on the table. Wire wrapped itself in neat little spools. Wicked-looking tools sat among a line of rusted pliers and a sharpened whittling knife. She followed patterns of bones arranged to shape doll bodies, the same as the figures nailed along the path from the lake.

"So he *is* making them," she whispered, "but why?"

Footsteps creaked overhead, followed by the low lilt of the Ossifier's voice, too quiet to make out the words.

"Maybe he's bored," Keeper muttered.

"Must be it," Finder answered flatly, pressing her abdomen to try and ease its throbbing. She ran a fingertip along a slender bone, pale and amorphous. "Can you imagine how many creatures he had to kill to get this much bone?" she wondered aloud. Then she froze, finger pressing hard into a neat little wing joint as the realization dawned.

"It was him."

"What do you mean?"

"He slaughtered the chickens," Finder said, "to make these."

With a sweep of her arm, she knocked the bones from the table, scattering them across the room. They clinked to the ground and Keeper flinched hard. Footsteps crossed the floor again, slowing as they crept closer to the cellar door, and Finder curled her grip around the handle of the whittling knife.

"What the hell are you doing?" Keeper whispered fiercely.

"Listen to me closely," she said. "When I tell you to grab onto me, you do it. No matter what."

"Finder—" he started, her name tart in his mouth.

"Promise me," she hissed, circling his wrist and tugging. The door at the top of the stairs rattled and a key clicked into the lock. She shook him, hard. "*Promise.*"

"I promise!"

Finder clutched the knife in the hand that wasn't touching Keeper, her grip sure around the hilt. She glanced down at the speckled gleam of the blade, the ragged edge of her dress already bloodstained. If she could make a cut—if she could spill enough—

The door creaked open. A trickle of yellow bounced down the stairs. Finder squinted against it, barely illuminated but bright enough to make her eyelids ache.

"Hello," the Ossifier said pleasantly, and then he pushed something down the stairs.

They staggered back as it thumped. When it hit the ground, it sprawled wide, a twist of flesh and cloth. It let out an enormous, pained whimper. It was Mother Mab.

The Ossifier descended behind her, his steps eerily soft and lingering. He took them two at a time. He held a lantern, golden and gleaming, and it lit up his face like scattered shards of glass. The skin around his right eye remained dark even in the light; she'd blackened it. Satisfaction curled in her stomach.

"Have you both been good down here?" he asked.

Mab looked a lot like Finder imagined herself to appear, hair matted with blood, dress torn and stained. "I command you," she said, sharp as splintered wood. "I command you to—"

The Ossifier hopped down the last stair and delivered a swift kick to Mother Mab's abdomen. Finder cried out like the hit had landed on her. She held little love for Mab, but loyalty was a strung-out thing. She'd never had anyone else to pledge herself to before.

"*I* command *you*," the Ossifier said brightly, "to break the ward before I cut it open myself."

Mother Mab could only whimper and curl in on herself. Finder had never seen her look so small.

"What is he talking about?" Keeper asked, at the same moment that Finder said, "We know what you've been constructing." She eyed him, warning him to stay quiet, to honor his promise and follow whatever she asked of him.

"Well, it's decently obvious," the Ossifier said, still grinning. "I assume that's what you spent your time frolicking after in the woods? My trinkets?" He nudged Mother Mab with the pointed toe of his boot. "Did you happen to run into anything else along the way? Serpents? Creatures? Things that go bump in the night, with hooves and horns?"

All Finder could do was watch the lines of Mother Mab's face, her knotted hair, her pleading eyes. Finally, when it appeared that the Ossifier actually wanted her to speak, she answered: "I don't know what you expect me to say."

"It's a breadcrumb trail!" the Ossifier exclaimed. "It's a constellation map!"

Finder waited, skin numb around the slick handle of the knife. She held it out in front of her as if suddenly remembering it was there, trying her hardest not to shake.

"Cute," the Ossifier said. His lantern flickered against his glassy stare. "Allow me to teach you something. Pain demands pain. Suffering demands suffering. Everything is an exchange, power given for power. That's how magic works. You can't ask for something without giving something away." His eyes darted across Mother Mab's supine form. He set the light down beside his feet, burning against the ground. "It's an offering."

"Don't," Finder pleaded, feeling dizzy, like she might crumple at any moment. "She's your family. She takes care of us."

He reached down and tugged Mab up by her hair. The old woman cried out, thrashing, snarling. Her eyes met Finder's, and her fury flamed with the kerosene. The Ossifier flicked out a little blade. His preferred whittling knife, handle worn smooth from hours of use. It glimmered among the lamplight and the shadows cut his face into pieces.

"There is a creature that waits in the woods," he said, smiling wide. "I know her name."

"Good for you," Finder spat.

"I know her name and she knows mine. That's an offer, Finder. Don't you love to take notes? We made an *offer*. And as a part of our bargain, she provides me power. She makes me strong and ancient. I will never do something so pathetic as dying. And in turn, I feed her, and watch her grow. She has called to me, and she has told me that it is time. She is ready to eat."

Mother Mab twisted and cursed in the Ossifier's grip.

"Mab here thought she could keep this creature away, but you can't keep a demon from its rightful place."

"You will regret it," Mab hissed, "you will lose everything."

"You think you're so powerful," the Ossifier chided. "You thought you could stop every witch that came to your door. You thought you could banish that girl and her mother, that you could keep Finder ignorant. You've failed every time, Mab. They always slip through your grasp."

His fist tightened against Mother Mab's scalp.

"And you've learned from her over the years, haven't you, Finder? I've watched it happen. She's taught you about the magic she holds. Witchery. Kitchen spells. How to cloister yourself away from the world and grind your bones down into dust."

Finder kept her mouth pinned shut, knife still outstretched. Her eyes locked on Mother Mab's and the hand knotted in her hair. They were evenly matched.

"Fine, then," the Ossifier sighed. "Tell me, Mab. Does she know how to break the ward?"

"Just kill me already," Mother Mab ground out.

"What do you think, Finder?" the Ossifier asked, buoyant and jovial. "Would you like for me to kill her? Break the ward myself? Or will you help me, and save her life?"

The problem was—the fact of the matter was—Finder didn't know what he was talking about. She knew Mab had abilities the rest of them didn't. Knew her to be wise beyond the years and years that clung to her, that rooted deep within her. Knew there must have been something protecting the house from darkness all these sunless days, if creatures like the one that paced the perimeter of the fence hadn't crossed the threshold yet. And while she'd washed the windows with buckets of cinnamon-heavy water and rags soaked in lavender oils, while she'd boiled orange peels on the woodstove and drunk deep cups of chicory root, while she'd read book after book and tried to understand why the world operated the way that it did, Finder had never been taught the mechanics of magic, the reasoning behind it, the meaning that held it in place.

"Don't speak, Finder chick," Mother Mab said. It was a final command, her last chore. Mab's mouth was a thunderstorm. Blood ran down her chin. The wicked scar that bisected her cheek had a fresh cut running beside it. Finder felt grief splice her apart, welcomed the sting of it.

"You've forced my hand," the Ossifier said wistfully, and he cut Mother Mab's throat.

Keeper cried out. Finder went limp, the knife landing on the dirt floor. The sound that left her mouth belonged to some other girl's voice, some other animal's pain.

It was over quickly. The blood bubbled from Mab's throat across the floor in a black pool, lamplight flickering against it.

The Ossifier raised his hand. Blood trickled down his white wrist. "Come," he sang, and Finder was prepared to argue until she realized he wasn't speaking to her. It seemed for a moment that the shadows in the room flocked to his waiting palm, the dusk deepening, corners of the basement stretching and bending. Distantly, a scream sounded, a nightmare coming to life. "Feed on what I offer you."

"Keeper," Finder said, still staring at Mother Mab's limp form. "Grab onto me."

Keeper did as she asked and the Ossifier laughed. It was the dry sound of paper crinkling in a flame. "He has a name now?"

Finder bent to the floor as the Ossifier stalked closer to them. Her body groaned in protest, her mind whirring, her eyes shockingly wet at the corners. She wanted to catch the tears that waited there, bottle the salt.

"I thought the first time might have taught you something," she said roughly, all bravado and bile in her throat. Above them the house shuddered, caught up in an unnatural wind, shutters banging and doors thudding open. Keeper's skin was so warm against her arm. She grounded herself in that feeling as she pushed her splayed fingers into Mother Mab's blood.

Please, she thought. *Let it work. Let me be capable. Let her life be worth it.*

The Ossifier realized a beat too late. He lunged at them, snarling as a roar sounded around them again, closer now, in the house.

Away, she thought to the mirror of Mother Mab's blood, her heart an empty chasm.

Together they flickered. The Ossifier's hand wisped through the memory of Finder's throat.

42

Secrets Sewn in Fraying Cloth

Is this what her sister had felt in those final moments, what the end looked like? Fear, sharp as a spark in Frankie's chest. Betrayal cooling deep. Goose bumps rising along her arms—dread.

The trees were lush with last season's dead growth. Kudzu ate everything. Frankie's shoes sank where rain had churned the ground to marsh over the past few weeks, never enough light poking through the leaves to sap the water back skyward. Each footstep made a dull sucking sound. Honeysuckle rose hot and lazy among the green and wasps torqued between them as they walked, single file, toward the house slumping atop the hill.

Cass led the way. Marya stayed close behind. Frankie followed and tried not to feel the world imploding around her as Mrs. Glasswell remained at the rear with her gun raised. Frankie glanced back once to see if the sheriff followed, too, and received a prod in the back with the barrel. She caught only the top of his ugly hat, but it was enough to confirm her fears.

"Keep moving," Mrs. Glasswell insisted.

Frankie conjured a million retorts and stuck with biting down on her tongue until she tasted blood as an answer.

Past the line of trees, the house rose splintered and angular against the unshattered blue mirror of sky. The porch drooped like the shoulders of a weeping woman, caution tape fluttering in the breeze from the skeletal columns. Flickers of open space shone through the shattered windows, and she could almost make out branches where the tree had torn through crumbling walls.

As they walked, she held her elbows across her chest. Twining her fingers together made little roots of pain sprout from her knuckles to the spots beneath her ears, and leaving them to hang at her sides felt like losing control. Soft breeze bit into her skin, made the hair on her arms stand on end. It had been a breezy night when Sofia disappeared. Summer just a dead green. The fire rising too high. Frankie remembered the aftermath, how she'd stepped outside the next morning and found the petals of peonies scattered across the yard, torn from their stems and tossed into the wind.

Maybe, years before, Sofia had been led here like Frankie, the doomed Lyon girls, each of them meant for nothing other than annihilation.

In some ways it was an omen, in others, a comfort. It was that dream that kept Frankie's footsteps steady. She hadn't been permitted a goodbye, but she could have this—an echo, a repetition, an exchange of energy.

"We don't have all day," Mrs. Glasswell urged, and Frankie's steps fell into place with the sheriff's as they climbed the porch stairs.

Inside, the heavy heat was absent. Darkness made everything cool and damp. Frankie shivered, the black chill seeping down to the core of her, that same bone-deep fear she'd felt the night something slipped inside of Poppy's body and cooked Frankie's hands. The only sound was the lowing of the rotting floor beneath them. Frankie took careful steps behind Cass and Marya as they were goaded toward the kitchen where the tree waited, where she waited, where—

Cass let out a ragged cry at the sight of Poppy curled in the belly of the tree. She rushed to it with hands outstretched and Frankie reached to stop her, remembering the pain darting through her nerves.

But Mrs. Glasswell beat her to it. The gun made a slick sound as she trained it on Poppy. "Sit or I'll shoot her," the woman commanded.

Poppy bloomed against the bark and the chrysanthemums. Faint trickling light crawled its way through the house and made stained glass out of her dark skin. Her eyes were shut, knees drawn up, shirt stained and dirty, jeans torn at the knees. Her chest rose and fell—too slowly, too still. Frankie wanted to hold her. Frankie wanted to burn the whole house down.

"Sit," Mrs. Glasswell repeated. This time her voice shook.

Frankie sank to the floor and its roots, the three of them lined up like targets on a fence post. Beside her, Marya pressed her knee up against Frankie's, and the near warmth of it was enough to slow her heart a little. Cass's leg bounced restlessly up and down until the vibration shook the room.

Mrs. Glasswell held the shotgun tight to her chest. It rested on a worn leather strap, a stark contrast against her gauzy blouse and the pearls in her ears. The sheriff stood beside her. He touched the edge of his hat in a manner that seemed born out of habit as Mrs. Glasswell cleared her throat. "Before we finish this, I want to know why."

"I don't understand the question," Cass answered.

Mrs. Glasswell swung the gun back to her shoulder and pointed it at Cass. There was a smudge in her lipstick. Some irrational part of Frankie wanted to reach out and fix it with her thumb. "Why did she choose my son?"

"Who?" Frankie asked, just to hear her say it.

"Don't act ignorant," Mrs. Glasswell snapped. "Your sister sent that horror after him. She's the one who made it want him in the first place. She ruined our entire lives. He loved her so much, you know that? He told me that he wanted to marry her one day."

Frankie felt too hot. "What are you talking about?"

Mrs. Glasswell's face fractured. There was something pinned beneath all her sharp words—fear, curdled and astringent. She tugged at a strand of her hair. Anxiety radiated off her in waves. "Why bother lying when all I'm asking is to understand?"

"We're trying to understand too," Cass insisted.

Mrs. Glasswell tilted her head, questioning. It was a strangely inhuman sight. "I thought I could help her. I thought that if Lucas wouldn't break it off with her, then I would have to keep them both safe."

There was a beat when Frankie felt her body shift to stone and thought she might become heavy enough to fall through the floor, passing down into the earth until there was nothing left of her but a chasm where she'd once been.

"You killed her," Frankie whispered, just to set the words free.

Mrs. Glasswell shook her head, but her mouth folded in on itself. She sucked in a staggered breath. The mask of her bravado slipped, and suddenly she was pitiful. "Your sister was dangerous. She made us all a part of this mess."

Frankie said it again, with venom. "You killed her."

Mrs. Glasswell smiled faintly, as if trying to console a crying child. "I didn't mean to."

"Marcia," the sheriff snapped, grasping her elbow. She shook him off immediately.

"It's not like any of them will leave here alive," she bit back. "I will have an answer. Tell me why she did this to *him*."

The room kept turning, no matter how many times Frankie blinked and swallowed around the sickness rising in her throat. Lucas's mother killed Sofia. She was looking at her sister's murderer. "What do you mean you 'didn't mean to'?"

Mrs. Glasswell tucked her hair behind her ear, and when it slipped free, she tucked it again, shaking. "You're not a mother. You don't know what it's like to watch your child grow and then see him throw away the life you built over a relationship with someone who isn't good for him."

Her knuckles went white around the stock of the gun. "Lucas told me about the ritual she did, and that *creature* she made a deal with. He wouldn't give her up and let it go. I tried so hard to give her a better life, so she could be the kind of woman worthy of my son. Your sister had the devil in her, Frances. Do you know the kind of toll an exorcism takes on someone? How it can break down the body?"

An exorcism. Frankie held her head—she couldn't look at anyone, couldn't stop the awful feeling of falling. "You didn't know anything about her," she said to the floor.

"I was helping her," Mrs. Glasswell repeated. "I wanted to banish the evil she had invited into herself, but she just wasn't strong enough to handle it."

"You're delusional," Cass said, strangled with pain.

How had Sofia suffered? What had they done to her? Frankie wanted to weep, wanted to snatch Mrs. Glasswell by the shoulders and shake her until something important snapped. She wanted to pick the Glasswell family apart until nothing remained. Instead, she dug her nails into her forearms, trying to pin herself to the nightmare of her reality.

Mrs. Glasswell's voice was wet. "I was giving her a chance at a better life. I wanted her to make it."

"Stop talking," the sheriff grunted out. "You never know when to shut your mouth."

Marya's eyes clung to the tree. "We just want to take Poppy home. We'll forget this ever happened."

Frankie could never forget. She would ruin everything they held dear. They had taken her sister from her. Though a slippery reminder fluttered at the back of her mind—*a sister you did not know*. Because Sofia *had* been different at the end. And they had learned secrets already, buried in the grave of Sofia's heart, kept from Frankie where they would fester and rot. What did she have left? What could she possibly trust?

Mrs. Glasswell's face crumpled. "I'm sorry, but I can't let you do that."

Rage burned up Frankie's throat, atomic. There was a sickly reciprocal kind of motion to this argument. She felt, suddenly, like she'd been in this exact moment before. "Why the fuck not?"

"It's an offering," Mrs. Glasswell whispered. "Your sister raised a demon. She was going to send it after my family, and I—when the light fell from her eyes, the creature spoke to me." Her voice was reverent. "She gave me her name and her terms. I asked for my son's life to be protected in exchange for another. I didn't have a choice."

"You had every choice," Frankie said. She shook with the effort of restraining her hatred. "You murdered her."

Mrs. Glasswell pointed the shotgun at Frankie. She stared down the barrel, coaxing it to shoot. Maybe Sofia had done the same before they crushed the tender shell of her skull. But Mrs. Glasswell lowered the gun again and looked to the sheriff. He nodded at her and turned to the tree, where Poppy's form curled in the trunk.

"Don't touch her!" Cass shouted, the words close to a sob.

"Your sister did this," Mrs. Glasswell said. "She made a deal she couldn't uphold and now the rest of us are paying the consequences. You ruined it when you left this tree empty and gave it nothing to feed on. We could have been fine. We could have all left this unscathed. But you know what Lucas told me? That the demon asked for the blood of someone she loved in exchange for the life of another. I wouldn't let it be him. Never him. So I'm giving her your friend, and I'm protecting my family."

Her hands shook, with anger or fear or a mixture of the two. "He's my only son. You have to understand that."

Frankie felt herself split open, a chasm between who she had been before and who she was now. Maybe in another universe there was a version of herself unsullied by this emptiness. But all she had was this world. All she had was the tender wound of her mind.

"You're lying," she whispered. Marya's hand brushed hers and Frankie felt her heartbeat in her fingertips. Her vision went spotty, radiated with life. Achingly, she could see it in her mind: the dirt that wouldn't come out from under Sofia's nails, hours spent away from home where she slipped back into her room late at night. The gaps in time, the trips to the Fissure, a whole other life unspoken.

Mrs. Glasswell bent close to Frankie. Her gaze was mournful. "I know you wanted to keep her safe. Trust me, I tried. But she wasn't a good person. Look at all the devastation she's caused, all the lives she's ruined, even when she's gone. Sometimes loving someone doesn't do any good. Sometimes, it's just a mistake."

Frankie wrenched in pain. She imagined her mother, buried alive, face down in the dirt. Was that fighting? Or was it desperation, a coiling viper of a mess that Frankie had only been destined to step into, a trap set to snap the bone and leave her unable to go on alone? Who would she have been if her mother had fought for her like this? If she had been willing to kill whatever stood in her daughter's path instead of lying down in front of it?

It wasn't a question—her mother had sacrificed, and this woman had killed—and now she would say anything to set herself free and slip out of this mess. Frankie wanted to argue, but her throat was burning, and she found she couldn't breathe.

"Shut up," Marya spat for her, ragged.

Mrs. Glasswell shook her head. "You know as well as I do that it's true."

Frankie watched Marya swallow. It turned her throat into a machine. When she spoke, the words thrummed through the air, alive on their own. "It's not. She wasn't like that. I would know, I would have felt it when I—when I saw her."

Mrs. Glasswell's expression was pitying. "We build ideas of people in our head, don't we?"

Frankie tried to keep up with the words; they slipped away from her, thin and nimble as black snakes underfoot. She blinked, shivered, tongue throbbing behind her teeth. *Saw her?* What was Marya talking about?

"You know," Mrs. Glasswell said softly, fixing Frankie with a hard look, "you two are nothing alike up close. She was a frigid thing. You're all fire."

Frankie was electric, fuzzing, mutilating herself from the inside out. "What did you mean by that?" she said, snaring the words, tasting blood.

"I'm trying to say that—" Mrs. Glasswell started.

"Not you. Marya, what did you mean by that?"

Marya wouldn't look at her. Cass's eyes were full of tears, flickering between them.

"What do you mean you *would have known?*"

Mrs. Glasswell's brow furrowed, the gun clutched in her arms. But Frankie only had eyes for Marya. Their thighs pressed together, sticky with humidity. She couldn't bring herself to pull away and make it real.

"Frankie, please," Marya started, and Frankie felt her mind stutter and stop.

Her heart thrummed and took flight like the bird she and Sofia found stuck in the attic one summer, beating its wings against the little round window overlooking the lake. The thump and thump and thump, the desperate shrill sounds of its panicked breaths. The hard thuds of its body against glass.

"Tell me," Frankie demanded.

"I just had this feeling—" Marya started, faltering.

"Tell me the *truth*," she demanded.

She wasn't going to cry. Not again, not here, not like this, Poppy tucked away in the belly of that tree, gun waiting before her.

"I can see the dead when they haven't yet passed over. When they're still spirits."

Frankie's nails cut past gauze. "And you've seen her before."

Marya's eyebrows furrowed, squinting like she might cry, and it wasn't fair, because all Frankie ever wanted to do was cry and all she could ever do was grit her teeth and drink it back like poison, swallow that lump in her throat and keep going because there was a person who took her sister's life and she was going to kill them herself she was going to tear them apart she was going to bring about the end of worlds if it meant a headstone for her sister and sleep without dreams but—

But here was the woman claiming to have killed her right in front of them, admitting, speaking it aloud, and all Frankie could think about was the fact that Marya had lied to her the whole time. That Cass had betrayed her. That Poppy had abandoned her. That Sofia had always been a little closer than it seemed, and always out of reach.

"I've seen her ever since we met," Marya said, eyes fluttering closed. "She used to follow you everywhere."

Since the beginning, since it started.

"You could have—the whole time, you could have told me she was fucking dead before they even found her, you could have helped her, you could have talked to her, asked her questions!"

"It wasn't my place to tell you that," Marya whispered. Tears clung to her lashes. Marya wouldn't look at her. Frankie wanted to steal the truth from her mouth. "I tried to talk to her! She couldn't speak to me, there was something holding her back, and then she started to disappear, and I didn't know what was happening, and I thought I might have imagined it or something and it was too late for me to tell you. You wouldn't have believed a word I said."

"What do you mean, used to?" Frankie's voice betrayed her pain. "You—you don't see her anymore?"

She felt the loss all over again. Here she was, holding her sister in her hands and watching her melt between the cracks.

"I don't know where she went," Marya admitted miserably.

Frankie's vision blurred with furious tears. She needed to get away. She needed to see—god, she wanted to hear Sofia's voice, wanted to feel the laugh come bounding through her chest and the rise and fall of her breath there beside her, the sound of a sister.

She tore her eyes away and saw into the cracked mirror leaned up against the wall, her reflection taunting her. It felt like decades had passed since she'd last seen herself. The familiar was gone. All this time it'd been everyone else in the world feeding her a lie, watching it drip down her chin. So what if her sister was a monster? So was Frankie. So was the sun. So was the endless turning world.

"Please just let us go," she whispered roughly.

Mrs. Glasswell sighed. A breeze pushed through the house and ruffled her sensible skirt. "Everything demands a sacrifice. Sofia's death was a necessary accident to keep us safe, and now that her body is gone, there's nothing standing between this creature and the hold your sister gave it over Lucas. If I offer your lives instead, it will be enough to set my family free. It's you or it's us, and I'm not willing to let it be us."

"But—" Cass said, strands of hair clinging to her damp cheeks, "we didn't do anything."

Distantly, the wind made animals out of air. It was a ragged howl, agonizing and drawn out. The sheriff perked up like a dog and Mrs. Glasswell turned to him, face full of fear.

"What was that?" Cass whispered.

It came again, a guttural wailing. The silence inside the house was too still. Marya sat ramrod straight and Mrs. Glasswell's eyes went wide.

"We need to satisfy the bargain," the sheriff said. "Now."

But Mrs. Glasswell was frozen. Her hands shook around the gun.

"*Now*, Marcia," he insisted.

A distinct crack sounded beneath them, and Frankie thought of the bonfire, flames glinting in her sister's eyes, so much unsaid between them. The way the house had fractured beneath Tommy's body—the porch biting into him, drawing his blood.

"What's happening?" Cass whispered.

Frankie watched as the roots of the tree started to writhe. They pulled themselves from the boards they had grown into, leaving jagged gaps in the floor. The tree's shadow, a wide thing cast across the room, began to grow bigger, darker, deeper.

The shape of it curled against the ceiling. It peeled away from the bloated plywood and rotten paint and gouged trunk. It swelled with mass. The scent of burning filled the air, choked her nearly breathless.

Frankie tipped her head back and took in the terror.

43

THE CRUX OF THE WORLD

From the sky, she's a know-it-all. She looks through the blue like glass. They are ants beneath her, her family, her women, their lives mapped out like flight patterns, their stories imprinted on the ground.

Sofia walks through time.

In the distance rises the demon's call. Her shadow looms over her, strengthened now by the demon of its origin, the tether between them strained with hunger. This is the moment where it becomes blurred—once she was alive and once she was a ghost and now she is a monster of the bisect where her body straddles the line, breathing through dirt, her mind just the imprint of a girl.

It would be a mercy to be eaten whole. Heaven knows her shadow's been trying to pull her back from this plane—black matter ripping for the memory of her heart. But she's the one who gave it a master in the first place, who carved the path for it to claim them. She's the one who took her options away. Who left herself no choice but to hold the one she loves in the tree and feel it devour them both.

From a certain angle, the simple unraveling of their lives was her doing. Or maybe it was her mother's, or her mother's mother's, or the splice in time through which they were born, or the recollection of a bird's egg in a forgotten nest. Maybe she is a bird. Maybe she is the bird's killer.

There's a moment she remembers, nonsensical, in her sister's voice, at points distorted to sound like her own: *No more birds, coyote.* Her mother standing at the porch railing with her fingertips digging down into Sofia's hair, whooping toward the clouds.

She glides through air. Pieces of her stick in time, caramel caught in teeth. Sofia haunts her life.

There she is in Lucas's bedroom, his love falling over her like dead leaves. His words rot between them, harsh as the temper that used to curdle him sour. There she is in Poppy's bathroom. There's Poppy's breath across her stomach. There is the soft dark tank of her eyes, the tender inside of her mouth. There she is with Cass's head cushioned in her lap, the easy closeness of her, laughter tremoring against Sofia's legs. There she is slamming the door in Frankie's face and then rushing to press her ear up against, to listen and wait and see if Frankie will walk away. She doesn't. She waits. *No more birds, coyote.*

Sofia takes up space, has mass. Sofia is lighter than air. Silos spread across the countryside, towers of grain, sleeping giants. Finches flock to higher ground. Sofia wants to fly too, so she—

Goes tumbling through the air. There across the chasm sits a church, forgotten. The steeple stands crooked, its cross leans into time. She watches it fall on repeat.

She is her mother's daughter. Once, she learned the magic, performed the proper steps.

She is her sister's twin. She keeps her secrets to herself, and of secrets Sofia is familiar.

Her first: she made a deal with the devil.

Maybe she *is* wicked. But Sofia has always admired her mother's work. Before she was a dead thing, the spell work that scared Frankie thrilled Sofia, made bees out of her blood. She liked the whimsy of it, the flick of a card, burning herbs, sigils drawn in soot above the mantel.

She slept with a bay leaf beneath her pillow. She relished telling Frankie about the dreams she'd had, her hair pooling on the pale sheets as she leaned across the bed, a harpy in the night. She liked to have her palm read. She savored the flavor of snuffing out candles with freshly tasted fingertips.

Her mother wrote recipes for heartbreak on the backs of grocery lists that looked like *poke root, hops, rose petal, essence of Queen Anne's lace*. In her living hands, Sofia held them to her lips. She mouthed the words to the mirror. She sucked cloves under her tongue and shut her eyes to properly savor the taste. In mugwort dreams she saw the starless sky, a great black glassy sea waiting for her touch, and a creature rising out of it like a portent of the end.

She remembers her first dive into the lake behind Oph's house, sinking past the reeds and silvery little fish, hearing her mother's voice like a home video instructing, "Part the fabric of the universe and step into the space that you've created." She remembers coming out of the water to find the world gone red. Sofia is her own monster, emerging, water running off her back.

Now she time-walks again, memories of other lives coming to her quicker than her own. There is her mother, a child on her knees in the dirt, burning oak leaves against matches and clasping her hands to the earth and wishing on something bigger than the world she knew.

There is Lucas, looking at her like he would take it all back in a heartbeat.

There is Frankie, Sofia's shirt clutched against her, shaking hard enough to bite her tongue. There she is in the bathtub with Cass and Poppy taking her into their arms, holding her above the water.

There is Oph standing in a night-dark cellar, younger than Sofia ever remembered her being, a shovel slung over her shoulder and a fault line for a mouth.

There is Finder taking Sofia's hand in her own and pressing it to the trunk of the red tree, smile igniting her face like a firework.

But in the landscape of her mind, the mountains remain like heaps of ash, a range of raked embers burning in wavering lines. Once, she was alive, and once, she knelt by a hearth, watching wood become searing coals. The thought of warmth is so delicious that she dreams of chewing the sensation between her teeth.

Towers of dust, tumultuous waves across the countryside of the dead. An ancient stone wall that separates the fields, shriveled grapes crawling up the hills. A constant ache like a souring tooth that drives itself from the roof of her mouth down to the heels of her feet. Blink and the sun is eaten whole and the woods are alive with howling creatures. Blink and she sees it all, the nonlinear formation of her universe, her mother and her sister and her aunt and her lovers and her friends and her longing, spread thin, dripping across the landscape.

There is a girl dying in the tree. Once, she could have said the same about herself. Now she is a whisper. Now something eats away at her even as she fights it, chews on the sinews of her haunt-skin. Something that infiltrates every dark corner. Something even her shadow is afraid of.

Sofia's in the room with her. No, in the room with them. The house groans against their life, so loud and bright. There is her face, her sister, her body repeater. There is the one she's held close to her heart. There is the witch who sees her for what she is.

Her body waxes and wanes. She leans into the tree, brushes her lips against a cold forehead. That feathered feeling is excruciating, nearly makes her gasp. She wants more. She can't bear the pain.

Poppy, name like a flower.

My fault, she thinks, bittersweet, her fingertips on the cheek of her love manifest. *My fault.* Sofia made the deal with the devil because the devil was alive and standing in the mirror, her own face looking back at her, sculpting her hate. Because she understood how it felt to know yourself—to discover what you want and be willing to take it. Because she'd learned that she had a choice, and she wanted to make it. Because she might have been afraid, she might have felt lost and out of control, but magic she *knew*, and there was something so sweet in making the world do your bidding.

Her mother showed her the ropes. Call it a summoning. Sofia gave herself to a boy she thought she was supposed to love, because she couldn't understand any other way out of her own life, and in the process she left her heart behind. It was a compulsive need to prove she was capable. It was the path she'd been predestined to, the one that would save her from herself.

But she could only lie for so long. The truth tasted like Poppy's thumb on her lips, pursing for a kiss.

She cut her palm open over a flame, and she tipped her head back to the beams of a barn, sun making slats across the white line of her neck and the rolled-back expanse of her irises. Her shadow staggered away from her body the moment the blood sizzled in the heat, ripped apart by a demon's hand.

"I have walked the Fissure, and I have seen your face," she said to the fire. "I call upon you, Heilacte. Undo the wrongs I have done. Sever me from his heart and return my own to me."

The dark figure bending to face her, its jaw falling open, her gaze lost in that endless cavern.

And then, like her mother taught her—

"I have a sister," she whispered with a voice that belonged to another being, "and I pray she may outlive me."

Now Sofia presses her cheek to an ancient tree in the house of her death and prays again.

Her fault. She is too weak—too foolish, too rash. She wants to take Poppy into her arms, to carry her into the dark, where she never has to be alone again. But she will have to be brave. She will go into that black and cleave its hold on the one she loves.

Rustling emerges down the hall among the noise of life and fear. It whispers across the creaking floorboards, heavier than footsteps and light as bird bone. Terror reaches down her throat to curl a fist around her heart. She squeezes herself up against the trunk and tries to hide, the outline of her not-skin trembling against the peeling bark. She can feel Poppy's breath through the wood, the unsteady rise and fall of her longing.

She chooses. A life for a life. *Listen,* she thinks, *it will be morning before you remember me.* And she hopes for sun.

Time ticks like tally marks past her. A minute becomes a day. She feels the color leach from her mind, looks at the absence of her skin. Where flesh and sun-bleached bone might have once waited, there is nothing but shimmering air.

A creature fills the room like soot from a choking fire. She is found out.

44

TREE-BOUND, STAR-CLUTCHED

Poppy knew she was still alive, because being dead would have been less painful.

Her head thrummed with the distant echo of past hurt. Her eyes were too heavy to blink, stitched shut by her own stubborn skin. Her tongue stuck to the roof of her mouth. She should have been dead by now. The nearness of her oblivion was as familiar as the sensation of sleeping in too late, waking to find the room a little brighter than expected. Behind her eyelids, soft plumes of color bloomed in spotty patterns.

She could smell it on the air: the hot damp of a far-off storm, humidity running down the walls. The cooked scent of magic, a scattering of ozone. Around the gnarled roots of the tree, deep puddles remained from the last rain, inky black between the fuzz of her eyelashes. She wanted to dip a finger in them. Wanted to feel the water trail across her wrist, remember what it was like to be a girl who tipped her head back and let the rain run down her cheeks.

Poppy Loveless. A label for the collection of skin and bones she had become, curled up like a bird in an egg waiting to be cracked open. Brittle as first frost crawling across the surface of a lake.

I WILL LEACH THE LIFE FROM YOU, COLOR AND LIGHT SUCKED FROM THE SURFACE OF THE SUN.

Her mind seeped away, coffee staining pale cloth. The scent of smoke clung to the air—cedar and breath, choking and green.

Underwater voices swelled wet around her. Someone was crying—it could have been her if she really considered it. She was a great exposed vein just waiting to be pressed and spurt blood.

I WILL DRINK OF YOU WITH MY ROOTS IN THE GROUND AND I WILL TURN THE DARK WORLD INSIDE OUT.

The crying grew louder, the air around her trembling with the dull hum of change. Poppy leaned into it. The room moved muffled and slow, every floating organism stretching and bending and taking advantage of incandescent particles.

"Poppy, can you hear me?"

She could, she wanted to tell them, but her body wasn't hers, wouldn't ever be hers again.

Her eyes tore open to find a tree reflected in front of her.

No, not quite a tree—but it had growth, spinning tendrils that curled down from the ceiling like its roots were reversed, like someone had torn it from the ground and flipped it upside down. Gouges ripped down the sides of it. Long-fingered hands stretched out at the ends of gnarled arms, branches become limbs, the shape of the trunk twisted as if it'd grown through an old iron fence, an imprint of life left behind on its gray skin. It had split from the trunk where it had been born. The phantom shape peeled itself up, and it stood.

I WILL RAZE THE EARTH AND DRINK OF YOUR LIFE.

This time, the voice came from outside of her body, beyond the confines of her own thoughts. It sluiced from the figure before her—she couldn't find a mouth on that colorless form, a creature like dust and ash and dead fauna curling in on itself.

Sofia, Poppy thought, a pathetic plea bouncing around in her mind. *Help me.* But the room full of doomed living people felt dead and cold, and even among all the sound there was silence forever.

I HAVE COME AGAIN FOR THE GIRL IN THE TREE.

She turned her head just in time to watch something crawl from the cracked mirror.

45

ARCHAIC MEMORIES OF THE DAISY FIELD

Finder sliced her way through worlds.

Time dripped, her one hand tight in Keeper's and the other tearing its way through unfamiliar light. Her body gone slippery and taut. She wondered if she was drenched in Mother Mab's blood, the cost of dimension-hopping through a pool of someone's exsanguination, but when she looked at her arm she found it the same clean and warm tone it'd always been, like a healing bruise, like crushed fruit.

"Don't let go," she tried to say to Keeper, but the words stole from her mouth and tumbled into the open air. When she blinked, the backs of her eyelids were rosy. When she opened them again she saw stars. Blink, roses, blink, stars, blink, roses, blink, sunlight—

Sunlight. A memory sweeter than berries squeezed between fingers. Splintered green. Sticky, too, and everlasting, warmth on her skin, warmth like the memory of a basket and a bear and a house with a tree growing straight through its stomach. Her body fragmented, scintillated, Keeper's voice just a whisper in the wind. She pushed on, wailing. *Don't let go don't let go don't let go just HOLD ON—*

They stepped into reality and found hell instead.

She felt like she was standing in a miniature, the world blown up around her, the expansive open of her dreams a swelling crescendo around her. Her skull pounded with refraction, mystified. It had *worked*.

It was her house, the place where she had grown and changed. It was Mother Mab's kitchen. But it was destroyed, colorless and dead.

And there in the center of the room stood a tree, and a creature before it rose tall and warped, horned, *no*, not horned, those were branches, no, roots, no, those were claws stretching out toward her ready to take her throat in its hands just like the Ossifier. She heard the thick crack, watched its body snap itself free of the tree's roots, spine bending, and expand to fill the room with choking shadow. So she'd left one death and walked into another.

He had called it to life. Whatever he served had walked between worlds.

There was a girl curled inside of the tree. There were people gathered before her like they'd collapsed in prayer. It took her a clarifying moment before she realized they were the same women she'd saved from the Ossifier's wrath in the basement. So much for that sacrifice.

She had never known so many faces at once, had never been forced to prepare herself for so many inevitable ends.

Finder drank it in like sour sumac, like chicory gone bitter, like dregs of kerosene: a nightmare and all around it the sun, falling across her like speckled pieces of starlight, bright enough to cup and marvel at. Not red like it'd once been but the color of flaxen hair, of candles on glimmering water. She nearly fell to her knees. Only Keeper, still clutching her wrist, was enough to keep her upright.

A voice boomed around her until it seemed it'd crawled inside of her head.

I AM HEILACTE, BRIDGE BETWEEN FISSURE AND UNDER AND ABOVE, AND I HAVE COME FOR THE LIVES THAT HAVE BEEN PROMISED TO ME.

Finder stared, tilted back her head to take in the creature standing before her and the pockets of its body where gray smoke gathered, the gaps where she could still make out the tree's bark beyond the storm of its limbs. It was too much belief to suspend. When it tilted forward and let out a single grating cry, stone against stone, rockslide down an ancient mountain, her blood ran cold. The house and its branches trembled beneath the sound.

An offering, the Ossifier had said, for a creature that ruled over them all.

It seemed that among all their time-running, the monster had beat them there.

46

THE HEART BEATING BENEATH THE FLOOR

The air around Cass went oppressive. It was the sensation of bumping into that figure in the basement, of standing in the kitchen as Poppy's head rolled, of seeing a creature loom in the sharp glare of her headlights. Now the shadows had a mind of their own and they crept insectoid up the legs of her pants. She swatted frantically as the propped-up mirror began to tremble. She flinched at the sight, already anticipating a new devil.

But a familiar hand plunged past the glass. Her eyes landed on Finder, and the boy from the Fissure, and she blinked and accepted it as fact.

Desperation made the house darker, even as morning sun pockmarked the floor. Wailing blended with the grating voice of the creature. Cass tried to focus on anything other than inevitable death, but her eyes were useless glass in her head. Nothing made sense, nothing was right, nothing would ever be the same again.

"Please," Mrs. Glasswell said, clearing her throat. Cass recognized the sound of someone trying to spit their fear out like the pit of a cherry. But the woman's hands shook as she slipped the gun's leather strap off her shoulder and raised it in surrender beside a placating palm. "I offer you these lives. I give them to you in exchange for the safety of my family."

Cass took in the form of the being before her, its rooted head, the maw of its mouth, spliced lines of matter wriggling inside of it. The eyes were caverns: gouges left for the suggestion of a face, like staring into the dark corner of a room until your mind invented something awful to fill the space. The tendrils of its head prodded around the room, ripped through the ceiling, crawled through the air to find Cass frozen in place.

After all this—after finding them again, after coming home—she desperately did not want to die.

She grabbed Frankie and ducked as the creature lunged. A moment hung in the air, trapeze caught. Its virulent roots slashed through where they'd been and plunged into Mrs. Glasswell's body. The point went through her abdomen and bloomed from her spine, tendrils arching like fresh spring leaves. The shadows held her like a doll, writhing between the inner mechanizations of her body, the warmth of her blood and life and weight.

The sheriff let out a broken scream. Mrs. Glasswell hung suspended by the branch. Her mouth fell open with an anguished gasp and the gun clattered to the ground. A trickle of blood ran down her ashen chin, dotted her blouse like a sentence.

The sheriff tipped his head back to the ceiling and the branches tearing through it. His cry came out ragged and awful. "I'm upholding our bargain, we gave you the girl, I gave you everything, you can't . . ."

The air thrummed. Somewhere distant and haunted, a voice carried past the creature as it loomed over Mrs. Glasswell, the sound of grinding metal. It careened through Cass's mind.

I WILL EAT AND I WILL EAT AND I WILL EAT.

"You can't do this," the sheriff moaned. He reached for his wife, his hands soaking in blood as he pressed them to her abdomen, his panicked voice saying, "Give her back to me, please, oh God." The branch kept twisting and goring, parasitic, and it tore its way up through Mrs.

Glasswell's throat. A spiny point burst from her mouth in a bloody unfurling.

Cass's mind went quiet. All she could think—all she could summon— was *someone needs to tell Lucas*. Grief trickling through them, a downstream collapse. There was a sort of rift in the room, a slice in the atmosphere. Cass's heart keened in her chest. They had to run. They had to get Poppy.

The sheriff reached for the gun. He snatched it up, turning to them. When he spotted Cass, she ducked away. The wide whites of his eyes darted between them and landed on Frankie, and the gun in his hands trained on her head. "You caused this," he whispered. "You killed her. You summoned this creature and doomed us all."

HE DOES MY BIDDING HE SERVES ME ALONE I HAVE COME TO BE FED AND WHEN YOU FALL I WILL EAT AND EAT AND EAT AND RAISE YOU AGAIN TO SERVE ME TOO.

Cass had to duck her head to keep the sound from boxing her ears. The creature lunged forward. She watched shadows split and shrink, grow and change, expand and inflate.

There was a moment where she felt the world stop. Where Cass's breath hung outside of her. Where Frankie started to get to her feet, eyes locked on Poppy beyond the clouded creature. Where Marya turned with her face in pieces. Where Finder rushed forward. Where creatures writhed and lashed and clawed for them, and this time when Cass heard a scream she was sure it was coming out of her own mouth and when the gun went off it sounded like—

47

PANG AND PANG AND PANG AND PANG

It sounded like Sheriff Glasswell's voice tore the earth in two with his guttural scream, leaving the halves to hang broken in black swaths of space.

The gun fell with a thud as he slid to his knees. It bounced once, metallic and clattering. The echoing shot had blown a hole in the ceiling, the house trembling and its body splitting open around us, the smell of copper washing over everything. Mrs. Glasswell hung above it all, her body nearly severed, the slumped form of her figure pinned by the branch. Her blood ran down to its end and dripped with a wet thud against the rooted ground.

In that severed second, we felt the shift—the moment we went from Frankie and Cass and Marya and Poppy and became an amalgamation of *us*.

If watched from the sagging ceiling and its bullet-blown wounds, we would have moved like one animal with the same neural paths, like limbs sprouting from one beating heart, like a chorus of women called to attention. It was a new awareness of self. Of presence. We were in that room together, interlinked and tracing back to one another, a network of roots and thoughts and hopes and desires.

We looked at each other, wishing for solace, afraid of the dark and the emptiness to follow it. We tilted back our heads. We took the apocalypse in.

It was a devastating sight—the chasm of Mrs. Glasswell's gory stomach, the sheriff on his knees begging the creature for mercy, the tree imposing behind them. The colossal shadow shape reared its rooted head back and crooned an awful sound. Our hearts kicked their legs up our throats. The floor wriggled with dark matter, worms after rain, the air rippling thick and wet.

Something slammed into the house. A spilling artery opened in its walls. It was a bullet, a gunshot, a killing blow—

Not a bullet. It was the ground around the tree itself. The being bent and slammed its head into the warped roots that held Poppy. The vines snaking from its skull tore through the floor and started to twist into the old tree. The trunk began to peel and die. Curls of bark fell to the ground like confetti.

I WILL EAT AND EAT AND EAT.

The voice tore through our mind and took our thoughts into its mouth. Heilacte, whatever power or history that name had, tried to chew us from the inside out. The shadows twisted and coiled. The house gave an impressive shake as the creature thrashed against the floor.

A SACRIFICE FOR A SACRIFICE. I WILL GORGE MYSELF ON THE DIVINE.

The mass of us lunged for the tree.

Poppy curled inside, her mouth open in a frozen gasp. Her skin was the blue-tinged hue of water after dark, all the warmth drained from it, lips cracked and bleeding. Her still hands folded under her chin as if in prayer.

One of us sucked in a breath and said, "Is she—"

But we shook our heads. Kept shaking them, even as we kicked black snaking matter away from the stampede of our feet. Not after all this. Not after everything.

One by one we plunged into the gouge, slipping an arm under Poppy's knees, another behind her head. The carved-out center of the tree pitched and spread, seeping up sleeves and skin. The choking gray engulfed us. We fought through haze, felt it infiltrate our throats and eyes, stinging where it met untouched flesh. Every breath was a fire. It cooked us in and out.

STAND UP.

Sheriff Glasswell was still sobbing, a broken echoing sound. He shook his head hard. "I can't," he said, "you took her away from me."

STAND UP. I AM NOT FINISHED.

"You said you only needed the girl," he wept. "Just the girl, and you would leave us alone."

I HAVE A BARGAIN AND IT WILL BE UPHELD. I WILL EAT AND EAT AND EAT AND EAT AND EAT AND—

Finder stepped up to the being. In this light, she was a vengeful spirit, blurred around the edges, bright as swallowed embers. We watched her raise a hand and call the creature's attention to the warm brown of her palm. It circled us and brayed, something low and rusty and summoned from a new world. It kept the blank carving of its eyes on her. It filled the room with black matter and thrashing dust.

When we screamed it was a shattering glass, an implosion of sound warring for control with the creature's commands and the sheriff's broken howl. We linked our arms, elbows hooked, heads bending together. We made ourselves a chain. Our bodies went molten, interlocked, alive with light. Our cries haunted the air. Shadows inked their way up our throats.

The circle of the tree's belly seemed to deepen and stretch, a forever cavern, Poppy preserved inside of it. The colors of her eaten up and away. Her eyes a pure and unblemished black, sclera erased, fragile veins of gray coiling up her throat. Our hands pulled at her, slipping, desperate. We entrenched ourselves in that endless dark.

Something shuddered out of the tree. Pale fingers pushed through Poppy's fetal form and landed on the edges of that gouge, borne out of the black.

We saw it as a symbiotic one. Our eyes found Sofia's as she stepped through the trunk and her shadow rose frantic behind her, twisting and tearing at its own skin as it grew across the tree to join the hulking apparition of Heilacte's monstrous form. Their lines became indistinct—the shadow contorting and collapsing and fizzing at the edges—and that fragmented piece of Sofia fed the creature new energy. Together they let out an echoing bellow, the ground vibrating with sound.

Sofia's toes dragged across the rotten floor. Her mouth was open in a cry that matched ours, mirror images even in death. The outline of her body was frayed and sanguinary against the blue valley of her scream.

The thing we had become didn't pretend to have power. Our capability lay in our capacity for belief—in each other, in goodness, in the way we loved one another. We just reached for her, the room moving beyond the pocket of her cracked skull. *Use me,* one of us said into the shaking air. *I am your seer.*

The words passed down our thread. We took them into our mouths. *Use us,* we insisted, fervent, awake. *We are your seers.*

Maybe it was an awful idea and we'd all die regardless. But we were together. This thing between us was a violent tether, an impossible bond. We wanted to be good for something, in the only way we knew how. Something would always be destroyed in the end. We would try our best to make sure that it wasn't us.

The terrible symphony rose and fell. Sofia stepped into our orbit. An overwhelming wash of cold dipped down into the warmest parts of us, stealing from our bellies, wicking the heat from our mouths. With one hand in ours, Sofia stretched the other into the tree. The universe slid away. The moment stretched from now to eternity. We slipped deeper into the tree and the demon's thrall, into a place that shouldn't have existed and yet flickered in front of us, red and wrong and endless.

It was this: Sofia Lyon tearing into the tree, a girl with her mouth open in a terrible scream that rattled the earth.

It was this: a man on his knees before us, screaming as Sofia did, come to kill us. Flickering visions of his hands withered with Sofia's blood, our eyes kaleidoscoping through shards of the past.

It was this: Sofia's face shifting from something meant to terrify into softness once again, the skin blinking back into place, pulling from strings of memory to make itself right.

It was this: Poppy lifting her head from her chest, rolling back to the present. It was Sofia, real before her, no less alive just because her body had been stolen from her. Sofia touching with skin that drained away all warmth.

It was this: Sofia a breath away. Poppy tipping up to meet her.

It was this: Sofia pressing their lips together. It must have been a matter of seconds, the cold seeping through the room like a drink of water, but it became forever, the same moment repeating itself, kiss and kiss and kiss and kiss.

"This is all I can give you," Sofia whispered, and we looked away. "I hope it's enough."

Sofia fizzled, electricity along a live wire. The man on the ground pulled his head from the razed floor, looking at us with sap dripping down his cheeks like tears and shadows dancing around him in roiling vines.

Sofia began to laugh. The sound was so bright that we winced away from the impossibility of it. The sheriff reached for Sofia and found nothing beneath his hands but a collection of sound. Darkness ran from his ears, too thin to be blood. Poppy tipped her chin up and looked into the brilliance of Sofia's grin until her open mouth was gone.

Gray shapes bled away slowly, trickling back toward the center of the tree. Our tears ran like an afterthought, our arms desperately clutching Poppy and her body refusing to be pulled from the tree. Maybe the cavern had grown into her skin—maybe there was no separating left to be done.

I WILL EAT! I WILL EAT! I WILL EAT! I WILL EAT!

With one unified tug we tore her past the gash in the bark, jubilant until we began to choke.

Sheriff Glasswell ripped us away from the tree and severed our chain. He pulled Frankie to the ground and grasped her throat. He was still weeping as he did it, all of him shaking with the fingers crushing Frankie's windpipe. The air seized between us. We fell with her, Poppy across our laps, held breathless against us.

Frankie scrabbled at his wrists. Her face shifted and purpled. We screamed and tore at him, pulling at his shoulders, ripping at the fabric across his back. We cried loud enough to shake the house. But maybe it was just the sound of the world ripping itself into jagged sections where we were not dying and where we were.

A crash echoed through the room, and our eyes landed on Finder—she'd brought the mirror down on the ground with one great swing of her arm and now it lay in a puzzle of shards. She snatched one up, long and wicked as a dagger.

"Keeper," she snarled, glass offering in her palm. Everything about her was vicious and alive, her teeth bared, blood on her dress.

Keeper took it from her. He stalked forward, one step, two, took the mirror shard point down and thrust it into Sheriff Glasswell's arm. The sheriff's hold faltered as he cried out and Frankie gasped for air, clawing at her throat and his loosening hands. Keeper stuck him with the shard again and again, even as the sheriff swung at him, even as he cowered.

We pulled Frankie into us and felt the moment our breaths became one again—hers heaving in our chests, prickling with desperation.

"Go!" Keeper called, but we'd left them behind once before. We wouldn't do it again.

The sheriff pressed his fingertips over the gore. Every slice pulsed blood along his bicep and through his tremoring hands. Sap boiled from the empty tree in dark clots. Poppy coughed in our arms and the same substance dribbled from her lips, running down her chin. We pressed Poppy's head to us, heaved breath after breath after breath. The creature twisted against the ground with guttural roars. Finder kicked the gun away and it skittered to land at our feet.

It was a wrenching loss, as Cass slipped from us and snatched it up. She held it tight to her chest. Debris fell like snow, dust caught up in the thick air.

The sheriff struggled forward and snatched Finder's wrist. She tried to rip it free, beating helplessly at his blood-slicked grip.

"You need to go!" Finder shouted to us, an echo of Keeper.

We helped each other stand, entangled. Everywhere we touched was sharp and alive. The mass of our minds remembered the sensation of being one. We couldn't delineate our boundaries. We rocked together like that, a step forward, then another.

Mrs. Glasswell's body hung suspended in the center of us all. The house gave a mournful shiver and shook her like a snared animal in a trap.

Cass raised the gun at Sheriff Glasswell as Finder struggled to slip free, but her hands shook too hard to keep it steady. "I can't," she whispered, "I can't do it."

"Cass," we pleaded. "Now."

Cass spared us a look, her eyes wet and afraid. She tried to fire the gun, but it only clicked, nothing left to shoot and no bullets to feed the barrels. Sheriff Glasswell laughed deep in his throat.

"Hey," Cass called, her voice breaking. "Hey!"

Every head swiveled. We watched her wave the gun and call the demon's attention. It met her eyes and bent to her, to us. The hands that knuckled into roots felt across the floor. Dark curls of shadow snared our legs, prodded the thin skin holding us together.

YOU HAVE TASTED IT.

Heilacte's voice fell to a purr, the soft roll of tires on asphalt, the dull grind of metal on metal.

YOU HAVE SHARED A LIFE WITH A LIFE, YOU BINDER OF SOULS, YOU HEART OF HEARTS, YOU WHO HAVE CROSSED THE MIRROR AND DEFIED WHAT I DEMAND.

We looked into the maw of its mouth. There, in the distant tunnel of its throat, there was a faint red light—like the promise of a life beyond all that darkness. Something quelled an understanding of what Sofia might have once seen in the demon's offer—the idea of a future without weakness. A dream untethered.

THERE IS A DEAL AND IT MUST BE SATISFIED.

"I'll make you a new one," Cass said, and we could feel the thudding of her heart in our veins too. The vined ropes of Heilacte's body prodded their way through the air, seeking Cass, curling at her feet. She pointed the gun at the sheriff's kneeling form. "Offering for an offering."

The creature hissed. It slammed its splintered claws down into the floor. The wood cracked in a great circle around the tree, Mrs. Glasswell's body and the sheriff contained within it, Finder pinned among them. She delivered a final kick to the sheriff's torso and stumbled backward. Cass caught her as the circle split and we fell into each other once again, complete.

The house cried out like a hundred felled trees crashing to the ground, fracturing into shards.

We knocked aside debris and lashing ropes of shadow, ducked under collapsing doorways and fat sections of swollen ceiling. The porch bucked beneath our feet as we held Poppy upright between us and made for the road, the grass so solid and green, the dirt path through the woods warm and waiting. The sun made coins of illumination against the earth, everything bright and beautiful. We were so grateful for the light and so afraid of what could be waiting for us in the forest.

The echoing crack stopped us at the edge of the trees. We turned and almost regretted looking, the image forever burned behind our eyes.

The house caved in.

48

THE CROOKED MASTER OF THE DARKEST CORNER

It was a wonder to own her body again. Frankie's hands still prickled with feeling, seeping along the heart lines.

They found the Ford waiting down the dirt road, the sight of it sweet enough to make Frankie's heart sing. The wheels hiccupped out of the mud as Cass wrenched at the clutch. Frankie could barely see the road through a veil of salt, everything a dampened blur. She just had to trust Cass to get them home.

The thought would have been simple and senseless once. Just trust them. Just trust. She was afraid that she'd never believe anyone again, she'd never get the feeling of them out of her head, she'd never be the master of her own spiraling mind.

"What do we do?" Mucus mixed with dried blood turned Cass's nose into a patchwork of bodily evidence as she spoke. "She's barely alive. What was the point of all this if someone was just going to die anyway?"

"Don't say that." Frankie's words rattled as the truck or its driver took a violent turn. "She's not dead."

She cradled Poppy's velvet head in her lap. Her shoulders rocked as the Ford reared, an unruly horse. Gray sap dribbled past her lips, stark against Frankie's thigh. Frankie couldn't bear to look and still she wiped Poppy's chin clean, one aching palm resting where Poppy's waist dipped.

"What the fuck was that thing? How did we—how did it know we could hear each other?"

"I don't know," Frankie said, her throat aching.

Cass scrubbed under her eyes. Her cheeks were pink and splotchy, her brown curls matted at the end with blood and sweat, shirt stained with the same mixture. There was a wicked slice down her forearm. Frankie didn't remember it happening, couldn't separate herself from the rest of them, from that room and its disaster and the mass of energy they had become.

She turned her head. Her cheek cooled against the rear window where Marya's head was propped beside the people from the Fissure. Her breath left a fogged-up circle on the surface, a halo around Marya's hair. There was a pause where the only sounds were the whine of the Ford's tires and the rattling of Frankie's teeth in her head, chorused by Cass's sniffles, and she could almost pretend that they had rewound time and none of this had happened. But Poppy's life was thin and tenuous in her arms. The shotgun and its implications sat on the bench seat between Frankie's thigh and Cass's gearshift.

Frankie traced the tattered edge of Poppy's shirt and held her as still as she could. Her chin pointed defiantly back at Cass, pleading with her to hold on to hope for a little bit longer.

Then the girl from the mirror world laughed past the glass. Wind whipped her wild hair. She lifted her arms skyward as a ray of sun illuminated the blue mountains, burial mounds for some ancient god. "It's real!" The boy laughed with her, throwing an arm across Marya to take the girl's hand in his own. For a second, their joy was enough to make her feel unburdened.

Frankie could just make out the farmhouse in the distance, a sight that nearly tore her breath from her throat with the force of sudden emotion that swelled inside of her.

Muttered words fell past Poppy's mouth, hollow in the air. There was a rough echo to them—the grating sound of Heilacte's voice and its claim on her.

"Why is it still inside of her?" Cass asked, her voice hiccupping with the same cadence as the rumble of the truck's engine. "Shouldn't the Glasswells have been enough to get it to leave us the fuck alone? What if it never stops following us?"

Frankie stroked Poppy's head and felt her anger swell over, though she didn't know who to be upset with, where to direct the tight desperation in her chest.

The Ford lurched into place beside the house, sun making trapezoids across the dry grass. Frankie was out of the cab before it had fully stopped, pulling Poppy with her. Cass's door thudded shut before she circled the truck to grab Poppy's legs and help ease her out. Poppy heaved, body arching with the threat of expelling something from the pit of her stomach, and Frankie watched Cass cover her own mouth on instinct.

"I can't do this," Cass said in one unbearable sob.

"We don't have a choice," Frankie snapped.

Marya leapt down from the bed at Frankie's side. "She needs to get it out."

Frankie couldn't look at her, couldn't summon the words to say anything other than *not yet*, couldn't stop thinking about her arm in Marya's and her eyes on her sister's corpse crawling from the belly of a tree.

Marya avoided Frankie's internal implosion and slung one of Poppy's arms over her shoulders. Together they hobbled to the front door. The house stood like a mausoleum, its shape cast across the forsythia bushes now blue and muggy. Frankie wondered if her family was inside. If they'd accepted her leaving, and the rift she had torn between them. If they'd gone looking for her. In a rushing pang of regret, Frankie wished she had somewhere else to go where she could feel safe. But this was all that remained.

Sissa opened the door. Frankie felt the fury stoke hotter inside of her. She would never trust them again. She would never trust anyone for as long as she lived. But what did she have if not them?

She was not strong enough. She would never be good enough to make them safe. But no one had ever thought better of her for being the best at hating herself.

Sissa took them in, six now, gathered but barely standing. "Foolish," she said. But she kissed her fingertips and brushed them over Frankie's forehead.

"Tell us what to do," Frankie said. Because she didn't want it, but Poppy was limp in her arms, and she needed to see her open eyes more than any honest magic in the world.

Sissa smiled, forlorn. "Take her to the water."

When Frankie thought about home, she saw the lake, the glass of its surface. Red clay sucking her shoes down into the earth. Driftwood washing up like ancient bones, whittled and smooth. In that perfect picture she saw Sofia floating on her back in a bathing suit that had been Frankie's the year before. Algae tangling around their ankles, seeking light and phosphorus. Her mother had been baptized in that water as a kid. Oph had taught them how to hold their breath. It had nearly taken Frankie's life once. She adored it even more for spitting her back up.

Poppy's arm hung over her shoulder, its fever warmth pressing against the nape of Frankie's neck. With Cass beside her jogging to keep up and Marya propping up Poppy's other side, she was pressed in, close, contained.

They carried her past the flower beds heavy with blooms, across the sloping yard, all the way down to the shore. Sissa followed beside them, silent and reserved with her arms folded over her chest. Frankie wanted to ask where her aunt was. She wanted to say something that might matter—wanted to accuse them both, or question them, or beg them to turn around and shut off the lights and fall asleep, to wake to a new day where they could forget the ways they had betrayed each other.

The lake was pure and still. From yards away it appeared a mirage, one of those spots far down the road that made it seem like the asphalt was underwater. But the closer they got, the realer it became, and Frankie loved it again. This part of her world that remained unchanged.

The water shimmered beneath the sweet hues of the sun, mandarin and peach and turmeric. Finder ran ahead of them. She still had blood on her chin when she turned to look at them, her body aglow.

They brought Poppy to the shore where the grass gave way to silt. As they lowered her to the lapping water, Frankie pressed her hands to the heat of Poppy's cheeks, soothing away the pressure. Cass waded further out with her hips above the surface, looking back anxiously at Frankie. Together they turned and faced the house.

Sissa stood at the edge of the water. She was a stranger to Frankie, a spirit in the body of a woman she'd once known. Frankie's first instinct lent itself to anger; she wanted to scorch the great and green universe. She wanted to reach for Marya and Cass and shake each of them, wanted to shout and scold her family for leading her down a path that had never given her a choice.

All her life she'd been recalibrating, debilitated by the instinct to retreat inside herself.

In that last year, Sofia had tried to bridge their gap. After the drowning, and the weird, stilted silence between them, after all the nights Sofia never came home and never called, Frankie used to sit down by the water and toss stones into the place where stagnant growth gathered, pebbles shattering the algae and sending water bugs skidding. Sometimes she cried. Sometimes she flicked through text messages, thought about sending one to Sofia. Considered admitting how afraid she was to be alone. How desperately she wanted to know that Sofia's leaving wouldn't change everything. How pathetically she hoped that one day her sister might come home and tell her she regretted going, that she'd always had everything she needed, right there, at home in the farmhouse and sleeping down the hall.

But Sofia found her there before she could type anything out, moon making eyes on the water and Frankie's stones settling to the bottom of the silt. The collar of Frankie's sweatshirt was drawn up over her chin to wipe the place where tears had gathered. Sofia sat down beside her and left a space between them where something unsaid could sit. Frankie had dragged a stick through the gritty clay there, mostly for something to do with her hands, partly to draw a line down their center.

She didn't recognize Sofia's shirt. It could have been Lucas's, or the product of a day spent shopping somewhere Frankie couldn't reach her. It exposed her freckled arms and the spot where a bandage stuck to pale peach fuzz. The hair at the nape of her neck was shorter, the makeup around her eyes smudged and dark. "Talk to me, bird," her sister had said. "If you tell me what's wrong, then maybe we can fix it."

How to speak without letting it kill her. Frankie opened her mouth, but nothing would come out. Sofia dug her heels down into the earth and hung her head. In the dark she looked like one of those angelic headstones, where someone might leave flowers. Frankie wanted to lean over and put her head on her sister's shoulder. She wanted to feel her rise with an inhale.

"Go to bed," she said instead, and when Sofia finally left her behind and walked back to the house, she dried her cheeks again with damp fabric and dug her knuckles into the soft indentations of her shuttered eyes.

Frankie couldn't stop failing both of them. It seemed she never would.

Now she ignited with pain, a scarecrow girl with a straw body, perfect for kindling. The four of them stood in the water. It was too cold for summer. Frankie shivered immediately, feeling everyone's eyes on her. She wanted to say: *don't look at me, I'm on fire, you lied to me and I have nothing left but this moment in my ruined hands.* Instead, Frankie burned, burned, burned. She sucked a breath through her teeth and the sound died before it could leave her mouth. Feeling too much. Giving too little.

"What—" she started, calling to Sissa on the shore, but she could hear the distant and warped sound of thrumming like hummingbird wings in her head. "What do we do?"

49

Mountains to Move, Miles to Eat

Poppy floated, breathless, buoyant. The water touched her like silk. Reeds bent to her will. She was warm, alive, cooked, alight.

Her head boomed with the distant voice of the demon. Its never-ending croon called her back and begged her to stay, promised to flay her open and make use of her tender heart. But beyond the threat she could hear something else—a voice like Sofia's, telling her to focus and breathe. Poppy let her head loll back, sucked in the noise, drank it down like cool water.

In the fabric of that tangled dream, Poppy watched planets turn, felt cosmic heat. The sky was a forever blue. A black ring threatened to eclipse the sun overhead, feathered with red around the edges. Through the smattering of light, Poppy saw the line of forest where the shore sloped to meet Frankie's house. The trees stood up.

No. Not the trees. The shapes in between them. Shadows that stretched arms out from their sides. Fingers with tendons made of absent space. Heads like ripped-up roots, gnarled and earthen. They crawled forward on bent legs. Knelt toward the water. Pressed their heads to the molten earth.

The darkness pulsed. Hundreds of figures crouched before her, pressing their foreheads to the dirt, and in the midst of them one great column of swirling matter grew until it was nearly five times her height.

I AM HEILACTE, RULER OF WORLDS, AND I HAVE COME FOR THE GIRL IN THE TREE.

When she closed her eyes, she saw through the lids. The sun was magma hot.

A DEAL LEFT UNFULFILLED WILL ONLY EVER BE A RECKONING. WILL YOU GAMBLE YOUR LIFE FOR TOMORROW'S SUSTAINED BREATH?

Poppy pushed through the water to the murky banks, sinking into the muck and dirt. She pulled free and felt her skin beat with an invented heart. The water made rings around her, ripples red and grisly. She thought about her parents alone in the little house where she'd been born, thought about Sofia curled inside of a tree. She thought about being held in a very soft bed. She thought about Oph in Frankie's kitchen, once telling her "do nothing if not with intention."

She had so many intentions. It was hard to choose only one.

Make it safe. Make it safe. Make it safe.

Where she'd crawled the banks of the lake, ink bled into the earth, seeping away from her body. She thought for a moment she was crying, something dripping across her face, but when she touched the wetness there she found graying sap leaking from her eyes and nose.

Poppy looked back to the water.

The creature stood in the lake. It was a massive thing, solid and rippling and strong. The roots of its skull prodded the surface of the water as it bent its head to her. A cavern tore its way through the center of its tree-body.

WHEN YOU WAKE YOU WILL WISH THIS HAD BEEN A DREAM, AND I WILL WAIT IN YOUR UNSHAKEN CORNER, AND YOU WILL FIND THAT ALL THINGS ARE OPENED AND CLOSED BY MY HAND.

Poppy couldn't tell if she wanted to scream or sob or gag, so she—

Dove under the water, exhaling as she went, bubbles crawling along her cheeks. *Let it be safe,* she thought, pushing past river grass. She held herself beneath the surface for as long as her lungs could bear. Cold snaked down her throat and through her veins. It rendered her immobile. She felt herself go light with it. Like the water was plunging past her, scrubbing her clean, sapping the dark thing coiled in her belly and bringing it skyward once again.

Poppy came up coughing. The world flickered. For a moment she saw them—Frankie cupping her cheek, Cass's hair clinging to her throat, Marya holding Poppy's body up to the surface.

"Let it be an exorcism," Sissa said, voice like a memory.

Was it wrong to be afraid? To want to crawl from this feeling? To remember the pitch world through the mirror and suddenly long for it? Maybe she'd find Sofia there. Maybe they'd forgive each other for all their hurts.

The creature groaned. The shadows wavered and flickered. Every place that its body made contact with the water became oily and slick, disintegrating, breaking down in motes. Its serpent-rooted head thrashed in the water near Poppy, trying to snare her in its grasp.

"Let the water cleanse her," Sissa's incantation continued, distorted. "Let the sky revolve thrice on its never-resting axis. Let it expel the forces that claim her."

"She can't handle this," another voice pleaded, desperation in the words. "It will kill her."

Sofia was the one who taught Poppy to swim. They were thirteen, Poppy all legs and self-conscious laughter. "Don't worry," Sofia had said, "I'll hold you up."

Now the water went iridescent. Shimmering organic. She watched the cavern of the creature's mouth submerge, roiling as it went under. She could feel it slithering through the water, devouring matter in its wake. It slipped lower until it was just the suggestion of a nightmare with its head prodding the surface like the roots of a mangrove. Poppy went under again. She would take the sanguine darkness and churn it into something all her own. She followed it, the two of them sinking down into the green lake. Everything was black and enormous, a sunken world, a dreamt utopia. Her chest pinched with the desire to breathe, or to expel something poisonous. Bubbles ran out of her nose. She could feel hands all over her, even when she couldn't see them, even when she couldn't pull herself up.

She didn't want to look beneath her—afraid, scrambling for air—but she kicked against something ensnaring, unable to see what lashed itself around her ankles. She clawed for the surface and spared a glance down.

It was everywhere, a network of roots and vines, black lines like the veins of the world snaked against the murky bottom of the water. It spread in every direction. And there, below her legs, was the open hovel of its mouth, like a bowl for scrying, that endless desolate ripple and its promise to swallow her up.

Make it safe, she said into the water, cold sliding down into the core of her and gray matter oozing past her mouth. *Make it safe make it safe make it safe.*

Something echoed her warbled call, a distant scream muffled by the close pressure of liquid. She kept hallucinating figures in the water with her. She kept wishing one of them was Sofia, that if this was her end at least they'd live it together. But they were indistinct, ghoulish, like rays of light pushing past algae. Poppy tilted her head back.

Overhead, pinpricks of sun made fireflies along the rippling lake. Rings of color shifted to deep purples, thick blues. She kicked hard against the hold on her legs, feeling those phantom hands pull her higher, her heart rising all the way to her mouth. One desperate thrash and she knocked herself free. She pushed skyward and parted the water.

The shadows on the banks wisped away on the breeze, became bits of dust in the air once again. Through the haze of her lids she saw a daytime moon fall like an eye from a socket. It landed somewhere in the water of a dream, dissipated and clean.

They were all over her again, tugging at her clothes, holding her close, pulling her from the bottom of herself. Only the cicadas were left to scream.

She was a part of them again. One fragment of that whole. They were a joint in her body, a critical component of her system. There was no way to pull herself free without leaving herself incomplete.

When she opened her eyes, she found her still face reflected in the water where it shone green and gold and burning brown.

"Let her breathe!" someone called, and Poppy sucked in a gasp, suddenly aware of her life, her body, her lungs. A cheek pressed to her shoulder. Hands fisted in her shirt. It took a moment for her to recalibrate. Not a dream, but life.

They swept her into a clutching hug, a tangle of limbs. She knew them by touch alone, even amaurotic and dripping, her chin trembling with cold. The damp ends of Cass's hair caught in her mouth. Frankie's cheek pressed warm against her throat. Marya's palm held the crux of her neck. Her family. Extensions of her body, like pieces of her spread across the earth.

Poppy pressed her forehead against Frankie's chest and marveled at the beautiful rise and fall of it with each breath. Her lungs swelled with life.

She shut her eyes and remembered peace. She remembered the soft lull of their presence. She remembered this lake, and driving Sofia home the day before the bonfire, and looking at the water past the silhouette of the house. Summer had just started to die, the grass dry and starched. The trees were a green so vivid that it was nearly black, and Poppy loved it, how color became so rich that suddenly it was every hue poured into one.

Something had been off the whole time they'd spent at the bookstore together, Sofia with a pencil held between her lips, sweet and kissable, and Poppy rearranging titles until they made off-kilter sentences. She'd crafted the self-help section into a stanza that read *HOW TO-BECOME YOUR BEST SELF-IN THE MORNING-OF BETTER DAYS-ENDLESS NIGHT-DECADES OF FOREVER.*

In the car they were quiet. Oph's house was out of her way, but she'd always loved the drive, the simple delight of Sofia warm in the passenger seat beside her. Maybe they'd been a secret to everyone around them, coming together only in the moments that Sofia and Lucas were apart, but this was the most honest Poppy had ever been with herself. She loved Sofia, and Sofia loved her. She'd take the drifting moments that she could manage to catch.

"I'm going to miss you so much," Sofia had said, forlorn. Poppy watched her fiddle with a bandage, half-obscured by Sofia's curling fist. She wanted to ask where the cut had come from—she could see the irritated gash of it beyond the peeling pink edge. But Sofia's mouth twisted up into something wounded, like she was seconds away from crying.

"Hey," Poppy said, tracing the line of Sofia's ear with a thumb. "I'll come visit you all the time. We'll spend so many days together that you'll be sick of me in the end."

"It's going to be different," Sofia whispered to her lap.

"Only if you let it."

Sofia shook her head a few times until the ends of her hair fell sloppily around her ears and half-obscured her eyes. In that evening air, with the windows rolled down, she was the most beautiful person Poppy had ever seen.

"I won't remember who I am without you," Sofia said at last.

"I'm right here," Poppy said. "I'm with you. I wouldn't be me if I wasn't."

Then Sofia was kissing her. Just a press of her lips, parting for a breath, one of her hands warm on Poppy's knee, palm pressing down into bone as she tried to slip closer. Gentle fingers grazed her scalp and ran down her neck.

When Sofia pushed the door open and slid out into the grass, Poppy caught her wrist. Sofia looked back at her. Poppy suddenly didn't care if anyone saw. She smiled at Sofia. Sofia smiled back.

Then the car door shut. The porch creaked beneath her and her shadow passed the living room light, a patchwork ghost.

Poppy would leave in a week, and Sofia would disappear the next night. There was a time not so long ago when all she could hold was her grief, so heavy in her hands. Now it was wonderful to hold the memories at all. She clutched them close.

Now she had loved someone who'd never be alive again, and the future was the eye of a needle before her, her body too angular to fit through it. Poppy had seen things more daunting than she could have ever dreamt. And here she was, the same as always, throat a little raw, eyes a little wet, but she was surrounded by people who cared about her, and she was alive, and she wasn't going to waste that reality again. That was what her heart wanted most. To know that maybe tomorrow they'd leave, go their separate ways, but the next day they'd come back.

She sighed, and felt Frankie's hand rest on the nape of her neck, and she was grateful for the way it anchored her to herself, pinning her in place.

"Pops?" Cass whispered, as if afraid she might not receive an answer.

"Right here," Poppy said. "I'm okay."

Cass threw her head back and laughed. "We're alive!" she cried out to the sky, to any bird that would listen.

"What happened?" Poppy asked, past the mess of her mouth. Her voice was rough around the edges. She coughed once, twice. "How did it work?"

"We fucking exorcised you or something!" Frankie exclaimed, her scarred hands lifting Poppy's face to meet hers and the relief there softening every harsh furrow. There was so much joy in the gleam of her eyes, in the soft way her eyebrows peaked above the slope of her nose. An overwhelming warmth of belief. Poppy bared her teeth back in a triumphant grin. Marya fussed, checking her pulse along her throat and feeling for injuries. Frankie cupped her skull and held fast. Poppy breathed a loose sigh of relief and then she was hacking again, sludge falling past her lips and into the lake between them.

"Way to ruin a moment," Cass gasped, falling back into the water.

Poppy found Sissa watching them from the shore. She met them at the edge of the water. "Frankie," she began as they sloshed toward the rocks, hands outstretched to halt them. The breeze whipped her hair across her cheek. "I need to speak with you about something—"

"Not yet," Frankie said, firm.

They started toward the house. At the bottom of the stairs Poppy caught sight of the boy and the girl from the Fissure. They looked so strange beside the farmhouse, their timeless clothing bloodstained and tattered, everything about them jewel-toned against the washed-out wood.

"What are they still doing here?" Poppy asked, the sound raw.

Cass tightened her arm around Poppy's shoulders. "I'm wondering the same thing."

They helped Poppy up the stairs. Frankie pushed inside first, setting sun casting a grid across the dining room as it shone through the door's glass panels. When she froze, the rest of them stopped behind her.

A woman crouched on the table, the mirror that used to hang over the fireplace now splayed over the ringed surface of the wood and fogging where her breath fanned against it. Her hair hung down over her wan face as she stared into the black reflection there. From where Poppy stood in the doorway, the woman was feline and hunched. Her knees were two sharp and framing points on either side of her body. She tipped her head to face them, one pale green eye peeking past a swath of red hair, iris shining the color of real jade under sunlight. Her smile stretched feral and wide.

The woman leaned back to take them in. Her knees slid forward onto the glass. Her wrists were bound with a deft knot across her chest, red and raw where they kissed against one another.

The cellar door creaked behind her. Sissa darted past them just as soon as it opened, her hands reaching and placating, as if hoping to pin the door shut again.

"Frankie," Oph said from the top of the basement stairs. Her clothes were covered in dirt. Hair stuck to her cheeks and caught her mouth. There was a shovel in her messy hands, like an apocalyptic weapon from a past life. "I didn't know what else to do. She told me to never touch her—she said it would destroy everything she had built—but I had to try and fix it, for you, for all of us . . ."

Oph faltered, her face falling open, desperation cracking through her words. "You were going to die out there. She was the only person who might know how to fix it."

"Frances Jude," a voice said, crackling like a record player. It was the woman, chin tilted defiantly high. Her hair was matted with dirt. But her jaw had the same hardened line Frankie's got, when she was tired of defending herself.

Poppy looked at Frankie's mother. Then she looked at Frankie, frozen in place, a butterfly pinned in a shadow box. Her eyes two mirrors. Her mouth a cavern for night birds.

"I've missed you, kid," Fiona Lyon said in her haunted voice. "Where's your sister?"

50

SALT THE EARTH, LICK THE PALM CLEAN

The Styx had given Frankie her first awareness of pain. As kids, they were unbridled in their love of it. Sofia hopped from rock to rock, barefoot in the sweet heat, and Frankie followed the damp prints she left behind. Cass marked up the limestone with knobs of sidewalk chalk, runes and sigils and stars. Poppy liked to swirl her hands along the green current and catch bait fish by the tail. It continued this way until it didn't, when Frankie leapt from one stone to another and the serrated edge tore her sole open. She remembered the rippled surface of the stone brackish with her blood. The torn-up skin full of dirt. How it hadn't hurt at first, not for a long time, creek water rushing over and blotting away pain until it was time to limp home and bandage it quietly in her room. The way it didn't ache but instead drained all feeling, like her body had been swelling and that slice was the moment where it let go. Then the healing—the stitched-together heat wound of her beating heart, scar running down the heel.

Her mother kneeled on the table with her hands knotted beneath her chin and stole away Frankie's last semblance of sanity. That same cold, empty feeling washed over her, left her a void.

The room changed with Fiona as she leaned forward. Light shifted the planes of her face and the scuffed dirt on her jaw, the ragged ends of her nails, the too-big and too-bright pupils of her eyes, sclera all wrong.

Oph leaned her shovel up against the cellar door and stepped up to her sister's side, the floor creaking quietly underfoot. She gently touched Fiona's shoulder and they angled their heads together with a hum, a waking cicada emerging on the thirteenth year. They looked at each other—something unspoken passed between them—and for a moment Fiona looked so much like Sofia that Frankie imagined her sister had been the one to follow them out of that collapsing house.

Sissa circled around to Fiona's other side. They made a strange triangle with Frankie's mother at its apex, dirt turning her bruised and blue under the warm overhead light.

Sissa took Fiona's fingers and brought them to her lips. Frankie watched her switch out a blade at her hip and raise it, until it was flush with Fiona's ribs—then she arced it up and sliced through the rope. Dirt-stained twine fell away and left lines along her wrists. Fiona held her hands to the light, turning and examining, and then she fixed her eyes on Frankie.

"Come here," she said, "let me get a good look at you."

But Frankie stayed in the doorway, rooted in place. "You're not real."

Fiona's grin widened. "Want me to prove it to you? Sissa, pass me that knife. I'll show you how I bleed like you do."

Sissa pulled away and kept the knife close to her chest, eyes flicking warily back and forth across Frankie's mother's face like she couldn't believe it was real either. Frankie made fists at her sides, dug the nails all the way down to the hard heel of her palms.

"What did you do?" she whispered.

"Frankie," Oph said, her voice wet with emotion. "If I could have done anything else . . . if I could have helped in any other way, I would have done so. We tried what we knew. Your mother was the only one—"

Frankie's fury threatened to split past her ribs. "I'm not fucking talking to you."

Her mother's head cocked to the side, curious. There was something so distinctly inhuman about her, a shifty and frantic quality about the edges of her skin. The figure in front of Frankie was a poor imitation, a woman with some important piece removed, propped up and puppeted with a hand up the back.

"They woke me up," Fiona said, rubbing her wrist absently. "I went into the mirror. You wanted it to stop, didn't you? You wanted it out of her?"

Fiona gestured to Poppy. Frankie remembered falling asleep with that hand in her hair, breathing in the close clove warmth of her mother's shoulder. Her heart howled like a dog in her chest.

"That was you?" Poppy asked, voice woven with wonder.

For a moment Frankie had thought—hopefully, recklessly—that they'd been the ones to save Poppy. Like their will had been enough to keep her safe, there, in their arms.

Fiona's tongue darted out to wet her lips. She dragged a fingernail down the glass of the mirror beneath her. In the past, scrying always made her mother distant, like she had reclaimed her body and given something valuable away in the process. Now Frankie struggled to align this version of Fiona with memory at all. She was afraid of the gaps, and all the places her mother's self hadn't returned to.

"I made a new bargain," Fiona said.

Oph's head swiveled to face Fiona. Frankie watched emotions file across her face—shock, doubt, despair. "What are you talking about?"

Fiona rolled her neck, head lolling from one side to another with a satisfied *pop*. Her knuckles pressed down into the mirror and the glass curved away from her touch. Frankie was afraid to trust her eyes; she blinked rapidly, as if the action might set the room right again. The afternoon light on her scalp made her head hot and dizzy, and something dried beneath the feeling, stiff and mineral tinged. She wanted to scrub herself clean enough to kill the sensation. She wanted to snatch up the shovel and bury her mother back in the earth she rose from.

"You were the one who asked me, Ophelia. You said do whatever it takes."

"I told you to *kill* it," Oph spat, her voice falling low and harsh, "not give it something new to feed on. What good is a bargain, after everything we've done? After it took you the first time?"

There were tears in her wide eyes. Oph scrubbed them away furiously, as if offended to find them there. Fiona looked at her sister through narrowed lids and frowned. Her mouth was red with the memory of her teeth biting down on her lip. Frankie felt as if she were seeing the two of them for the first time, a reinvention of women they had been before she existed.

"I'm a woman," Fiona said roughly, "not a god. I can't *kill* Heilacte." The name sapped light from the room. Frankie could still feel the weight of it, hear the sound of its voice tearing from Poppy's throat. "Nothing can. I already gave her what I could offer an eon ago, and that was barely enough to keep her from slaughtering the rest of you in search of more. Power has a cost."

She slid off the table and left the mirror bare. The glass reflected the chandelier overhead and refracted it around the room. Sissa took a minuscule step away from her, mouth an uncertain line.

"Then tell us what you did," she said, knife still clutched in her hands. Fiona's gaze flickered down to it.

"What, would you really stick me with that? I'm impressed. You can put it away, I told you already that I'm not a threat."

"Let me make that decision," Sissa said.

Fiona laughed and rolled her shoulders again, like she was trying to coax feeling back into her body. Sissa didn't move. "I went to Mab's house, in the mirror."

Finder made an involuntary sound behind Frankie—a sharp inhale of breath, the kind that hurt. Frankie held the edge of the dining table and tried to steady herself.

"Oh God," Oph said.

"I didn't kill her," Fiona corrected, eyes slitted in Sissa's direction. "She was already dead when I got there. The house was empty, and the sky was black and sunless. I left her body in the basement and I told Heilacte how to split her wards."

"Wards?" Oph asked, frozen in place.

"Mab spent her whole life keeping the villages there safe," Fiona said. "She taught me how the wards worked, a lifetime ago. It's a simple spell if you know the mechanics of it. Heilacte's wanted a way to break them down since before I was buried. Some of them were tethered to Mab's life, and likely fell when she did. But there were others. All it takes to break them is the destruction of a sigil."

Fiona held her fingers in the air and twisted them together, back and forth, back and forth. Frankie thought about the snakes on the barn door and around Poppy's neck.

"The end of the world," Keeper whispered. His voice, strangled, picked up volume. "Those were innocent people. You killed them."

Fiona's placating expression was cruel. Oph pressed a shaking hand over her mouth.

"You told me to fix it, and this was the answer. Their lives for ours. Heilacte's just . . . hungry. She needed to eat. Haven't you ever starved for something before?"

Frankie's mouth worked, trying to summon words, but the sound kept catching in her throat. There was something about the way her mother spoke about the demon—with a certain pacified reverence, or affection. She wanted to leave that room behind and turn to a past self, one with no concept of resurrected mothers or starving portents or dead sisters. But there was no going back, and no untouched place to return to.

"Mab was a stronger witch than I could have ever been, and she still lost," Fiona continued. "Someone asked for too much and gave Heilacte permission to devour, and she eclipsed the light. It could be why she's stronger now, and why she needs so much more energy to sustain herself."

"It was probably your daughter," Frankie interrupted. Her mouth was dry with anticipation. Her hands pulsed in pain. She thought about that basement in the Fissure, the severed bodies of bone dolls, the pale man thumping down the stairs. She thought about Sofia slicing her skin open over a flame and giving herself over to a demon. She wondered what could have been so terrible about them—about *her*—that Sofia would destroy her whole life to be granted a new one, somewhere in a distant world where Frankie couldn't travel.

Her mother smiled at her. "Sofia wouldn't do something like that. I taught her better."

But you didn't teach me, Frankie thought, letting the idea wound her. Aloud, she said: "Well, you weren't around to make sure, were you?"

"It could have been the Ossifier," Finder said, her first words since they'd stepped into that room. Frankie turned to her, watched the trembling outline of her mouth. "He told me that he serves Heilacte. He killed Mother Mab and offered her life in exchange for his own power. As far as we know, he is still somewhere in the Fissure and capable of destruction. He might try to find us or send her after us again. This could all be temporary while he figures out his next move."

"The Ossifier?" Fiona asked, eyes gleaming with curiosity.

"The—bone creature," Finder continued. She stumbled over the words. "The pale man."

"Oh, yuck, that creepy bastard," Fiona said.

Oph started to shake her head, the hair tucked behind her ears slipping forward and falling into her eyes. Her arms were covered with dirt, and there was a smudge across her forehead, above the rosy bridge of her nose and the damp shine of her eyes. Frankie wanted to hate her—and she did in some ways, deep in the pit of her, with a resentment that felt more like grief than any of the familiar anger. But she also wanted to wipe the dirt from Oph's brow and press her head into her shoulder. Frankie crossed her arms over her chest instead.

"This is never going to end," Sissa said weakly. "Fiona, you've—you've entrenched us in this cycle. Fine, a life for a life. But what's the limit? How many lives can you give away?"

"I bought you time," Fiona said, low in her throat. "You'd be dead otherwise."

Time turning on one spinning axis, time digging down into the meat of Frankie's heart and waiting for her to feel the sting. She kept trying to anticipate the pain, as if that would make it easier to bear. Was she supposed to be grateful for a life she couldn't call her own? "I spoke to you for so long," Frankie whispered, the words catching. "I tried to resurrect you myself and you were here? This whole time?"

Fiona stared back, impassive, waiting.

"We—she needed you. We could have prevented all of this from happening in the first place."

"I was asleep," Fiona said, her voice landing somewhere in the distance.

"She's *dead*," Frankie said raggedly, as if Fiona hadn't spoken at all, "and I went under the water to find you and you let our lives implode instead."

"I did what I did to keep the two of you safe," Fiona answered immediately, so viciously serious that Frankie took a step back, afraid. She collided with Marya, who righted her again, grasp lingering around a wrist. "It's not my fault you threw it away."

"Threw it away? Are you serious? You *ruined* us. You said 'I have a daughter and I pray she may outlive me.' *A* daughter. One." Frankie pointed at herself, hard, fingertip digging into her chest. "What was I supposed to do here alone?"

The promise of tears was a burning stone in her throat. All she could hear was the blood-thump of her heart in her ears.

"Frankie," Fiona said finally, sardonic. "I never intended for you to be the one who remained."

Frankie flinched as if hit. Two fast betraying tears fell down to her chin. Sissa had a hand on one of Fiona's, but she started, pulling back. "Fiona," she said, disbelieving.

"But I did it right," Frankie whispered. "I followed all the steps. I watched you scry in the mirror and I did exactly what you did and it still didn't work. You could have, I don't know, warned me, or taught me something worthwhile."

Her mother grimaced. "What would you have done with a gift like that? You didn't even want the world I handed to you."

Frankie's lips parted, eyelids stuttering. She squeezed her fists and dropped them to her sides again. She couldn't catch her breath.

"Christ," Cass said, "could you get off her back?"

"It's a fact, not a criticism," Fiona said. "You survived, didn't you? Of course I hoped Sofia would be the one who remained. She wanted to learn. She had the potential to bridge the gap between the Fissure and our plane. She could have built so many beautiful things, mastered the scrying passage, created something symbiotic and lasting. She could have sated Heilacte's hunger and kept us in her favor. Clearly, I over-estimated her capacity for understanding. But I don't care anymore. It doesn't matter. We're alive, and we're here, aren't we?"

"I care!" Frankie cried, voice breaking. "I fucking care!"

Fiona took a step forward. Poppy hooked around Frankie's bicep and tugged her into her side, blocking her mother's advance.

"Stop," Oph pleaded. "We're all upset right now, and there's a lot to take in. Let's just sit down and talk this through."

"You know," Fiona said to Frankie after a beat of silence, her face lined with pity, "throwing a tantrum isn't the way to bring her back. But I could show you how if you really wanted to learn this time."

"No. We're not listening to this," Poppy snapped, her face alight with a fury Frankie hadn't realized her capable of. Her hand slid down Frankie's arm until they fit together and she pulled her from the room, a chorus of protests rising from everyone except Fiona, solid and eerie under the chandelier's light. Cass and Marya followed, Finder and Keeper right behind them in motley solidarity. Oph called after them. The door muffled the desperate break of her voice.

Frankie dazedly trailed Poppy down the porch stairs, where Cass's truck waited in the drive and the sun made everything a violent gold. She gave one last look over her shoulder as the screen door slammed shut. Past the windows and the living room lamp, she could make out the silhouettes of the women's heads, gathered and stooped.

Poppy stopped and clutched Frankie by the shoulders.

"If you want us to leave, tell us now. You can go back in there and you can have your time with her, and you can decide if you want to listen to what's coming out of her mouth or not. I know she's your mom, Frankie, but I can't listen to her say that shit to you." Poppy's thumbs dug down to the bone. Frankie couldn't stop staring at the enormity of her pupils and the angry furrow of her brows. "So you can ask us to go. Or we can leave, together. We can deal with the consequences if they come."

"What if it hurts you again?" Frankie whispered. Tears caught in her mouth. She tasted salt, felt it sting.

She said *you* and meant *us*. Their simultaneous unraveling, their entangled threads, the lines between them blurred beyond uncrossing. They'd hurt each other so irreparably, in ways only they knew how to. They had dissolved any semblance of trust, swallowed every secret, burned every boundary.

Poppy almost smiled. "I guess she bought us time to figure that out, didn't she?"

The laugh bubbled out of Frankie's chest—it was all so ridiculous, some story warped and woven between different mouths. But she looked at Cass leaning against Marya in exhaustion, and the matching pair that was Finder and Keeper staggering just behind them. She could leave. She could go with the family she'd built for herself, and she would learn how to believe them again, and she would become someone worthy of giving their trust to.

They piled into the Ford. They left the house behind, with the sun setting in its belly and the once-dead haunting its halls.

51

SÉANCE FOR WISHING

That night, they went to Marya's. She was nervous with them all gathered in the little space she'd carved out for herself, but they didn't seem to mind the places where she had shoved dirty laundry into piles for later sorting, or the fat crack in the shower tiles, or the understocked refrigerator, fruit all rotten and forgotten. They settled in like they were welcome. And they were. For the first time, she wanted to show them that internal part of her world.

Marya rooted around in her closet for clean clothes and extra blankets. Her pajamas were a gown on Cass, doll clothes on Poppy, unbearably satisfying on Frankie, and hilariously out of place on Finder and Keeper—but they'd have to do. In the kitchen they bandaged the wounds on Cass's head and the oozing cuts on Frankie's arms. They heaped onto the couch with the sea of quilts and sheets with cups of tea and decaf. They were a crowded knot, ankles crossing over ankles, calves pressing against thighs.

"Thanks," Poppy said after they'd hovered a while in the quiet, voice rusty with disuse, "for coming back for me."

Frankie rested a palm against Poppy's knee and a cheek against her shoulder. Cass propped her feet in Marya's lap. Begrudgingly, she let her fingers rest around an ankle and sank deeper into the warmth. Finder and Keeper perched on Marya's thin rug, posture too perfect to suggest comfort.

"I meant what I said back there," Finder admitted, fiddling with the hem of the shirt Marya had given to her. "The Ossifier is dangerous. Without Mab there to stop him, he's capable of anything. And if your mother really cracked those wards, every soul and spirit living in the Fissure will likely be devoured. All that energy inside of Heilacte is . . . a terrifying thought."

Marya plucked at the hem of Cass's pants and shivered, trying to disguise it by fidgeting in her seat. The lives of just a few—Sofia, and the Glasswells—had been enough to give the demon a bridge to their plane and an invigorated power. She couldn't imagine the amplification of a thousand spirits, fed into one starving creature.

"If they come for us, we'll deal with it," Frankie said.

"We're putting you in danger by staying."

Poppy shrugged. "I don't know if I'd call us safe either way."

"What I'm trying to say is—we can go," Finder said. She sat stiffly. Marya imagined she'd never been comfortable in her life.

"Where would you go?" Marya asked.

"It's our responsibility to deal with the Ossifier," Keeper added, looking green. "We can't sit here and wait for disaster."

"We shouldn't have gone to the Fissure either, but we did that," Cass said around a mouthful of tea. "You helped us. Let us help you."

Keeper looked at Finder. A silent conversation passed between them, and then Finder nodded.

"We should sleep," Marya said, touching Poppy's arm as if trying to reassure herself of reality. "We'll feel better in the morning."

Cass sighed. "That's the best idea I've ever heard."

They couldn't bear to separate. They gave Marya's bed to Finder and Keeper, who found the fitted sheet an entirely strange concept. Then they made up the living room floor to be one great bed, blankets on every surface. There was no discussion about how they'd sleep: they collapsed together on the floor, slotted like sardines, Marya then Frankie then Poppy then Cass, back to front.

That was how they passed the days to come—trying to live like people, making the most out of discomfort and distrust and the casual immediacy of each other's presences. They talked around Frankie's family. They kept a light on all the time. They tried to fashion a new normal, even without the trust, even with the knowledge that they could be living on borrowed time, on the precipice between their world and its inverse.

Sometimes they took to the road. Even Marya, a known shitty driver, took her turn behind the Ford's wheel and stalled a few times. They went to the Styx. They went to the mountains and skinny-dipped at the foot of waterfalls. They went to work. They were despicably happy and irreparably sad together. They got trashed, a few times. They slept it off and ate donuts out of the supermarket box and drove again when their heads finally cleared.

They went to the old house, a crime scene all over again. They looked at the mess of it, the pile of wood and timbers, the tree still standing despite the ruins of roof and parlor and master bedroom. They tossed matches into wreckage. Nothing ever caught.

"I'm never going back to Oph's again," Frankie told them, viciously alive, every part of her awake. Marya believed her. They cooked dinners on Marya's finicky stove. They found horror movies strangely comforting, the gore and prosthetics now so disconnected from the terrors they'd witnessed that they played like bedtime stories. Still, sometimes Frankie wouldn't meet Marya's eyes, flinched lightly under Cass's grasp. Mostly she was quiet and avoidant, nestled inside of her hurt. But she stayed. That was enough for Marya—that the potential for repair remained present.

So the road again. So the mountains. Marya's bed, messy and unmade, light slanting in through her crooked blinds. Poppy's bed starched and quilted. Cass's, a mattress made up on the floor beneath glow-in-the-dark stars stuck to her ceiling. Never Frankie's, never the farmhouse, never the lamp left on in the living room window.

They were rarely ever apart, that week of aftermaths. They took Finder and Keeper everywhere. It was easier to show them the world through brand-new eyes than it was to address the past.

In the studio Frankie spun mugs and Marya played sudoku and Cass taught Keeper how to recycle clay, softening misshapen plates back into blocks of buildable earth. They ate in every diner across the county, where Keeper found that he loved hot sauce on bacon. They drove up the hill where Finder cried when she saw the sunrise and Cass cried when she saw the tears on Finder's cheeks.

They made meals together, cooking late into the night, drinking wine that Cass filched from her mom's house, cheap hangover fodder. Poppy sprawled on the couch beside Keeper, who went pink after a single sip. Finder refused to try it; instead, she flipped through a tarot deck she'd found on Marya's bookshelf, peering intently at the illustrations. Cass mixed wine and juice and cheap liquor, a sight that made Marya's stomach turn, and tipped it back with a deferent grin.

Marya got tipsy and they all danced around her apartment and once, for a split second, Frankie allowed herself to be tugged into Marya's arms, hair smelling of the basil and tea shampoo that she'd pilfered from Marya's shower. The shock of it, the impossible knowledge that Frankie forgave her long enough to be held, pushed Marya over the edge from tipsy to drunk. They pressed close. Marya put her hand on Frankie's waist. The heat of that casual touch, tank top under palm, turned her electric. The music boomed like distant fireworks and Marya felt them explode in her heart.

"You didn't have to let me stay here," Frankie said, voice low.

Oh, what that sound did to her.

"We're friends," Marya answered beside her ear, even as the words felt strange in her mouth. Friends, but she was hungrier, needier, wanted more. She looked at Frankie's bare shoulder and fought the urge to press her mouth there.

Frankie watched her for a long moment. "Thanks," she said at last, around a flicker of a smile. The appreciation warmed something in Marya's chest. They stood so close. She tugged on a lock of Frankie's hair. The movement felt dangerous. Risk buzzed just under the surface of her skin with the bass thrum of music. The strand twined beautifully around her finger.

"I thought if I stayed behind and kept it together, I could better myself. Become a good daughter, or a good sister, or a good friend," Frankie admitted.

Good, Marya thought. What a word. Marya had never felt completely good in her life, in any definition. She'd thought once that she might have the potential. But she'd let her mother rule her emotions from states away and left Nina behind when those feelings became unruly and too real, still couldn't rein them in and stop them from hurting Frankie, even when that was the last thing Marya wanted to do, even if the thought of it alone was enough to nearly kill her.

"I thought I could make up for all the ways I failed," Frankie continued, unaware of Marya's internal spiral. "I couldn't go to college or have a boyfriend like Sofia, and I'm not—pretty, or sweet, or easy. But I could keep the studio running and find out who did this to her, and I could make it right."

"Didn't you?" Marya asked, her cheek against Frankie's hair. She felt Frankie inhale in her arms, long and tired.

"I guess," Frankie said. "I don't know."

Her arms tightened behind Marya's neck. Cass said something that made Poppy laugh, and the sound melted into the music. When Frankie spoke again, her voice was barely more than a whisper. "I'm afraid that I'm just a bad person, and this whole mess is happening because deep down, I deserve it."

The music nearly ate the words. Marya felt it all, just under her skin—the pounding of her heart, the nearness and immediacy of Frankie, the close encouragement of the song.

"Why do you think that?"

"It all comes back to me," Frankie said, "and to Sofia. I should have helped her."

"Someone should have helped *you*," Marya corrected, suddenly alight and defensive.

Frankie just shook her head. Her cheek rubbed Marya's shoulder. She wanted to bring a hand up and cup the back of Frankie's skull, to hold her there, to feel her rise and fall with Marya's nervous breaths.

"What are we going to do now?" Frankie asked. She was so tense, as if suspicious that any movement would set off a chain of events that neither of them could control. Her throat bobbed as she swallowed.

Marya was afraid. Always had been. She hated not knowing how to solve a problem, and here she was, just a maker of more.

"We can be bad people together," she murmured, because the bravado was simpler. "And if our time runs out, then we'll go hunting for more."

She let the strand of Frankie's hair slip from her finger and landed on Frankie's waist again, sweetly familiar. The words must have reminded Frankie of her distrust—she stepped back out of Marya's arms, pressed her fingers over her mouth to smother the smile. Marya let her go and took a sip directly from Cass's wine bottle, untethered.

Marya had known the consequences when she kept her mouth shut. She had learned Frankie, knew what her secret would do to them all. But there had been a moment where she hoped that maybe they could have something without binds.

And she was lonelier now than she had been when she was truly isolated—suddenly a part of whatever strange group they had formed, sure, but inhabiting a different world. The man was gone. She expected him every time she ran the sink. When she showered, she stared at that split in the tile and remembered the mournful mask of his face. The one thing that used to make her feel like she had some kind of power in the world had been taken from her.

She looked for Sofia in the cracks. Waited for her to appear in a closet, a shower, indigo and alone and aching. Watched for her shadow in the flitting trees as they flew down mountain roads, imagining it upright and running once again. But the two halves of Sofia slipped away, elusive.

Still—Marya stared extra hard in the mirror, hoping for a glimpse of red light.

52

LURE THE VOICE DIVINE

Cass Sullivan was conditionally happy.

Sure, everything had fallen apart. But look at her now, surrounded by the people she loved. The world was a massive thing, full of life. It was the way she always came back to them. It was how she felt touched by Poppy's laugh that she reserved for only when it was the four of them together. It was Marya's tentative comfort in their newborn family. It was Frankie, different now, but finally smiling when Cass looked in her direction.

Inevitably, there came an end.

On the nights she went home, she lived a different life. The sheriff's station fell apart after the Glasswell family's funeral, and the deputy had to pick up the slack. Alex kept to himself. Cass would sit at the dining table with her fractured family before sequestering herself in her room, where she lasted about an hour before slipping out to find the others across the world, needing rain-heavy clouds, the moon an overhead light, something round and electric on the radio.

How had she ever been without them? They were extensions of her body, the lines between them indistinguishable.

They had secrets and hurts that only the four of them knew how to impart on one another. She wasn't naive enough to think that they didn't. But she kept things to herself too. Tell too much and there's nothing left when it inevitably implodes.

Like Alex behind the crack of a black door, curled childlike in his bed, color drained from his face. Some nights Cass peeked into that opening, wishing for the chance to prod at him like she used to when they were kids. Usually she just slipped back to her own bed, where she'd count phosphorescent stars until she couldn't stand it. But he'd leave for college soon. He would keep moving and growing and changing until she could barely recognize him, until the people they had once been would remain only in photographs.

Now it was a hazy after-dinner evening. She crept up the stairs. The thin house was quiet. Flimsy blue light filtered out under Alex's door.

She hesitated, sucked in a breath. Rapped on the door.

"What?" Alex called, muffled.

She entered. "I didn't say you could come in," he muttered, curled on the bed. Tinny sound emitted from his laptop and the screen painted his face a deep cobalt.

"You think I'd listen to you?" she answered, teasingly, but her heart had claws and it tore its way up her throat. He deflated. She crawled into bed beside him even as he pushed her away. But Cass wrapped an arm around him in a constricting hug.

"Don't fight it," she said, jabbing his arm with a pointed finger. "You know I give the best hugs."

He fell silent. For a few still moments they watched the reality show on his screen together, taking in a girl's elimination process.

"Everything okay?" Cass asked against his hair.

"Don't be weird," Alex answered. They were silent again. Then: "What would you care, anyway? I feel like I've barely seen you since you came home."

It was true, but it hurt. Her traitorous mind imagined Alex in that tree, never to be held in this moment again.

"Of course I care, jerk," she said, but she squeezed him again affectionately. "You heard about everything with the Glasswells, right?"

"Obviously," Alex answered.

She wondered what his perception of the event might be—local sheriff and his wife run into a crumbling house thinking their son is trapped inside, just to die in the house's collapse. There was no mention of the rest of them. No reports of demons and inky things lurking in the corners. Just a weak foundation made worse by the erosion of roots, and the shock of someone inside the house after all those empty years.

When he remained silent, Cass said: "Are you—okay?"

"Why wouldn't I be okay?"

Words crept to the edge of her tongue, threatened to spill over. *I was there in that room. His mother held a gun to me. I watched her die.*

She said, "I'm just trying to figure out why you're mega depressed."

He shifted away from her. "Can you get out of my room?"

"C'mon," she pleaded, sitting up. "Can you tell me what's going on? Please?"

Alex twisted back to the show and yanked the comforter up to his throat.

But his phone buzzed beside them on his bed. He eyed it for a moment before answering the call. "What's up?" A beat of silence. Then he turned to her, unreadable. "He wants to talk to you."

Cass blinked. "Excuse me?"

But Alex pushed the phone into her hand and she held it up to her ear, heart thudding in her chest. "Hello?"

"Sullivan," Lucas Glasswell's vacant voice said. "Come outside."

"What?"

"Quickly, please. I have places to be."

She slid from the bed and hovered for a moment, wishing there was something she could say that would soothe the gray look on Alex's face. But in the end, she slipped from his room, jogged barefoot down the steps, and stole out onto the front porch. Twilight made everything lavender and bright. The air was muggy, a passing storm leaving its tender touch. He waited at the bottom of the stairs, his dusty hair purpled in the evening, a jacket thrown over his T-shirt and jeans. She'd always thought him eerie—now he was cryptic.

"What do you want?" she asked, and then, feeling rude, added: "How are you doing?"

He shrugged. She hadn't gone to the funeral. She wondered what Lucas thought of his parents' death, if he believed what the police had reported, the evidence that they found—that collapsed house, just the tree standing in the center of it all.

He had given her a truth. She could give him one back. But it was a precipice, one she had already crossed, one she could never crawl away from.

"Look, I just came by to give you something."

She waited. "Thanks, I guess. What is it?"

Lucas held out a hand. In it was a small wooden box, just big enough for his palm to encompass it. Between his fingers she could make out the ornate carvings, gold filigree. Then he extended the other, a stack of leather-bound books clutched there. "You wanted her secrets," he said. "If they're in here, I can't make sense of them. But maybe you can."

She took the box and the books. They were warm as a beating heart, worn smooth from handling. She cradled them against her chest. "Thank you," she said again. "Really."

Lucas nodded. "Whatever. I'll see you around."

She watched him step up into his truck, listened to the engine ignite. Then she clicked the door shut behind her. Back in her bedroom, stars petered out overhead. She perched on the edge of her duvet and flicked on the lamp. She undid the little gold latch across the box's front in a rush and flipped it open.

Jasmine, cedar. The scent of it was overwhelmingly Sofia in a way Cass thought she had forgotten. Inside was a thin gold bracelet, one Cass had picked out for her birthday when Sofia turned sixteen. At the sight of it Cass smiled, despite the thorns in her veins. There were little tinctures in brown glass bottles, a satin satchel, and a folded piece of paper beneath it all, covered in Sofia's looping scrawl. Cass blinked tears down her cheeks and held the paper to her nose, taking in that scent before it could fade. She shook as she unfolded it, pulse a bird-wing beat.

It was a recipe—no, it was a spell—no, it was a summoning, *HEILACTE* scratched across the top and beneath it: *I have a lover and I pray she may outlive me.* Under the folded paper was a smoky little compact, the mirror russet and glazed. It was cold in her hands. Cass thrust it back into the box and locked it again.

She touched the journals next, reverent. The leather was worn so smooth it almost felt like skin. She thumbed one open—every page was covered in tight, dark scrawl, interjected with Sofia's frenzied cursive. It would take weeks to read them. The ink had purpled with age, the words were cramped and foreign. Cass stopped on a black silhouette where the scribbling was so hard that it tore through the paper in places. The shape was dwarfed by a massive depiction of what Cass assumed to be Heilacte, the creature horned and rippling with ink. Beside it, Sofia had scrawled: *She took my shadow with her. I don't think I'll ever be able to get that part of me back.*

Her mind raced. She drew her knees up to her chin, trying to catch her breath. Sofia had summoned Heilacte on her own and left part of herself behind in the Fissure. Why hadn't she warned them before she was—gone? What had Marya seen in that glimpse between worlds? What did Poppy know about the space between life and death that they might not?

She had to show the rest of them. She couldn't tell anyone. She had to burn it all and forget it ever happened.

They had finally made peace with all their fears. If she showed this to Frankie, it would only make the ache worse. It would destroy her to see the physical proof that Sofia had kept something so huge from them, that she had remained unknowable in the end. But they had to understand why Sofia had called Heilacte back to the surface of the earth when everything in their blood sang against it.

The scent of Sofia's perfume clung to the air and she had to press a hand over her nose to focus. She'd show it to Frankie—she'd tell all of them what she'd seen—but first she'd ask Finder exactly what she knew about a dead girl's demise.

Cass sucked in a deep breath and practiced a grin in the mirror over her dresser, even as the reflection terrified her, even as the shadows in her room went lurid. She fished her phone out of her pocket and called Poppy's number. It picked up before it could ring twice.

"Where are we going next?" Cass asked, with the box and journals tucked under her arm, close to her heart. She thrust the window open and hauled a leg over the sill before Poppy finished speaking.

53

HER HAIR FALLING DOWN HER BACK

Finder didn't understand mothers, the sun, the earth, the blue-green of growth, lakes without masters, animals without secrets, witches without hate, lamps with electric bulbs, twins with shared faces, cars, tenderness, mirrors with trustworthy reflections, tortilla chips, or pop music.

Sleepless, nightmares of the Ossifier kept her up, his blade cutting cleanly through Mother Mab's throat, bloody nose running across his teeth. She imagined him crawling past every reflective surface. Dreamt of Sofia reaching for her in the woods, tugging her closer to the water.

Sofia, her name like a prayer. Some nights Finder scried for her—stared in Marya's bathroom mirror for hours, a candle lit below her chin, the rest of the house asleep and unknowing. Maybe if she could call her close. Maybe if she could keep some small piece of her clinging to the Fissure. Just to understand and watch it bloom.

When Keeper looked at her, she felt seen, so she stopped meeting his gaze.

Sometimes, in the dark where they were most familiar, he'd reach for her. She'd allow the touch. Let the soothing warmth of his body beside her lull her from her fears.

When at last she would sleep, surrounded by strangers in the shape of women and Keeper's grounding presence, she dreamt of blooming trees and the sun shining high above them. Sofia came to her behind her eyes. They went for walks.

Frankie asked a favor of her, just once. In the week since they'd dug up her mother from the basement, Frankie had refused to return to her house. She'd turned to Finder—asked if she'd be willing to go inside for her, to grab her a change of clothes and a book she'd been reading.

"It would mean a lot to me," Frankie said, and suddenly Finder could feel her sister in her. The tender upturn of the corner of her lips. The weight of her eyelashes, low and sad.

"Of course," Finder said.

She slipped through the front door, clicked it shut. The house was shady and emptied in the late afternoon. They'd tried to find a time when no one would be there, and now Frankie waited outside with Cass parked in the driveway. Ready to run.

She hadn't yet learned the bellows of this house—where she'd known every creak and cranny of Mab's house, here her steps were clumsy. In the dark, she climbed the stairs to Frankie's bedroom. The door sat ajar. She could see the shape of a body inside, just past the hanging knob.

Fear curdled in her, instant and all-encompassing. But she was different now. The master of her own world.

She found Frankie's mother sitting on the bed, running her hand over the quilt. She looked up at the sound of Finder's footsteps and smiled.

"Look at you," Fiona Lyon said, "marvel of a thing."

Finder felt that if she stood out of the light's reach maybe she could ghost through this room, avoid the eerie feeling of being watched. Fiona looked as if she'd been crying. She kept speaking like she'd known Finder all her life.

"Do you know what it's like to wake without a daughter? To know that you gave up everything in the hope that she would live, and still destroyed her in the process? Do you know how it feels to lie beneath the dirt with only your mind for company?" Her fingers dragged over embroidered florals, shades of yellow and green. "I imagine you would understand better than anyone. You lived there, in the Fissure. Do you miss it, Finder? That's what they tell me your name is. It's lovely. Fitting."

"I don't know," Finder said at last, feeling that an answer was demanded of her.

"Good girl," Fiona said. "I like when you tell the truth. I don't know if I miss the dirt, either. It seemed easier than whatever this is. Well, go on, take what you need. I won't ask you to tell me about Frankie. I'd rather she come to me when she's ready."

Finder faced the bookshelf and flipped through titles, scanning for the one Frankie requested.

"I would like to ask you a favor though, if you're willing," Fiona said softly. Finder prickled. All these Lyon women asking something of her, always wanting more.

"What?" Finder asked, impatient.

"You knew her," Fiona said.

Sofia. First girl. First friend.

"Of course," Finder answered.

"You call to her."

Finder didn't answer, feeling scrutinized.

"It's written all over you. All I've ever had is time to think," Fiona said, "and you can see so much when you adjust to the dark."

Finder hovered over the books. She touched the corner of her eye, feeling it prickle. "What do you need from me?"

"It's just a desire," Fiona said, listless, "just a dream. My daughter isn't made for death, Finder. You should know that about her by now."

It seemed a Lyon would never die. It seemed they already walked the boundary, detached from sensibility.

"Come here."

Finder obeyed. She'd been raised to listen, felt it like puppet strings around her wrists.

"You're a conduit," Fiona said, tapping Finder's shoulder. "I can see why Mab clung to you. You can find the thin places, can see the shift."

"I don't understand," Finder said.

"I want you to bring her to me," Fiona answered. "When you scry for her in that mirror. I want you to bring Sofia forward in your body. I want you to become a mirror for her to look through. If you're interested, I'll teach you how." She smiled, toothy and wide. She had a gap in her teeth just like Sofia's. "You would make an excellent student."

Finder tried to hide the way the praise hit her, how it swelled like a wound. But she could feel herself glow with it. "I can try."

"Good. You're very good, Finder." Fiona patted her shoulder, her expression distant and strange. "You'll have to be careful. Come and see me when you can slip away. I don't find much use in sleeping, nowadays. You can use the door whenever you need."

Finder stepped away, all of it too much to take. But Fiona clucked her tongue. "You should get your book. My Frances is observant, and she'll miss it."

Finder nodded and snatched the title off the shelf. She turned out of the room before Fiona could speak again, hurrying down the stairs, the volume pinned under her arm.

"There you are," Frankie said when Finder stepped off the porch. "Did you forget the dress?"

She hadn't even thought to look. "Right," Finder said, going pink. "I'm sorry. I thought I heard someone coming home."

"No worries, I'll steal something from Cass," Frankie answered, taking the book with a smile. "Thank you. I appreciate it."

Finder nodded. She let her body be wedged between Cass's and Frankie's in the truck, everyone else waiting for them to come home, *home*, still feeling untethered and uncontained and hating the feeling of the road beneath her. Everything strange, everything possible, everything made beautiful and terrifying with the sun in the sky.

It was a sleepless night again. She stared into Marya's bathroom mirror until her nose began to bleed.

54

THE SPIRIT RIOTS AND THE BODY GLOWS

Past the fields of grapevine, crawling up the mountain. Beyond the fertile valley. Echoing over the creeks and under the red rising sun, through the trees, just down the road from the ruins of a house where they found the shell of her body in the cradled hands of the tree.

Across the landscape, ancient stone walls mark out property lines, separating the hills and the grapes and the corn. She wants to lean down and breathe in lavender. She wants to scoop bouquets of earth. Fireflies take to the sky, lanterns to ferry her beyond her dreams.

Remote: even the beasts can barely find it.

There sits a church, abandoned, some relic of a past where the pagan was preferred. Its rotting steeple rising high. The crooked cross propped atop it like a birthday candle, prepared to burn.

Sofia spirit-walks through an overgrown graveyard, all shape, split shadow. Soon they'll move her body again and she'll have a headstone among the moss and fern, where a stone with her mother's name waits to guard a still-living heart. Soon she'll hang from the sky while the stars pull her along, marionette, watching as her family lowers her bones into the ground. She'll never wake in that body again, never own that mind. Once, she was a girl. Now, she is—

Anything but. Scent in the air, the pop of fruit between teeth. She steps between the pews. Touches pocked wood with ethereal hands. Her shadow stands in the corner and watches her on its haunches, a wicked attempt to hide.

In another world, where she once ran among the other beasts in a Fissure split down the center of the universe, a man made of bone returns to the house and buries an old witch's body in the basement. He obeys the orders of Heilacte. The creature crawls the sunless land and eats, and eats, and eats. He rises up those damp stairs, walks through the woods along a path lined with swinging creatures, takes his first steps into the black mirror of the lake. When his head goes under, Sofia staggers, tries to hold herself together. She wants to go home, but it's a word made of dust. She can see through her veins. She has no master, only the recollection of heartbeat.

Overhead, birds roost in the beams of the ceiling. The moon pokes holes between them and makes a white pupil out of a puddle in the pulpit. Her weak shadow crawls closer to it, hazy around the edges. Sofia tilts the idea of her head back and takes in the pinkened light. Stands along the edge of worlds. Flickers between here and Fissure, there and Fissure, here and there and the split down the middle.

Once, she made a bargain with a demon, so no one she loved would ever be hurt again, even if it meant her own demise. She would do it again. She's halfway there, if only she can pull herself together, one final time.

Sofia works through the mechanics of lips and teeth, imagines a smile. A whistle carries through the air, then a thud, the sound of the cross taking its tumble, leaving the steeple bare. It sounds through the forest with an echo.

She goes, seeking—

Nothing but a pause, a place to lay the heavy thoughts floating where her head would be. She's laughing now, no, just whistling air through an imaginary chest. Magpies sing in the dark. An image of her mother flashes through her mind quick as a striking match, a woman who looks like Sofia if she'd had the chance to grow up, her head tossed back as she howls to the trees. *No more birds, coyote.*

Sometimes she sinks, the world so soft, the boundary thinned. Sometimes she blinks and finds that she's looking through the eyes of another—sees Frankie lying awake on a couch she doesn't recognize, Cass putting her hair up in the Ford's rearview mirror, Poppy's sleeping head cradled in Frankie's lap, Marya standing in her kitchen and staring at the sink's faucet, fixing a cup of evening coffee.

Oh, Mother! Sofia thinks, no longer certain of who she's speaking to. Her feet, or the concept of them, press into broken wood, and she kneels before the altar. *I saw heaven in the red glow of the sun. Grant me your favor; let me grow here, through the floor. Let the glad ground gleam with crimson light.*

In the center of that pitch puddle, a white head rises. Fingers push over its edges, dripping. Strands ascend with him. Snaking tendrils latch into the shattered foundation of the church and lift him into another world. Her shadow screams at the sight of him, an endless sound, a forever recollection of all her fear and pain. He catches it like an animal, by the loose fabric of its neck. He tugs it skyward and turns his milky gaze on Sofia.

"Found you," the Ossifier says.

Under the glow of evening, the moon is a big unblinking eye above her.

Here, it is dark and quiet. The whole world has roots.

ACKNOWLEDGMENTS

This is a book about friendship, and I am rich in love. With all the generous support I've received over this book's inception, there will never be enough words and appreciation and adoration. Still, I will try.

When *We Ate the Dark* was born, before it cycled through a few different titles and several scrapped drafts, I was a terrified college senior living in a house in Brooklyn with my best friends. I cried every time I thought about graduation—I couldn't imagine a world without them steps away from me. I knew their dreams, and their fears, and the absurd things they found funny, and the music they loved, and the places they wanted to go. They saw past the self I'd built for presentation and gave me a new language for love. I started this book because I wanted to make us a record. Over the years, we've spread across the world and a few streets over and down the hall, and it never gets old, even when we joke about the ways that we do. Let the years come—I'll love y'all in the next life, too.

I am forever indebted to Bailey Tamayo, the agent of my dreams. You understood me from day one, and you honed this story into something special. To my incredible editors Adrienne Procaccini, who took a chance on my queer little novel, and Tegan Tigani, who shaped it into something worth reading. To the talented team at 47North for providing my witches with life—thank you, thank you, thank you.

This is also a book about family and all the forms it can take. To my wonderful parents, for raising me in a home where we can't leave a room without saying "I love you." I can't express how thankful I am that you never balked when I told you that I wanted to be a painter, and that you still supported me when I wrote a book instead. To my grandparents and my great-grandmother, near and far and in my heart, for teaching me our mythology and calling to remind me of our love through generations. To Taylor, for being the kind of brother whose kindness and humor taught me who to be, and for marrying Jenny, my sister and friend and a beautiful soul. And to Ella, for giving me the gift of sisterhood in the first place, for mulberries and persimmons, for seeing the world like I do. Let's go to McKay's.

All my appreciation and all my heart to Alex, Amy, Lucy, Monica, Nico, and Nina; you give me the kind of friendship worth writing about, and I'll spend the rest of my days telling everyone how in love I am with you, even when they're tired of hearing it. To Erin; you are my Virginia and the other half of me that took too long to find. I want to sing Dolly with you every time the wisteria blooms. To Emma; your brilliant mind and radiant presence make me a better writer and a better friend. I'm so lucky to know you. To Aly, who has been by my side since those first years without fail, and believed that this day would come long before I did. To Abby, Anna, Julie, Lainee, Mace, Rachel, Solaja, Suzie, Virginia, and all my hometown hearts, for your friendship through every embarrassing phase of my life. You are the golden hour of growing up. To Cecilia, for your endless support and inimitable heart, and for forming our friendship through Bookstagram DMs. To Joanne, whose companionship and care is poetry incarnate. To Andrew and Sally and the whole Gombas family, for always treating me like one of your own and welcoming me into your joy. To Xaveria, without whom the concept of this book would have never left the Stiefvater Critique Partner discussion forum. And to my Pratt painting crew, for encouraging the early illustrations that inspired much of this book, and for all the late studio nights. The next book's for you.

The names listed here and so many beyond them make me the happiest woman among all women. I could go on about the length of love for the rest of my life. It still wouldn't feel like we had enough time to celebrate that kind of magic.

About the Author

Photo © 2022 Justin Borucki

Mallory Pearson is a writer and artist portraying themes of folklore, queer identity, loss, and the interaction of these elements with the southern United States. She studied painting and bookbinding, and she now spends her time translating visual art into prose. She is an avid fan of horror movies and elaborate stews cooked in big witchy pots. Her work has appeared in *Electric Literature*, *Capsule Stories*, and *Haverthorn Press*, among others. Mallory lives in Brooklyn, New York, with her dearest friends. For more information, visit http://mallorypearson.com.